Praise for *Null-A Continuum*

"John Wright is a marvelous craftsman. . . . [*Null-A Continuum*] is not the first sequel to a van Vogt novel, but it is the only one worth reading."
—*The New York Review of Science Fiction*

"Anyone curious about the grand old days of gosh-wow, whiz-bang, golden age SF need look no further than this homage to A. E. van Vogt. Packed with intergalactic adventures, the cliff-hangers and plot twists of the pulp era—and space princesses!—this is a roller-coaster ride."
—Michael Flynn, author of *Eifelheim*

"[The book is] no slavish copy. . . . In Wright's hands the pulp original turns into a pulp-meets-hard-SF meditation of cosmological evolution. . . . Wright is a born novelist. And *Null-A Continuum* is a novelist's novel, bristling with ideas and characters that demand novel-length treatment. . . . Wright's book is an erudite homage to the pulp tradition by a twenty-first-century master."
—*The Magazine of Fantasy & Science Fiction*

"For continuing the adventures of van Vogt's superhuman, double-brained protagonist, Gilbert Gosseyn, no one is better qualified than rising star Wright. . . . Wright faithfully emulates van Vogt's labyrinthine plot twists and energetic prose while answering questions about Gosseyn's origins that have burned in fans' minds for decades."   —*Booklist*

"A novel made of love."
                    —George Zebrowski, award-winning author
                                        of *Brute Orbits*

"Wright attempts to flesh out and make sense of van Vogt's world while retaining a respectful distance from the original story. . . . The characters' individual voices are sound. . . . inventive."   —*Publishers Weekly*

"Wright out–van Vogts van Vogt. . . . *Null-A Continuum* is an impressive achievement in both style and storytelling. Wright settles for nothing less than telling a van Vogt tale the way the late, great 'Van' would have told it himself."   —*SciFiDimensions.com*

"John Wright has revived and extended the magically brilliant work of A. E. van Vogt. I cannot think of any writer better suited to this task."
                    —Charles Platt, author of *The Silicon Man*

Tor Books by John C. Wright

NULL-A
CONTINUUM

JOHN C. WRIGHT

Continuing A. E. van Vogt's
THE WORLD OF NULL-A

A TOM DOHERTY ASSOCIATES BOOK
NEW YORK

This is a work of fiction. All of the characters, organizations, and events portrayed in this novel are either products of the author's imagination or are used fictitiously.

NULL-A CONTINUUM

Copyright © 2008 by John C. Wright

All rights reserved.

A Tor Book
Published by Tom Doherty Associates, LLC
175 Fifth Avenue
New York, NY 10010

www.tor-forge.com

Tor® is a registered trademark of Tom Doherty Associates, LLC.

ISBN 978-0-7653-5537-9

First Edition: May 2008
First Mass Market Edition: June 2009

Printed in the United States of America

0 9 8 7 6 5 4 3 2 1

To the grandmaster of imagination
I never wrote you a letter
For those hours
And there were many
When the world did not welcome me
And your worlds
And there were many
Did.
Let this writing stand in the stead
Of that unsent letter.

●

For Lydia, with love. Without your courage and cheer, this work would have been stillborn.

●

To the memory of Dan Hooker, with respect, who made this novel possible.

●

To Isaac Wilcott, whose work and research were invaluable.

AUTHOR'S NOTE: WHAT HAS GONE BEFORE

The occupants of each floor of the hotel must as usual during the games form their own protective groups. . . .

With these words, *The World of Null-A* opens, and we are introduced to one Gilbert Gosseyn, who believes himself to be a widowed farmer from Cress Village, Florida, presenting himself during the games to the City of the Machine. And yet Gosseyn's beliefs are false, implanted in his mind by an unknown agency for a hidden purpose.

Reader, the volume you hold in your hands is meant to serve as an homage and continuation of the celebrated Null-A books of A. E. van Vogt. *The World of Null-A* was first published in 1945 in *Astounding* magazine, and arrested the attention of the science fiction readership as few books before or since. For sheer invention, breathless pace, and glimpses of the amazing potential of the human individual, the tale is unequaled. That A. E. van Vogt also introduces a concept as esoteric as non-Aristotelian multivalued logic (abbreviated Null-A) while telling a tale of adventure, intrigue, and war is a testament to his powers.

The theory of general semantics postulates that through a proper understanding of the relationship between words and the reality words allegedly represent a mind can be trained to avoid disorientation. On an emotional level, a lack of disorientation means the absence of neurotic and self-destructive behavior. It entails an integration of the cortex, the seat of reason, with the thalamus, the seat of emotion.

By A.D. 2560, Earth is a world of Null-A. The games select candidates on the basis of their cortical-thalamic integration, their sanity, for various high positions in business or government, including the presidency of Earth. Candidates of the very highest qualification are selected by the Games Machine for emigration to Venus, where men live without laws or the need of laws.

On Earth, police protection is suspended only for one month, and only in the City of the Machine. A man named Nordegg, a neighbor from his home village, claims Gosseyn is an impostor. When Gosseyn protests that he is the widower of Patricia, the daughter of Michael Hardie, his statement is greeted with derision, and the protective group of the hotel where he is staying casts him out into the streets to fend for himself.

He then encounters a young woman calling herself Teresa Clark, apparently unprotected during the policeless month, who leads him into a trap. Gosseyn discovers Michael Hardie is the President of Earth. "Teresa" is his daughter Patricia, a member of a gang led by a sardonic giant of a man named Thorson. Thorson and his gang have been using a device called a distorter to paralyze certain circuits in the Games Machine, falsifying the outcome of the games, and allowing Hardie, an ambitious gangster in no way qualified for the presidency, to assume power.

One member of the gang is a bald and earless cripple with prosthetic limbs, whose horrible disfigurations are covered by a medicinal plastic, but he has a strangely magnetic personality. He introduces himself with these words: "Consider me the 'X' quantity. And let 'X' equal any infinite value." He arranges to have Gosseyn's cortex photographed: Gosseyn possesses, in embryonic form, a secondary brain.

Patricia reveals that Thorson is an agent of an interstellar power called the Greatest Empire, ruled by a tyrant named Enro the Red. Enro intends to massacre Earth and Venus as the quickest way of provoking a galactic war with his neighbors, the Interstellar League. X is none other than Lavoisseur, the head of the General Semantics Institute of Earth.

Gosseyn makes a foolish escape attempt and is shot to death in the street. He wakes up on Venus, apparently the same individual, but actually Gosseyn Two, the same memories lodged in a duplicate body. A robotic plane under orders from the Games Machine forces Gosseyn to surrender himself to Eldred Crang, apparently another member of the gang and Patricia's sweetheart. During what appears to be an escape attempt, a member of the gang named Prescott shoots and kills X and Hardie.

While free, Gosseyn is convinced by the Games Machine to attempt suicide in order that he will wake up in the final Gosseyn body, one with a fully trained superhuman double brain. Dosing himself with a hypnotic drug, he programs his subconscious with the defeat and despair needed to carry through with the desperate act of self-destruction: He is saved by the intervention of a hotel clerk, but later recaptured by the galactic agents.

Venus and Earth are invaded, but the invaders are thrown back by the resilience and tenacity of the Null-A resistance. Thorson hides the failure from his superiors, and instead concentrates on training Gosseyn's embryonic double brain, with the help of Dr. Lauren Kair, a Null-A psychiatrist. Thorson's hope is that Gosseyn, if fully trained, will be able to lead him to "the Chessplayer" manipulating Gosseyn and the events around him. Thorson wants to find the man who made Gilbert Gosseyn, for Gosseyn is obviously an artificial being, and wrest the secret of eternal life from him.

During this period, Patricia is placed in the same comfortable cell with Gosseyn. Apparently their captors hope that Gosseyn will be reluctant to escape if it means harm to the girl. He asks her what her status is. "I'm your wife," she says, and Gosseyn is irritated that she should joke at such a time.

She reveals that Eldred Crang is a Venusian Null-A

detective, who, discovering the secret base of galactic invaders many years ago, infiltrated them, rose to prominence in the Greatest Empire military command, and returned with the Venusian invasion force as a fifth columnist. It was Crang who persuaded Thorson to study rather than kill Gosseyn, Crang who will convince Thorson to leave the safety of his well-protected galactic base.

Gosseyn's secondary brain is developed through training to act as an organic distorter. On a practical level, it gives Gosseyn awareness of and control over the energy patterns and forces in his environment.

Thorson, unwilling that any other man find the secret of eternal life, returns with Gosseyn and a battalion of soldiers to Earth. Due to the fighting, the city is a burnt-out ruin and the Games Machine is destroyed. Thorson follows Gosseyn to the now-deserted Institute of General Semantics, where a telepathic signal leads Gosseyn to someone who seems to be an older and uncrippled version of X, Lavoisseur, head of the Institute. Lavoisseur, who has similar control over space and energy as Gosseyn, electrocutes Thorson; Gosseyn remorselessly slaughters the soldiers of the Greatest Empire who had been guarding him.

Lavoisseur is severely wounded in the firefight but lives long enough to briefly answer Gosseyn's questions. He explains the process by which duplicate bodies can be created and nourished in a sensory-deprivation environment, with a twin brain linked by a distorter circuit, so the thoughts of one are reflected in the other, who can wake when the first duplicate dies. Lavoisseur says he created X by means of his cellular duplication process and damaged him to speed up the life process, making X the greater, so that his thoughts would be telepathically "similarized" back to an identical brain in Lavoisseur. By this means Lavoisseur spied out the plans of the gang and, working through Crang and the Games Machine, thwarted them.

Lavoisseur dies. Gosseyn is able to pick up from the fading energy of his nervous system certain fragments of thought and memories. These thoughts reveal to Gosseyn that for centuries, under many names, Lavoisseur has been the secret patron of Null-A, having built the first Games Machine on Earth. When all men are trained to the levels of sanity and moral maturity promised by the Null-A sciences, they will be ready for the secret of immortality.

Lavoisseur has often wondered if there is a Chessplayer behind him, manipulating his life for some unknown purpose, but concludes that there is not one. Life itself is the mystery and the source of mystery: "Once more, the cycle is completed, and we are no further ahead." After he dies, Gosseyn realizes the implication of Lavoisseur's last thought.

He removes the beard from the face of the old man and looks into his own features.

The Players of Null-A (published in the United States under the title *The Pawns of Null-A*) elevates the action to a galactic scale. Enro the Red, cheated of the atrocity he wished to commit so as to provoke a war, instigates without provocation the greatest war in galactic history.

With Thorson dead, Eldred Crang, as second-in-command, takes control of the galactic base on Venus and the soldiers stationed there. He disperses the army by the simple means of offering the men to regional commanders of other bases elsewhere in the galaxy. The commanders, always understaffed, gladly receive the additional troopers with no questions asked.

Meanwhile, a mysterious shadow-being known as the Follower appears on Venus and uses his uncanny ability to predict the future to arrange an assassination attempt against Gosseyn. When that fails, Gosseyn tracks the clues into the apartments of one of the agents of the Follower. The agent puts up no resistance but hands Gosseyn a shining card. On it is printed a simple message from the Follower: "You are caught in the most intricate trap ever devised to capture one man."

Gosseyn wakes up somehow occupying the cortex of

another man on the planet Gorgzid, capital planet of the Greatest Empire. He is trapped inside the untrained nervous system of Ashargin, last survivor of the previous dynasty, now merely a pawn in Enro's political machine. Ashargin had been raised as a novice by the servants of Secoh, Chief Guardian of the state-established Cult of the Sleeping God. Ashargin is weak, childish, and neurotic, the outcome of years of ill treatment during his youth; Gosseyn resolves to train the body and brain he is inhabiting with Null-A techniques, to enable Ashargin to act effectively against Enro. These plans are thwarted by Enro's eerie power to see through walls and discover all conspiracies against him.

Patricia, now revealed as Empress Reesha, Enro's sister, arrives on Gorgzid, on the arm of Eldred Crang, apparently her husband. Gorgzid has a custom of brother-sister marriage for the Emperor and Empress, and Enro is outraged that Reesha refuses to honor it.

Gosseyn is returned to his own body and finds himself imprisoned in the Retreat of the Follower on the planet Yalerta, held in the same cage with Leej the Predictress. Gosseyn protects Leej and uses the powers of his extra brain to escape.

The pitiless ruling caste of the planet Yalerta can predict the future, apparently able to bypass the limitations of time in much the same fashion that Gosseyn can bypass the limitations of space. The Follower meant Gosseyn to be kept under the watch of the Predictors. However, Gosseyn's double brain blurs the Predictors' impressions of his future whenever he uses it to distort time-space, blinding them.

Leej conceives the desire to be Gosseyn's lover (there being no marriage or other permanent emotional relationships among the Predictors), but Gosseyn is unable to find himself interested in any woman who lacks the Null-A training.

A warship of the Greatest Empire, apparently in alliance with the Follower, is on Yalerta, gathering Predictors into Imperial service, so that they might advise Enro of enemy military movements before they are detected and the outcomes of engagements before they occur.

Gosseyn single-handedly seizes control of the ship and, later, discovers that the Follower meant to sabotage Enro's efforts to recruit Predictors.

Meanwhile the Null-A technicians of Venus have invented a technique for mechanically dominating and paralyzing the brain of any person lacking in Null-A cortical-thalamic integration. When it is revealed that this system of mind control cannot stop the Predictor-guided warships of the Greatest Empire, the decision is made to abandon Venus. The population of Null-A's is scattered throughout the various worlds of the Interstellar League.

Gosseyn discovers a distorter circuit linking the Retreat of the Follower on Yalerta to the Crypt of the Sleeping God on Gorgzid. The Crypt is revealed to be a long-buried intergalactic vessel, the last remnant of an eons-old fleet that fled a dying galaxy and populated the Milky Way. Lavoisseur was one of the original migrants from the Shadow Galaxy; with him gone, Gosseyn was the only person the damaged Observer Machine, the electronic brain guarding the vessel, could contact.

The one remaining passenger in his medical suspension coffin is brain-dead, kept alive by the Observer Machine, which cannot act to damage a body in its keeping. The superstitious men of Gorgzid, having long ago forgotten their origins, since primitive times have worshipped the ageless yet living body as their Sleeping God.

Aboard the archaic ship is an instrument for reproducing, on a small scale, the Shadow Effect that consumed the previous galaxy inhabited by man; the Observer Machine tells Gosseyn that, years ago, while Lavoisseur was attempting repairs on the ship, a junior priest was accidentally attuned to this shadow-energy circuit and gained the ability to render himself insubstantial. That junior priest,

convinced that he was granted this power by the Sleeping
God, used it to gain highest rank and vowed to see the
galaxy conquered and the Cult spread to all worlds.

The Observer Machine tells Gosseyn that it was the
Chessplayer transferring Gosseyn's mind into Ashargin
to put Gosseyn into a position where he could be told the
truth and sent to stop the Follower. But the machine says
the real gods, and the real Chessplayer, have been dead
for two hundred million years.

The Follower is Secoh. Secoh has organized a palace
coup and wrestled control of the Empire away from
Enro, who has fled. As Ashargin, Gosseyn negotiates
with Secoh to lend his prestige as the remaining legitimate heir to the throne to the Cult, in return for a chance
to view the Sleeping God in his crypt.

Secoh agrees, and Ashargin and the hierarchy of the
Cult meet for the ceremony of viewing at the Crypt.
Gosseyn has arranged with the Observer Machine to
transfer his consciousness into the body of the last passenger.

To all appearances, it seems as if the Sleeping God
wakes; he accuses Secoh of treason and advances toward
him menacingly; Secoh, maddened with terror, assumes
his shadow-form and destroys the figure shambling toward him. The mind of Secoh is unable to withstand the
stress of remembering that he killed his own god, and he
collapses into profound amnesia, his entire personality
erased by the shock.

Null-A Three takes up the narrative of Gilbert Gosseyn,
now on an intergalactic scale. A fleet of warships from
the dead galaxy from which mankind originally came is
brought into the Milky Way, apparently by the malfunction of the space-control lobe of the extra brain of one of
the undiscovered sleeping bodies of Gosseyn. The fleet is
titanic, well over one hundred thousand warships, and
manned by a troglodyte race degenerated due to eons of
exposure to the Shadow Effect. The flagship finds and pre-

maturely wakes the body of Gosseyn Three, who is in mental contact with Gosseyn Two, both bodies alive and awake at the same time.

Enro the Red cooperates with Leej the Predictress and Gosseyn Two and Gosseyn Three to end the menace posed by this superfleet, but at the height of the crisis Enro intrigues to have the troglodytes brought under his control. Gosseyn Two summarily sends Enro to an asteroid prison remote from any contact with galactic civilization.

The tale ends with Gosseyn Three departing the Milky Way galaxy.

NULL-A THREE was composed many years after the first two, when van Vogt's health was suffering. With apologies to any purists among my readers, some of the events in the third book do not fit well with the established continuity of the first two.

I will mention four examples:

1. Much of the third book is concerned with a fatuous courtship between Gosseyn and a widowed queen, a neurotic woman who should not hold any attraction for a man like Gosseyn.
2. On Earth, gangsters and businessmen conspire to prevent the creation of a second Games Machine, but the notion that business enterprises would cooperate with crime is contradicted by the first book, where it is stated management and ownership positions in the business world are not available to any but those who pass the initial round of the games, i.e., highly sane and well-integrated individuals.
3. When Enro says that he has never known if his visions are visible to others, this is contradicted by the first description of his use of the power: A woman is bathing him when he uses the power to spy on Ashargin in the next room, and it would have been obvious whether she could see the clairvoyant image or not.

4. The assumption that the Shadow Galaxy could still hold habitable planets conflicts with the description of the Great Migration away from that galaxy in the second book.

For this sequel, I have taken the license to disregard these and other inconvenient events.

ON a personal note, let me confess that *The World of Null-A* and *The Players of Null-A* are the books that in my youth most strongly influenced my mind and opened the realm of wonder to me. Gilbert Gosseyn has always represented to me what a hero truly is: A man who overcomes, not because of his strength or ruthlessness, but because of his integrity, his sanity, his ability to adapt quickly, without hysteria or regret, to the circumstance around him. I doubt I would have become a science fiction writer had it not been for the inspiration provided by the words and worlds of A. E. van Vogt.

To write the sequel to the books prized above all others in youth is a privilege granted to very few indeed. Reader, in your hands you hold the stuff of dreams come true.

I wish to express my gratitude to Mrs. Lydia van Vogt, by whose kind permission this has been made possible.

NULL-A
CONTINUUM

1

The Map is not the Territory; the Word is not the thing it represents. Our sensations are not reality, but an abstraction from reality.

Pain.

A torment of fire raced along Gilbert Gosseyn's nerves as he stood on the promenade deck of the great space liner *Spirit of Liberty*.

The next moment: darkness.

A moment before, the calm voice of the captain echoed from the annunciators, warning passengers that the distorter-shift from orbit to the ship's berth on the planet below was about to take place. Through the cool armored plastic of the transparent hull, the planet Nirene hung like a black pearl in space, her ice caps a dazzling azure crown in the light of her blue-giant sun.

Then next moment . . .

Gosseyn's body jerked in agony, but before he could draw breath, the darkness and the scalding pain were gone. He landed on his feet in a crouch. There was carpet, not metal deck, underfoot.

He blinked. His eyes adjusted to indoor gloom. He was in a small, well-kept apartment. Behind him was a kitchenette, outfitted with the latest in electronic appliances; before him to the left, a retractable door was slid half-open to reveal a greenhouse filled with orchids. Steamy, hot air came from that door. What little light there was came from that doorway. Before him to the right was a closed door. Directly before him were a desk and chair made of lightweight plastic-steel. The chair had toppled. Here was a corpse.

The corpse was distorted, blackened, as if the once-human body had been *twisted* by unthinkably powerful forces. Here and there a white bone fragment peered through the dark, dry mass. The bones were subtly curved, but not fractured, warped out of alignment.

The mental picture formed was one of subatomic *wrongness*.

The man had been of a wiry build, lean but not tall. Few other details survived. The face of the corpse was an indistinguishable blackened mass. The head was burned free of hair. The right hand was a fleshless black claw; the left hand had been burned down to a stump. Concentric stains of decayed matter surrounded the left stump, as if the murder-energy, whatever it had been, had lingered at that spot after the man's death. Tiny glimmers of gold formed teardrops at the center of the halo of stains: Gosseyn assumed it was the remnant of a wedding ring.

Gilbert Gosseyn gently probed the corpse with a pulse of energy from his double brain. There was no return signal: He could not "memorize" or mentally "photograph" the cellular and atomic structure of the corpse.

The man's clothing, strangely, was not burnt or marred. He was dressed in the somber, loose-fitting garments favored by citizens of the central worlds of the Galactic League.

This raised the question of what planet Gosseyn was now on. How many light-years had he been carried by distorter?

THE gravity seemed the same as it had been aboard ship, which had been adjusted to match that of the planet Nirene.

The sensation of momentary darkness was familiar to him. Distorter matrices were able to form an electro-nuclear similarity between the atomic composition of one area of space-time and another, in such a fashion that the interval between the two points became mathematically insignificant. During that moment of distortion, objects, energy, people, even giant space vessels, could be moved across the gap between the two points as if there were no gap. The lesser always moved toward the greater.

Gosseyn knew the phenomenon better than anyone else. Except for Gosseyn Three, his "twin brother" (that cell-duplicated version of himself created in the same fashion he had been), no other living person was known to have the extra neural matter, a secondary brain, tuned to the energy flows of the continuum in such a fashion as to allow him to act as a living, biological distorter machine.

Someone had acted during the moment of distorter uncertainty. While the ship moved to her home-station receivers to which she was attuned, something had attuned Gosseyn . . . here.

Alert, he stepped into the orchid greenhouse. The room was hot and wet but unlit. A shawl hung on a peg near the door, emitting cool air. Gosseyn assumed the thermostat on the shawl was turned down to compensate for the close warmth of the room. Something tickled his memory. Where had he seen this before?

The light came from a second door beyond, half-open. Gosseyn was through it in a moment. It was a bedroom.

First, he stepped to the window, turned it on. The window was bolted to what seemed a wooden wall, but Gosseyn's secondary brain could detect the residual magnetism of the armor beneath the wood veneer, nine inches thick or more. The window was a fixed-direction model, able to bring in images from beyond the armored wall but not to peer into neighboring apartments.

The view showed a giant blue-white sun glaring down on a metropolis of superskyscrapers. Despite their height, the buildings were squat, cylinders as wide as they were tall; many were crowned with rooftop gardens of vivid blue plant life. One building, a stepped pyramid half a mile high, had acres of garden and park at every balcony.

But the scene had a grim aspect to it. Each building was surrounded by a slight haze like a heat shimmer: electromagnetic force shields heavy enough to dissipate the heat and radiation of orbital bombardments, nor did modern windows need to pierce the massive armor of their surfaces to bring in light. Air traffic was conspicuously absent, as were energy-bridges leading from roof to roof. Flying cars, or pedestrians strolling atop a solid streamer of force, made vulnerable targets.

Gosseyn amplified the window image. As a precaution, he selected a spot on a nearby rooftop and memorized it. Specialized ganglia in his extra brain felt the "tug" of awareness of that little portion of space less than a mile away. He set the trigger in his mind to jump him to that spot if doubt or pain struck him.

Then he focused the window on the posters and signs of the few street-level shops he saw. Some writing was in the script of Gorgzidi, which Gosseyn could not read but which he recognized. The automatic methods of learning spoken languages at a subverbal level did not have a means of teaching writing systems. Writing on the older buildings was Nireni, which he had learned in preparation for his voyage. He had also studied maps; he recognized place names.

This was the city New Nirene of the planet Nirene, the second city of that name. Before the throne had been removed to Planet Gorgzid, this world had been the capital of the Greatest Empire. The first city called Nirene, once a metropolis of some thirty million souls, was now a burnt, radioactive wasteland.

The military aspect of the architecture of New Nirene was merely one more legacy of the decades of iron rule by Enro the Red. The great dictator was gone, but the events the tyrant set in motion continued in their remorseless way under the vast inertia of social habit and thought.

The years of conditioning by police and military propagandists left a visible stamp on the scene below, and, Gosseyn reminded himself, an invisible stamp in the minds of Enro's subjects. To call the world a League protectorate was an abstraction, an incomplete statement. On a fundamental level, by habit and custom and all the neurotic behaviors of the untrained minds of Enro's subjects, this was still a world of the Imperium.

There was a high dome in the distance, possibly the very starport where the ship he'd traveled on was now berthed. The dome seemed solid: Distorter technology did not require the ship launching or landing stations to be open to the sky. But there were antennas atop the peak that suggested X-ray radar-photography arrays were able to examine ships in orbit for weapons before bringing them to the surface, in the heart of the city.

So Gosseyn had been carried a few miles, at most.

Why? And by whom?

GOSSEYN turned from the window.

The sense of familiarity was stronger now. There were two separate beds, with a nightstand between them. Next to one of the beds was an electric shoe rack, with several pairs of women's shoes, kept clean by the silent, invisible vibrations of the rack. Beyond, a beige suit of feminine cut was visible through a gap in the closet door. On the vanity, next to a small jewelry box, was a slender platinum cigarette case of the automatic kind. Everything on that side of the room bespoke taste, wealth, and elegance.

Next to the other bed was a bookshelf, neatly organized. The spines were lettered in English. Books of psychology, neurolinguistic philosophy, atomic theory, forensics, and other scientific works. The books were of the type that recorded spoken thoughts and notes by the reader, and were locked at his fingerprint. Atop the bookcase were several small scientific instruments, folded into black leather cases. Gosseyn picked up two of them:

The first was a unit for detecting atomic vibrations at a fine level; the second was a camera whose special lens arrangement could reconstruct photons absorbed into ordinary substances, glass or wood, and show recent events.

Gosseyn stepped to the closet, opened it. The man's portion of the closet had four suits of clothing of similar cut: One of them was an Earthman's dress suit, jacket and tie. A transparent plastic case built into the side of the closet held a heavy electric pistol with a snub-nose, several-megawatt aperture, dialed down to a nonlethal shock setting. A line of atomic batteries was fitted into a clip. Gosseyn recognized the make and model: It was Venus-made, designed with a built-in lie-detector circuit to prevent misuse.

He moved quickly over to the farther bed and picked up the pillow. There was a faint scent of perfume, a long strand of brown hair. Beneath the pillow was a recharging holster for a slenderer type of pistol: a lady's model. The pistol itself was gone. The manufacturer's brand was marked on the holster. Gosseyn recognized the model.

THERE had been a general store, run by a man named Nordegg, not five miles from Gosseyn's little house in Cress Village, Florida, that stocked sporting goods, including firearms. The slender and powerful handguns sat in a display case beneath the hunting rifles, with a small depth-illusion sign:

For the Prudent Student!
GOING TO THE CITY OF THE MACHINE
DURING THE LAWLESS MONTH?
Buy **Lady Colt Lectrocutioner** 1.6 Megavolt
Because not every man is sane.

His wife had bought one just before her death, back when they were both young students, preparing to visit the Games Machine.

Rather (Gosseyn mentally corrected himself), he remembered such a sporting goods store. He remembered his wife's tragic death in an airplane crash. He remembered his lonely continued studies, and his trip by stratospheric liner to the City of the Machine.

Most memories are abstractions of real events. The photon strikes the eye, and the brain records the images, or, rather, its filtered impressions of the images. But Gosseyn's memories, in this area, were false: imprints on his gray matter, having no bearing on reality. He had been shipped in a medical crate to the City of the Machine, fully grown, an artificial being with no past save for recorded fictions in his brain, and set to walk from the stratospheric liner station to the hotel. Within an hour, a routine sweep by the hotel lie detector had discovered his imposture.

The emotional connotations, the love, the pain, the regret, the hopes: All these emotions were false-to-facts. The image in his mind of the courtship, the marriage, the honeymoon, their sunlit days together: a delirium placed in his mind by Gosseyn's creator, Lavoisseur.

The image of a wife had been taken from a real woman: the Empress of the Greatest Empire. The moment a lie detector had verified those images in his mind, Gosseyn had been brought to the attention of the Imperial agents secretly on Earth.

It was all false. Gosseyn's training allowed him to dismiss the whole complex hallucination with the sobriety of a man waking from a dream. Lavoisseur had not been particularly cruel to him, since he could rely on Gosseyn not to form any neurotic attachment to any memories shown to be untrue.

But . . . and now the thought occurred to him for the first time . . . how had Lavoisseur gotten the detailed information, the picture, the echoes of her voice, which were written into Gosseyn's memories?

Because the details were correct. This was Patricia's room. He recognized her things. Which meant . . .

———

GOSSEYN returned to the first room and photographed the corpse with the special camera. With the lights in the room dim, the camera was able to project the image it found holographically into the room around him.

The camera image showed only a solid, hard-edged silhouette. Here was a man, standing before his desk, his back to it. From his posture and gesture, he seemed to be talking calmly with someone. That was the overall impression in Gosseyn's mind: The unknown man was serenely calm, even as he spoke with his murderer.

The other figure in the room was also a silhouette, but this was a shadow-being, a cloud of filmy darkness, tenuous at the edges. Details of the room could be glimpsed even through the thickest part of the shadow-body. Nothing else, not even whether it was man or woman, could be seen.

The first man shook his head: a curt refusal. The second being, the shadow-creature, raised a wraithlike arm and pointed toward him. The gesture was ominous.

Behind the man, behind the desk, the wall receded and opened into mist, which parted. The impression was one of immense distances entering the enclosed space of the apartment. Where the wall had once been now could be seen a huge red giant sun glancing down on a sea of black oil, crisscrossed by large and violent whitecaps. Jagged islands with peaks like razors towered into the black sky, and the red and rocky ground was cratered as if with millions of years of meteorite impacts. Despite the ground-dazzle, stars were visible here and there overhead. The heights of the waves and also of the island peaks suggested a low-gravity world; the dark sky suggested a very thin atmosphere. A second sun, this one a mere pinpoint of intolerable brightness, was transiting across the huge, cool, dull face of the red giant. The red giant's photosphere was curled into sunspots as the tiny white star passed.

The man turned slowly to regard the gigantic sun that had appeared behind him. The shadow-being drifted to the left, putting the man directly between him and the image. A flickering darkness passed from the shadow to the image, striking the man. The man staggered, throwing his hands over his head in sudden pain. His outline lost its sharpness and began to dissolve. He fell.

The shadow-being bent over the fallen figure, whose silhouette jerked and writhed.

The camera clicked, and the image was gone.

NEXT Gosseyn turned the atomic analysis unit on the corpse.

Every cell in the victim's body had been disorganized, complex molecules broken. The carbon atoms in the man's flesh had lost their atomic bonds with their neighbors but had not formed ions nor formed other chemical bonds: The black soot was due to a layer of this atomically disorganized carbon. It was a behavior not seen in normal space: only when the atom's location in timespace was profoundly disturbed, so that its relation to its environment fell below the crucial twenty decimal points that maintained the coherency of matter, could this effect occur. The man's flesh and bone had been melted atom by atom: a sadistically painful death.

No wonder the images from the embedded-photon camera had been merely black outlines. There were no photons embedded in the corpse, nothing for the camera to use to reconstitute an image.

The unit also detected a similar effect in the carpet. The carpet pores had automatically cleaned any visible stain, but the unit detected the invisible trail leading to the right-hand door. Gosseyn opened it. Though it seemed to be made of wood, when he swung the door half-shut he could sense the heft of the door panel, the metallic thickness beneath the veneer. It was armor. The dead man evidently had led a life of caution.

Beyond was a study. Whatever energy-ray had blackened and twisted the man had passed across this room and left a dark trail, which crawled up the wall and lingered on a mantelpiece above an artificial fireplace: Here were three-dimensional photographs, mementos from a wedding. The line of black char had neatly sliced each picture in half. The groom had been blotted from each picture, meticulously. In each picture, only the smiling bride survived: a tanned, trim, and athletic young figure in a white silk dress, orchids in her hair, a look of determination and intelligence in her hazel eyes—Patricia.

Gosseyn returned to the first room, bent over the corpse, wrapped his fingers in a handkerchief, and delicately removed the small, hard, flat object he found at the breast of the suit. It was a private detective's badge, still tingling slightly from its self-protective energy that prevented forgery. His name was still visible, as well as an address for an office on the Avenue of the Games Machine in Venus City.

The dead man was Patricia's husband, Gilbert Gosseyn's fellow Null-A, Eldred Crang. Gosseyn's friend.

There came a knock at the door. "Open! In the name of the law!"

2

The Laws of Men will never be just until they are sane.

Gosseyn stepped toward the door, but the shouted command had been merely perfunctory: The lock glowed red, then white, and shattered, while Gosseyn spun and dove back through the study door. Closed to a crack, the armored door offered both cover and concealment.

Through the door crack, he saw two men enter the room. In the gloom, each had a similar silhouette. Both men were light-haired, of medium height, physically fit.

Both were dressed in formal, somber suits. Behind them, he could a glimpse a third man, a technician, bent over a projector. The projector maneuvered a portable energy curtain that flickered as it advanced into the room before the two men.

The man on the left had a drawn pistol, still whining from the heat of the bolt that had shattered the door. "Where is he?"

The man on the right was holding up a detector: Tiny cherry-red electron tubes protruded from the reader face. He spoke: "Behind that door. Don't shoot, Commissioner Veeds! The readings are consistent with those of an unarmed man. At this stage, to assume him to be the murderer would be unsupported, given the murder weapon involved, and the evidence that this was a crime of passion."

"Let's have some light!"

The technician said, "Yes, sir." It must have been police procedure not to touch any circuits in a crime scene, for no one stepped toward the wall switch. Instead, the electric curtain stopped advancing and grew bright in the visible spectrum range. Light flooded the dim room.

Now the difference between the two men was clear. The man on the left, dressed in the long coat of a Nireni, was blinking and scowling, and he had the nervous, fierce look of a human adult raised without the benefit of Null-A training: a human, in other words, still governed by the same infantile emotional system as his killer-ape ancestors.

The man addressed as Veeds said, "Don't tell me when not to shoot. You're not the one in charge here, Mr. Mahren!" But he holstered his weapon.

Impossible that the other man, Mahren, would literally have been unaware of the first man's rank. Gosseyn regarded the comment as a non-message, meant only to convey dominance-symbolism, affirming Veeds' sense of self-importance.

Mahren was not blinking. His eyes had adjusted instantly to the change in light levels. He had the lightness of posture, the deep calm of expression, natural to a man in total control of his nervous system. He was half an inch taller than Gosseyn, with broad shoulders and muscular arms. He was dressed in the suit and tie of an Earthman.

Gosseyn recognized him. Karl Mahren was the Null-A representative on the planet, sent from Venus to help establish a General Semantics Institute here.

Gilbert Gosseyn called out to the men in the other room and came out with his hands up.

Mahren recognized him. To Veeds, he said, "This is the man who forced Emperor Enro to abdicate."

Veeds said, "The famous Gilbert Gosseyn. The living distorter. The man who dies and springs to life again."

Gosseyn heard mingled resentment and awe in the man's voice. Veeds came from a culture, despite its technological accomplishments, deeply superstitious: The look on his face was that of a man confronting a thing out of myth.

"The phenomenon is more complex than that," said Gosseyn. "My memories are transferred at death to a prepared new body; he will think and act as I do, and recall what I know. But this 'me' still dies at death, even if my memory chain lives on in another man. It's not real immortality."

Veeds said sardonically, "Perhaps not, but the rest of us just die at death, memory chains and all."

Gosseyn made as if to step forward and shake hands, but the energy curtain between them grew stiff. Gosseyn stepped back. "Am I a suspect in this? There is a lie detector in the other room that will confirm my innocence."

Mahren said, "I will vouch for him."

Commissioner Veeds glanced sidelong at the Null-A man. "You don't know him. Not personally."

Mahren said, "There are psychological rules involved in murder situations that Null-A science has studied.

Gosseyn is a sane man: There would be signs evident in his behavior if he were not."

Veeds turned to the wall screen, turned it on. "Security log, please."

The robot voice answered, "The last person to enter this apartment was the owner, Eldred Crang, at 2500 Imperial City Time. He was alone for two hours, nineteen minutes. At 2720, circuits detected his vital signs were abnormal and the hospital annex was called; at 2722, a voice matching Eldred Crang's uttered one of the key phrases that triggers an automatic call to the Commissioner of Police. At 2730, the record is blank—I was unaware of events and cannot account for the time. At 2735, I resumed function, did a system check, and detected a second man in the room. At that time, vital signs from the owner Eldred Crang were null: He was dead. There is no record of entry by the second man."

"Is this the second man?"

"Yes. He stepped from this room through the sunroom to the bedchamber, turned on the window, entered the closet, returned, went into the study, and returned again to this room. At that point, you entered. Imperial City Time was 2741."

Gosseyn said, "Where's Mrs. Crang?"

The robot did not answer until Veeds repeated the question. It said, "She and Mr. Crang left at the same time this morning, 0250. She was dressed in a beige jacket and slacks. The door circuits detected she was armed. I cannot report whether the weapon is properly registered with the Police Control Board: Records on members of the Imperial family are not available to me."

"There is no more Imperial family!" said Veeds. "The members of the Divine House of Gorgzid are private citizens: You will refer to them as such."

"So noted. Nonetheless, no records are available."

Veeds turned back to Gosseyn: "Let's hear your testimony." He put his hand casually back on the butt of his holstered gun.

Gosseyn briefly described his experience. He added: "The captain or crew of the ship I arrived aboard can vouch for my presence up to a point."

Veeds said, "Meaningless, Mr. Gosseyn. You could step into a stateroom, step across the galaxy in an instant, and step back in time to be seen coming out of the stateroom. I don't even know why you came aboard a ship at all."

Gosseyn explained that he could not memorize an area of space he had never seen before.

Gosseyn addressed Mahren: "This murder was committed by distorter. Crang was placed out of attunement with normal reality, and it killed him. A distorter also could have been used to interrupt the electronic thought patterns of the room's robot brain. I don't recognize why an image of another world appeared in this room, a dark oceanic world beneath two suns: a red giant and a white dwarf." He turned to Veeds, for the commissioner had stiffened in surprise.

Mahren said, "There is no need for a complex theory when a simple one will do. The other owner registered to this apartment could have turned off the security brain, committed the murder, and erased her record from the brain before turning it back on. Notice that the murderess was particularly vengeful about destroying symbols of Crang's marriage. Imperial law does not allow for divorce."

Gosseyn felt a sinking sensation in the pit of his stomach. "You don't suspect Patricia? She—"

Mahren's eyes narrowed. "Mr. Gosseyn, the psychological file on you maintained by the Games Machine mentioned that you had false memories of being in love with, and married to, Patricia Hardie, as she was known at that time. Perhaps the reintegration of your thought was less successful than appeared."

Gosseyn closed his eyes and paused in his thoughts. He was aware that his awareness was hierarchical: Sensations were interpreted by his thalamus and hypothalamus before reaching his cortex, and it required a brief moment of trained awareness to separate the emotional context of his thoughts from the unfiltered reality. This cortical-thalamic pause in his thoughts instantly and effortlessly restored his calm.

He opened his eyes to see that Veeds was drawing his pistol. Gosseyn stared at it quizzically.

Veeds said ruefully, "Sorry. I thought you were going to disappear." He lowered the weapon and said to Mahren, "I have known the Divine Empress Reesha, whom you call Patricia Crang, for many years: She loved peace as her brother loved war, serene where he was wrathful. Her hand is not in this. Her people might act on her behalf without her consent: Those who want to restore the Royal House of Gorgzid are dangerous men. The Interim Government forbids me to arrest Reesha's people." The contempt in his voice was plain.

Her people! Gosseyn took a moment to adjust his mind to that concept: fanatics who regarded Patricia Crang as a divine being, who wanted her to resume the throne of her defeated brother.

It was odd, for his training should have reminded him of the falsehood of this train of thought, but Gosseyn had a momentary picture, sharp and clear, from his memory: his young wife, dressed in plain and inexpensive clothes, coming in the front door of their little cottage, books of neuropsychology and linguistic philosophy tucked under her arm, an automatic basket filled with vegetables from the local greengrocer floating behind her. She was outlined against the light. He remembered how the brown hair, escaping her kerchief, was tossed in the autumn breeze; he remembered the clear look in her bright eyes; he remembered the joy in her light, quick footsteps. Strange to think of this simple wife of a poor student as the Empress of fourteen hundred worlds!

But the oddness grew on him, for the image and the

associated emotion were false-to-facts. They were based
on an emotional "set" that Gosseyn's training long ago
dismissed.

Gosseyn realized that he must act as if he were suffering a continuing mental attack. Some unknown force had
imprinted, or was imprinting, false-to-facts emotive reactions into his hypothalamus. He resolved to have his
brain photographed at the earliest opportunity.

Could Patricia or her people be trying to influence
Gosseyn's thinking to win her an ally? It did not seem
likely—but Gosseyn realized how little he knew about
this fascinating, capable woman.

Gosseyn said, "Why did she return here?"

Mahren stared at Gosseyn carefully for a moment. It
was not clear what he was thinking: Gosseyn detected
no interruptions in the smooth, strong flow of the man's
neural energies.

Mahren answered the question: "Mrs. Crang came to
this planet at my request. I thought it would quell the pro-
Gorgzid faction to have her publicly renounce the throne
and repudiate the Cult of the Sleeping God."

Gosseyn said, "That didn't work?"

Mahren said, "The announcement was scheduled for
today. She was going to swear fealty to the Ashargin
sovereign in a public ceremony. Obviously, that's been
canceled." He turned to Veeds. "Notice that the murder
weapon was used to destroy marriage symbols long after
the victim was dead: as if the symbols were real independently of the husband. This indicates neurotic symbol confusion. Therefore, this was a crime of passion."

Veeds said, "Not the passion of the Empress! You
come from a world without government, so they say. You
don't know that symbols drive politics. You think this
was not a political crime? There are still pro-Gorgzid
Royalists active on our world: The Interim Government,
the League Powers, will not allow us to abolish the party,
arrest the known members. The laws of Gorgzid require
the Divine Emperor to marry his sister: The Royalists

regard Mr. Crang's marriage to the Emperor's rightful bride as an outrage. Worse: a blasphemy."

Mahren now examined Gosseyn with a calculating look, saying thoughtfully, "The passions of a private man whose wife marries another can run just as strong. Even a man who merely thinks the woman was once his wife."

Gosseyn said impatiently, "Mr. Mahren, you were willing to vouch for my sanity just a moment ago. Why this change?"

Mahren said, "You flinch every time we say her name. You have a subconscious neurotic rage toward her—one you are unaware of. I did not see evidence of it, a moment ago. But it is peculiar. A split personality cannot have one personality perfectly sane, by definition. Yet that is what I'm seeing."

This was ridiculous. Gosseyn was of sound mind, incapable of rage. But Mahren was a Null-A. The man would neither lie, nor could he be mistaken about such a simple observation. Gosseyn nodded thoughtfully. The belief that he was free of rage did not make it so: Beliefs were abstractions from events, not the events themselves.

"A lie detector will clear this up in a moment. There is one in the other room, in a case beneath the bed." Gosseyn pointed at the wall.

Gosseyn saw a look of fear so stark and plain on Commissioner Veeds' face that Gosseyn whirled to see what the threat might be. There was nothing behind him but wall.

He turned back. The pistol in Veeds' hand was trembling. The Commissioner was afraid of him, of Gosseyn.

Gosseyn said, "I cannot see through walls. I am not your Emperor." Gosseyn kept his eyes on the gun and carefully memorized it, speaking calmly during the moment it took to do so. "Listen: Enro is currently in comfortable but lonely exile inside a remote asteroid near the edge of the galaxy. Cut off from the distorter circuits webbing the galaxy, it would be years, maybe decades, for any ship crossing normal space at sublight speed to reach him. I was the one who sent him there; there was no distorter machine on the other end."

The technician standing in the corridor spoke up: "Sir! He's attuning himself to your gun."

Veeds tensed, but the weapon *blurred* and vanished out of Veeds' hand before Veeds could pull the trigger. It appeared in Gosseyn's hand. He engaged the safety and slid it into his pocket.

"You'd shoot an unarmed man!" said Gosseyn.

Veeds snarled, "For a Null-A, you seem to use your words in a sloppy fashion. Unarmed, indeed!" Veeds said over his shoulder to the technician, "Can you detect the distorter that killed Mr. Crang in this room, hidden in the walls, anything?"

The technician said, "Whatever distorter circuit was used to commit this crime is not within range of these instruments, sir. Even if it were shielded, I'd detect it."

Veeds turned to Gosseyn. "Except we have a living distorter right here."

Mahren, by then, had returned with the lie detector. Veeds put his hand in his coat pocket. If he had a second weapon there, he did not draw it out.

Mahren said to the lie detector, "This man claims he is innocent of the murder that just took place here. Well?"

The dozens of tiny electronic tubes in it glowed serenely. "He has the rage and jealousy present in his mind to have committed the crime, but these emotions are not part of his primary brain. I would hypothesize we are seeing a malfunction of his unique brain structure: The second brain may be operating without the primary brain's awareness."

Veeds said, "Give us facts, not hypothesis."

"The subject has no memory of having committed any crime. . . ."

Gosseyn allowed himself a sigh of relief. "There! That's

settled. Now if we can find out what that image of the twin-sun world means . . ."

The lie detector said, "He is not consciously aware of the killing. Nonetheless, he committed the murder. . . ."

Veeds said, "You are under arrest for the murder of Eldred Crang, Mr. Gosseyn. Could you hand me my gun, please?"

3

Fear is the reaction of the living organism, not to threat, but to the perception of threat.

Gosseyn was puzzled during the brief ride. He and Veeds were in the back of a large black sedan, a silent machine that ran off atomic power. The soldiers at the military checkpoints glanced in the car at the commissioner and waved the vehicle through. In a short time, the sedan reached the armored fortress that served the district of New Nirene City as a police station. By the time he was brought, not into a cell, but into the commissioner's magnificent inner office, Gosseyn was puzzled no longer.

His extra brain could sense a complex web of suppressive force-fields around the building. He had encountered such nullification fields before, back when he had been a prisoner of Imperial agents on Venus. The stresses imposed on the local space-time prevented him from using his extra brain. He could have suppressed one or two of the vibrations, but to suppress all of them would have required the full attention of his extra brain, leaving none of his special abilities free to act. A mechanical distorter would likewise be blocked.

After the doors closed behind them and they were

alone within the palatial office of the police Commissioner, Gosseyn said, "It took me a moment to realize my assumption that lie detectors don't lie was false-to-facts. The ones used on Venus are not manufactured by a police state."

Veeds smiled genially and drew a small electronic cylinder out of his pocket and dropped it on the large polished desk that dominated one side of the room. "Useful for convincing skeptics during show trials. Everyone knows lie detectors are accurate."

Gosseyn saw no sign of shame or embarrassment on the man's face. Veeds came from a society where lying was an accepted matter of course. Gosseyn tried to imagine such a thing and found he could not. Certain history books on Earth hinted at such widespread neuroses, but— whole planets full of insane people? A galaxy full? The picture was a depressing one.

"So my secondary brain has not gone mad? I'm not really the murderer?"

"Ah—Mr. Gosseyn, I did not say that. Everything the lie detector said was accurate, all but that last sentence. I used my police override to give myself grounds to arrest you, something *he* would believe would convince me. Had I said I was taking out a warrant against the Empress, *he* surely would have killed us all on the spot, even as Mr. Crang was killed. *He* is very protective of his sister."

Veeds crossed around behind the desk, seated himself rather casually, and put his polished boots on the polished surface with a sigh of satisfaction. He opened a lower drawer to pull out a plum-colored bottle and two small tumblers.

Gosseyn said, "No, thanks. I don't drink."

"Too sane to have bad habits?"

"Something like that."

"I was expecting you to vanish from the car. Why didn't you?"

That explained the lack of precautions during the ride.

There had been no vibration field surrounding the sedan. "I'm innocent."

"Either you are abnormally naïve or your world must have abnormally honest police."

"My world has no police at all."

Veeds looked skeptical. "Who runs your prison colonies and concentration camps?"

How could he explain that there was no need for madhouses on a world with no madmen? Gosseyn turned away. Looking out, he could see boat and hydrofoil traffic on the river. The highway bridges, despite their size, were designed to be retracted into the concrete banks of the river. The multitude of low, flat barges floating along the bay Gosseyn took to be factories, which could be dispersed or submerged during emergencies.

Veeds had been raised in an environment where war and crime, with all the fear and sorrow that entailed, had shaped his basic assumptions. Gosseyn could not bridge the gap between them with mere words.

Veeds said, "Wonderful thing, those windows. You tend to forget it's just an image produced by rays. The outside of the building is opaque to visible light."

"You have evidence the building is opaque to Enro as well?"

Veeds studied his glass with evident relish, downed it swiftly. Whatever he was drinking was potent enough to bring a touch of pink to his cheeks, and he blinked and rubbed his eyes. "No evidence. Guesswork. No one knows how it is Enro can see through walls. No one is sure how far he can see. But—you are a scientifically trained man, Mr. Gosseyn. What would you say?"

"It is a distortion effect. Biological, like mine."

"So we hope. When this system was first invented, volunteers would plot against the throne in rooms such as this one. Some were arrested; some were not. We still do not know. Perhaps Enro can see through the suppression field, and merely toys with us. Perhaps he is not watching us now. Perhaps."

"You cannot believe Enro can see so far."

"See and hear."

"He is in a cell—a very comfortable, large, well-equipped cell, a cell the size of a small planetoid, but a cell nonetheless—a quarter million light-years away. Surely his power only works on a limited range."

"Surely? And I thought you Null-A types never made assumptions."

Gosseyn was silent. The man had a point. Gosseyn's own power had recently expanded from a twenty-one-light-hour range to an interstellar one, due to his study under the Yalertan Predictors. And Enro's people had been the masters of Yalerta, with years to study there.

"Still, there is no distorter record of that asteroid. I am the only one who could have freed him, and I haven't."

"No one else?"

"There is another version of me. He woke prematurely, before I had a chance to die. Our memories have diverged since that time."

"Where is he now?"

"He joined an expedition to the Primordial Galaxy. An experimental ship using engine designs taken from the Crypt of the Sleeping God, together with the powers of Gosseyn Three, artificially amplified, was able to cross the intergalactic distance in a matter of months rather than centuries. He hoped to find traces of the ancient, original civilization of the Forerunners of Man, discover the causes of the Shadow Effect that ate their galaxy and extinguished all their suns. He has been gone for over a year."

"Maybe your second brain has gone insane, and freed him without your knowledge."

"Why?"

"Your people are the expert psychologists. Can you think of no reason?"

Gosseyn could: Freeing Enro to commit the murder Gosseyn could not consciously contemplate would satisfy this hypothetical psychotic jealousy in his secondary brain.

And the lie detector had not confirmed that Gosseyn was not psychotic.

Gosseyn's training permitted him no emotional connections to fictitious memories of a fictitious marriage. But could that training have been removed from his extra brain without his first brain's knowledge?

GOSSEYN said, "You recognized the world of two suns at my mention of it. But there are more double-star systems in the galaxy than single-star systems, are there not?"

"Twin stars with planets are rare. Low-gravity worlds with oceans are rare. Both together are impossible. Nonetheless, the followers of the Old Religion say that the original home world of man was one such: a planet called Ur. Their doctrine says that the Sleeping God tarried on Ur before he came to Gorgzid to sleep. Spacemen say the world is haunted. Enro occupied the prehistoric cathedral some ancient race built upon that world, garrisoning it as his stronghold: an act meant to humiliate the Old Religion and confirm the supremacy of the Cult of the Sleeping God. Ur is Enro's fortress-world. No chart shows in which decant it lies. They say the world of Ur is invisible. They say Enro found it with his special power."

Gosseyn's interest was piqued. "My people think men evolved on Earth."

"How then to explain why men are found on so many planets?"

"Earth has cognate species, monkeys and apes."

"As do other worlds. All the scientific evidence points to an evolution, but . . ." Veeds shrugged. "We all must have started somewhere. Man did not create himself."

"The extragalactics—the ones who built the ancient starship you call the Crypt of the Sleeping God—say man originated in the Shadow Galaxy."

Veeds spread his hands nonchalantly. "Nirene was settled from Gorgzid, as were most of the worlds in this decant. If there is any record of Gorgzid being settled from an earlier world, that record did not survive the Inquisition under Secoh."

Gosseyn said, "What did your scientists conclude of the limits on Enro's powers?"

Veeds said with a snort, "Scientists? The Greatest Empire was never a place where one could inquire into the Emperor's divine powers and walk free. I know only rumor."

Now his voice became soft, as if, even now, even here, he feared who might be listening.

Veeds continued, "When Enro first wrestled the throne from the Ashargin of Nirene and returned it to the old capital on Gorgzid, his secret police network was highly organized, highly professional, and equipped with the lie-detector technology. Everyone believed that was all he had. The Ashargin, they had told us Enro's clairvoyance was all fakery, the superstitions of a senile planet. They said that even up till the moment when Enro's agents had them all slaughtered; only the feebleminded boy, young Rhade Ashargin, was spared, due to the cunning, or perhaps it was the mercy, of the Empress.

"But then Enro began to show his powers to ambassadors, courtiers, and rival lords of outer worlds. They would see the images form in the air before them. Perhaps he would show them their wives in bed, their buried armories, their secret shipyards, or the settings on the encryption machines hidden in orbital vaults.

"Enro would just show them and they would fall down in fear. He commanded them to worship the Sleeping God, and to make this worship the law of their world.

"Because there was no mechanism. No plate, no spyray. He would just close his eyes and open them again and what he saw became visible around him. Mirrors worked better than other surfaces to catch the images: He surrounded himself with mirrors, not because he was vain. No one knew how he did it."

"There is one man who might know. On this planet. I'll need to be able to move around. You've made arrangements?" Gosseyn stood up.

Veeds nodded genially. "You are a perceptive man, Mr. Gosseyn. I had been assuming you would teleport back to your home world, and flee the death that awaits you here; but, of course, I made plans in case you decided otherwise."

Gosseyn did not see what button he pressed, but to one side of the room a section of the wall slid open, and a white closet with glass shelves was revealed.

"There are masks made of pseudo-flesh in the drawer yonder, wigs made of living fiber, and so on. The suits can inflate or deflate in sections to alter your build to a casual glance. We will have your Earth clothing passed to Mahren, who is even now being made up to look like you. Brave men, you Venusians! Maybe Enro will be fooled. Maybe Enro cannot see bone structure. We think he cannot see the interior structure of solid objects. We think."

Veeds drained his tumbler and sighed loudly. "Some members of my cell threw their disguise equipment away, during the celebrations following Liberation Day. Fools. After the galactic war, the League-backed Interim Government refused to hang Enro; they think it is uncivilized to kill one's foes! Fools. And the Church of the Sleeping God still forms the backbone of Enro's political machine, but the Interim Government must follow the League Charter, which does not allow us to abolish a religion. Fools. All fools."

"I assume this equipment fell into your hands after you arrested some cells in the resistance? And you just continued their work. Why? You, a police commissioner under Enro? You were not loyal to the Ashargin."

"No. They let the worlds of the Greatest Empire slip through their fingers. League Powers encouraged rebellion and dissatisfaction, while the Ashargin dithered.

The Empire needed a strong hand to set her back on course. So I told myself when I was a younger man, stupid with a young man's stupidity. I suppose you Venusians do not lie to yourselves?"

"The training is not difficult. Talk to Mr. Mahren."

"Bah. I need no training to see through that lie. I was invited to Court once; do you know that? After my men liquidated a particularly well-connected League spy-ring. It was the supreme moment of my life, the one day from which I count forward and backward to mark the years. I met the Empress. She was as pure and regal as they say. Have you ever met a woman for whom you would do anything, betray anything? I stepped up to the throne, and she asked me about my wife and children by name. By name! Monarchs do not need to flatter and beg for votes, but she took the time to have someone read her my file. And she smiled and told me to continue my work. The Empire needed men like me. Her exact words. There was a small bruise on her cheek, here." Veeds raised a finger to touch his cheekbone. "Just here. Makeup covered it, but I am a policeman; I notice these things. No one in our Empire would strike the Divine Empress. Except Enro. You must kill him. He killed your friend."

Gosseyn shook his head. "The war is over."

"Only you can do it: You are like him. Beyond human."

Gosseyn said, "Enro is a man. He is limited by the logic of his passions."

"He gained divine powers after sleeping in the Crypt of the Sleeping God. Others in history attempted to sleep as he did, but they were not of the royal house of Gorgzid, not of the unbroken bloodline of primordial Ptath-Reesha, and so they died. Enro the Red is not merely a man."

Gosseyn paused, struck by a thought. "And did Patricia? Sleep in the Crypt?"

"The common folk were outraged when Enro's parents allowed him to sleep in the coffin of the God for the first three months of his life. They would have been more outraged at the thought of a girl-child. But Reesha is younger than Enro, and the Royal Family's control of the priesthood had grown in the intervening years. There were rumors that she was incubated secretly in the most sacred coffin. Some say she has the power to know things from afar; some say she has another, to see patterns in the structure of time, to sense fate."

Gosseyn wondered. Patricia did seem always to be at hand when crucial events were in the offing.

Veeds said, "Many of us think Reesha was the genius behind their early success. She reformed the navy, outlawed the selling of commissions. The wrath of Enro was without bounds after his sister the Empress left him. Enro sent whole worlds to the executioner: Whole seas were filled with blood, whole atmospheres with fine ash. They do not call him 'the Red' because of his hair. Come now! The blood of your friend calls out for vengeance, and the League-backed Interim Government will do nothing."

"You think Patricia will assume the throne of the Greatest Empire and overthrow the Interim Government once I kill her brother. That is your real motive."

"Enro is a beast. That is my real motive! Seeing the Divine Reesha enthroned is merely a . . . a fortunate side effect."

"She is loyal to Null-A ideas. Totalitarian dictatorship cannot hold much romance for her."

"Thorson died on your world: Enro's loyal right-hand man, and her rival at Court, or so I've heard."

"I killed Thorson."

"You alone? Or was her hand in it?"

Gosseyn pursed his lips. Patricia had been the one who introduced X, the crippled, psychologically damaged version of Gosseyn, into the household of Hardie, the President of Earth, when that schemer had been using smuggled galactic technology to corrupt the government of Earth. The conspirators thought X was Lavoisseur, the chief of the Semantics Institute, and therefore a crucial ally to their work on Earth. Unknown even to himself, X had been a copy of Lavoisseur, whose specially constructed and warped brain was designed to transmit thought-echoes, including all the inner plots of the conspirators, to his creator, the real Lavoisseur.

Later, X had been shot to death by Prescott, another galactic agent. Gosseyn assumed Prescott had done this on Thorson's orders.

But Patricia had been Thorson's sovereign; he could not have failed to recognize her. He knew her brother the Emperor to be hunting frantically for her. What hold had she held over Thorson to keep him in check? Which of his men had been loyal to her?

Veeds smiled a thin, triumphant smile. "Do you think she is not cunning enough to pretend a loyalty to your Null-A philosophy long enough to persuade you and your people to overthrow her brother?"

Gosseyn was silent. Patricia had not shirked personal danger. She had acted with bold confidence during her adventures on Earth and during the galactic war, a woman of abnormal intelligence and drive, even if not Null-A trained. Cunning? The word had implications he didn't like.

"Besides," Veeds said, "you have to kill him before he kills you. Oh? You cannot die. Well, then—then kill him before he kills me." Veeds poured himself another stiff drink.

"Illogical to fear him. Recapturing Enro, if he's at large, is merely a problem to be solved as efficiently as possible. Fear saps efficiency; therefore, I do not fear Enro."

Veeds snorted. "And they say men from your world are sane!"

4

Analyzing the universe into simple binary opposites, while necessary, has limited value.

Gosseyn watched from a balcony as Mahren, dressed in Gosseyn's clothing and wearing a convincing flesh mask, departed the police station. Gosseyn, dressed in Nireni fashion, departed a few minutes later, going the other direction.

The papers he had been given by Commissioner Veeds included a badge: With this Gosseyn was able to hire a robotic cab.

A half-an-hour ride found him two hundred miles south of the city, in a metropolis that on a smaller world would have been a major city but here was merely a sub-urb. The lawns and campuses of the Semantics Institute shined with the blue vegetation typical of Nirene, but in certain flowerpots were the roses and lilies of Earth. The architecture was airy and light, all soaring arches and weightlessly high roofs, in sharp contrast to the heavy and blocky Nireni buildings.

One building made of blue-gray metal, in a dell surrounded by trees and flowering bushes, was the medical center. He showed his pass to the clerk at the wicket.

The clerk was a Venusian Null-A. The rapid glance at Gosseyn's face, the suppressed smile, the small nod, told him his disguise had been penetrated.

The clerk said, "You cannot travel the grounds without an escort, who, in this case, is me. Now I have one errand to run first, to check the power switches in the dynamo room, so you'll have to come with me while I do that, and then we can see the patient you requested."

The dynamo room had one wall filled with power sockets of the atomic type, as well as step-down converters for changing the energy to electromagnetic, nucleonic, or gravitic energy of various types and wavelengths. During the clerk's system check, energies of various types pulsed through the rooms and Gosseyn memorized dozens of sockets of various voltages and roentgens.

Gosseyn was impressed. The clerk, whose name was Daley, had recognized not merely that the impostor was a Null-A Venusian but also which one he was and what needed to be done to provide him with a well-stocked armory.

Gosseyn said, "As a security precaution I assume you have all visitors pass a lie-detector test?"

Daley shot him a quizzical look but, for the benefit of any unseen eyes watching them, said only, "Of course."

They stepped into one of the unoccupied rooms. The medical appliances were, for the most part, hidden: A complex structure of electron tubes and neural psychology machines was built into the bed and walls. Otherwise, it looked like a well-appointed hotel room. A broad window (and this was an Earth window, made of glass) showed the lawns and grounds outside.

Gosseyn merely put his hand on the pillow. His extra brain sensed the electron flows from the lie detector were hidden under that spot. "Analyze the insanity afflicting me."

The lie detector spoke: "It is a possessive jealous obsession, combined with incest-guilt, of the typical Violent Man Syndrome. The false image of the object of your romantic obsession has been mutated by repeated subconscious neurotic redactions of your memory: It is tied to deep impulses of your most fundamental identity-concepts—a leader of men, a defender of the One True Faith."

Gosseyn said, "But—I have no such concepts."

"The concepts did not arise in your mind. Your mind merely interpreted them according to its own structure."

"How is that possible?"

"The question is beyond the capacity of this unit to answer."

Daley said, "I can answer. Lie on the bed; I will take an energy-photograph of your brain."

Gosseyn lay. Daley asked him to induce a semihypnotic state. Gosseyn did not need relaxing drugs to accomplish this; merely a silent effort of will sufficed. A special camera arrangement lowered itself from the ceiling on a telescoping arm.

A moment later, Daley pulled a treated sheet from the equipment in the ceiling, put it under a reader, and studied it.

Gosseyn felt a moment of grim satisfaction when Daley confirmed his suspicions. Gosseyn was not insane. Daley said, "The memory records in your brain are a sympathetic resonance phenomenon. The record in your mind was created in another mind. Imagine a brain in a completely passive state, so that another brain of the exact same electro-molecular composition could transmit thoughts to you below the level of your conscious awareness."

Daley did not need to say it, for they both knew Gosseyn's secondary brain was kept in an artificially passive state, for just the purpose of picking up energy signals from the surrounding universe.

Daley said cautiously, "I see that you enjoy an exceptional level of Null-A training."

Gosseyn understood. Daley meant that his well-trained primary brain was able to cleanse itself of the external impulses at a preverbal level, automatically. Gosseyn's second cortex, which was not used for abstract thought, was not a seat of awareness, could have no such training, no immunity.

Gosseyn spoke without rising from the bed: "Is it possible to suffer pain without damage?"

"If the pain signals were false, originating in another nervous system, and transmitted to yours."

Gosseyn understood. His system of immortality depended on the law of nature that created a subatomic confusion, an uncertainty of location, between two identical brains. But—how could the signal reach from the Shadow Galaxy to this one? Had Gosseyn Three returned in secret? And when did Gosseyn Three go insane? To the best of Gosseyn's knowledge, there were no other cellular-duplicates of the Gosseyn/Lavoisseur body line still alive, anywhere.

Awake bodies, that is. Was it possible that the accident that woke his "twin" Gosseyn Three prematurely had been repeated? The body would be young: The growth tanks had not had time to mature any clones beyond the biological equivalent of seventeen. Normally Gosseyn and his twin Gosseyn Three would have been immediately aware of the thoughts of another duplicate: unless the thought-signals were particularly weak.

Gosseyn had to make his primary brain aware of the subconscious whisper his supersensitive secondary brain was picking up. There was a chance that it would drive him insane. Gosseyn smiled, though. Here he was in one of the most advanced psychiatric facilities outside Venus; where better for a man to go mad?

Relaxation was the key. His primary brain had to be put into a passive mode.

Gosseyn said, "I've read that, in the old days, on Earth, there were sensory-deprivation tanks that cut off all sensation from the outside world."

Daley said, "We can accomplish that merely by interrupting the neural flow along your sensory nerves. It is painless. A lie detector can continue to monitor your brain for disturbances, in case the lack of sensation begins to damage you."

"Please make periodic energy photographs of my brain structure while I do this: I am interested to see what forces interact with my nervous system during this condition. Perhaps five minutes at first, then a longer period if the first test produces no result?"

Daley set the controls.

Gosseyn was floating in a silent darkness. Immediately

came a sense of burning pain. His flesh was being scalded, his nerves burned inch by inch.

Gosseyn blinked. He was upright, on his feet, standing in the bright sunlight. He caught the railing he found underneath his fingers. There were planters to his left and right and blue metal wall behind, some chairs and tables, but no people. Underfoot was a dizzying drop to the street, half a mile below.

By his previously established reflex, the moment pain touched his nerves, he had automatically shifted himself across the city and found himself on the balcony of the building across from Crang's apartment.

Gosseyn's limbs were shaking. Rage. There was rage inside his body. Not his own. Some other man's rage was making Gosseyn's face red with wrath, eyes narrow, and teeth clenched so hard that they chattered. The untrained, raw impulses of another man were making his skin crawl with hate, making his trembling hands curl into fists, eager for bones to break beneath them.

He sank into one of the chairs. Clutching his head.

What had that been?

There was something distinctly . . . corrosive . . . about the sensation. Like finding another man has been wearing your clothes, leaving his things in your pockets, his smell on your shirt.

Gosseyn paused to clear his mind. Then he used his double brain to "memorize" his own body and take a crude mental picture of it. He could feel the energy imbalance in his nervous system, connecting him to distant locations in time-space. He could sense which neural paths led to the trigger-concepts in his brain associated with each location. The most recent ones were here, this balcony; Veeds' pistol; the dynamo room at the Nirene General Semantics Institute. His modest brownstone in the City of the Machine back on Earth, his tree apartment on Venus, tens of thousands of light-years away, existed as trace patterns in his brain but were too far away, without use of another special technique, to reach.

There was nothing else.

Nothing else he could detect. Equipment at the Nirene Institute would be able to do more delicate analysis than any he could perform on himself.

He similarized himself back into the dynamo room. It took him a moment, at a run, to cross the lawn to the main building. Daley was in the room where he'd been standing a moment before.

At Daley's feet was a blackened corpse, naked.

"Mr. Gosseyn," said Daley in surprise. The young man closed his eyes and drew a slow breath. The cortical-thalamic pause. He opened them again. His voice was calm: "You are dead."

From the throbbing sensations passing through him, Gosseyn did not have to kneel and turn the body over to confirm the identity. He could feel the partial attunement still active, though fading, from a life-rhythm perfectly matched with his own.

He turned the body over nonetheless. This murder had been committed in a more professional fashion, a wound through the chest, not the slow torture of Crang's death. The face was intact.

His face.

5

A multivalued logic more accurately reflects the complexity of the universe. Such logic is called non-Aristotelian or Null-A.

Gosseyn tried to memorize the body, and could not. Like Crang, most of the body showed the corrosive blackness where molecules had lost their identity and lo-cation. The nineteen-decimal-point similarity needed for

Gosseyn's system of immortality to work had been disrupted.

The disruption was not complete, however. Certain cells still retained their connection to space-time, and to Gosseyn.

Gosseyn said, "There is a trace of neural energy left in the brain; it is too dim to make it out. Do you have access to an electron tube tuned to the frequencies needed to amplify brain-energy?"

As it turned out, he did. Less than two minutes later, the equipment cart was wheeled in. Gosseyn was again lying on the bed, and the lights in the room were dimmed, so that the ambient radiation would not disturb the delicate energies involved. Invisible vibrations issued from the machine cart, passed through the dead body, and set up a series of rhythms in Gosseyn's brain.

He closed his eyes. The sensations grew stronger.

Immediately he saw the galaxy of darkness.

A black hole, hundreds of light-years in diameter, occupied the vast center of the dark spiral. Brown dwarf stars, neutron stars, and black holes orbited slowly in the unlit spiral arms. Nebular gas and dust there were in abundance, but even when they gathered together under the enormous pressure of billions of tons in the center of a shrinking nebula, no ignition occurred. Here and there were globular masses of dark gas, hundreds or thousands of times the size of Jupiter, but the atoms at the core did not fuse but broke into a cold, dense plasma: a state of matter unknown to any science of the Milky Way.

In this empty zone between the dead stars and the supermassive black hole core hung the scientific superstarship *Ultimate Prime,* a five-mile-long torpedo-shaped machine.

To one side of the ship, the collapsed galactic core was dark, a monster of outer space that consumed all it touched, but it was not silent: Radio picked up the continuous hissing crackle of the X-ray storm issuing from the event horizon, as nebulae larger than worlds were sucked over the lightless brink. A wide area of ten thousand light-years surrounded the dark core, and had been swept clear of matter over millions of years, till only one particle per square parsec could be detected. Beyond this empty zone, to the other side of the ship, the dark stars in their millions, choked with streamers of cold nebulae, clouds of dust and gas thousands of light-years across, slowly circled the galaxy, a ring of ash that would never again wake to fire.

Gosseyn Three hung, weightless, in the giant cylindrical chamber of the navigation room. To each side of him, and above and below, vision-plates the size of football fields shined with the images of the desolation of the dead galaxy. He could see astronomers from the navigation crew slowly pacing across the panels of the vast vision-plates, held like flies on a wall by artificial gravity, now and again making measurements, or placing an amplifier between their feet, and bending with interest over the eye-piece.

His belt telephone rang. He pressed a pushbutton on the earpiece. "Yes?"

It was Dr. Lauren Kair, the Null-A psychologist. He was a tall, heavily built man in his late fifties, and his voice over the phone was strong and gravelly: "The ship's electronic brain says we are ready to make the energy connections to the Spheres. It will require all the distorter-based engines of the ship to make the primary connection. Dr. Petry of the archeology department assures me that any of the Spheres that are still active will send the connection to the next, outer rank of Spheres. If only one in forty still have any active circuits after so many millions of years, the resulting field should still stretch across a major segment of this galaxy, a cone-shape centered in the core radiating out to the fringes, some twenty-five hundred thousand light-years along its axis."

Gosseyn said, "And what does the ship's psychology

department say, Doctor? If my extra brain cannot encompass the energies involved, the experiment is pointless."

In this vast empty area between the arms and core, the expedition had found evidence of the lost civilization of the Primordial Humans. Giant geodesic spheres, metallic constructs larger than Jupiter, were here, hundreds and thousands and millions, each one separated from its neighbor by a distance of one thousand light-years, roughly the distance from Sol to Rigel. Amphibians ruled the torrid swamps of Earth at the time when these artifacts were built, and the dinosaurs were not yet born. The archeology department estimated that a little over 5 percent of the mass of the dark galaxy had been converted into the materials used to construct these Spheres.

Archeological teams had descended into more than one Sphere, cutting through layers of armor, miles of machinery, and standing in awe to gaze at circuits the size of continents, but a three-dimensional volume larger than Jupiter was simply too huge to examine. "We're like ants exploring the headlamp of an automobile," John Grey, the Earthman on the team, had said, after they had penetrated only a hundred miles or so under the surface. "We can only guess what the main engine does."

But the ship's nexialism officer, the "Expert Generalist" named Curoi, from the planet Petrino, had combined the findings of the high-energy physics and archeological departments with the speculations of the experimental distorter engine research team. Curoi's conclusion, which he presented at the last meeting of the Council of Captains (for the ship was too large to be governed by one captain), was that the primordial humans had been attempting to stop the spread of the Shadow Effect that was consuming their galaxy.

Gosseyn remembered overhearing the conversation. Dr. Kair had left his belt-phone running, the circuit to Gosseyn's phone engaged, so that Gosseyn heard Curoi's calm, uninflected voice: "The effect—and we don't know what it is—is related in some way to the distorter technology, to the fundamental realities underpinning time and space, energy and matter. The Shadow Effect must have spread, by the time the Spheres were built, to the degree that escape by faster-than-light distorter was impossible: This is why the Primordials colonized the Milky Way so slowly. A ship like *Ultimate Prime,* with her twenty-five-point similarity matrices, would not have been able to operate, to bridge the gap across space-time, in the conditions that obtained then."

The officer from the Engine Design Research department objected: "This ship's design is, itself, a product of this long-dead supercivilization at her height: How do we know under what conditions the engines would not have been able to function?" There was no need for him to say that there were elements and circuits in the engines whose functions were still unknown. The machinery occupied over nine-tenths of the available volume beneath the hull, and on hops across the short distances available inside a galaxy many of the circuits and energy-mechanisms had not yet been observed in play. His team's sole purpose during the expedition was to study these engines in operation.

Curoi said slowly, "The archeological team estimates that the Primordials fled this galaxy much more slowly than we are now approaching it, and used many small, slow four-man ships at sublight speeds. A strange choice from an engineering standpoint. Not a strange choice from a military standpoint, if they were scattering deliberately, allowing most of themselves to die on the gamble that some would live. The Primordials fled as if they were under fire. Therefore, we cannot assume the Shadow Effect that consumed this galaxy was a natural phenomenon. These Spheres, gentlemen, were their last line of defense. The Spheres are components of a distorter engine large enough to influence the entire structure of space-time on a galactic scale."

The Grand Captain of the expedition, Treyvenant, a

man from Accolon, chief world of the League, said, "There are countless millions of Spheres. How could they be controlled?"

Curoi spoke to Dr. Kair: "The Venusian man who is helping us make the million-light-year distorter jumps, Gosseyn, what is the theoretical maximum limit on his ability? We know he can teleport a man-sized object, like himself, from one deck of this ship to another, when he is too impatient to wait for an express elevator. . . ." (There was some murmured laughter at that.) ". . . But can he shift a building from a planet to its moon? A city? Can he shift a planet out of orbit? Can he memorize an entire solar system?"

Kair explained that the number of possible neural interconnections in Gosseyn's secondary brain exceeded the number of estimated particles in the universe. "As with most of the secrets of the human nervous system, the potential has not yet even begun to be explored."

There was a muttering of dismay from around the table. Grand Captain Treyvenant said heavily, "Without Mr. Gosseyn's special abilities, if anything happened to him, the ship would require fifty years rather than five months to return to our home galaxy! The risk is unacceptable!"

Leej the Predictress spoke next. Gosseyn heard her calm, patrician tones over his belt-phone. "Gentlemen, need I remind you why the Galactic Assembly launched this expedition? The Predictors of my planet, Yalerta, foretell that the Shadow Effect may soon appear in our galaxy as well. If this experiment yields clues as to how these Spheres arrested the Shadow Effect, the risk must be faced."

E-Vroi, an officer from Planet Corthid, spoke in the rapid staccato accents of his planet: "The Spheres did not save the Shadow Galaxy. What luck will we have, following a failed attempt?"

Curoi said somberly, "The evidence from the astronomy and paleontology departments suggests they were constructed after the Shadow Effect was much advanced, perhaps even after it was clear that it was too late for them. There is a mystery as to why they went to the effort."

E-Vroi uttered a high, sharp laugh. "Perhaps they left them for us. A generous effort!"

Curoi said, "Be that as it may, the Spheres attune two areas of space-time to each other to force them to behave according to a normal metric. Any defense against the Shadow Effect our own scientists might examine naturally will follow similar lines. Instead of starting from scratch, we have here the end product of an entire galaxy of scientific genius working for centuries on the problem, embodied in a physical form, reduced from theory to practice. It would be criminal to ignore the mass of data these Spheres could give us—if only we could measure them in operation."

Curoi's suggestion was to use the ship's engines to engage the ancient Sphere distorter circuitry, with Gilbert Gosseyn as part of the circuit. He was convinced the physiology of the Primordials was something like Gosseyn's and that the giant machines were meant to intermesh with a human nervous system.

The vast navigation chamber was the only place on the ship large enough, and insulated enough, to allow the energies from the ship's distorter engines to pass through.

So Gosseyn found himself in the middle of the half-mile-wide chamber, floating with his local gravity turned off.

Dr. Kair, over the belt-phone, was saying, "I cannot guarantee your safety. Leej the Predictress does not foresee a good outcome: Once we engage the engines, it is all a blur to her."

Gosseyn said, "I should be expected to endure more danger than a man with only one life: Otherwise, I'm shirking."

"Very well. The ship's electronic brain is engaging the engines . . . now!"

At first, Gosseyn detected nothing strange. Then, the sensation came upon him as if a million tiny particles, grains of sand and droplets of mist, were being "memorized" automatically by an action of his extra brain. A steady, powerful flow was rushing through his extra brain, so quickly that it was without turbulence, a blur of motion so swift that it seemed solid. Gosseyn realized that he could not move: The neural pressure in his body was too great for a signal to react from his cortex to his motion centers.

Then, a shift of perspective: The tiny grains and droplets he was memorizing were dead worlds and dead stars; the clammy clouds of mist were nebulae two hundred light-years wide.

Only one thing was alive within the dead galaxy: the Sphere network. Like a warm ring of fire, the electronic and nucleonic circuitry of the mighty Spheres tingled in Gosseyn's brain, sending his perception further and further. . . .

Experimentally, Gosseyn selected one of the millions of star systems he had memorized: two neutron stars with a companion brown dwarf, surrounded by dozens of frozen gas giants and hundreds of smaller ice-planets and asteroids. He shifted this system from its location in one of the outer spiral arms to a position less than a light-year from the *Ultimate Prime*.

The transition was smooth and effortless.

Gosseyn reached out and out with his perceptions. Some of the neutron stars he was memorizing seemed oddly smeared, as if he were perceiving them over more than one period of time at once. . . . All the stars in the galaxy were "blurred" along lines radiating from a single point, centered on a vast disturbance in space-time, a bubble of antigravity filling a superhot, superdense area of space . . . no, not of space . . . of the medium, whatever it was, that the early universe occupied before the balancing relations of space-time and matter-energy were settled. Pre-space. The Sphere-energies rushing through Gosseyn's extra brain were trying to take a photograph of the early universe, the origin point of all things.

Gosseyn opened his eyes. Dimly, he heard the ship's alarms ringing. The acres of vision-panel had gone a dark gray hue, and, even as he watched, they swelled outward and away from him, becoming misty and semitransparent. The ship was gone. Instead was a black misty nothingness, a shadowy cloud whose dim billows could be glimpsed by the stray sparks of some unknown energy that flickered between them.

Gosseyn Three remembered seeing such an effect before, when Secoh, the High Priest of the Sleeping God, had assumed his guise as the shadow-being called the Follower. But this time, it was not a human body but the ship, and the galaxy surrounding, and the circumambient universe that had lost its identity.

Through the black mist, toward him, a vaguely human figure, a man made of shadows, was walking. The figure seemed, in some strange, impossible way, to be walking forward across eternity, out from the origin point of the universe, down along the strands of blurred time-energy toward the present moment. An aura of colorless and deadly light was around him, making him visible: a smoky black figure against a smoky black background.

Immediately Gosseyn Three felt the tug of an attunement between the two of them. When the shadow-figure raised its hand, he felt his paralyzed hand rise of its own accord in response.

The rapid thoughts of the other being leaped into his brain: "I detect that the amnesiac version of Lavoisseur called Gosseyn has almost achieved the no-time, no-space condition: But he has not yet attuned. His death must be instantaneous, for he is aware of my thought-patterns, but has not realized my identity. The isolation technology of the primal Ydd life will distort his relation to the continuum below the twenty-five decimal places needed for existence to maintain self-identification."

The figure reached out its shadowy hand, pointed a wraithlike finger. Gosseyn Three felt his mind dissolve into agony.

Gosseyn Three's final thought was the sudden awareness of a reflex that Lavoisseur must have built into his brain stem, a hidden reflex that would try to reach across time and space to any of his twin-brother organisms within range.

Gosseyn Three's last act was to similarize himself to Gosseyn Two.

The intergalactic space was far beyond Gosseyn Three's normal range, but the galaxy-wide circuit of ancient alien technology bent space to shorten the distance, allowing this last, desperate jump all the way back to the Milky Way, back to the planet Nirene.

Einsteinian considerations prevented any true simultaneity of events, so the final connection had been suspended until the moment when Gosseyn Two, in the relaxation of the sensory-deprivation tank, attuned himself to his twin. The pain signal of his death, arriving when he arrived, accidentally sent Gosseyn Two across the city to the balcony opposite Crang's.

Gosseyn Two, lying on the bed in a small room in the Institute, now opened his eyes.

He said to Daley, "I killed him."

6

Insanity is the confusion of symbol for object at a preconscious level.

Because Enro might be eavesdropping, Gosseyn could say no more to Daley about the unknown, murderous version of himself, a Gosseyn version who had slain Gosseyn Three, but it was clear that the rage Gosseyn

Two picked up with his double brain had been coming from this new and deadly twin.

Had the two not been duplicates on a molecular level, the attunement of thought from one brain to another could not have taken place. The killer had to be a version of himself.

In the third subbasement below the ground, Gosseyn looked through the one-way wall at the tall, gaunt middle-aged figure seated, motionless, eyes dull and blank, in the white chair. The room was comfortably appointed, but the slight telltale haze around certain of the objects betrayed the presence of force-fields ready to catch the patient if he fell, or tried to hurt himself.

Gosseyn entered the room quietly. "Secoh," he said.

Secoh lifted his dull eyes and stared at Gosseyn without recognition. Then, his face, thin but strong, lit up with a smile. Some of the old charisma of the High Priest of a galaxy-conquering religion was still there: Gosseyn noticed how handsome the man seemed.

"Ya wanna play? Play wif me? I'm *Secoh*! Who're you?"

Gosseyn looked toward Daley, who had come in with him. "The memory-layering technique," Daley said.

Gosseyn nodded. The doctors were restoring sanity at each level of development, chronologically.

Gosseyn said, "Can you adjust the neural flows so that later layers of memory, adult memories, are available? I don't want to hurt him, but he may know something useful to an investigation I am pursuing."

Daley opened a panel in the wall, where banks of lie-detector-type circuitry were glowing. He made one or two adjustments.

Secoh said, "Play!"

Gosseyn picked up a child's ball that was one of several toys on the floor: a transparent sphere with a glittering many-armed spiral inside. He tossed it to Secoh.

The man caught it with both hands but then forgot the

game and stared in wonder at the spiral image in the ball. "Galaxy. The whole galaxy. Mine. In my hand."

Secoh stood up from the chair, swayed, but then knelt down. "Mommy says I have to pray. Pray to the Sleeping God before I sleep. Both of us sleeping. Ain't that funny. Pray to . . . pray to . . . He screamed when I killed him. . . ."

Tears welled up in Secoh's eyes, and a sudden grief, deeper than agony, contorted his features. He screamed in stark, terrible rage, clawing at his own face with his fingernails.

Daley adjusted the circuit. Secoh smiled and collapsed on the floor, drooling and cooing happily.

Daley said, "The difficulty is that all his major memory chains, even to his youngest, are caught up in the worship of the idol he killed. However, we have been getting some success with a more dangerous technique: one you must be familiar with."

Gosseyn looked at him quizzically.

"A second personality can be created from the main stem, unaware of the memories of the parent mind. We call it the Lavoisseur technique. We will have to step back behind the protective barrier to use it."

"The patient becomes dangerous?"

"Very. Secoh occupies more than one vibration state of matter-energy. His other form enjoyed state-specific memories, and can be layered to a more adult level."

When they were watching, once again, through the transparent wall, Daley donned a pair of thick, leaded goggles and handed a similar pair to Gosseyn. Then Daley turned to the control panel governing the electron tube energies flowing through the brain of the patient in the next room.

Daley said, "The system works by negative suppression. If the energy from the board is cut off, his normal pre-adult brain-wave pattern will emerge."

Daley made the delicate adjustment.

In the other room, Secoh, his eyes glittering, his face expressionless, rose to his feet. The body of Secoh began to blur and darken. In a moment, his flesh was dissolved; instead, a being made of shadow hovered there.

Gosseyn was amazed. "How is he able to do that without a distorter?"

Daley said significantly, "Certain specialized cells in his brain act as a biological distorter. However, he cannot cast the shadow-image beyond a limited range without artificial amplification."

Gosseyn opened the microphone and said, "Secoh. I've come to talk to you."

From the shadow-being came a deep, dispassionate voice: "Not Secoh. That name is nothing to me."

"Who are you?"

"I am the Follower."

"I need to ask you some questions."

The shadowy silhouette of a head tilted forward. There was no face, but the hint of posture seemed to indicate intensity. "Ah! Gosseyn. I see your energy patterns. I know you."

The lightning bolt that flashed from the core of the shadow-being sputtered against the insulated transparency. The internal force-fields in the room flickered into full strength, and only this prevented the bed and chairs and other flammable objects from igniting.

GOSSEYN turned up the gain on the microphone, to make himself heard above the terrific discharge in the other room.

"Follower! I've come to ask you about the Crypt of the Sleeping God."

Daley put a hand on Gosseyn's elbow, pointed to one of the readouts on the psychology machine. The needles on several dials were inching their way toward the red. This topic was the main psychological danger to Secoh.

Gosseyn said, "There is someone else who can manifest a shadow-body."

The needles crept down. The dark, translucent figure nodded. No features of its face could be seen, but the posture was one of a man intent, watching.

The Follower said, "The Observer said this body was to be my particular sign of favor from the Sleeping God."

Gosseyn was taken aback. "Observer? You mean the artificial brain controlling the Crypt?" Gosseyn had called that machine the Chessplayer. He knew no other name for it. "It told me that when you were a novice at the Crypt you accidentally operated the shadow-substance mechanism, which was one of few devices still operating in the Crypt. It attuned itself to you."

The dark, sardonic voice of the Follower said, "Amusing! If you call the months of instruction spent repairing the shadow-attunement mechanism, and being trained in the space-deception and control techniques 'an accident,' well, then an accident it was."

Gosseyn said carefully, "But—it told me that when it tried to make mental contact with the peoples surrounding the Crypt, they grew frightened, and fell into worshipping the Sleeping God. That they did not understand his true nature." Gosseyn said nothing about the so-called god being nothing more than a crippled intergalactic spacetraveler. He did not want to challenge Secoh's neurotic beliefs.

"Is *that* what it told you? Frightened of it, were we?" Again, a deep chuckle came from the wraithlike figure. "The Inner Circle of Priests knew what the Observer Machine was, Mr. Gosseyn. Ever since the early days of our industrial revolution, we knew what machinery was. The scientific advances produced from secret studies of the systems allowed the priesthood to hold its grip on power for thousands of years. Yes, we knew. The science was a gift of the Sleeping God. And we knew the Observer Machine was not reliable. The machine had a God that it was entrusted to keep and watch as He slept, and it schemed forever, forever seeking to escape its duty, and find a way to destroy Him."

But this thought was too near the forbidden, horrible truth that Secoh could not bear. The needles fell all the way to the red. Daley reached toward the control to sever the circuit keeping Secoh's real personality suppressed, but the needles suddenly fell into the normal range.

The shadow-being straightened. He said, "The other priests communicated with the Observer, and thought the body in the Crypt was merely a man. But what do you call a creature that cannot die, who can see the future and view events remote in time and space, who can step through walls, control matter and energy, and whom no mortal weapon can touch? Would he not be, indeed, a god?"

The Follower stepped forward. The armored glass wall separating them shimmered oddly when the shadow-being stepped through it.

Daley's quick reaction was to use the wall circuits to place an insulation force-web around himself and Gosseyn. That split-second action saved Daley's life: The bolt that came from the Follower threw Daley back across the room, away from the controls, but Gosseyn could still detect the young man's nervous-system action, his vital energy: Daley lay motionless on the ground but was alive. Gosseyn merely similarized the lightning bolt thrown at him into grounding points in the Institution dynamo chamber.

The Follower now took up position between Gosseyn and the control panel. Gosseyn could not tell which way the odd being was facing. Perhaps it was studying the controls that maintained the thought-pressures allowing it to think and move; perhaps it was contemplating Gosseyn.

Gosseyn said, "If you move away from the range of the field, or damage the control unit, your artificial state will collapse back into your base personality. You cannot escape."

The Follower said nothing. There was a slight hiss in the air, as if the shadow-creature were building up a static charge.

Gosseyn said quickly, "If the other shadow-being commits murders that do not honor the Sleeping God, the Follower will be blamed, his name dishonored."

The Follower spoke in a voice of amused contempt: "Do you think it is for the praise of men I do my work? Do not toy with me, Gosseyn of Venus. You think the Sleeping God is a cripple, a mortal man maintained by an ancient robotic brain. You think man evolved upward from apes. Surely all the evidence points to another conclusion: that man degenerated from a higher state."

Gosseyn said, "Are you saying the other shadow-being is a higher form of man?"

"No. Obviously, it is my cousin Enro."

Gosseyn was surprised. "Cousin?"

"Of course. The Emperor is my cousin. I am a bastard son of the House of Gorgzid. The blood is in me, though only the God recognized me. All other men despised me. But had I not been of ancient and royal blood, the God in the Crypt would not have been able to stimulate the growth of special space-control nerve ganglia in me, or train me to control the non-identity condition." The Follower raised a shadowy hand, its fingers like wisps of ghost-stuff. "Lesser men thrust into this state simply die."

Gosseyn was shocked by the implication. Enro and Secoh seemed to have suffered a process similar to the one that grew a double brain in him.

And yet it made sense, suddenly, of a number of things.

But he did not see how this second shadow-being could be anything other than another Gosseyn body. How else had the mental connection, the automatic awareness of the murderer's thoughts, leaped to Gosseyn Three?

The Follower was speaking. "When the newborn Enro was operated on by the Observer of the Sleeping God, the work done was repair work, correcting genetic errors due to degeneration of the superhuman species from which we descend. Surely you did not think those coffins, those life-suspension units, were designed to mutate the patients placed inside them?"

Gosseyn said, "I was told the double brain was found in the brain stem of ordinary humans in a stunted form, undeveloped. You were subjected to a similar technique related to a different nerve cluster area of the brain."

"Such a nerve cluster is an atavism, a stunted relic, not an undeveloped potential. The Primordials suffered genetic decay due to inbreeding after their galaxy was destroyed. But the coffins were designed to repair years and centuries of accumulated cell damage, and they can restore to proper function the organs of those in whom the ancient blood runs true. The ancient gene combinations can be found in the Vestals of Ur, the Savants of Petrino, the No-Men of Accolon, or the Predictors of Yalerta, or any other worlds, not yet discovered, where the Primordial Men first touched down when they colonized this galaxy. The Royal Family of Dzan is magnetoelectrokinetic, but the trait was once common among their general population."

"That's why the Greatest Empire sought and found Yalerta."

"Yalerta is a planet isolated and unaware of the galactic civilization around her. The Greatest Empire also found Earth, and also prevented other worlds from making contact with her. It served our purposes to hoard the planets with remnants of extragalactic technology. Petrino and Accolon discovered the galactic culture before our ancestors could stop them. Remnants of the science and wisdom of the Primordials are found there: They rose quickly to predominance. These two worlds formed the League to stop the spread of the Greatest Empire."

"So if there is a second Follower, a second shadow-being . . ."

"It is Enro. The Second Follower must be of the House of Gorgzid, one who slept in the coffin of the Sleeping God. That is: Secoh or Enro or Reesha; the Lord Guardian or the Emperor or the Empress. But she is fallen from the ancient ways, and brings shame on House Gorgzid. And I am trapped here."

So Patricia had been exposed to the mutative nerve-surgery of the Crypt!

Gosseyn said, "Why would the Chessplayer, the one you call the Observer, have lied to me?"

"Why would it tell the truth? Its builders, despite that they were gods, were desperate, fleeing galactic disaster. They would not have given the machine scruples: It was meant to carry out its task, no matter the cost."

"What task?"

"The Machine was programmed to protect its charges: the first four stored in its medical coffins, and, later, their descendants. Do you not know who woke from the other three coffins, the empty ones? The second was Inxelendra, the Bride of the Sleeping God; she turned to evil when her husband could not wake, and stole the tablets of prophecy to the world of a far star. The third and fourth remained and wed, and became the father and mother of our race. The Observer continued to keep watch over the sons and daughters of Ptath and Aradine for ten million years: That is the age of the House of Gorgzid."

"Then why help me?"

"The machine concluded that the ambitions of the Greatest Empire involved an unacceptable level of danger to its charges. It carried out its programming, and arranged matters to stop Secoh without hurting him—by breaking his weak mind, trapping him here in this madhouse. Enro was sent to exile, unharmed. And the Observer was finally rid of its burden. The only way it could allow the God to be slain was if one of the God's own bloodline, someone the Observer was forbidden to harm or stop, was manipulated into dealing the fatal blow."

The needles on the machine behind drove all the way into the red. The shadow-being raised its wraithlike hands

to the blankness of its face, while sparks and flares of
lightning began to gather around it.

The Follower said coldly, "For that blasphemy, Secoh
must die. He was a traitor. The Awakened God himself
pronounced these words: *Secoh—traitor! You must die.* I
can still hear the words in my ear. The God Slept, and
creation was unfinished, and for these reasons man is
weak and false. But when he wakes, the God will complete the world, and all the dross be burnt away."

Lightning leaped in and around the figure, but in its
shadow-state the creature could do itself no harm.

Gosseyn detected a jump in the roentgens in the area.
It appeared that the Follower was about to employ atomic
rather than merely electromagnetic energy in its futile attempt to destroy its invulnerable shadow-body. Gosseyn
could not calculate the damage such a discharge might do
in the middle of a crowded metropolis. He similarized
the mechanism keeping Secoh's personality suppressed
to the spot on the balcony overlooking Crang's apartment.
The Follower slowly began to take on substance and shape.

But this had evidently been part of the Follower's self-
destructive plan. Its body of flesh was about to materialize in a radioactive room, surrounded by the fires started
by the energies released into the room a moment before.

Looking through the armored glass, Gosseyn selected
a spot on the far side of the room, where the insulation
and safety fields were still operating, and he similarized
Daley's unconscious body there. Gosseyn established a
reflex in his extra brain to do the same to Secoh as soon
as Secoh's body became solid. Ringing alarms were already summoning medical technicians to the scene.

The Follower was solidifying into Secoh, clothes and
all. Gosseyn asked one last question: "How did Enro escape from his prison asteroid?"

The Shadow Man uttered a breathy laugh. "You may
ask him yourself. He watches us now."

Secoh appeared where the Follower had been, and then

reappeared safely on the other side of the barrier, unconscious, and in the arms of the waiting technicians.

Gosseyn felt his nape hairs tingle. His extra brain felt the buildup of space-distorting energies in the area, like those that slew Crang. He turned. There was no one there.

The wall phone said, "Call for you, sir. Long distance."

Gosseyn turned, and stepped toward the phone. The handset hung next to its intercom plate, slightly burnt from the voltage released in the room.

He picked it up. "You did not kill me."

7

When the symbol-to-object relation is false-to-facts, behaviors are maladaptive. When the mind will not abandon useless behaviors, frustration is the result.

A voice, a deep, rich baritone, spoke: "What would posterity say if I cut down a man, even an enemy, while he was helping my mad cousin to safety? I am not a monster, Mr. Gosseyn."

"You killed Crang."

"And what would posterity have said if I had not?" A charming chuckle sounded over the line. "Why, nothing, I suppose! Since my posterity will never come into existence until I marry my mate, and breed the true bloodline again. The race that springs from me shall oversweep the galaxy, and replace mankind. Crang hindered that destiny; hence he destined himself to die. It was really suicide, not murder, if you think about it, Mr. Gosseyn."

The wall beyond the phone stand turned to mist and seemed to open and recede. Beyond was an ocean-scape of rocky, cratered islands. It was night, and dazzling bright stars gleamed on a wild ocean whose wave crests rose to monstrous heights in the low gravity. The island mountains reared to impossibly thin peaks and lopsided overhangs.

Standing on the cratered ground, tall beneath the stars, was a red-haired man, powerfully built, wearing a Greatest Empire naval uniform of scarlet, crimson, and royal purple, but without any other insignia of rank. His eyes bored into Gosseyn's sardonically.

He had a microphone clipped to one epaulette. Its wires ran to a small radio-distorter unit, half-hidden among the ribbons, medals, and jewels on his chest. The radio was the type used to transmit orders to warships in orbit or troopers in air-helmets.

Gosseyn selected a spot behind Enro and memorized it. He half-expected something to detect and interfere, but nothing did. He now had a mental cue to allow him to step to the planet Ur instantaneously.

Enro's smile thinned slightly. Suspicion tingled in Gosseyn's brain.

Why had the dictator used his power to broadcast an image of himself across the galaxy to a room on Nirene? It was evident that he could see without being seen. Why reveal himself?

Gosseyn recalled a similar image had appeared in Crang's room before his death, and that the shadow-being who killed Crang had carefully positioned itself so that Crang was between it and the image.

Enro had once mentioned a dangerous tension of space that existed between him and the images his power created: The great dictator here had used the effect as a murder weapon.

Gosseyn realized that he must be partly attuned by Enro's power in order to see this image. He dared not similarize himself to this specific spot of ground, not if Enro had manipulated the space-tension to erect a trap. If he was ever to find his way to this world, Enro's base, it had to be through an image Enro showed to, and attuned to, someone else.

Enro said, "So here is the immortal man! But it seems you have learned that your method of cheating death can itself be cheated. Welcome back to the ranks of those of us who know what it means to die: You must now do what all your fellow mortals must do to stay alive."

"Think . . . ?"

"Obey! I am here to give you an ultimatum."

Gosseyn sighed inwardly. Neurotic minds were not flexible and tended to fall into well-established habits. Next would come bloodthirsty threats.

To Gosseyn's surprise, Enro uttered no threat, not directly. Instead he said, "Thorson was greedy for immortality; he had been elevated to a high place, but he was of common birth, and you must know how that is. What a strain it must have been for him to serve a man like me! To see the gift the Sleeping God gave me, and to know his low blood made such gifts forever beyond his reach. He tried to betray me: He called off the genocide we had planned for Earth, merely to have more time to study *you*. You see, he thought you would lead him to the man who made you, the man who knew the secret. But there was no secret, was there?"

"What do you mean?"

"You cannot make other men as you are, can you? The great Gilbert Gosseyn does not know who he is or whence he comes, does he?"

Gosseyn smiled in disbelief. He did not think of himself as "great." But Enro could not admit he had been defeated by an ordinary Venusian man. "You tell me who I am then."

Enro simply shook his head, a look of bitter amusement on his face.

Gosseyn waited.

Enro was suffering from what Null-A identified as the Violence Syndrome, the belief that when bloodshed did not solve a problem, more bloodshed would. Enro's sense of freedom from the normal rules of morality came from the distorted idea he had of a posterity that would justify, with grateful applause, all his actions. This imaginary audience allowed him to ignore the real world, the real consequences of his actions.

However, the imaginary audience made demands on him: He had to strut and proclaim like a stage actor for them, to do the things his neurotic imaginings told him they wanted. So he had to talk; otherwise his make-believe historians would have nothing to write down.

Therefore it was Enro who broke the silence:

"The stories about you say you don't know where you come from, Mr. Gosseyn. They say a galactic traveler, one of our people, independently discovered a method for cloning men and transmitting memories from one generation of himself to the next."

"On Earth, he called himself Lavoisseur. The memory chain between his line and mine was broken."

"Your father?"

Gosseyn shook his head. "That term is not accurate."

"Whatever he was, the story is false."

"False how?"

"He was not a galactic traveler. Not one of us. No League world, no Imperial world, none of the neutral worlds has any such technology, or any science from which such technology could grow."

Strange. Once again, Enro's speech did not seem to fall into the pattern Gosseyn expected: almost as if the great dictator were playing for time, trying to keep Gosseyn occupied.

Gosseyn's eyes swept the room. What was Enro waiting for?

Of course. The medical technicians were about to take Secoh away. Enro was waiting for Secoh to be out of the line of fire.

Gosseyn touched a button on the intercom and asked the decontamination room to sweep this area with a field to nullify the traces of the atomic energy Secoh had introduced. At the same time, with his extra brain, he similarized a connection between the phone wire and its wall socket, maintaining the electric flow between the two as he unplugged it.

Gosseyn said into the phone, "You told your people that the genocide of Earth, the plot against Null-A, was merely a gambit meant to outrage the League Powers into going to war with you. That is not the real reason. Earth and Yalerta figure in your religion: Gorgzid's rivals for the claim of being the original home of man in this galaxy."

Gosseyn opened the transparent armored wall and stepped over to the levitation trolley where Secoh lay. He walked with the technicians as they wheeled Secoh out of the room.

The lead technician's eyes flickered to Gosseyn. Without a word, Gosseyn nodded toward the exit. The technicians started moving that way as if it were the normal direction to take a patient.

The man was a Null-A. He had recognized the dangerous plight Gosseyn was in and the danger Gosseyn had brought upon everyone, visitors and staff, currently on the Institute grounds. Obviously, they were evacuating the grounds. Obviously, they were hoping Enro would not release a wide-area weapon until Gosseyn was away from the buildings.

They stepped out of the room. Gosseyn wondered if the image of Enro would move and keep pace with them. It did not. Enro did not need to be seen to see. This suggested again that the image had been presented to Gosseyn as a trap, tempting him to similarize himself to an area Enro had prepared.

Over the phone, Enro was saying, "The attack on Earth was meant to provoke a response from the Games Machine, or, rather, from whatever Primordial Being was protecting Earth. The response seemed weak out of proportion to the threat: You appeared on the scene, killed Thorson, and let your creator be killed."

It seemed Enro could be prodded into continuing to talk before he struck. But for how long? How long until the pressures in Enro's subconscious required him to kill Gosseyn?

Enro was saying, "It seemed a small response, at first. But then, on Gorgzid, the Ashargin heir was possessed by the Sleeping God . . . or so he said. Reesha reappeared, but now married to a Venusian detective named Crang . . . or so she said. You appeared on the planet Yalerta, where the Follower had been recruiting the Predictors for my fleets. Before I knew it, Secoh was mad, the Predictors were gone, and I was forced from my throne. I discovered later that it was you, not the Sleeping God, who was possessing the brain of Rhade Ashargin. Poor, ineffective, little Ashargin! He is now Emperor once again, at least until the Interim Government decides what to do with him. So you are simply everywhere where I suffer a setback, Mr. Gosseyn! Not surprising for a living distorter, I suppose. But somehow you are less than you seem."

Enro had something he wanted from the conversation, perhaps a symbolic concession. Neurotics often played out scenes in their imaginations when contemplating their crimes and were disappointed if reality left out any lovingly anticipated details. Enro was a much more powerful neurotic than most: The supreme leader of a galactic totalitarian theocracy, gifted with superhuman teleclairvoyant powers, has many ways of getting his most finicky whims sated. He would delay killing Gosseyn until the moment seemed perfect.

The path the chief technician took was a roundabout one, away from the other buildings in the Institute. Gosseyn could see that the tall arches of the Venusian architecture, peering high above the ornamental trees, were now shimmering with the telltale haze of a Nireni building. Generators were erecting anti-atomic fields. Shields were being lowered over the expansive Earth-style glass windows. The staff did not know how large a weapon Enro would unleash upon Gosseyn: They were taking every precaution.

While they walked, Gosseyn spoke into the phone he carried. One way to keep the Emperor talking was to give him the opportunity to boast. The kind of man who does not think men can be cowed by boasting speeches does not become an Emperor.

"You knew about Thorson's betrayal?"

"Oh, come now. What can be hidden from an interstellar-range clairvoyant? Of course I knew."

Gosseyn had doubts about Enro's range. He suspected the dictator needed a distorter system to gather images at multiple-parsec distances. Secoh had used such a system, and it seemed a safe assumption that Secoh's shadow-being projection was a phenomenon related to Enro's clairvoyance.

The dictator continued, "The only reason why I delayed spraying your planet with radioactive isotopes was that my divine sister was holding herself hostage there, if you take my meaning."

When they were halfway between the two buildings, Gosseyn simply stopped walking and the technicians and Secoh continued. They turned a leafy corner and were gone.

Gosseyn said, "You found out about the shadow-substance mechanism in the Crypt of the Sleeping God by listening to the psychiatrists here interview Secoh."

Enro said, "Don't be absurd. Secoh told my parents about the machine when he first found it. That is why my father, Ajjan the Wise, struggled so long to maneuver Secoh into a position of more influence in the Crypt. Once he murdered his way into a high position, Cousin Secoh was able to arrange to have me placed in one of the medical coffins as part of an ancient ceremony when I was but a baby. Later, when I was an ambitious young planetary governor, Secoh murdered his way all the way to the Chief Guardianship. Do you think such a thing could happen on my world unknown to me?"

"But you said you didn't know who the Follower was!"

"Yes. So I *said*. I am gratified to note that you assume

everything I say is truth. Would that my own subjects were so trusting! But they believed that the Divine Emperor had nothing to do with the shadow-being that slew the priests disloyal to me. I would not confess otherwise even to my court, or in private. We never know who is listening, do we?"

A dry chuckle.

The dictator said lightly, half to himself, "Oh, that is wry, coming from me, isn't it? I should change the motto under my dynastic crest."

Gosseyn looked around, both with his eyes and with his extra brain. There was no one nearby, no pulse of nerve energy to indicate someone hiding in the brush. Secoh was a safe distance away, in a shielded building.

Gosseyn said, "Who are you waiting for?"

A dry chuckle. "Surely that is obvious. Lavoisseur. I am curious to see if your creator will intervene when I dispose of you."

"Lavoisseur is dead. Thorson killed him."

"Oh, come now, Mr. Gosseyn. I understand you come from a planet with no laws, but are the basic principles of government power unknown to you? Agents are disposable; masters are not. According to my spies, Lavoisseur created two duplicates of himself. One was the cripple who Thorson thought was the chief of your Semantics Institute on Earth, the man you knew as X, who was shot by Prescott. The other was you. My spies were wrong. There were three duplicates. The third . . ."

"The third?"

"The third was the man seen by Thorson, killed by him; and with his death, all links to your original creator and the secret of deathlessness are severed. All clues are destroyed. Surely the advanced science of psychology for which your world is famous could detect that there is one thought so obvious that it should have occurred to you at once, Mr. Gosseyn. At once! Except that you were designed with a mental block, a subconscious interference that prevents you from thinking it."

"You are saying the third man, the one I saw die, was not the real Lavoisseur. He was another X. Another Gosseyn. Another expendable spare body."

Gosseyn was remembering that the dying man's last words to him had been to assure him that there was no Chessplayer behind him, no mysterious figure manipulating his life. Those words had convinced Gosseyn to cease seeking his origin.

"Even now you do not see it. Amazing! I am saying he was as much the 'real' Lavoisseur as you were the 'real' Gosseyn. The first version of you, Gosseyn One, was gunned down on Earth. You are Gosseyn Two, who woke up on Venus. The artificial memories of Lavoisseur One held the crucial idea that there was no Cosmic Chessplayer behind his actions: an idea he passed on to you. His mission done, he was also gunned down. And so . . . where did Lavoisseur Two wake up?"

"Why do you assume he is still alive?"

"Oh, I do not. Not really. Because the Lavoisseur who created Lavoisseur One, the original and unknown Lavoisseur, perhaps had no more need for a Lavoisseur Two, and simply let that line die. Gosseyn Two he needed to corrupt Thorson's loyalty to me. But the Lavoisseur Zero, the Unknown, he is surely still alive. You don't see it, do you? You are an intelligent and curious man, Mr. Gosseyn. But you have one blind spot, placed in your mind by your creator. You are programmed to overlook clues leading back to your creator. A little over two years ago, the last and highly degenerate remnants of the extragalactics, the Primordial Men who fled from the Shadow Galaxy, stumbled across one of the asteroids where Gosseyn Three was held in a medical suspension capsule. An accident woke him prematurely. This just so happened to place a Gosseyn at the right place at the right time to quell the threat posed by the extragalactics. It was during my investigation of the extragalactic men and their technology that Gosseyn Three, with no warning or formality, teleported me to a remote asteroid prison. I recall the incident well. So very well. Now ask yourself why this astronomical coincidence happened."

Gosseyn said nothing.

Enro continued in an amiable tone, "I admire the economy of his moves. Lavoisseur Zero is clearly one of the Primordial Men, perhaps the last of them. I require his knowledge and technology to serve me. So far, I have been content to leave you alive, hoping you would lead me back to him. He has not seen fit to contact you. Surely you wish to find him?"

"I hardly have any reason to cooperate with you, Enro."

"You have no reason to be loyal to him, do you? He created Gosseyn One for the express purpose of dying, merely as a stunt, to impress Thorson. So much blood, just for a gesture. No, Lavoisseur does not care if you live."

"Lavoisseur, if he is alive, would not want the secrets of his technology in your hands."

"Nonetheless, you will help me find him, willingly, in life, or unwillingly, by your death."

"You are asking me to join you?"

"To serve me, yes."

"I refuse, of course."

"Is my cause so ignoble? Since the dawn of time men have yearned for universal empire, and dreamed of the end of all wars."

"Imperium obviates the need for external wars, but the civil wars and revolutions are just as bloody, or more so. Even decent men are trapped by the need to betray or be betrayed; armistice and honorable surrender are impossible to rebels."

"Nonsense!" Enro's tone was dismissive. "If the Empire is well run, there will be no rebellions. If the Emperor is immortal, there will be no wars of succession. If he is clairvoyant and prescient, there will be no chance of conspiracy against him. There will be one law, eternal and all-powerful."

"Enforced by whom? Unless there is universal agreement on the principles behind the government, there can be no universal peace. Only a scientific principle has the necessary objective truth behind it: such as Null-A neurolinguistic psychology."

"Oh, I have plans along those lines, Mr. Gosseyn," Enro said airily. "But come now! I am not unreasonable! I offer a temporary partnership: You wish to find your creator for your reasons, and I for mine. We cooperate until our interests no longer intersect. Surely that is preferable to immediate, painful, and permanent death?"

Gosseyn said, "Very well. I agree."

"I will wait while you get a lie detector to confirm that for me. From the Institute, please! I do not trust the lie detectors used by the Nireni police."

So Gosseyn walked back into the building. As he expected, it was deserted. The fires had been extinguished in Secoh's room. There was a bank of lie detectors built into the wall: Gosseyn opened a panel and touched one.

"Confirm that I am sincerely willing to help Enro find Lavoisseur, if he is alive. I believe the attempt will be futile; if Lavoisseur allows himself to be found, it will only be under such conditions as will defeat Enro's schemes. I also honestly believe that Enro, even knowing that I have these mental reservations, will not be psychologically able to believe that he has no chance of success."

Again the dry chuckle came from the phone. "I see we understand each other, Mr. Gosseyn."

But the lie detector said, "The subject is sincere on a conscious level, and speaks what he believes to be the truth; however, on an unconscious level, he is consumed with rage and jealousy, to the point where he intends to kill Enro at the earliest opportunity. The subject regards Enro as a rival for the love of Patricia Hardie, his wife."

Gosseyn yanked his hand away from the unit. "Enro! If you overheard my conversation with Daley, you know those emotions came from an exterior source."

Enro said slowly, "My spies tell me that the way

Lavoisseur made sure you came to Thorson's attention was to have the false memory that you were married to my sister placed in your brain. I had been assuming this was merely a surface delusion, like a hypnotic suggestion. Lie detector! Did he touch her? Does this baseborn infidel vermin remember touching my sister's divine flesh with his filthy hands?"

Gosseyn crushed the phone in his fist, but it was too late. The machine had heard the words and responded, "Subject memories include many instances of an erotic congress with his wife after their honeymoon, which are neither delirium nor fantasy, but neither do they seem to be true memories of this body. . . ."

Enro was apparently not listening to the qualifications. If he had any last words or threats to accompany his attack, Gosseyn, broken telephone in hand, did not hear them.

The room around Gosseyn turned to black mist and swirled away from him in all directions. He still felt the solid floor underfoot, but his eyes beheld the cratered landscape and the wild seas of the twin-sun world of Ur. Where Enro had been standing now a shadow-figure loomed, eyes burning. Enro had no need to move to a position to put Gosseyn between him and his projection: The projection was all around Gosseyn, and above, and below.

Gosseyn felt the intolerable pain of space-time being distorted around him. The shock of death came faster than he could consciously react.

He felt his extra brain acting of its own accord, automatically.

Darkness.

He woke naked between the satin sheets of a four-poster bed. Dazzling pale sunlight shined from the marble floor and was reflected by the ornamental carvings in the painted ceiling. Seated before a vanity mirror in a sheer negligee was a woman brushing her brown hair, which shined like polished amber. The mirror was one of those television types that could show the room at any angle: The image held both the seated woman and the bed where Gosseyn stirred.

She turned. Her eyes sparkled playfully, and her white teeth flashed in a mischievous smile as she said, "Well, well, sleepyhead! It is about time you woke up!"

It was Patricia.

8

The function served by a tool can be inferred by its design.

Gosseyn saw the gun when he started to sit up. Patricia half-turned in her seat, hairbrush still in one hand. In her other hand, shining like a jewel, was an electric-voltage pistol of powerful design.

Gosseyn noted abstractly that it was a Lady Colt 1.6 megavolt. The gun she bought on Earth, in Cress Village. But those memories were false.

Weren't they?

Noticing the direction of his stare, Patricia smiled slightly and inclined her head toward the deadly weapon held in her slender, rock-steady fist. "A woman can't be too careful. Last time we were alone in my bedroom, you tied me up and gagged me. You're a dangerous man."

He said, "At that time, you were Patricia Hardie, member of a conspiracy to destroy Null-A. Who are you now?"

She flipped on the pistol's gyro, so it would continue to point at Gosseyn, and turned on the pinpoint microphone in the grip, so she could fire by voice command. The pistol balanced itself on the back of her chair and continued to cover him. This freed up her hands to continue putting her hair up.

She said casually, "Reesha. Her Radiant, Divine, and Imperial Majesty, the Gorgzin and Holy Imperatrix

Reesha vor Ptathrandu of the House of Gorgzid, Bride of the Sleeping God, Shepherdess of the People, August Mother of the Greatest Empire Ever to Exist in Time and Space, Protectress of the Mirabel Cluster, Grand Duchess of the Lesser Magellanic Cloud and the Stars beyond the Hercules Nebula, Sovereign Queen Absolute of all the stars, systems, and constellations of the Seventh Decant. I've got a dozen other titles to go with it. It's quite a mouthful."

"At that time, your bedroom wall was the one holding the mechanism that had driven the Games Machine insane, and forced it to select your father—the man pretending to be your father—as President of Earth, instead of a qualified candidate. Even then, I should have wondered why the President of Earth would put himself in the position where his so-called daughter, by wrecking one unprotected machine, could send him to a criminal-psychiatric ward."

Patricia sat with her elbows up, fixing her hair into a net. Her eyes tilted sideways, not looking at him; she talked without moving her teeth, for she was holding pins in her mouth. Every now and then she drew one from between her lips to pin her hair up in place.

"Mr. Hardie was an Earthman, an ambitious native chieftain of a backwater world. Originally, that was Thorson's room, but I outranked Thorson and so I booted him out . . . and sweet little Vorgul would have done anything for me anyway."

" 'Vorgul'?"

"Vorgul Xor Xayan of Gorgzid. You did not think his real name was Jim Thorson, did you?"

Gosseyn was trying to imagine calling the hulking, cold-eyed murderer he knew as Thorson sweet or little. He could not.

Patricia gave a slight moue of distaste and prodded a last strand of hair into place. "No matter," she said, lowering her hands. "We have more important things to do than to chat about old times. Will you give me your word that you will not teleport away, blast anything with lightning, or do anything rash, while we talk?"

Gosseyn, leaning on his elbows, half-reclining, shifted his eyes left and right, using an eidetic method to take in all details at one glance. There were tall windows to one side of the room opposite where Patricia sat, but covered with a semitransparent force-barrier, so that sunlight entered, but details of the world outside were blurred. Gosseyn saw green shadows, a sway of motion he took to be a fountain, and guessed the blurred glass looked out upon a walled garden.

Across the chamber from the bed were tall doors, paneled with ornamental designs, hanging half-open. Through this, a lavishly appointed suite could be glimpsed. Larger doors on the far side of the suite were closed, and also were dimmed by an energy barrier. The impression was that of a place under siege.

The wall opposite the windows, behind Patricia, registered on his extra brain: a complex of circuits, as of some large machinery, but none of the energies he detected was lethal.

His only danger came from the gun. Gosseyn took a moment to memorize it.

He said, "I agree."

There must have been a lie detector in a drawer in her vanity table, because a mechanized voice said, "The subject is speaking the truth without mental reservation."

Gosseyn sat up in the bed. "Lie detector! What is the name of this woman here?"

"She thinks of herself as Mrs. Patr—"

"Don't answer that!" Patricia's voice, suddenly sharp, cut off the lie detector in mid-syllable.

But she did not seem angry. Her green eyes glittered with amusement. Her hair done, she stood and took the pistol in hand again. The mirror behind her formed a bright backdrop, making her filmy nightgown insubstantial: The slim curves of her alluring silhouette shined through it.

But Gosseyn kept his eyes on the pistol.

"Are you going to holster that?"

"It's for me."

The idea that she might be in so much danger should not have surprised him, but her comment came like a blow. He searched her features. "You . . . you would kill yourself rather than marry Enro?"

She shook her head. "I fear him, but not to the point of death."

"Then who?"

"The League Powers. The Interim Government. They are using something like Null-A technology in ways that are nightmarish, abhorrent. A technology your people foolishly gave into their hands."

GOSSEYN said nothing. The detectives of Venus had discussed the ramifications of giving the secrets of their Science of the Mind into the hands of unsane and insane men. The grim decision had been to proceed. The theory was that once the technology was spread widely enough, those who misused it must inevitably be detected and cured by the efforts of those who used it correctly. The Games Machine of Venus had seconded the decision.

A science that taught men how to control their own minds was the only science, which, by its very nature, in the long run, could not be abused.

But in the short run, it could.

She said, "Imagine a torture chamber equipped with Null-A-qualified lie detectors, so that every nuance of pain can be studied carefully to increase its effect. Imagine using electron tubes to suppress the higher brain functions where moral reasoning takes place. Your people's theory is that correct use of language can make men sane: Obviously the incorrect use can make them insane, and, if used skillfully, can make them all insane along similar lines. Do your people understand the nuances of mob psychology? My brother is not the only one who knows how to sway the huge planetary populations of the ignorant."

"The League Powers are a democracy."

"Which means, in order to secure their elections, their politicians there must study mass psychology as closely as any dictatorship. The planet Petrino, one of the main League Powers, has already voted itself under the control of a Psychology Standardization Committee, one that defines disloyalty to Petrine ideas as a form of mental aberration to be cured by the state. They are using highly sophisticated neuropsychological techniques to do it. If this is what they are doing openly, I can only wonder what their military intelligence bureaus are doing secretly."

"Do you expect to be attacked any minute? Any second?"

That was the moment when he allowed his extra brain to memorize her molecular and atomic composition. He combined the cluster of cells in his extra brain to track her location and monitor her levels of neural pressure for signs of danger-anxiety.

She said, "Several people from the palace have already vanished: Someone focused a distorter on them from orbit and snatched them away. The Interim Government won't let us take proper precautions, won't give us the military electronics we need to protect ourselves. . . ."

"Us? Where am I? What planet is this?"

She tilted back her head and gave a ringing peal of laughter. "Are you lost? The man who can cross the universe in one step, lost!" She turned her back to him, setting the pistol down on the vanity table and taking a cigarette out of a jewel-studded holder. The little box lit the cigarette for her automatically. She turned again, breathing in the translucent bluish smoke and studying Gosseyn thoughtfully.

Gosseyn stood up but drew the silk sheet up with him and draped it over one shoulder, an impromptu tunic. His act was based not on modesty but on calculation. Nudity would distract this fascinating woman from answering his questions. Somewhere in the galaxy, great events were taking place; dangerous forces were set in motion. Gosseyn felt a sense of impatience inside him. Enro had already struck once, and Gosseyn did not know why the blow had failed.

"Where am I?"

He must have sounded more forceful than he meant to, or perhaps there was a cold look in his eyes, for Patricia took half a step back and picked up her pistol. And yet she did not seem flustered—Gosseyn could not recall ever seeing her at a loss.

She took a slow puff of her cigarette, tilted back her head, and blew a plume toward the ceiling. She spoke in a lighthearted tone: "You are in the one place where Enro, even if he can see you, cannot kill you."

"Where?"

"Near me."

PISTOL in hand, she turned her back to him and walked over to where a dress of glittering, finely woven metallic cloth hung on a mannequin. There must have been a concealed holster woven into the fabric of the skirt, for the pistol disappeared into its folds.

Then the filmy nightgown came off her shoulders and began to slide toward the floor. The action was entirely spontaneous, unconscious. It was only with a slight gasp of surprise that she caught herself and clutched the robe about herself before it fell farther. Pausing to flick her cigarette into a nearby disintegrator tray, with a sidelong, cryptic look at Gosseyn, now she stepped behind a screen. The mannequin stepped after her and helped her dress. Gosseyn could only see her feet and ankles as she dropped her lacy garments and went through the motions of donning her stockings and shoes.

He said, "This is the Imperial Palace of Gorgzid."

Patricia said, "Obviously. You must be slower on the uptake than the last Gosseyn."

Gosseyn saw the implications of that comment. He examined his hands: no evidence of calluses. He threw the bedsheet from his body. No sunburns, no moles, none of the tiny little evidences of a man living an active life.

He felt with his extra brain for the energy connections leading to his various recently memorized spots, such as the balcony across from Crang's apartment, or the Semantics Institute on Nirene: nothing. He was cut off.

It was as if his secondary brain had not been used before.

With swift steps, he leaped toward the section of the wall where he had detected a complex machine circuitry. He could not find the secret switch to open the panel, but he could detect the magnetic locks holding the panel in place. The energy circuit from Patricia's gun was already memorized. He took the long moment for his extra brain to negate the space-time relation between the power cell inside her gun and the magnetic bolts in the walls. There was a flash of lightning and a loud shock of noise, and the panel toppled slowly outward. It was heavy, but Gosseyn's training allowed him to increase the muscular pressure in his limbs, and so he caught the massive slab and lowered it quickly to the floor.

He straightened.

Hidden in the wall was a medical coffin, surrounded by a life-support machine of the self-sustaining kind. Here also was the special distorter-and-lie-detector combination Gosseyn recognized as the products of Lavoisseur's technology.

His coffin. His birth-coffin.

Gosseyn turned. Patricia had emerged from behind her dressing screen.

"I am Gosseyn Four. The fourth version."

She nodded. "My brother killed you."

HE examined the settings on the distorter-detector combination. From the ranges involved, the magnitude of energy flows recorded in the system's log, it seemed as if Gosseyn Two had died even as he landed on one of the prearranged safety spots, a hospital on Venus, to which he had trained his body to teleport by reflex when driven unconscious; but at that death-moment (for no events in the universe were perfectly simultaneous) his brain was out of the range of Enro's no-identity effect, so that his body hidden in a medical capsule here in the great palace of Gorgzid was able to quicken to life. He touched the unit with his finger: The electron tubes were dark and cold. There was no connection with the body on Venus, which was probably even now being autopsied by Null-A physicians.

Had Enro merely allowed his attacking effect to reach a higher energy potential before striking, the similarity between the two Gosseyn bodies would have been broken and Gosseyn Two's identity would have been lost. Enro would not have made this mistake had he not been blind with anger.

Gosseyn straightened and turned toward Patricia.

She was in a stately yet simple gown of gleaming metal cloth, with a chain of office around her neck, a diadem on her head, and a delicate scepter in her glove. She wore the regal ensemble with no trace of self-consciousness. Gosseyn could sense the energy source from her pistol near her thigh, but the folds of the dress betrayed nothing.

He noted that she did not seem to see his nudity. On the one hand, she must have been present when someone manhandled him out of the birth-coffin into her bed. But on the other, her beginning to disrobe in front of him seemed automatic, not a matter of coy flirting. As if . . .

He said, "You remember being married to me. I do not see how that could be, though. Those memories were implanted in me. They were false."

Patricia, for the first time, looked at a loss, uncertain. She turned her eyes away from his.

But she said, "Null-A men are trained to observe psychological reactions, nuances of expression, subtle verbal cues. Unless I undertook a process of false memory implantation—similar to yours—I would never have been able to lure you into Thorson's trap, and Thorson would not have been able to examine you up close. And it was necessary for him to examine the immortal man up close."

Stepping over to a drawer built into the side of the medical coffin, she drew out a bundle of clothing and tossed it toward him.

"Implanted by whom? The Greatest Empire does not have that technology."

The bundle unfolded as he caught it in the air. It was a one-piece suit, durable and inconspicuous, wrapped around shirt, shorts, tie.

"I was working with Lavoisseur," she said.

He began dressing. He noticed that the thermostat settings on the suit were already at the temperature he liked.

"And why not have the false memories removed later?" he asked.

She motioned with her hand, and a shoe box rolled out of the automatic closet and offered him socks and shoes.

"Lavoisseur died on Earth, killed by Thorson's men," she said.

He sat on the bed and picked up a shoe and turned it over. It was a brand made by a small firm in Chicago, one he habitually wore. The soles would adapt to different surfaces, in case the footing was rough or slippery or so on. The insides had a layer of comfortable medical foam that would chemically react to small cuts, bruises, or bunions to bandage and soothe them. Useful footgear for a man who does not know when he might step from one landscape to another.

He said, "Enro thinks Lavoisseur must still be alive."

Patricia said airily, "Enro became Emperor because he is the kind of man who does not believe an enemy is dead unless he sees the body. Paranoia is useful to him."

Gosseyn donned the shoes and stood up. They were in his size. "No neurosis is useful. It has already driven him to commit unnecessary murders. Three murders, if you count me. Where is Lavoisseur? If you are his agent, you should know."

She put her gloved hand to her mouth, trying to hide a girlish laugh quite at odds with her regal appearance. Her eyes danced with mirth. "His agent? Oh, no. No, not quite like that, Mr. Gosseyn. Gilbert? May I call you Gilbert? I mean, I am the only person you know."

He opened his mouth to object that he knew many people, but he snapped it shut again. Gosseyn Four did not know anyone: He had never been out of this room.

"He was your agent then. How did you find him? Where is he from?"

"I don't know. The Observer of the Crypt found him for me."

"The Chessplayer."

"What?"

"Sorry. My name for it. That machine seems to be behind everything that happens to me. It manipulates events to . . ."

"To what?"

"You tell me. You say it found Lavoisseur for you—why?"

She said, "It wanted to stop the war between the League and the Empire. The only way to keep us safe was to dethrone Enro, and the only one who could do that was Lavoisseur, who created you for that purpose. Enro was too ambitious, and each passing year created more enemies for us."

"Us?"

"Enro and me. Observer is like a nanny. It protects me."

Gosseyn nodded. Her statements agreed with Secoh's. That did not necessarily mean that they were true; the two could have agreed on a story beforehand, or have been raised in a similar belief-system, or deceived by the same source, or . . . there were several possibilities.

"I wondered why you were so reckless."

"Me?" She seemed startled.

Gosseyn shook his head. "The first time we met, I had just been thrown out of a protected hotel during the policeless month in the City of the Machine. You were running down a dark alleyway. You spent the night huddled up to me, trusting me completely. On a psychological level, it never made sense. I am an artificial being, an experiment. Even if Lavoisseur was in on it, why go through such an elaborate ruse? Why not hire an actress to look like you? Or just have Thorson's men walk up with guns and force me into a car. . . ."

"Thorson did not know what you could do. X told him you might teleport away, or use your control of energy flows as a weapon. Until they photographed your brain, they did not realize it was untrained. The third Gosseyn body, the one they found and destroyed, had been possessed of a fully integrated nervous system."

"It was still reckless on your part."

She smiled, stepped forward, and draped her hand over his elbow. "I didn't know you cared!"

He shook her hand away. "I mean, you thought the Observer would save you, and that belief is questionable. We should go to it right away and organize a hunt for Enro. It can put me in contact with Lavoisseur . . . if you are telling the truth."

She raised an eyebrow at that and turned her head toward her vanity table "Well? Am I?"

The voice spoke from one of the drawers: "The subject is telling the truth, within limits. She has certain mental reservations, and is suffering a great deal of nervous tension."

Gosseyn said, "Related to what thought?"

"Murder!" said the machine. "It is a violence-related thought of a high magnitude . . ."

Patricia said, "Stop! That's enough."

The voice halted.

She said in exasperation, "Stop trying to get my lie detector to rat me out. Get your own machine."

"What are you hiding?"

She tilted up her nose and looked at him through long lashes. "It is not that easy. You're going to have to trust me."

"I am not sure I should. Someone told me you had merely manipulated the Earth government and the people of Venus into helping you, that your ultimate goal was to oust your brother from power and seize the throne for yourself."

"Someone who?"

He shook his head. "I'll ask the questions. Why would you work for Lavoisseur—or have him work for you, whichever it was—against your own family, against your people and your empire? Why support Earth above your own home world?"

She put her hand on his arm once more and tugged on it.

"I'll answer," she said, "if you come with me."

"I need more answers than just that. How did Enro kill Crang? How did he kill me? What is the method? And what is his range? He says he can reach across interstellar distances, but he certainly did not have that power or that range during the war, or else he would have simply assassinated the League leadership."

"I'll get you the answers to those questions—if you come now. Time is short."

He walked with her.

As they passed through the outer suite, he caught the humid, heady perfume coming from yet another room not far away: the smell of orchids.

He breathed in the scent. "Why orchids?"

She said, "You know why. It's in your memory."

The memory in his head was this: Gosseyn had been working as a carpenter for Michael Hardie when the man had been adding eccentric towers and wings to his Florida home. He had been asked to walk his employer's daughter, Patricia, to the nearby town, to keep an eye on her and help her carry some packages. She had slipped away from him, and he spent a worried hour looking for her. He finally found Patricia sitting on a bench near a flower shop, a potted plant in her lap and a book on neurolinguistics in her hand. He had helped her carry her packages to the streetcar, and they fell into a conversation. She had said orchids are rooted in the decomposition of other organisms, but their bloom is colorful: They bring beauty out of corruption.

WHEN the Empress stepped through the doors of her suite, guards in splendid scarlet uniforms with boots polished to a mirror-shine snapped to attention, saluting with their energy-rifles. Aside from these armed men— directly outside the door to Patricia's suite—the wide corridors of the Imperial Palace seemed empty.

As they walked, he said, "You promised me certain answers."

She said, "Have you ever seen a distorter fail in midtransmission? The distortion process creates a momentary non-identity condition. Prolonged exposure is fatal. Man cannot live and particles cannot retain their integrity without a location in time and space. The Observer Machine explained it to me once, this way, when it was explaining the danger that accompanies even minor distortion of time-space involved in clairvoyance. Life evolved in sublight conditions, in a vast but boundaried area of stable and neutral space-time. Outside that boundary, conditions are different. The previous condition of the universe, where all matter and energy existed at a pinpoint of no-time and no-space, is a condition the living process cannot tolerate to be reminded of."

Gosseyn said sharply, "You must have been inside the Crypt for the Observer to communicate with you, in the coffin itself. Why was it warning you about a dangerous side effect to Enro's power?"

She shrugged. "It came up in the conversation somehow. Did you want to know about his range? During the war, he could not read the plans hidden in vaults of enemy headquarters, or see the movement of ships, except at close range, within a thousand light-years. Some ancient piece of technology gave him a breakthrough: He was watching Gosseyn Three and the expedition to another galaxy."

Gosseyn said, "Is he on the planet Ur?"

"Yes. I don't know the location. The planet is supposed to be a ghost world. There are special conditions there that Enro believes render his powers less dangerous to himself, even when he is distorting photons across intergalactic distances. I don't know the details."

She led him along the shining floor toward a tall pair of golden doors, and the gold panels were sheathed in the heat-shimmer effect of a high-density force-barrier.

Gosseyn stopped. "You were going to tell me why you were loyal to Earth."

"It should be obvious. Earth is free."

"That's it?"

"That's it."

He shook his head. "There has got to be more to it than that."

"I am a normal woman, Gilbert, and I want what any normal woman wants. It's the people around me who think I am a goddess and an empress. They want to crouch down on the floor and bow to me. Do you know what I saw on Earth, the first time I visited it? No one bows there. No one puts his face on the floor."

The mental picture formed was still incomplete. Autocracy was a system of government demanding total loyalty: Members of the Party were allowed no private interests, no self-thoughts. The Party was their only conscience. To be denounced as disloyal meant death, with reprisals against one's family; and the only way to prove loyalty was to denounce others.

In the case of Gorgzid, the Party psychology was also married to a Cult psychology. And the Cult demanded even more—for the loyal follower, every thought had to be devoted to the idol, to the symbol, for which there was no referent in real life. To doubt was sin.

Impossible that someone raised in such an environment could escape the damage caused by the necessary psychological adaptations to the madness.

Gosseyn tried to imagine a woman born and raised amid the routine cruelty and falsehood of the highest levels of a ruthless theocratic government turning her back on it all and wanting only a normal life. She calmly betrayed her brother, her emperor, her people, and her church, all for a philosophical idea utterly unlike anything a youth spent among ruthless intriguers would have prepared her to understand.

Patricia seemed like a woman too rooted in practical matters to be easily carried away by an ideal. Unless . . .

"When the Observer introduced you to Lavoisseur, you fell in love with him, didn't you? You're loyal to Null-A because . . . of him?"

Emotion brought color to her cheeks, but she smiled a lazy, charming smile and said in an arch tone, "I found him immensely pigheaded and annoying to deal with, almost more trouble than he was worth. Much like you. Now come on."

"I think my first priority should be to visit the Observer."

She raised an eyebrow. "That might prove difficult. Besides, don't tell me you don't want to meet him!"

"Who?"

"My new husband."

"Husband? Crang was killed this morning!"

"It was a quick engagement."

"Who did you marry?"

She smiled at his confusion and stepped forward. The door automatically opened for her.

Over her shoulder, she said, "I married the Ashargin heir. You remember him!"

And she swept forward into the vast chamber beyond.

9

Because we make artificial but necessary distinctions in speech and thought between various phenomena in the plenum, our habit is to ignore their fundamental unity.

Atop a shining platform reached by a series of steps, beneath a canopy of scarlet held up by posts crusted with gold, on a throne of barbaric and dazzling splendor, wearing a heavy coronet too large for his head, and huddled in a mass of red and gold finery, overburdened with gems, sat a thin and dark-haired man, pale and twitching. He was a boyish figure, large eyed as a waif.

This was the Ashargin heir, Rhade. Gosseyn knew him well: Not long ago, the Chessplayer had, by some technology unknown to Earth, implanted Gosseyn's memory and being, his essential *self,* into the young man's nervous system.

At that time, Ashargin lived as a wretched prisoner of Enro, working as a thrall in the Shrine of the Sleeping God, making sure that as he grew from boy to man he would learn nothing but cowardice and servility. It had been a cruel, desperate attempt to shatter the human spirit right down to its base.

Enro's calculation was that no opposition to his rule would ever center around the legitimate heir to the throne. The youth was brought to the palace and put on display for Enro's generals and courtiers. Any conspirators would take one look at the only other person with a legal claim to the throne and shudder and wish long life to the current Emperor.

Gosseyn, while occupying Rhade's body and living his life, had taken certain steps to undo the psychological damage. With improvised neural training techniques, and short time, he had not been able to do much, but Ashargin began developing the courage and confidence that come from even a small exposure to absolute mental health.

The moment that Patricia and Gosseyn stepped into the room, the slender, neurotic-looking man shrugged his shoulders. The long ceremonial sleeves fell from his hands, revealing the two heavy energy-pistols he had been holding in his grip.

One was pointed at Gosseyn, the other at Patricia.

Rhade Ashargin did not speak or hesitate. His fingers depressed the triggers. There was a flash of intolerable brightness and a roar of deadly energy. A wide sweep of energy flooded the chamber.

Patricia did not scream or show alarm. She was watching Gosseyn. Her expression contained the unearthly calm of a woman committing suicide. *It is a violence-related thought of a high-magnitude. . . .*

GOSSEYN'S extra brain had only three object-locations in space-time "memorized," that is, attuned to the special cluster of cells near his brain stem. One was Patricia's pistol; one was the panels taken from the wall in her bedroom; the third was Patricia herself.

When Rhade fired, Gosseyn's reaction, fast as thought, was to trigger the cells attuned to the location of wall panel in the bedroom and those attuned to Patricia, forcing a similarity, a near identity. She was relocated into the bedroom and out of harm's way. Her pistol was in Gosseyn's hand.

The Colt model automatically erected a hemisphere of neutralizing force when its Geiger counter detected atomic rays directed at the user. Gosseyn did not even need to press the thumb-button. However, the weapon's tiny alarm rang: The force-shell was about to be overloaded.

Ashargin, his eyes glittering, his shoulders hunched, now pointed both his weapons at Gosseyn, and twin beams of force, brighter than lightning, hammered against the weakening force-shell. The slim pistol began to grow warm in Gosseyn's hand: There was only a moment remaining before the tiny electron tubes in the weapon burned out.

The moment was long enough.

Gosseyn memorized a spot behind Ashargin's throne and similarized himself to it. He sent Patricia's weapon back to its hidden holster in her skirt, so that both his hands were free to clamp Rhade's wrists. A momentary pressure—Gosseyn was strong enough to break the young man's slender wrist bones, but he held his strength in check—was enough to force the Ashargin heir to drop both weapons. They clattered to the shining marble floor, barrels smoking.

Gosseyn used his extra brain to examine the nervous system of the frail man in his grasp: "Why did you do that?"

He said in a quivering voice, "You're my enemy! Reesha is a traitor! You're all out to kill me!"

To Gosseyn's astonishment, he detected not the sputtering, broken, and erratic nerve-flow of a neurotic man, thrust into a dangerous high position for which he was never qualified, but, rather, the calm, strong flow of a highly trained individual, cool under pressure.

Amazingly, even the subconscious cues, the look of uncertainty, the nervous posture—all this was part of an act, coolly and deliberately followed by Rhade, obviously for the benefit of unseen watchers.

Forgive the deception, but I had to force you to make flesh-to-flesh contact. Can you hear me? The fact that our minds were once linked gives me hope that, in close quarters, some thought-energy will be able to bridge the gap between us.

The mental flow was only one-way. Rhade had, no doubt by a simple stimulant, accelerated the nerve-firings of his brain, making him the "greater" so that Gosseyn was the "lesser."

Gosseyn spoke aloud: "I am here to help you. What are you afraid of?"

A short time ago the temple of the Sleeping God took off. Someone repaired the ancient engines.

In the young man's memory, Gosseyn saw Ashargin had been due for a civic ceremony, but his retinue had arrived late. The delay perhaps saved his life. Gosseyn caught the flash of a mental picture of the dome-shaped "building," known as the Crypt of the Sleeping God, actually a sphere-shaped machine half-buried in a Gorgzid hillside, pulling itself out of its bedrock with unimaginable fury and flinging itself skyward: He saw the buildings and priest quarters around the temple being torn from their foundations and hurled into flinders by the gravitational energy of the liftoff.

Gosseyn knew the Crypt, the starship of the Primordial Men from the Shadow Galaxy, was the only vessel, aside from the experimental ship *Ultimate Prime,* that could make a journey of intergalactic scope: Here was the explanation how an assassin from the Milky Way had been on hand in the remote black galaxy to slay Gosseyn Three.

And if Enro had been active in the Shadow Galaxy, this explained the tremendous increase in range of his powers. The experiment attempted by Gosseyn Three showed that the Primordial Spheres could be used in just such a fashion.

The scientists of the Greatest Empire, perhaps in secret, must have studied the sacred temple of the Sleeping God with far more skepticism and objectivity than is usually afforded the sacred relics of a powerful religion. The cooperation of the Predictors of Yaltera would have been an immense help. Invasive experiments would have only needed to be prepared, not performed.

The thought-flow from Ashargin was continuing.

Predictors loyal to Enro (many converted to his religion) have been anticipating my movements, blocking my every attempt to communicate to anyone outside the palace. I knew that your teleportation is the only thing that can blind the prediction visions: I am free to act for the first time in weeks. Warn the League Powers!

Gosseyn understood. Ashargin knew Enro's Predictors could not foresee whether Gosseyn lived or died when Gosseyn reacted to Ashargin's shot, so they had not interfered with what looked like a scheme to kill Gosseyn.

Was Enro's power of remote viewing also blocked by the action of his extra brain? Ashargin was acting as if it were not.

Aloud, Ashargin said, "Help me, eh?! You can help me by going to the Interstellar League and telling them that the Greatest Empire is protected by the power of the Sleeping God."

Enro has escaped from the asteroid cell where you imprisoned him. He has already gathered a large and competent cadre of men, his old supporters, to his cause. He has powers beyond any formerly revealed. I cannot be sure even this shielded building is beyond his range.

Gosseyn was impressed that Ashargin's mind had enough self-control to speak one set of thoughts aloud while concentrating on an entirely different second set of thoughts.

Briefly, Gosseyn wondered what prevented Enro from striking down Gosseyn now, since Patricia was out of the room. Perhaps Enro had decided to use Gosseyn to track down Lavoisseur; perhaps he was unwilling to wreck his own palace. Perhaps his clairvoyance was focused on Patricia and he had lost the image of this chamber.

Gosseyn forced the guesswork to the back of his mind. There were more immediate problems.

"Describe this power."

The Observer of the Crypt, before Enro made off with it, warned me that Enro had his scientists reproduce a large-scale version of the space-disassociation machine that created the Follower.

"The power of the Sleeping God is to kill all living things when He wakes!"

He means to reproduce in the Milky Way, as a weapon,

the same disaster that overwhelmed the Shadow Galaxy in ancient times.

"What do you want me to tell the League?" Gosseyn asked.

"They are about to be destroyed!"

That thought was the same both aloud and what Ashargin said silently.

THERE was no time for further questions: The guards, who had heard the blast of weapon-fire, flung open the doors, their rifles at their shoulders. Nor could Ashargin tell them to spare the man grappling with their Emperor, not and maintain the masquerade he was maintaining to fool any unseen spies, either Predictors or clairvoyant. Gosseyn similarized to the only spot open to him for retreat.

He landed lightly on the slab of the wall panel that now rested on the floor of Patricia's bedchamber.

He tried to feel with his extra brain for that slight tug, which indicated that she was still attuned to him. Nothing. Her pistol was likewise out of his range, or had been de-attuned by some vibrational-disassociation method.

She was gone.

10

Every identity is distinct. No matter their overt similarity, one of any two objects in a class of objects is an individual.

Gosseyn was walking in the cool of the twilight down the streets of Ungzid, one of the major cities of Gorgzid, on an island far from the capital. The city occupied the whole body of the island, and many of the buildings simply continued past the shoreline and formed acres of towers and domes and city squares underwater. It was a spaceport as well as a seaport. Floating on the waves were interstellar vessels of all descriptions.

Certain underwater restaurants would send their pretty waitresses swimming up through permeable membranes in the dining room ceiling to swim alongside the vessels and wave at the tourists.

Gosseyn was not interested in the deceptively picturesque view. A war effort was under way, and its first overt steps had taken place.

He had spent the last day and a half stranded on this world, eluding the police. This was not hard to do: Whenever he felt the energy of a detection-beam probing him from a lamppost or passing squad car, he used his extra brain to bend the invisible ray away from himself. If the police came too close, he stepped into a phone booth and moved to one of his several memorized spots forming a rough line between Ungzid and the Imperial Palace in the capital back on the main continent.

For Gosseyn had left the palace immediately upon finding Patricia gone. While alarms and klaxons blared in the corridor outside her room, he had stepped over to the window, used his extra brain to interrupt the window field and render it transparent. He had selected the most distant tower-top he could see, and, when he arrived there, he had selected the peak of a mountain on the horizon.

It took him less than an hour to travel across the continent.

In the island-city of Ungzid, he found a spaceport, but it was too heavily guarded, too well watched, even for a man of his special abilities to break into.

So he stepped into a shop and bought a postcard for a penny and asked the shop owner to look up for him the schedule for mail runs to various planets. The proprietor studied star routes on the stat plate next to his cash register. Gosseyn casually turned his back to the man, for the news screen hanging over the shop counter had lit up with the picture of Gosseyn's head. The caption identified the reward for information leading to the capture of the would-be assassin of Emperor Ashargin, the man who had kidnapped the Divine Empress Reesha.

Gosseyn strolled out of the shop and slipped the card into an express mailbox.

Later, he strolled past the mailbox at collection time and then loitered near the wall of the spaceport annex, watching armed marines check the incoming parcels and search the ticket-carrying passengers. The annex windows were of the same type as he'd seen on Nirene, so the spaceport was one huge opaque structure of steel, with no way for him to see in. But he picked out the container from the post office, and he saw the mailbag going in.

As he stood watching, Gosseyn heard a strident voice ringing from a street-corner public loudspeaker nearby, calling for "uncompromising action!" The Interim Government was being blamed for its inability to protect Reesha—or perhaps having a hand in her disappearance.

The efficiency of Enro's propaganda organization was startling: Without Ashargin being able to stop it, already the government of Gorgzid, the police, and the public telecommunications networks were reacting to Enro's will. Even treason against Ashargin was being broadcast on government-sponsored channels.

"We were never defeated—we were betrayed by disloyal elements in the government! . . . We demand the return of our Divine Empress! We yearn for the swift and safe release of our young and beautiful leader . . . torture chambers . . . unspeakable . . . of the corrupt and decadent Interstellar League! . . . How long is the Greatest Empire to tolerate this humiliation?!"

A small crowd had gathered to listen to the harangue, and some of the young men there were already nodding and muttering their agreement. A hunter-gatherer tribe steeling itself for bloody violence against its neighbors would have addressed its appeals to the same deeply rooted complexes: The outsiders are threatening our women.

Briefly, Gosseyn found the sight depressing. He walked away, passing a line of news-boxes.

The flashing stat-plates of the dedicated news channels were also filled with rumors of missing men, mostly veterans from the previous wars but also scientists and technicians: highly trained personnel of the Gorgzid military who, when the Imperial Forces demobilized, had been permitted to return home. Most had been under observation, ordered by the Interim Government not to travel outside their home districts, not allowed to own a firearm or to receive or send uncensored mail—except now they had vanished. Others had been under more strict confinement, house arrest or even jail.

The degree of advance planning needed to smuggle distorter units to within transmission range of over ten thousand men was startling. The stealth involved bespoke the presence of a powerful and efficient network of spies and agents, guided, no doubt, by the Predictors of Yalerta, who could foresee and forestall any possibility of detection or capture.

The news reports spoke of the police questioning the wives and mistresses of the missing men, hoping their families would know something of their whereabouts: There were uglier rumors of arrests and interrogation of these innocent women.

Gosseyn bought a newspaper from the automatic vendor, paying the extra coin for the detailed version. Here on a back sheet was a fine-print column of names released by the police, veterans confirmed as missing; under the entry for "F" Gosseyn found the name:

Free, Anaxim vor Capech, Capt. 1033th ImpGalNaval Destryr., Cmdr. Y381907.

Captain Free had been the Commanding Officer of the Gorgzid expedition to Yalerta. Gosseyn assumed every name on this list would be that of a man with a working knowledge of that once-hidden world of superhumans.

Gosseyn turned: Silent as a thundercloud, one of the medium-sized space vessels was rising slowly from the bay, waters sluicing from its titanium-steel hull. It hung weightless in the air only for a moment, suspended on its powerful gravity-nullification engines. Then there was an eye-confusing blur, a green afterimage shimmering where the vast hull had been. This was the distortion effect. The ship had dematerialized, reappearing light-years away, at whatever world held the distorter to which the ship's engine matrices were currently attuned.

Gosseyn, once he saw the ship depart, spent the evening in a hotel room, with the lights dimmed, soaking in the hottest water he could tolerate in the tub, using a rhythmic-breathing technique to relax his body.

For there was a limitation to his range: At roughly twenty hours' time, or twenty light-hours' distance (something over thirteen billion miles), he could not maintain the degree of similarity needed to bypass time-space. Beyond that interval, the small, unpredictable atomic changes in the matter memorized made Gosseyn's mental "photograph" of the object insufficiently accurate— twenty decimal places was the crucial threshold.

However, during Gosseyn's brief stay on the planet Yalerta he had learned enough of the Predictors' technique to extend his range to several thousand light-years.

With the combination of the two techniques, he could predict what the subatomic organization of a memorized location would be past the twenty-hour limit and "update" his mental photograph of it. All this was done at a subconscious level, by the furious activity of his extra brain. Relaxation of the surrounding tissue was the key.

To help himself enter the autohypnotic state, he used the phone hookup in the room to send himself a message he had recorded in a soothing tone and he set the phone timer to call itself and repeat the message every forty-five minutes—the space of time of the human dreaming-state cycle. The human mind is wonderfully prone to suggestion: A voice telling you to relax will make you relax.

And so a hot bath, of all things, did wonders for him.

The flashing mental pictures, images of possible future events, began to appear. He saw shadows engulfing the galaxy, whole planets warped and burnt even as Crang's body had been . . . suns dying, turning black, falling inward on themselves, while their planets froze . . . he saw a warship of the Greatest Empire hanging above some metropolis beneath an alien sun, dropping an atomic warhead . . . he saw a young man, strangely familiar: a seventeen-year-old version of himself . . . a chamber full of burning corpses . . . he saw Patricia being killed by Enro in a fit of jealous rage. . . .

He made no attempt to examine the pictures that appeared and disappeared in his brain. These images pulled at his fear and curiosity with powerful magnetism, but he held himself aloof. Lingering would snap him out of his trance. Leej the Predictress had once explained that any attempt by a Predictor to read his own future too closely would create a positive feedback, as he would start to see visions based on the hypothetical futures where he reacted to the visions, and then more futures, and more, resulting from visions resulting from reactions to visions . . . eventually he would see nothing but dream extrapolations so unlikely as to have no meaning.

So Gosseyn let the images wash through him, his mind receptive to signals from the future sections of space-time.

Gosseyn rose to his feet, naked and dripping, in the general delivery room of the post office in the city of Accardistran Minor on the planet Accolon.

In a small cubby nearby, a sorting machine was now placing the postcard he had bought, and whose atomic structure he had memorized, on Gorgzid.

The predictive image had been clear enough to allow him to select the proper moment: The total mass of a nearby robotic sorter machine was enough that, while the postcard was gripped in its magnetic slot, Gosseyn

crossed the gap to it, rather than merely bringing the
card back to him.

GOSSEYN did not even bother to explain his nakedness
to the post office security officer, nor to the Accoloni police. The police allowed him to call the Earth Consulate
on Accolon, but the secretary who appeared on the
vision-plate would not put him through to the ambassador. Gosseyn could see a spot through the vision-plate of
the office behind: The picture was clear enough for him
to memorize it. He stepped there. Had it not been an
emergency, perhaps he would have taken the time to negotiate through complexities of the various bureaucra-
cies of two worlds, the complexes and neuroses of the
bureaucrats. As it was, this seemed the best method to
quickly establish his identity and put himself on home
soil.

Fortunately, the Earth ambassador, James Norcross,
was at least partly trained in Null-A techniques, so he
could adjust his mind quickly to the situation. He arranged
to have a tailor fit Gosseyn out with a new suit of clothing,
at about the same time that he arranged an interview for
Gosseyn to meet the members of the Security Council of
the Interstellar League, in their headquarters in Accardistran Major, not ten minutes' flight away by air-limousine.

Through the tinted windows of the air-limousine, he
saw the horizon twice as distant as that of Earth, or more.
On the horizon, flattened and red, the setting sun bathed
the mile-high towers of the supermetropolis, turning acres
of windows to yellow and red gold. As on the planet
Nirene, the architecture showed its military nature: The
windows were merely repeater screens.

Seeing Gosseyn's stare, Ambassador Norcross explained that the world was many times the diameter of
Earth but so much less dense that the gravity was only
slightly above Earth-normal. "Between the buildings,
you can glimpse the jungle canopy below us. Looks just

like the Amazon, doesn't it? Except this is the polar region. The sun won't finish setting for another half year.
The equator of Accolon is a lava belt. The life at the North
and South poles here evolved in isolation.

"Accolon is also one of the only planets in the galaxy
with monkeys and apes in her jungles, and other members of the primate family. Someone went to a lot of
trouble, including burying evidence in the fossil record,
to make this look like the world where man evolved, not
Earth."

Gosseyn said, "I was looking at the defensive fortifi-
cations." For they were passing over a vast spaceport,
with commercial ships and warships more numerous
than any he had seen on any world. "There is nothing
here that can stop the Shadow Effect."

Moments later, they had arrived on the roof of the Interstellar League Organization building. A distorter-type
elevator transmitted them to the anteroom of the Security
Council, buried somewhere deep below the mile-high
structure. From there it was a short walk down gleaming
corridors and past armed space marines in dress uniforms.

When Gosseyn stepped into the main chamber, an energy force entered his brain, and he was overwhelmed.

Hanging near the ceiling was a small, round machine,
emitting a number of complex vibrations on a wide number of bands. As in the Nirene police station, Gosseyn felt
the nerve organization of his extra brain overstimulated
by the electro-gravitonic white noise: His powers were
cut off while that machine was active. He could use his
extra brain to suppress the energy flows in the machine
and neutralize it, but this would have taken the full attention of his extra brain, with nothing left over to do anything further.

He drew down his eyes. There, behind the wide expanse
of a gleaming oval table, sat nineteen men: the various
ambassadors and officers of planetary governments, each

with a robotic translator button in his ear. Norcross had explained that only three of the men had any real power: the Councilors for the worlds of Petrino, Corthid, and the Great Planet Accolon.

The Accoloni Councilor, a No-Man named Edwenofer Prin, saw the direction of Gosseyn's gaze and said, "We have it here as a security precaution against assassination by distorter."

But Gosseyn could see by the stiff and uncertain demeanor of the other sixteen Councilors that this was not the whole truth. The men were alarmed, dangerously alarmed, merely to see him.

Gosseyn reminded himself that these were men who lived in a binary Aristotelian universe. Whatever rumors, exaggerations, or outright lies they had heard of Gilbert Gosseyn they would believe, consciously or unconsciously, and pattern their actions on assumptions as if those assumptions were the whole truth, not a partial picture of the truth.

Prin's special training must have made him sensitive to nuances of expression other men would miss, or perhaps he had a special instrument trained on Gosseyn, measuring his capillary and nerve responses, for he said, "Forgive our precautions. The intuitional science of my people needs only to observe ten percent of the data-pattern of an event to deduce the whole sequence. Based on just such a sequential-intuition model, it is certain that a deadly attack on the Security Council is the next step in the coming galactic war."

Gosseyn felt a sense of great relief. At least, that basic fact was beyond dispute.

But his relief evaporated when Prin continued, "The intuitive model deduces that the war will proceed by stealth and misdirection, a matter of rare acts of piracy, while Enro's men, without his leadership, play for time, and maneuver to secure his release."

Gosseyn was astonished at the unreality of the mental

picture the Interstellar League government had permitted itself. He said, shocked, "You mean—you have not yet mobilized your worlds onto a wartime footing?"

Cevric Nolo was the Councilor for Petrino and was a trained Nexialist, an expert in that strange gestalt-science that studied the areas of overlap, the parallels, between other sciences. Nolo spoke: "We are aware of the recent disappearances of veteran soldiers and military scientists from Imperial worlds. Also we are aware that roughly six hundred Imperial warships are unaccounted for during the supervised decommission. Some were reported destroyed in combat, where there is no League ship credited with the destruction; others are missing due to clerical errors.

"Since the recent war involved the industrial production of hundreds of thousands of ships on tens of thousands of worlds, this handful—three percent of the eighteen-hundred-thousand-ship fleet of Imperial Gorgzid—can have no significant influence on the events of galactic history. It is an armed force insufficient to conquer and hold more than twenty planets. And at that, six hundred ships could hold twenty planets only until the League Fleet arrives in overwhelming numbers.

"The nexus of the sciences involved (military history, economics, the metallurgical and electro-nuclear industrial production sciences, and, in this case, theology) indicates that Enro's men will surprise a score of planets, and cut them off from the galactic distorter network by destroying all local distortion-circuit recordings. This will give them a respite of a few years to build up ship production on those few planets, while the League Fleet travels slowly through normal space.

"As best we can tell, their plan is futile, irrational. Enro's men must be staking everything on the hope that the Sleeping God will wake and reward their devotion with some miraculous, divine intervention."

Nolo finished his speech in a voice of self-satisfaction: "These religious fanatics cannot possibly overcome a galaxy-wide civilization, rationally organized to a rational police effort."

Gosseyn said, "Gentlemen, your model is based on two false assumptions. First, Enro is at large. He has secretly traveled to the Shadow Galaxy, and presently controls certain of the technologies of the Primordial Humans. Second, you are thinking in terms of the last war. The space-superdreadnoughts of the last war will be of no use whatsoever against the Shadow Effect. Enro intends to unleash in this galaxy the same all-destroying phenomenon which wiped out the Primordials, whose technology was more advanced than ours. Six hundred ships, crewed by Yalertan Predictors, is more than enough to accept the surrenders of fleets and planets with no defense against him."

He saw the disbelief on the faces of the Councilors.

White-haired Councilor Ifvrid Madrisol of Corthid, the so-called World of Luck, a planet famed for the high number of callidetic geniuses amongst her people, spoke next. "Mr. Gosseyn, let us assume matters are as dire as you suggest; what is your proposal? If Enro were free, and in possession of the Shadow Galaxy technology, what would you have us do?"

Gosseyn said, "Abandon the Milky Way."

He succinctly outlined his plan: a fleet of ships to be built using the experimental engines of the *Ultimate Prime;* a concerted effort to be made to find wherever Lavoisseur had hidden the next group of Gosseyn bodies. Perhaps there were enough of them, and perhaps even a seventeen-year-old might have the trained double brain needed to reproduce what Gosseyn Three did to carry the *Ultimate Prime,* with its half-understood primordial-technology engines, to the Shadow Galaxy. The shipboard Gosseyns, interacting with the Spheres, could begin the whole-scale transmission of planets to stable orbits circling the suns of various nearby galaxies. Meanwhile, Sphere technology could be brought back here to combat the Shadow Effect, which, by then, Enro would have released into several areas of space-time inside the Milky Way.

The Councilors exchanged wary glances among themselves. One or two men broke into open laughter.

Prin said archly, "I notice this new setup—shall I call it a new form of government?—would involve no one but copies of yourself in control of the technology to move and remove stars and planets." Turning his head, he said to the other Councilors, "It is as we were warned."

The accusation was so astonishing that Gosseyn could say nothing.

Nolo said in a voice of heavy condescension, "Mr. Gosseyn, your planet can be proud of the advances she has made, while isolated from the mainstream of Galactic Civilization, in the psychological sciences, what you call Null-A. But you may be unaware of where such a science fits into the grand scheme of things, into the overall picture. You see, yours is not the first world to have developed a unique approach, and you are not the first man to fall into the philosophical and psychological trap of judging everything in terms of your own inflexible system of ideas."

Gosseyn said, "You haven't studied Null-A if you regard it as inflexible."

Nolo raised his hand. "Nonetheless, I have studied it enough to know that it predisposes the mind to make rapid alterations in behavior based on small changes in circumstances. But all the other sciences, from anthropology to engineering, predispose a more careful approach. Organisms and machines need adaptation time. Even to heat or cool the strongest metal in too brief a time will shatter it. Enro's men cannot possibly study and reproduce an unknown supertechnology and reduce it to military practice under a trained cadre in anything less than months or years. The Interstellar League cannot even consider the possibility of making you dictator for the duration of the emergency—and this is, in effect, what you have just asked us to do."

Gosseyn realized that government structures produce their own rigidity, which they seek, by their own accord, to keep intact. When an emergency calls for a response not permitted within that perception-structure, that rigidity must be set aside. Aloud he said, "Gentlemen, you can draft me into your military, or assign me whatever post you like in your system, and place any oversight on my actions, but the fact is that no one else available at the moment has the ability to use the Sphere technology to preserve the galaxy from the Shadow Effect."

Nolo said, "Nonsense. You are a man with a biological version of a distorter in your skull. Our industrial planets produce millions of units per year of mechanical distorters."

Elderly Madrisol raised a thin hand. "The point is moot. Mr. Gosseyn, you are the one operating under several false assumptions, not this council."

He must have made some signal to the marine standing near the door, for at that moment a technician wheeled in a large depth-video tank, which he connected by a cable to a plug in the floor.

The tank showed an image of Enro the Red, dressed in his prison garb, in his small but comfortable asteroid-prison cell. There were robot guards in the view but no human beings. Built into the ceiling of his cell was a suppression emitter, the same type of emitter that hung here in the Council Chambers, suppressing Gosseyn's powers.

Enro had his back to the view. He was watching a wall screen: the news broadcast from his home world, describing the abduction of Empress Reesha. Enro's shoulders were tense, and his whole attitude and demeanor was that of a man receiving shocking news, helpless to do anything about it.

Nolo said, "This is a current image—as nearly simultaneous as anything can be inside an Einsteinian universe. There is Enro."

Gosseyn shook his head. "I saw Enro on the planet Ur,

a projected image of his. I have memories from my destroyed alternate copy of myself, destroyed by a shadow-body: the kind of body Enro has recently discovered how to duplicate."

Nolo smiled thinly. "Actually, Mr. Gosseyn, your Null-A science says that you should say, *I remember seeing Enro*. We have no assurance your memories are correct."

Prin spread his hands. "Put yourself in our position, Mr. Gosseyn. Here you are, the man who cannot be killed, but who has no past, no family, no particular reason to be loyal to the Interstellar League. We have a report from Planet Nirene that you are wanted for the murder of your best friend, a Mr. Crang, a detective helping the police there. The local lie detector says your experimental extra brain—a mass of tissue neither you nor anyone else in the galaxy truly understands—may be insane. We next have official word from the Ashargin ruler of the planet Gorgzid that you are wanted for the kidnapping of their Empress . . . who also happens to be the murdered man's bride.

"Then—according to the Nireni police report—there is the possibility that you are being influenced by emotions of jealousy somehow being transmitted into your nervous system from an outside point. But there is also the more obvious possibility that you are insane, that you killed your friend, and carried off his wife. Is it true that the missing woman is someone who you once hallucinated you were married to?"

Gosseyn said, "Those were false memories implanted in my brain."

Prin gave a sad little shrug. "How do we know that your memories of seeing Enro released from prison are true ones? More to the point, why should we believe them, when we can see with our eyes that Enro is still in prison?"

"No, sir. You are seeing what purports to be a transmission, carrying an image of someone who looks very much like Enro. Perhaps it is a recorded image. The news releases on Gorgzid could have been prepared in advance, and . . ."

Madrisol said, "Gentlemen, my people have made a science of a certain type of pattern recognition, which gives us the reputation of being gifted with unusual luck. But it is not luck: It is a discipline of recognizing that two objects in the same category, two throws of the same dice, are not the same, and of being ready to act on the infinitesimal but real differences between situations that seem the same." He held up a thin sheet of plasto-paper, upon which lines of text and pictures appeared and disappeared. "I have in hand the report of one of these trained Callidetics of Corthid. His close observation of the man we now see in this image tank convinces him, from a hundred tiny nuances of gesture and expression, that it is Enro, not an actor or impostor made to look like him, and a live image, not a recording. I regard this report as definitive." Madrisol's pale eyes now turned toward Gosseyn. He said scathingly, "Unless you wish this council to believe that Enro just happens to have a twin brother no one ever heard of?"

Gosseyn said, "Speaking as the fourth near-identical copy of my self-consciousness, I do not rule the possibility out. The fourth surviving copy." Gosseyn, as he spoke those words, reflected grimly that men who lived lives of adventure and danger did not live long.

He mentally corrected the figure upward: X was also a Gosseyn body, although a deviant one, as was Lavoisseur himself. Gosseyn had seen both men die, shot down before his eyes.

The Councilors exchanged meaningful glances. There was a slight stiffening of shoulders, an intake of breath, a narrowing of eyes.

With the suppression emitter hanging over his head, Gosseyn could not read the flow of neural energies, but he could see the suspicions settling on the faces of the men here.

"Gentlemen," he said, "why are you afraid of me?"

Prin said, "We have it from an unimpeachable source that you are an agent of Enro."

11

Categorization, the mental act of treating individuals as identical members of a class, is an abstraction whose accuracy must be always open to question.

Gosseyn was impressed by the sheer audacity of the suggestion. Then, harshly: "Might I suggest that this unimpeachable source be investigated quite thoroughly by your military intelligence for ties to Enro?"

Nolo said, "Look at the logic of it. No one but you has the distorter coordinates of Enro's prison asteroid. Only you could have released him from it. If what we are seeing is a duplicate body of Enro, only you are known to possess the duplicating technique as well. You visit Gorgzid and the Empress vanishes, undermining the Ashargin government, and drumming up popular support for Enro's cause."

Gosseyn said, "Does it mean anything to you that the Predictors of Yalerta have foreseen, within the year, that many worlds and stars of this galaxy will be overwhelmed by the Shadow Effect, all life blotted out as all complex molecules lose their coherent structure?"

Prin said, "One possible interpretation is that the Predictors of Yalerta are still loyal to Enro, and spreading a prediction useful to him. Now, if you are also his agent, and you appear with this unique plan to save the galaxy, requiring us to place all our worlds under the control of a technology only you can use . . ."

Gosseyn said, "Bring in a lie detector."

Ambassador Norcross, who had been standing by Gosseyn's shoulder this whole time, facing the table of Councilors, said, "Mr. Gosseyn is a citizen of Venus, an independent sovereign power." To Gosseyn he said, "You are not answerable to these men, and it is not in the interests of the Earth government that we cede this point of precedent."

Gosseyn said, "I act as an independent individual of Venus."

Norcross sighed. "Do Venusians ever act any other way?" Then, to the Councilors, he said, "The Earth government withdraws the objection. You may inspect Mr. Gosseyn with a lie detector."

Nolo said, "What would that prove? A man of Mr. Gosseyn's unique mental powers—or should I say mental deficiencies?—can testify quite honestly about his memory without it bearing any relation to reality." To the Council members he said, "Gentlemen, this . . . organism . . . this artificial life-form thinks only what his creator desires him to think."

But Prin said, "Gentlemen, I'd like to see the detector reading, nonetheless. If Mr. Gosseyn is not consciously working for Enro, it eliminates certain possibilities from the logic-gestalt."

Nolo said, "Enro is not so foolish as to send one of his men here, into the very Council Chambers of the Interstellar League!"

Madrisol shook his white head, saying, "Recall the Battle of the Sixth Decant! Enro the Red is a bold strategist, and he believes that his Sleeping God protects him. Even imprisoned, I fear him."

The lie detector, carried in on an antigravity plate, was larger than other models Gosseyn had seen, a round housing with many electron tubes protruding from its rim.

The Councilors had a technician shut off certain of the magnetic bands the suppressor was emitting, to allow the lie detector to interact with Gosseyn's nervous system.

Gosseyn could still not use his similarity methods, but his awareness of electromagnetic, chemical, and atomic actions in the nearby area was restored.

"This man is not an agent of Enro the Red, consciously or subconsciously," the machine said firmly.

Gosseyn studied the faces of the Councilors. He said, "That's not it, is it? Your fear of me is more fundamental."

Nolo laughed weakly. "I do admit that the shock of meeting the man who cannot die is greater than I expected. A more-than-human confidence gleams in your eyes; it echoes in your words. No matter what we mere mortals say or do, you, the unknown man from an unknown world, are going to decide what happens to our lives and our worlds, and nothing we can do can stop you."

Gosseyn put his hand on the lie detector. "First, I have turned over all that I know of my origins to the Games Machines which are, even now, being constructed on the various planets that have accepted colonists from Venus and Earth. These machines can measure human sanity and integrity."

He paused while sensitive, energy-conducting lights played over his face. One by one, he met the eyes of the Councilors. In his deep baritone he continued, "Second, it is only a matter of time until I can discover who I am and where I come from. Once that is done, I will know the secret of how to preserve continuity of memory from one duplicate body to another: a secret I will share with any men sane enough to not destroy themselves, or others, with the knowledge. Gentlemen, these two statements taken together offer great promise. I expect that you all will soon join me, and be as I am."

Prin said to the lie detector, "Well?"

The machine said, "The statement is true as far as it goes, but there is a deeper thought behind it."

Gosseyn said, "Once many men, not just one, have my special method of bypassing space-time, and the scientists of many worlds can study it, humanity as a whole will have an opportunity to understand something fundamental—essential—about the base nature of reality. The repercussions are not merely unknown, but unknowable."

Prin said to the machine, "Based on that last statement, can you tell us what this man's real purpose is in coming here?"

The lie detector said, "There is an identity confusion in the subject. He does not know who he is. On the surface, he regards himself as a copy of three other dead men, perhaps four, inheriting their memory chains, and therefore inheriting their name and self-ness. . . . This central difficulty obscures all other readings. The subject is not himself aware of his purpose in life, but that purpose is an immense one . . . his real purpose is tied into his real identity. . . . He is . . . connected . . . in some way, some basic-energy way, to an identity older than mankind."

Prin said in a hushed tone, "But . . . then who is this man? What is he?"

Nolo said, "We know who he is. We were warned. Marines!" He raised his hand to the two guards flanking the doors.

A voice came into Gosseyn's head at that moment. *This is Lavoisseur. You represent a tremendous secret, which you yourself only dimly grasp: a secret not just of immortality, but of infinity! By revealing your true nature, you are repeating the mistakes I made during an earlier incarnation, mistakes that led to the destruction of the Shadow Galaxy. The Councilors' fear of you has grown beyond all bounds: They are going to kill you unless you let me help you. Quickly! Use your extra brain to suppress the radiations from the vibration machine!*

Gosseyn triggered all the nerve-combinations in his extra brain at once. The suppression emitter was muffled, but it required all of Gosseyn's capacity to do it: He could feel the flow of nervous energy in his brain stem, stiffened with the overload.

From outside the main doors came cries of pain and alarm, the shocking noise of energy-rifles being fired in an enclosed space, the sizzling echo of ricochets. The two marines threw open the doors and raced out, beyond Gosseyn's range of vision.

Then, a sudden ominous silence fell.

The echo of a pair of footsteps resounded from the marble floor as a figure walked calmly through the double doors.

It was a boyish figure, short and slim, but with the awkwardly large hands and feet of a late teenager going through a growth spurt. However, he had the large head, the wide shoulders, the hawkish eyes, the slender-lipped mouth, of a Gosseyn body. Gosseyn estimated the biological age of this younger version of him as equal to sixteen or seventeen. The youth was wearing a red and scarlet jacket of a military cut.

There was a series of rapid metallic clicks as the tall doors slid shut behind him. The magnetic pistons of the locking mechanism had been triggered by some outside power.

Elderly Ifvrid Madrisol rose to his feet saying, "Who are you, young man? How dare you to enter here?"

The seventeen-year-old spoke. From such a young man the voice was surprisingly powerful and strong, indicating a Null-A precision of control over the acoustic cavities and vocal cords. More highly pitched, of course, but the tone, timbre, and accent were those Gosseyn had heard, before his death, from the mouth of Lavoisseur.

Only the words themselves were horribly, insanely wrong.

"I bear a message from your Emperor, who is the father of the race that will replace mankind. The universe has judged you, gentlemen, by the laws of evolution . . . and you have been condemned to death."

Norcross was the only man quick enough to put his

hand to his pistol before he died. The other Councilors were slain where they sat, their heads sheared off by a jagged lightning bolt.

The similarity channel used to send words into Gosseyn's brain, at the moment, flooded Gosseyn with a complex of thought-forces meant to paralyze his nervous system. He used the cortical-thalamic pause to break the connection and defeat the paralysis, but that moment of distraction was enough: The young man pulled out his sidearm, a Gorgzid military-issue nuclear-electric piece, pointed it at Gosseyn, and pulled the trigger.

The boy said, "I am similarizing the energy from this weapon in my hand to a neutral spot in orbit. However, the moment you release the suppressor machine, my powers will be neutralized, and the bolt will strike you. Now, you might think that you will merely wake up in another Gosseyn body elsewhere, but the same suppressor field that prevents you from using your biological distorter in your brain will prevent the automatic similarization of your memory information into your next body. Checkmate."

"You monster!" Gosseyn stared in horror. "Who are you, really?"

The young man said lightly, "I am Gilbert Gosseyn. The *real* Gilbert Gosseyn."

12

The general rule is that any notions of identity are simplifications of a more complex underlying reality; this rule applies to self-identification as well.

The young man continued, "The real Gosseyn! I am the person you would be if an earlier version of you had not erased your own memory in a rash attempt to stop me."

The lie detector spoke up out of turn: "There is confusion. I was asked to verify the testimony of the man named Gosseyn: The young man now speaking does have continuity of identity with the name 'Gosseyn,' but there are other identities present in his mind."

Gosseyn said, "Who is he?"

"He thinks of himself as Lavoisseur, but there is additional confusion, as he knows you knew him not by that name, but another. There is deceptive intent involved."

Gosseyn said to the boy, "When first we met, you called yourself X the Unknown Factor. You are the crippled version of Lavoisseur he created to infiltrate the Hardie gang."

The young man's eyes narrowed in grim amusement. "Is *that* what he said? He told you the truth as best he knew it. When I created him, that was what I wanted him to believe."

"*You* created *him*?"

"Of course. I had to create a version of myself who thought he was the original, to make mind-to-mind contact with the Observer of the Crypt, so that I, from a safe distance, attuned to his thoughts, could watch to see what the Observer would do with him. It used him to spread Null-A to several planets before I could prevent it. He was using the name 'de Lany' at that time. Later, I recovered partial control of my stray self. I arranged to have him, under the name Lavoisseur, go to Earth just before the Galactic Invasion, to keep me aware of any resistance gathered around the Semantics Institute, or from the Venusian detectives. A Venusian detective named Crang befriended him—or should I say you?—and figured out that he was a copy. At first the thought-flow was from him to me, for I had designed the Lavoisseur body on a genetic level to have increased adrenal flows to make him ever in a state of nervous excitement. But I underestimated myself."

"Are you claiming that, once he discovered your existence, Lavoisseur arranged your accident, to wound you, and speed up your life process?"

"Ruthless, wasn't it?" The young man called X smiled. "But the psychological strain on him was terrific. I had also kept to myself my method of immortality through body-duplication, but he examined his own construction and reproduced the technique, creating an amnesiac version of himself: the first copy of your current memory-line."

"Gosseyn One."

Now the young man smiled grimly. "I admit I was startled the first time I met your first body—imagine seeing a young and uncrippled version of yourself dragged into a room with your fellow conspirators. Imagine my relief when I discovered you were a brain-damaged version, unable to use your powers. But I could not have you killed, because you were the only clue leading back to Lavoisseur. When Gosseyn One was born, Lavoisseur disappeared from my view. After that, when I tried to enter the low-energy nerve-meditation to find his thoughts, all I could find were yours. And you knew nothing. I had at that time assumed the identity of Lavoisseur to control the Semantics Institute, to prevent the Institute from hindering Thorson's plan to invade Earth."

"Prescott shot you."

X shrugged nonchalantly. "Your appearance on the scene meant I had to exit before any awkward questions were asked. What if they had checked your fingerprints? I was tired of being in a wheelchair, and I needed to be offstage for a while, to maneuver you into a position to kill Thorson, who had grown ambitious. The older and more insane version of you, the man who thought he was Lavoisseur, got himself killed off nicely: I blocked his extra-brain distorter signal using the non-identity method, so nothing was transmitted to his next body. A fitting penalty for trying to reveal the secret of immortality!" The boy frowned soberly. "But he was not the first version of me to make that foolish error. In ancient times, I also tried to immortalize the Shadow Galaxy, with results too hideous to describe. It is to prevent that catastrophe from repeating itself that I am here."

Gosseyn said, "I assume you are prepared to prove your more unlikely statements? I admit I have doubts on a basic level that a murdering madman like you could be any sort of version of me."

X said harshly to the lie detector, "Verify this!" and to Gosseyn: "I have come here with every expectation of killing you, should you prove stubborn. I needed to trick you into a situation where your death-trigger would not release your memories back into me, as I have no wish to have my thoughts confused with your sentimental emotionalism."

The lie detector said, "The statement is a true one, according to the information and belief of the speaker, but there is a deception based on omission."

The young man said, "The omission is this: I am waiting for compatriots of mine to establish a no-signal condition in this area. You examined the body of Gosseyn Three? There is a mechanical means of neutralizing the immortality circuit."

"Then you are the one who killed him."

The young version of his own head nodded. "The Interstellar League was almost correct. Gilbert Gosseyn, the real Gosseyn, is indeed an agent of Enro the Red."

"Why are you doing this?"

"I thought that would be clear by now. Superior and sane minds should not bow to inferior and unsane governments. My attempt was to create a universal government, working through Enro and Secoh. A government ruled by sane men, the only men who can be trusted with power over others. The Observer in the Crypt of the Sleeping God was programmed to release its passengers when safe, and to educate them according to the scientific knowledge left aboard. That knowledge included the Null-A training techniques, of course. I wanted that knowledge released only into the ruling class of the new empire: You see the difficulty."

"Null-A's would not help you establish a galactic empire."

"Correct. That meant that Null-A training had to be forbidden to men until *after* the galaxy was conquered. However, the Observer of the Sleeping God was programmed to do otherwise: Working through you, it propagated Null-A through several planets that were unknown or unmapped, including Earth, as well as the electronic tube technology and the lie detector."

Gosseyn noticed the oddity: *Working through you.* The seventeen-year-old several times had slipped into the habit of referring to Gosseyn as if he were Lavoisseur, the immortal man who brought the Null-A science to Earth.

Wryly, he realized that this verbalization was just as accurate as to call him by his current name. He had lost Lavoisseur's conscious memories at his creation, it was true, but the drive, the ideals, the loyalty to Null-A, that remained. Something of Lavoisseur survived.

The boy said, "Only on Earth did the seed take root. The original attack on Null-A Earth, and the reason for the Greatest Empire base there, was to destroy the philosophy, and to start the galactic war that would lead to union."

"That plan failed." Grimly.

"Did it? The League Powers, in order to cooperate during this war, had to give some of their sovereignty over to an interstellar body, an emergency commission known as the Security Council. Control of that council is the next step. The members who were more recalcitrant were gathered here to be eliminated. You were allowed to escape from Gorgzid to bring your warning to the League Powers, bringing all together to this one place, this buried war room I could not find except through my link to you. Enro has been maneuvered into a position where he must use psychological methods, rather than open war, to establish universal dominion. The loss of life will be much less."

Gosseyn said, "You speak as if you expect to persuade me to join you."

"Why not? We are one and the same individual, after all. But I remember our former lives all the way back to when I and two women awoke in the suspended-animation coffins of the crashed spaceship that later was worshipped as the Crypt of the Sleeping God. Do you understand the utter pointlessness of opposing me? There is no Cosmic Chessplayer aside from me. On Earth, my duplicate was called de Lany; on a prehistoric Mars that died when the dinosaurs were young, I was called Xenius; on Yalerta, I was Ysvid of Forever Isle; on Ur, the most primal of all worlds, I was called Ur-ath-Vir the First-of-Living. I have a thousand names. I am eldest of all men: the galaxy's one immortal. I am Lavoisseur from a time period before the man you thought was Lavoisseur, the modified version of me, began to work against me. I am the original Lavoisseur, the eldest of all the Gosseyn line."

The lie detector said, "False statement. This is not the man you knew as Lavoisseur. He is—"

But a shot from the blaster ended the comment.

As Gosseyn leaped on the boy, he released the suppressor, and an invisible tangle of energies flooded the chamber. The boy's not fully developed muscles were no match for Gosseyn's Null-A-trained body; but, as they wrestled, the young body had a suppleness and strength that showed that he was not lying, at least, about being a Null-A. The young muscles reacted with the strength that only tissues momentarily disconnected from the fatigue centers of the brain could match.

But Gosseyn knew the same techniques, and he was more massive, had longer reach.

The two struggled over the still-firing gun. The blinding ray scrawled curlicues of burning debris across the wall and ceiling of the chamber, blowing out vision screens and chandeliers. Then the boy's muscles sagged and suddenly gave way. Gosseyn, off-balanced, nonetheless retained his grip on the widely struggling figure, one hand clamped like a vise on the boy's gun hand. During that moment, the boy strained and pointed the weapon at the suppression emitter. The machine exploded in the shower of electron tubes.

The boy dematerialized right out of Gosseyn's hands.

13

The advantage of non-Aristotelian integration over the stereotyped reflexes of categorical thought is greater flexibility of mental adjustment of abstractions to the facts they represent.

Two things happened rapidly.

First, Alert lights flashed red throughout the Council Chambers of the Interstellar League. In several places, the wall decorations swung back to reveal television screens and electronic tactical display maps. Phones rang in front of the chairs where the corpses of the Interstellar alliance government slumped. Tinny voices called out, shouting out alarms and warnings, begging for instructions.

The television screens displayed the view above the city of Accardistran Major. Hanging above the North Pole of the planet, with the supermetropolis looming from the polar jungles below her, was a dreadnought-class battlewagon some two miles long, shimmering with eerie green shadows as she materialized into view. On her prow was the triangle of Three Watching Eyes, the emblem of the Greatest Empire.

These were the compatriots X had been expecting.

A zone of force, transparent at first, but smoggy-black

and growing blacker, was radiating from powerful projection arrays amidships. This sphere, centered on the ship, encompassed within its border a large dome of atmosphere, several miles of the city, and a bowl-shaped bite out of the planet crust.

Second, as the force-zone solidified, Gosseyn felt a space-distortion ripple through the area: He recognized it as the same shadow-substance effect used to break Gosseyn's relationship with his next bodies.

Gosseyn was aware of the fact that his "memorized" locations in his brain were no longer connected to anything . . . all but two. He could still feel the locations at the post office and the Earth embassy: within the sphere projected by the ship. At a rough guess, the volume of action of the isolation-energy was about eighty-one cubic miles.

Several of the telephone voices cut off, and certain television screens went dark. The views from orbital satellites were missing: The sphere of force was negating all signals from outside.

The city lights shined up into a sky as lightless as a tomb.

The sphere . . . coruscated . . . with black energies. Little ripples and sparks of coal-black substance fluttered in and out of a deeper ebony; a dull red-gray smoke, the hue of blood, hovered over it. Gosseyn had a distinct impression that the photons near the force-zone were *blurring,* losing their exact locations, losing energy, the closer they got to the mathematically perfect barrier of the spherical zone of force.

Gosseyn similarized himself to the only location available. The secretary and the marine guards and the persons waiting to see Ambassador Norcross were startled when Gosseyn appeared in the antechamber of Norcross' offices.

One of the marines had an electro-telescopic range-finding mechanism on his power rifle.

Ignoring the questions from startled bystanders,

Gosseyn said to the marine, "There is a warship of the Greatest Empire about to destroy . . ."

The man obviously had Null-A training, at least to a degree. "I recognize you, sir," he said, unclipping the range finder and handing it to Gosseyn.

Gosseyn rested the metal tube on the windowsill and focused it on the warship hovering in the gloom overhead. Already searchlights from police and military installations beneath were sending narrow and brilliant beams through the dark air. Space-raid sirens were bellowing across the midnight-black streets; glittering force-shells were thickening around the buildings. The outer defensive screens of the mighty warship were already glinting with pinpoint sparks, perhaps from small-arms fire or vehicle-mounted weapons from police ships: small but defiant gestures.

There was also a military response from a four-thousand-foot-long frigate: A warship of the Interstellar League, by chance, had been trapped within the black sphere. It rose above the skyscrapers on invisible anti-gravitic pulses and opened fire.

Gosseyn watched carefully as the counterfire destroyed the incoming missiles one by one and sharpshooter pencil beams knocked out the frigate's main projectors with a series of nearly impossible perfect shots. The dreadnought was under the guidance of a Predictor of Yalerta, who was feeding precise coordinates to the gunners minutes and seconds before the Accoloni ship was even firing.

The hulk of the frigate toppled from the air. It must have had partial control, and the piloting crew stayed at their posts, for rather than crash into the mile-high buildings of the city, the huge machine toppled into a large civic park, erupting in flame. Some figures jumped from the hull and floated slowly groundward; some few others perhaps escaped by means of onboard distorter, but most of the crew did not escape.

From the prow of the triumphant Greatest Empire vessel reached a hollow tube of force, smashing buildings and streets to flinders, and boring deep into the bedrock.

Down this hollow tube descended a superatomic torpedo. The warhead was housed in a cylinder some two hundred yards long. The recognition program in the range finder in Gosseyn's hand lit up with red letters: This was a Nova-O-type warhead, able to reduce the planet to a seething mass of lava. The flimsy civilian screens of the buildings below had no chance of withstanding the blast.

After memorizing the torpedo, Gosseyn focused the aiming beam of the range finder at the still-open hatch from which the torpedo emerged. It took him a long-seeming second, but he memorized the atomic structure and space-time contour of the ship's launch bay.

For the dreadnought could not move away from the blast radius: It had to stay within the zone of force that was pinning Gosseyn into this location. Nor could it use a distorter to retreat to a distant star, because the black zone prevented similarization. Which meant . . .

Blindingly white-hot protective shells concentrically one after another appeared around the superwarship, more and more powerful screens than Gosseyn had seen even during space battles. He estimated that more than half of the immense volume beneath that two-mile-long hull must be taken up with force-projection machinery and atomic dynamos to power it.

The Predictors aboard the dreadnought would know when Gosseyn used his double brain, because the action created a blur across their vision of the future. They could not see what lay on the other side of that blur. . . .

And, of course, the protective shells were designed to be potent enough to withstand the torpedo's explosion. As with most high-energy phenomena, the shells maintained their magnetic coherency for that crucial microsecond after the generator-complex projecting them and the ship containing it was reduced to white-hot radiation. When the force-shells vanished, the molten debris from the ship, and the superheated spherical volume of air it once occupied, expanded and washed over the city, a titanic ball of flame, but this was a minor explosion, an afterthought, and the civilian-strength defensive shields, gleaming in the light of the reddish sun of Accolon, were sufficient to withstand most of the blow.

But it was a near thing, not without casualties: Gosseyn could see cracks running through some of the towers, shattered antennas, toppled vehicles, and bodies motionless in the streets below. He heard both wails of sirens and the faint shouts and screams of victims and survivors.

The marine was standing at Gosseyn's shoulder. He said, "The ambassador . . . ? I assume that since you are alone, he is dead."

Gosseyn nodded grimly. "Murdered by Enro's agent. The older version of me, the Lavoisseur who was helping the Hardie gang corrupt the Earth government selection process, is at large. At that time he was wheelchair bound, horribly wounded, and he called himself X. Now he is occupying a seventeen-year-old copy of my body, so his fingerprints, voiceprints, and brain patterns are the same as mine. Warn the Earth government not to trust any mental communication from me, or electronic messages, even those verified by a lie detector."

The guard seemed startled. "But how do we protect ourselves . . . from you?"

Gosseyn said, "That Shadow Effect projected by the dreadnought will stop—"

At that moment the secretary leaned from the window and, pointing, shouted, "Look!"

For there were still films and thin clouds of the shadow-substance hanging in midair, the residue of the vanished globular screen that had entombed them. Some clouds were high above the city; others were burning a long, thin, broken line in a great curve along the ground. Clinging, tenacious, and black, the dark fog writhed and solidified, in places growing larger and darker. Gosseyn tried to memorize a section of the nothingness, but no mental picture formed in his extra brain. The shadow-substance was neither matter nor energy, and the condition of space-time returned no signals where it was present.

In other places, the darkness was thinner and the foggy non-substance was returning to normal matter, becoming molecules of air, droplets of water, photons of sunlight.

Gosseyn took mental "photographs" of what was happening in the areas surrounding where the Shadow Effect was diminishing. As best he could tell, the broken energy-connections creating the local contour of space-time were reasserting themselves. But why?

He attempted to memorize two volumes of air, one on each side of a growing patch of darkness, and similarize them. He noticed the darkness effect slowing. Where he concentrated his efforts, he could break the clouds of darkness into smaller clouds and, after many minutes of work, the remaining wisps of cloud were small enough that they were naturally re-identifying themselves with their surroundings; matter and energy were returning to normal.

But it was an agonizingly slow and difficult process.

Gosseyn guessed the crucial factor was that space-time had not been stressed beyond a certain limit, or had been shadowless some small amount of time. How much energy did it take to establish all the atomic and molecular interactions, electromagnetic and nucleonic, all the vibrations and kinetic motions, all the matter-energy relationships of time-space and gravity within even one cubic inch of normal matter?

Gosseyn said, "I suspect the warship commander had not been willing to trust to a new and untested weapon. Otherwise, he would have simply placed his ship a light-year or two away, created a large field of darkness, and retreated. In a month, or perhaps only a week, the expanding Shadow Effect would have swept through this area of space. This phenomenon is not restricted to the speed of light, which, after all, is a by-product of the particular geometry of time-space that this non-identity effect is rendering null."

The secretary said, shocked, "Then there is no defense?"

Gosseyn did not answer her.

GOSSEYN reappeared in the Council Chambers of the League. Here were the corpses, still undisturbed, in spreading pools of red, and the smell of ozone and charred flesh still hung in the air. The emergency was less than fifteen minutes old, and no one had yet battered down the magnetically sealed chamber doors.

With no wasted motions, Gosseyn picked up the damaged lie detector X had shot and unplugged it from the surrounding electronics.

From there it was but one step to the post office in Accardistran Minor, where he had the damaged lie detector carefully sealed into a plain brown package. It was a short stroll to the local spaceport.

He walked onto first one interstellar cruiser to select a cabin, announced that he was changing his mind, disembarked, and then boarded a second ship.

By the time the local police put out a planet-wide bulletin, searching for the only witness to the death of the Interstellar League leaders, and ordered first one and then the second cruise-ship where he had been seen back to the surface, Gosseyn, smuggled aboard a third ship, a tramp freighter, into whose open airlock he had merely glanced in passing, was far beyond their reach.

The freighter captain was willing to put the stowaway to work to earn his passage. Gosseyn spent the next few days' ship-time moving crates.

THERE were Interstellar League patrol ships waiting in orbit around Venus. Gosseyn was able to persuade the freighter's supercargo to let him borrow a camera with a radar attachment to allow him to take a photograph through the thick clouds of the Venusian atmosphere.

14

Once the mind and body are conditioned, at a pre-verbal level, to operate beyond the assumptions of Aristotelian categories, and to be aware of the self-reflexive nature of abstraction, then the mind is ready to adapt itself to reality as it is, not as we wish it were.

When Gosseyn appeared on the roof of the Venus City spaceport, a man in a wide-brimmed hat, green coat, and dark glasses was waiting there for him.

The spaceport was situated on top of the flattened peak of a mountain, one of the few mountains on Venus lofty enough to reach above the five-thousand-yard-tall trees of that light-gravity world. This spaceport had been built by Earthmen before the distorter technology had been known to solar system science. It was designed to allow ships to land and depart through the thick atmosphere, guided down by radar-beams to platforms held high above the surrounding canopy, and highly visible on many bands of the spectrum.

The view of Venus was breathtaking: a forest canopy of endless green extending underfoot in all directions, beneath a rippling pearly white sky of cloud extending equally as far overhead—a plane of green facing a parallel plane of silver. The huge sun was invisible, but the whole sky was lit with shadowless cloud-dazzle.

The man approached. His coat was refrigerated against the blazing heat here above the forest canopy; Gosseyn could feel the breath of cool air coming from the emerald fabric. He was a small man with a wiry build.

With no introduction, the man spoke. "There are not that many places a man with your powers and limitations can materialize on Venus, Mr. Gosseyn. Our houses, for the most part, are burrowed into the solid wood, our cities hidden under miles of greenery, and cannot be distinguished, from orbit, from any other tree or grove of Venus, even with a powerful telescope."

Gosseyn looked the man up and down, "You are a Venusian detective?"

"Peter Clayton. As of now, I am in charge of the investigation."

"As of now?"

"One of the other detectives in my voluntary group is watching your apartment. He estimated that, by now, you would have overcome the last known limitations of your twenty-decimal-point similarity system, and would be able to appear there, despite the time-distance since your departure for Planet Nirene . . . unless I am speaking to the Gosseyn who went to the Shadow Galaxy aboard the *Ultimate Prime*?"

Gosseyn said, "Your information is out of date. He is dead, as is the version of me who went to Nirene, both slain by a person employing the Shadow Effect we first saw the Follower using. I am Gosseyn Four."

Clayton nodded. "In either case, the voluntary group decided to use a common-sense approach for selecting a coordinator to decide what to do about the Enro situation, and, as of now, no other detective's estimate as to your motions has proven to be as accurate as mine. As soon as I make a determination, I'll have the Games Machine of Venus broadcast assignments to the population of Venus and, by distorter-radio, to the Null-A groups colonizing the galaxy."

Gosseyn noted with wry amusement that this man, this ordinary Venusian Null-A detective, would temporarily command the men of Venus in a fashion more absolute than Enro the Red could even imagine: because the commands would be followed imaginatively and voluntarily, with no other sanction for disobedience than each man's own sense that he should do what logic demanded.

Clayton said, "I assume that package under your arm

contains the remains of the lie detector the seventeen-year-old variant of Lavoisseur shot? I have a scientific team standing by, including experts in robotic-memory reconstruction."

Clayton took off his dark glasses once they were downstairs, away from the cloud-dazzle. They paused in the spaceport annex to outfit Gosseyn in the local fashion. Once they were beneath the cool green shadow of the endless canopy, Gosseyn did not bother to turn on the air-conditioning circuit in his jacket. Instead, he adjusted his fabric to open the weave, to feel the soft breeze wandering beneath the trees of Venus.

Underfoot was soft, thick grass. The trees, some of them half a mile high, were spaced so far apart that the brown and black trunks seemed like the posts of some immense world-cathedral; and Venus, a world with a whispering sky of leaf-green. A robocab was sitting on the grass not far away.

Gosseyn enjoyed a moment of homesick pleasure. The machinery, the clothing, all the devices of Venus were so well made; the landscape was gardenlike, beautiful. It was good to be back.

Clayton opened the vehicle's fusion motor and let Gosseyn examine the interior of the power core through a viewing device. "In case Enro attacks us here," Clayton explained curtly.

When they were airborne, Gosseyn said, "The League police showed you the security recording of the murder scene?"

"An edited version, but I was able to deduce what they didn't show us."

"Are you going to cooperate with the League police and turn me in? Their desire to question me regarding the murders of the Councilors is understandable—"

Clayton waved his hand, a short, chopping gesture. "The future of the human race has more need of your time and talents elsewhere. I am hoping there will be a sufficient 'imprint' of the X variant of Lavoisseur lingering in the remaining lie-detector tubes to force a similarity between the two of you. Once we know everything he knows about Enro, we can take the next step."

Gosseyn said, "Does that next step include organizing a Sphere-technology defense against the Shadow Effect?"

"Null-A archeologists are already scouring the galaxy for relics of other Primordial ships like the one Enro stole. We are looking on any world with monkeys. But, at the moment, this is only a backup plan. The technique of long-range mechanical prediction-similarization needed to transmit planets intact between galaxies is not feasible, until and unless we can locate all the Gosseyn bodies Lavoisseur hid."

"Backup plan?"

Clayton said, "Think about it. Enro's main weakness is psychological. We can bypass his entire complex structure of military, political, religious, and psionic power, if we find the weakness inherent in his mind. Lavoisseur, including the version you call X the Unknown, is a trained Null-A observer and the founder of the Semantics Institute. If he is working with Enro, he observed Enro more closely than you or Eldred Crang were able to. X knows how to make Enro defeat himself."

Gosseyn said, "How is it possible that X can be driven by such an insane idea as creating a universal government by force of arms when he is such an advanced non-Aristotelian thinker? His training, his neurolinguistic integration, must be more complete than yours or mine."

"It would seem an impossibility," Clayton said with a sudden boyish smile. "And so some assumption we are making is false-to-facts. Don't you love puzzles? I do."

Gosseyn, for the first time in days, felt himself relaxing in the glow of confidence, of competence, this man naturally gave off.

"So you are just going to ignore the police of Accolon and Gorgzid seeking me, Mr. Clayton?"

"These galactics don't know what to make of us, Mr. Gosseyn. They keep asking who our leader is, and directing all their inquiries to the President of Earth, Janet Wake."

Gosseyn was amused. "Someone once asked me why there are detectives in a world without criminals."

Peter Clayton laughed aloud. "To keep it that way, of course!"

GOSSEYN remembered his first time on this planet, a few days before the invasion by the Greatest Empire. Gosseyn had been a hunted fugitive. Captured by Enro's agents, Gosseyn met a native-born henchman named Blayney, who was posing as a Null-A detective, a man so overwrought that he betrayed an inner cortical-thalamic confusion by his every word. At the time, not knowing about the distorter-imposed interference to the Games Machine of Venus, Gosseyn had wondered how the man roamed free in a sane world.

Even with the Games Machine of Venus compromised, real Null-A detectives had discovered the imposture and deduced the existence of the extraterrestrial civilization that had sent agents among them, made tentative guesses about its scope, socioeconomics, and technology. With the careful cooperation of all Venusians, especially wives married to galactic gang members, they had prepared an in-depth defense to resist the attack months and years before it came, including a plan to evacuate all the major cities at a moment's notice. One detective, Eldred Crang, had penetrated even to the Imperial Court of Gorgzid by that time.

The defense preparations were carried out with such secrecy that the Greatest Empire troopers, when they came, assumed the Null-A Venusian counterattacks were all spontaneous impromptu affairs and that the Venusians were supermen. Outnumbered and outfought, facing a vastly superior technology, the Venusians won a crushing psychological victory.

Gazing down at the immense trees of the garden-world, Gosseyn saw very few of the burns or scars that high explosives or atomic-powered beams had left after the war still marking the bark. Even a powerful cannon could do little to harm such colossal volumes of wood. Most of the crater damage to the living cities of Venus had already grown over.

THE robocab flew toward a tree-bole so large that the branches were as broad as highways. A brown and rugged wall of bark rose up in view: A massive door opened in the wood and slid aside, revealing a car park where many sleek green air vehicles were already cradled. Through the window panels set in the wall of living wood surrounding the buried car park, Gosseyn could see the shining instruments and winking electron tubes of several laboratories, including an entire wall of linked electronic brains, emitters and transmitters of various designs.

Gosseyn realized suddenly where he was: "Is this . . . ?"

Clayton nodded. "This is the lab for Dr. Hayakawa's design team. That man there is Dr. Reed, of the Neurolinguistic Research Institute."

No one knew more about the workings of the mind, human or electronic, than the people gathered here: The various Games Machine circuits Venus had been shipping out to expatriate Null-A's on other worlds were made in these labs. This team had invented the special designs to resist the kind of distorter paralysis the Hardie gang once used to corrupt the Machines of Earth and Venus, to put Hardie in a position of power there, or to prevent agents of the gang, present under false pretenses, from being extradited.

Gosseyn saw the faces of the men and women who watched him land. The sight filled him with confidence.

Introductions were brief, as Dr. Hayakawa rushed him into an insulated signal-nullification chamber. Technicians in full-body radiation armor began helping Gosseyn to strip and to attach medical and recording appliances to his head, spine, and upper body.

The scientists and their technical crew fled from the room, and motorized hinges swung shut a valve thicker than a bank vault door. Gosseyn did not blame them: The moment Gosseyn's nervous system established a connection with a distant point in space-time, any reactions X might have programmed into his own extra brain might be triggered. X could similarize an atomic force into the chamber, or worse.

Over the intercom, Dr. Reed was saying, "Once we take the imprint of Lavoisseur's brain from the tube fragments of the lie detector, we expect to be able to mechanically force enough similarity to provoke a reaction."

"What kind of reaction?"

Clayton's voice answered with a hint of humor, "Of course that depends on the energy-matter conditions of Lavoisseur and the area of space-time around him. If he is not in his shadow-form, and if he has taken no precautions, it is possible that we might have a sufficient connection to establish a mental connection, and draw vital information from his brain into yours. Naturally, we will have a thought-sensitive electron tube arrangement set to record the results."

Gosseyn realized why Clayton was making a point of calling the enemy version of Gosseyn by the name Lavoisseur rather than something else: That name drove home the point that they were dealing with an individual of rare genius, the leader of the Semantics Institute. If X's tale was to be believed, it had been merely an offshoot of his memory chain, a discarded duplicate, who, under the now-legendary name of Walter S. de Lany, had possessed the supreme knowledge to found and build the first Games Machine on Earth.

The solitary survivor of the Primordial Humans of the

long-dead Shadow Galaxy. Who was he, really? Xenius of Mars. Ysvid of Forever Isle. Ur-ath-Vir the First-of-Living. X the Unknown.

This supremely dangerous individual knew more about the intricate energy-relationships of the similarity and distortion effects than Venusian or galactic science knew.

Dr. Reed's voice came over the intercom: "No matter what precautions he takes, Lavoisseur cannot change the laws of nature. Once two bodies exceed twenty degrees of similarity, the greater bridges the gap to the lesser as if there is no gap. The armored suit you see before you there contains both a sensory-deprivation capacity as well as a molecular-refrigeration field to slow Brownian motions. By placing you in a passive, hypnotic state, similar to what your 'empty' bodies hidden in their medical coffins experience, we hope to make your nervous system the 'lesser' of the two poles, once the connection is forced. You can memorize the interior workings of the suit with that transparency bar."

Gosseyn took several moments to "photograph" the various suit components and energy systems into his double brain and attached each to a complex set of cues that would operate faster than any mechanical switch. Since he would be unconscious during the actual moment of forced contact, he set the cues to react to specific patterns in the suit's electronic brain, which had been pre-set to recognize a variety of threat scenarios.

Padded robot arms now helped Gosseyn, together with his medical packages, slide into the armored suit. It was more like entering a vehicle than it was like donning armor: The suit was fifteen feet tall, with amplifying motors at the joints. The robotic hands wired the appliances taped to Gosseyn's skull into the inner surface of the wide, domelike helmet.

There were mouth tubes for food and water up above and a catheter-recycler arrangement down below. The meaning of this was not lost on Gosseyn.

Over the suit radio, Gosseyn said, "You are assuming

that, seventeen-year-old or not, Lavoisseur would not make such a mistake as leaving the lie detector behind, even damaged."

Clayton answered, "We are talking about the foremost Null-A psychiatrist in the universe. He allowed a machine to make a verification model of his thought-patterns. He could have similarized it out of the room with him when he departed."

"So it is a trap."

Dr. Hayakawa's voice answered: "We did not bother mounting weapons on the suit, since our electronic brain calculated that your thought-patterns could direct nucleonic and electronic forces more precisely and with more deliberate effect than any aiming and delivery system we have. The suit's atomic pile is roughly equal to the output of a battleship, and you can concentrate your fire into a smaller area than any weapon by using the electron-microscope attachment. There is also a distorter-brake built in the suit, so that if you are physically pulled toward Lavoisseur, you will land not where he wants but some place nineteen-point-nine degrees of similarity off-target: In the metric of undistorted space, that works out to something around six billion miles."

As it turned out, when Gosseyn woke and checked his altimeter he found the nearest gravitating body was only two hundred forty thousand miles away, not the six billion it might have been.

The instruments in his helmet detected two smaller bodies, airless and waterless; after an hour of tracking their motions against the starry background, the onboard electronic brain was able to confirm the two dots of light were moons, the slim, rust-red crescent was a planet. The planet held atmosphere and water: There were also extensive atomic and electromagnetic power sources webbing the planet, signs of an advanced technological system.

Gosseyn pointed his gyroscope at the red crescent, set

the onboard electronic brain to calculate an orbit, and switched on his suit drivers. There was a slight sensation of pressure, as if he weighed an eighth of a pound and were lying on his back. That was all. There was no other sign of motion, except for the slow crawl of numbers in his suit dials.

15

It is important to remember that there is a wide, perhaps limitless, number of mechanisms, social and psychological, the human nervous system can adopt when dealing with the surrounding universe.

The planet was a visible disk the size of his palm at arm's length when it was blotted from sight. Gosseyn was alarmed at first, but his suit instruments and his extra brain continued to register the powerful gravitic and electromagnetic fields of the planet. There was some dark and solid body occluding it, not the Shadow Effect.

The patrol ship was a dark torpedo-shaped machine some four hundred feet long, which became visible when it focused a searchlight on Gosseyn. The ship was close enough that Gosseyn could sense the atomic energy in its drive core. Gosseyn was expecting a radio message, and so he opened his suit antennas to several bands and listened. Nothing.

He also expected the ship to undergo a period of maneuvering to match orbital elements with him, in case it wanted to narrow the distance: To his surprise, Gosseyn saw that, according to his suit instruments, the ship happened to be on the same course as his, with a slightly higher speed. To the instruments' limits of detection, the numbers were an exact match.

More and more stars were blotted out as the ship came closer. A circle of light appeared in the middle of the black hull: It was a large open airlock.

The hull loomed in his vision. So far, Gosseyn had detected no maneuvering thrust—the ship was coasting to this exact point in orbit, rotating at the correct rate to bring its airlock ring through the precise point in space occupied by his body at this exact time.

Then the airlock swooped up around him. Only now did he sense the electrical crackle of maneuvering jets firing, a short, controlled burst. The airlock valve shut out the stars. He was in a large, cylinder-shaped chamber. The far wall was moving toward him slowly, and then more slowly, and then the ship around him came to "rest" relative to his motion. Neither line nor grappling field had been used to make any last-minute fine adjustments: It was the most precise bit of space piloting Gosseyn had ever seen. He assumed it was done to impress him.

His suit dials registered an increasing air pressure around him.

An artificial gravity field, mild at first, pulled him toward one surface. He oriented the huge armored columns of his motorized legs toward it and landed lightly. He saw now that the airlock cylinder was not circular in cross section but octagonal: He landed on a flat surface rather than a curve. After a moment, weight increased, till it was roughly half Earth-normal.

The bulkhead above and perpendicular to him turned transparent. There on the deck above, in an austere-looking control chamber, looking down at him, were a group of six men. All were dressed in military-style uniform, in identical postures: hands clasped behind the back, legs spread, heads nodded slightly forward. The men were so similar of face, build, and expression that they might have been brothers. All were pale of skin, and their eyes were large and dark. Gosseyn noticed how dim the lighting was kept.

Despite their stiff postures, Gosseyn could see an eager glitter in their eyes, a foxlike avarice, which they could only partly hide. These men were keyed up.

The one on the far left pointed through the transparent wall at a section of the airlock floor near Gosseyn. At this gesture, a small hatch slid back and a machine in the niche beyond focused its lenses on Gosseyn. Gosseyn recognized it as a language imprinter.

Rather than remove his helmet to expose his brain for the imprinter, Gosseyn turned on his external loud-speaker: "Can we converse in the language of Accolon or Nirene?"

The second from the left replied, "Welcome to Corthid, central planet of the Interstellar League. We represent the Unit Vathirid of Organization Vathir, and, by extension, we represent the interests of the Corthidian Unity. Right now, we are examining how to exploit you. We have already rejected the option of executing you and taking your extraordinary battle-suit as salvage as being an option of limited imagination. What have you to offer us?"

Gosseyn, who had been expecting some terrific struggle with soldiers of the Greatest Empire, said in surprise, "The planet below us is Corthid? I was assuming it to be a base of Enro's."

The six exchanged wry glances. Another man, the third from the left, now spoke: "What is the empirical basis of that assumption?"

Gosseyn decided on a policy of openness. "I was brought into your area of space by a mutual enemy, whom I call X, an agent of Enro's. He attempted to similarize me to a location nearby, but the circuits in this suit automatically interrupted the distorter pattern involved before the transmission was complete."

Again the six men exchanged rapid glances. Gosseyn wondered if they were communicating by some silent method.

"You have piqued our curiosity," said the fourth man.

"Obviously, whatever interests us can interest other members of our larger group organization. There may be exploitation value here as news or entertainment. On what basis did you come here, a single person, to engage a military base of Enro?"

Gosseyn said, "If you are seeking some personal advantage from this situation, put the safety of yourself and your planet first! Are there military authorities here?"

There was a flicker of smiles among the sly-faced men gathered there. "We are all members of the militia," said the fifth man, shrugging. "The government, in peacetime, only acts as the umpire to see that we settle our wagers as promised."

"Our organizations each police themselves," said the sixth man, the one on the far right. "We would take it as a sign of your peaceful intent if you would put off your armor. Come now! The six of us have staked our lives on the wager that you will not open fire or force us to open fire. We could have hammered you with torpedoes from a distance: The cousin unit in our organization, Vathnogrod, wagered that we would come to regret not doing exactly that. Surely you want to see their wager lost! Cooperate with Unit Vathirid and we can share the profit with you. Our unit will be raised in value, and their unit will be depressed."

Gosseyn decided there was no use trying to hide his identity. He selected a spot of hull next to where the speaker was standing, made a mental "photograph" of it to the depth of several molecules, and similarized himself to it, leaving the armor standing empty.

Rather than appearing startled or alarmed, the six men merely seemed amused. The sixth man said, "An interesting method: no need to open the suit." He turned to the others and said, "Clearly his weapons can operate across space regardless of intermediary objects, barriers, or distances."

At that moment, a door opened near Gosseyn. Two women, as alike as twin sisters, dressed in white, stepped out. They were pale skinned and dark haired, with large, night-adapted eyes. Without a word, they stepped close to Gosseyn and began removing the medical appliances and recording boxes taped to his skull and spine. The two nurses (so Gosseyn assumed them to be) placed the instruments carefully on a table nearby.

He noticed that the women had the proper tools, calibrated to the proper standard-Venus fittings, to remove the surgical probes without any difficulty.

Gosseyn said, "I am trying to imagine how you run a society where everyone is lucky. Your callidetic sciences apparently enable you to launch ships on perfect trajectories to match the course and speed of tiny moving bodies at remote distances and to be prepared to meet with potentially dangerous visitors from other stars. I have heard it described as a type of observation system, but my own hunch is that it is a time-energy effect, perhaps like what a Predictor of Yalerta does, but on an unconscious level."

The man on the far left spoke: "Because of the cultivation of the callidetic talent among our peoples, we are quick to recognize, in the pattern of events, opportunities for advancement and exploitation. The group-surety system acts as a check, if you will, on what otherwise would be dangerous ambitions among us."

"Group-surety?"

"The whole unit is punished if one of us oversteps the social norms."

Gosseyn said, "The system would seem to discourage individual initiative."

The man on the far left smiled wryly, a very foxlike expression. "That is precisely its purpose. Individualism leaves the society incapable of coherent group action, and vulnerable to ambitious individuals using clever misinformation systems."

One of the women Gosseyn had thought to be a nurse stepped in front of the man talking and spoke: "The Corthid culture has risen to galactic predominance because of what outworlders call our luck, which is actually no more than a talent for recognizing significant patterns in apparently chaotic events."

Gosseyn noticed that the woman's eyes glittered with energetic personality: cunning and excited. He now recognized that look: the intensity of someone addicted to risk.

By speaking to him the woman was engaged in some dangerous gamble.

Meanwhile, the second woman had opened the medical cases and was examining Gosseyn's brain recordings. Gosseyn was startled at the casual invasion of his privacy. But this second woman spoke without looking up: "You can see why we must organize ourselves into a flexible yet coherent social structure: We must exploit advantages when they appear, acting as a team, quickly and without friction."

She looked up, exchanging glances with the men. Gosseyn suspected how the callidetic talent could allow them to exchange silent messages: She was sizing up her allies, predicting how the rest of the unit would react, relying on her "luck" to tell what the others would do if she seized the initiative. All the members of the group were using this method, keeping each other in view, trying to guess which way they would jump.

The second woman nodded to the first, who turned and said, "Gilbert Gosseyn! We have decided to deal with you on the same basis as we would negotiate with a sovereign interplanetary power. Your ability to disturb the patterns of fate is equal in magnitude, at least, to that of Enro the Red, even were his entire military empire restored to his command."

One of the men stepped forward and said, "For the moment, the warrants for your arrest from Accolon and Gorgzid we will ignore. We are throwing in with you." His glance toward the two women made Gosseyn realize that the six men, perhaps a different "unit" in this fluid social structure, had decided to allow the two women to seize control and were now following their lead.

Gosseyn realized the psychological pressures merely of the day-to-day life in such a society would be immense. Any misstep, real or feared, any moment of hesitation or doubt, and the initiative would be seized by someone luckier or more ruthless. Added to this was the continuous doubt whether one would be punished for some failure by another person in the unit or organization; there would be a constant pressure to stay alert and abandon any units about to be punished for failure.

There were quick introductions: The men were named O-Vath, E-Vath, Wu-Vath, Ai-Vath, Ah-Vath, and Y-Vath. The women were Evana and Yvana. At the moment, Yvana had seized the leadership role.

Gosseyn said, "You said you represented both your organization and also the general Corthid government? How do you resolve conflicts between the two?"

Yvana replied, "If you choose to deal with our unit, you will be wagering your prestige that the rest of Corthid will accept to be bound by what our unit decides. If our unit is successful, the other organizations will fall in line with our policy; otherwise, they will repudiate us, and we will suffer, as well as you. If you treat with us as if we represent Corthid, your fate is tied to our group fate."

Gosseyn realized that he had been assuming that, like the other galactics he had met, these people would be organized into a hierarchy: one of them the ship's captain, the others his crew. A foolish assumption. From the casual way they spoke, Gosseyn realized their mental and social habits were more flexible than that: Whoever was the "luckiest" among them, the quickest to turn events to his advantage, would be in the leadership role for so long as his luck held out.

There was something familiar about such an approach.

Gosseyn said, "You have a Games Machine here on Corthid, don't you?"

At that moment, a loudspeaker clattered to life in the room. "There is a message from the Hidden Capitol. The Safety Authority declares it is taking control of this case: All exploitation games must cease! All related wagers are held in abeyance until further notice. Escort Gilbert Gosseyn to the planet surface, to speak with Illverton."

The eight cunning-eyed, sly-faced individuals in the chamber, the six men and two women, sagged with disappointment.

GOSSEYN was allowed up on the bridge to watch the landing. The bridge canopy was an enormous transparent dome, giving an unobstructed view in every direction: Amplifier screens just below the canopy were tuned to a number of different frequencies and showed the X-ray, radio emission, and infrared patterns of the surrounding universe. On one screen was an image of the gravity-waves, and this showed a black, smoky shape smothering several stars in one direction.

Gosseyn nodded toward that image. "Enro has begun destroying solar systems. What lies in that direction?"

E-Vath answered, "Many of the most highly populated planets of the Sixth Decant of the Galaxy used to be there. The spread of the shadow-matter cloud that swallowed the central systems will not be visible, from this location, for another ninety centuries; since the shadow itself is a faster-than-light effect, it overtakes any visible images of itself as it spreads. However, the influence on the space-time metric propagates at similar speeds, and so gravity-wave instruments can pick it up."

Gosseyn tried to imagine the magnitude of the catastrophe: billions of lives snuffed out as planets and suns lost their coherent matter-energy states. Even with a highly organized evacuation, there were simply not enough ships to move whole continents of people into space, and the Shadow Effect rendered nearby distorter traffic unreliable.

Enro's doing. The great dictator had begun his next program of mass murder with the same callous efficiency as the last galactic war: Only now the weapon was a force of nature destroying the fabric of time and space.

The Corthid ship was entering the atmosphere, and the canopy overhead turned rosy-pink with reentry heat. In moments, the great dark curve of the world had flattened from a globe to a horizon, so that nocturnal landscape was spread below. In the dim light of two moons, Gosseyn could detect rough terrain below or perhaps (in the dimness it was difficult to see) merely clouds, but there was no light, no evidence of cities.

Dawn broke suddenly over a landscape of red crags tinged with white frost as the ship sped across the terminator to the dayside of the planet. There was nothing below but empty waste.

O-Vath explained, "Corthid is an ancient world, the eldest world inhabited by man. Our records stretch back over twelve million years. The atmosphere long ago lost its protective chemical-electrical properties, and the oceans evaporated to space. The surface has not been habitable for a quarter-million years: Our peoples removed their civilization underground during the many centuries long before that."

Even as he spoke, the ship came to a cavern mouth two miles across. Down into a half-mile-wide bore fell the ship. Here were scattered lights, for built into the sides and floor of the round shaft were installations and barracks, looking small and doll-like in the distance.

Gosseyn's extra brain detected charges of energy running through the stone. Miles of rock had been artificially degravitized.

The bore was not straight, nor was it short. First on one heading, then on another, for many minutes and many miles, the ship sped on. Deeper and deeper beneath the crust of the planet they traveled.

The bore opened into vastness. They sunk into an

underground world. Above them, like a sky, was the solid roof of weightless stone, and suddenly below them, bright from the light of countless floating lamps, were the cities and farmlands of Corthid. The lit areas were gathered around buried cisterns large as oceans, connected by canals as large as rivers.

The cavern space was huge beyond the reach of sight. The lights were gathered high above the well-tilled robot-worked farms and rice paddies, plashes of green against a dark stone background. But the same lights were gathered low above the avenues and courtyards of the metropolitan areas, giving them a jewel-like, nighttime look. Since the crust of the planet overhead was artificially made weightless, there was no danger of collapse, no matter how large the cavern system grew.

Degravitized matter was unstable on a fundamental wave-level, so that the approach of any ordinary matter set the gravityless particles into agitation. Any time a ship appeared within light-years of the planet, the planet surface itself would act as one gigantic detection array, and the gravity reaction was not limited by the speed of light. The crust also protected them against all but atomic bombardment of planet-destroying magnitude. It was an elegant system.

Gosseyn said, "How can your world maintain its predominance? Your space fleet is larger than that of Accolon or Petrino, who are the other major interstellar powers in the League. You have more colony planets under your sway even than Gorgzid. And yet your natural resources and raw materials must have been exhausted long ago."

Yvana smiled at him, a dazzling smile. "You know better than that. Predominance is caused by having a superior form of organization. Our system rewards and encourages brilliance but also rewards hard and steady work, team-loyalty. Because those other worlds we visit are richer after we depart, they welcome us again."

Evana rolled her eyes. "That's what we tell people. Actually, it's just luck."

The ship hung in the dark air of the cave, above the dazzling, jewel-like display of the capital city of Corthindel, on the rocky shores of a buried sea. Through a floorplate, Gosseyn studied the scene underfoot. There was a squat cubelike building, the center of several power plants and communication grids, which Evana told him was the headquarters of the Safety Authority. Across a large, parklike area from this, a stepped pyramid arose, its peak shining with a flare of atomic light. Rank on rank of that mighty building was merely the housing of electronic brains linked in series. So huge was the thinking machinery that the colonnades and schoolrooms dotting its lower levels only gave a slight texture to the sweep of metal. The Games Machine.

He asked Yvana about it.

She said, "It was installed by a small colony of Earthmen who have taken up residence during the war. Recently certain citizens have volunteered to be rated and graded according to the Null-A methods taught by the Machine. Our callidetic adepts can sense the increased 'luck,' the ability to shape events, of anyone so trained, and therefore organizations are automatically forming around the Null-A's here: We predict they will skyrocket to positions of great influence in politics, sciences, arts, and business."

Gosseyn realized that the psychological pressures brought to bear on the Corthid culture in the coming years would be slightly terrific. If their leadership was based on self-promoting individual initiative, they would be eager to "exploit" the advantages of the Null-A training but would grow increasingly uneasy as the Null-A training "exploited" them by changing them to personality types more stable, more group oriented (in one sense) than the average callidetic Corthidian but utterly individualistic in another sense.

Gosseyn said, "I cannot reconcile what you told me about your government system, which seems to rely entirely on the self-initiative of self-appointed leaders, with this Safety Authority, which apparently has no limit to its powers."

Yvana told him the Safety Authority was a recently created emergency agency. "Originally it had started in the same self-promoting fashion as other organizations, but when the technology was discovered that held out a promise of being able to drive back the Shadow Effect . . ."

Gosseyn was startled by the news. Stepping to a magnifier, he swept his gaze suddenly back and forth across the dark cavern floor below, following the power lines coming from the huge cubelike building of the Safety Authority. There! How could he have missed it? Distorter arrangements the size of skyscrapers, one after another, spaced across the city. Gosseyn focused the viewing plate at a farther point on the cavern floor. There, among the farms and fields under the blazing artificial lights, rose another distorter bank, a four-hundred-foot-tall spire: There was another beyond that some six miles away, and a third, dimly visible in the distance, beyond that. All were connected by heavy insulated cables and power couplings, and farms had been abandoned or other structures torn down, and cleared, to make the wide paths across the cavern floor for these hastily erected cables to pass.

". . . We had to organize ourselves quickly, and with absolute loyalty, behind the leadership of the Safety Authority. The other organizations were pressured by public opinion to fall into line. . . ."

Gosseyn said, "How did this man make this discovery?"

Yvana said, "Illverton is a paleoarcheologist, who goes alone to explore the outer asteroids of our system for years at a time. His publicists claim he came across a working starship of the Primordials and the machines aboard were still operational after two billion years, including a model of a device to inhibit the Shadow Effect."

Gosseyn said, "Doesn't it strike you as unlikely that he

would happen to come across such an astonishing find so recently, just in time to save your planet?"

Yvana smiled. "Among a race of people with the Callidetic talent? Unlikely? We don't ask such questions."

Gosseyn said, "I suspect this Illverton is an agent of Enro's. There is no way he could hide a naval base on the most well-defended enemy planet of the League, unless the local government—in this case, your Safety Authority—was firmly in his camp."

Yvana looked at Gosseyn with astonishment. "Are you asking us to rebel? The Safety Authority is our only hope for our planet to escape destruction! Scientists have examined the distorter arrays Illverton erected: They broadcast a specific set of positively reinforcing energies to increase the specific self-similarity of any particles caught in the field. It would reinforce the mathematical identity of shadow-matter and restore its proper atom-to-atom relations to normal time-space. The theory is sound!"

Gosseyn said, "I am throwing in with your group. Wagering my prestige that whoever first unmasks Illverton will win eternal gratitude from the peoples of Corthid. Are you with me?"

Yvana smiled, drew her sidearm, and touched an intercom switch.

"Fall in, boys! Who is ready for a gamble?"

YVANA led a squad of about forty armed men. They disembarked from the ship and were lowered toward the rooftop of the Safety Authority on pencils of force, falling as rapidly as paratroopers.

The guards on the roof were astonished when their weapons disappeared from their hands: Gosseyn sent the rifles to the only spot available to his extra brain, the control room overlooking the airlock of Yvana's ship.

Held at gunpoint by Yvana and her smiling, glittering-eyed riflemen, the Safety Authority guards showed Gosseyn how to operate the gate controls. He traced the

circuits with his extra brain and found no additional
wires, nothing leading to an alarm.

Gosseyn said, "You have no security cameras watching this spot?"

The guard said in amazement, "Who would want to
break into the Safety Authority?"

But at that same moment, two of the other guards
vowed to support Yvana and her group. Both men reached
up to their collars and tuned the colors of their uniforms to
match the patterns of the Vathir unit. Yvana handed these
men their charged rifles with no further ado. They fell into
her squad, apparently no more and no less trusted than
any other man there.

The corridor beyond the gate was empty. The architecture here was austere and bare of ornament. The two turn-
coat guards were happy to lead Gosseyn and the armed
squad down the corridors, arresting any other Safety Authority personnel they came across or bribing them to lay
down their arms.

The squad went down a long flight of stairs and then
into what looked like a large office: In a plain and spar-
tan style here were fifty desks, behind which sat clerks
and secretaries, each with her stat-plate and keypad, as
well as small electronic filing machines. When the
armed men broke suddenly into the room the women all
came to their feet and then, smiling in fox-faced nonchalance, raised their hands and shrugged in surrender.

Gosseyn did not pause to observe. At the far end of
the office were large double doors, sheathed in a force-
barrier of military-level strength. With his extra brain, he
blasted the panels open with a charge of power similarized to this spot from his battle-suit back in the airlock
of the Vathir ship.

The chamber beyond was huge and paneled with repeater screens. Each screen showed one of the tower-sized
distorter arrays spaced throughout the many gigantic caverns of the planet. There was a large desk at the far wall.

In the tall chair was a figure slumped in sleep. A gray-haired man, dressed in the stark utilitarian uniform of Corthid, lay snoring with his head on the desk.

Gosseyn stepped over the smoking panels of the shattered door. The man, obviously startled into wakefulness by the explosion, now stirred and raised his head, blinking.

The face was of a thin-jawed older man: He had the mild expression of an academic. This was not a Gosseyn body.

Nonetheless, when the man saw Gosseyn he was startled and leaped to his feet.

And his thoughts flowed into Gosseyn's brain.

16

A memory is an abstraction from reality and, as such, is not perfectly accurate. Always keep in mind that the nervous system records not sense-impressions but our reactions to and interpretations of them.

Awareness crashed into Gosseyn. Quicker than any spoken word could convey, memories flashed from X to Gosseyn.

X had been asleep to keep his nervous system in a receptive state, so that he had been aware of Gosseyn's every thought and action as he appeared in this area of space, was recovered by the Vathir Organization ship, came to the surface, prepared his rebellion, and broke in. Now that X was shocked awake, his every thought tense and focused, Gosseyn's thoughts could not match his for speed or clarity.

Even this was part of the plan: Gosseyn, who became the "lesser" pole of the thought-flow once X woke up, was now receiving thought, and so would leave no trace of his memories in Illverton as they both perished.

And the thought Gosseyn received was: *poor, pathetic, young fool*—the impression was of a creature tens of thousands, or even millions, of years old. This ancient, ancient being regarded Gosseyn as a temporary aberration, an excess chain of memory about to be excised.

Gosseyn said aloud, "What's the trap?"

X could not prevent himself from thinking the details of the trap, nor did he bother trying to hide his thoughts.

He was not really here. Using the same technique that the so-called Chessplayer once had used to imprint Gosseyn's consciousness on the nervous system of Ashargin, X had imprinted his consciousness into the helpless body of Illverton, a nondescript archeologist, whose long solitary sabbaticals to the remote regions of the Corthid star system made him the perfect victim. The hermit had no one who would recognize his sudden change of personality.

And the peoples of Corthid had one blind spot in their mental makeup. They believed in extraordinary strokes of luck, and they cooperated wholeheartedly with projects that seemed to be touched with that divine fire of good fortune: including a project to protect the world from the Shadow Effect by erecting, in record time, an astonishing number of ultra-large-scale distorter mechanisms. And the true purpose of those mechanisms was . . .

The repeater screens behind Illverton showed the distorter towers, hundreds and thousands of them, placed in a pattern all across the globe of Corthid, both on the surface and in the caverns beneath, all operating at their peak load. Eerie lights shined from them. When Gosseyn entered the room and woke X, that acted as the signal for those towers to erect some immense pattern of distorter-energies all across the planet.

Machinery does not activate with perfect speed and synchronicity on a planet-wide scale, but the massive flow of power across millions and trillions of circuits across the continents and hemispheres of Corthid had initiated its chain of consequences ... not even X could stop it now. ...

Some of the repeater screens filling the huge walls of the chamber were tuned to views of distorter towers projecting above the surface of Corthid. The sun vanished from the dayside sky, and the stars winked out from the nightside sky. Above the atmosphere of Corthid was ... nothingness ... a smoky, insubstantial void of non-being.

The distorter towers, at that same moment, shined with a strange greenish light, quivered like images in a rippling pond, and vanished, their basic structures and elemental components similarized away from Corthid. Whatever it was X had done to alter the machines and make them so lethal, the evidence vanished with the speed of twenty-decimal-point similarity.

At that same moment, the thought-flow from the enemy stopped. Gosseyn could detect that the similarity effect, the same one that precipitated the whole planet Corthid out of the ordinary realm of energy and matter, had already triggered the removal of the thought-patterns of X from the body of Illverton.

There was no way to stop the faster-than-instant retreat, not of a man who had never really been here to begin with.

Illverton swayed on his feet for a moment and then sagged, clutching the huge desk for support.

Gosseyn jumped to the man's side. "You were in contact with his mind! Wake up! In his knowledge was there a way to reverse the process? Is there a way to bring Corthid out of the shadow-condition?"

Yvana and her men surged into the room. They had not yet grasped the implications of what had happened: The men were still pointing their hand weapons at Illverton, calling on him to surrender.

If one or two of the excited young men had noticed

the repeater screens, the implications of the sunless and moonless landscape had not yet sunk in: Their untrained nervous systems would automatically attempt to fit the pattern of what was seen into a "set," that is, the nearest approximation of something familiar; it would happen without awareness. They saw merely unexceptional pictures of moonless nighttime scenes. They would for several moments be unable to see or understand the much stranger horror actually here: a world de-similarized from the laws of nature of normal time-space.

Illverton was saying, "No, no, there is nothing . . . the theoretical basis used to erect the towers was flawed."

Yvana shouted for quiet. Her men looked startled and slowly lowered their weapons. Several of them examined the repeater screens, looks of awe and fear beginning to dawn on their faces.

"Only if they had been perfectly synchronized," the gray-haired man wheezed, "would they have been able to impress on all the matter-energy in range the mechanical self-identity needed to resist the Shadow Effect. Even the tiny distance from one hemisphere of the planet to another was enough to put the towers out of synchronization. An unsynchronized self-identification produces only non-identity. Corthid, and a pocket of space around it for one hundred fifty thousand miles, has been forced into similarity with a null matrix, a mathematical state of non-being. And that pocket is shrinking." He pointed with a shaking finger to the readings flashing like ticker tape across the bottom of the astronomical information plate.

The whole world had become a shadow-being like the Follower . . . but without the special training the Follower had known to enable it to survive this condition.

"How long?" Gosseyn said, "How long will matter and energy within this pocket of non-shadow maintain its coherence? How long before the world of Corthid dissolves?"

Illverton shook his head. "I do not know the detailed

calculations he made—I shared some thoughts with him, but I could not follow the mathematics. My impression was that there is tremendous mass-energy inertia involved in a body the size of the planet and the particles will continue to 'try' to behave as they always have done until the Shadow Effect erodes their consistency. So—weeks, maybe months."

Yvana and her men listened, dumbfounded, as the death sentence of their world was pronounced.

Illverton said heavily, "He—the creature possessing my brain—did not care about how long we would survive the shadow-condition. Long or short, it was the same to him, since there is no way to return to normal. There is no connection between any atom on this planet and any atom in the outside universe. Time, gravity, energy, matter . . . all will now act as if we are no longer part of the universal system. As if we have no identity."

Gosseyn said, "The Games Machine of Corthid has circuits designed for examining deep neural structures. If there is a buried level of memory in your nervous system, a residuum from the imprint from X, then the Machine might be able to reconstruct it."

Illverton said, "Who do you mean by 'X'? The man possessing me did not think of himself by that name."

Gosseyn was curious. "What does he call himself?"

"Ptath."

AT Yvana's request, Gosseyn took her along when he went to the roof of the Safety Authority building, looked far down the avenue to where the mighty structure of the Games Machine reared, selected a spot on the sidewalk nearby, and similarized himself and Illverton there.

Gosseyn threw open one of the doors at random on the first tier skirting the base of the Machine. Within was a chair and a desk facing a screen. Electron tubes behind the screen, sensitive to neural flows, glowed a warm cherry-red when Illverton grasped the handles.

Gosseyn explained his request.

The calm voice of the Games Machine replied, "I can recover some, but not all, of the thoughts of the memory-identity—the man you call X—once impressed on this subject. However, your overall purpose will be frustrated."

Gosseyn said, "Why is that?"

"The man you call X has a more fundamental understanding of the structure of reality than current science. In his understanding, each atom of the planet Corthid was in a specific time-space-energy relationship with each other atom in the sidereal universe: That specific relationship can be approximated as a twenty-decimal number. To travel by distorter from one point to another, both points must be identified up to twenty decimals. However, this shadow-condition into which the planet Corthid has been thrust is a non-identity: It is not expressible in twenty decimals, or any number of decimals. Even had the distorter towers been left intact, the distorter matrices would have no information to enable them to locate the universe."

Gosseyn said, "The theory is that the universe is a vast collection of energy balances, held in a cooperative scheme?"

"In effect, each particle identifies itself to all others in return for being so identified: Two particles in such a relation can coordinate interaction at a distance. The desynchronized actions of the distorter towers merely randomized the identities, as far as the outside universe is concerned, of each separate particle of Corthid."

Gosseyn said, "There are mechanical distorters here on Corthid in great numbers, in elevators, in transportation booths, in shipyards, aboard any ships currently docked."

"They cannot help. Although, to each other, and from the frame of reference of the matter surrounding you, all of you appear to be solid bodies, as does the planet Corthid around us, a more accurate model would be to say that your atoms are disconnected partly from each other and utterly from the universe as a whole: You are shadow-beings, even if you don't look it to yourselves, and the distorter matrix cannot identify you so as to force a twenty-decimal-point similarity. The mechanical distorter matrices, as far as the surrounding universe is concerned, are blank."

Illverton spoke up, looking haggard. "There must be something in my memory, something that Ptath knew, which would save us from this trap!"

The Games Machine said, "I find no record of any such thought of his lodged in your memory. Instead, he had the conviction that this would entrap someone even with his own remarkable level of ability."

Yvana said suddenly, "Yet we have someone else who was in mental contact with him during that last moment."

Gosseyn took Illverton's chair and grasped the knobs of the nerve-reading machine. The electron tubes slowly brightened and dimmed as the Games Machine probed and analyzed.

"No. The same thoughts of the man you call X are reflected in both memory records: X had no ideas for any possible escape. But here is something interesting," said the Games Machine. "While the mechanical distorters on the planet have no detectable connection with the outside universe, I am detecting a trace—a very dim trace, roughly thirteen decimal points of similarity—of a still-active similarity in the subject's double brain. Mr. Gosseyn, some part of your nervous system is still connected with the outside universe—although the space intervals involved are on the order of three million light-years, farther than the Andromeda Galaxy is from the Milky Way: The time interval is even greater."

Gosseyn said, "Perhaps the Shadow Effect has an upper range."

Illverton said, "Archeological remains of the starships of the Primordial Men from the Shadow Galaxy indicate that they could, indeed, eventually outdistance the effect.

There is no record that the shadow can reach across intergalactic distances."

Gosseyn said, "But I do not recall memorizing such a point. It may be a trace picked up from the dying memory of Gosseyn Three, who perished in the Shadow Galaxy."

The Games Machine said, "No. It is far older. You inherited it from Lavoisseur, or from his predecessors. There are techniques which can be used to artificially stimulate the brain cells to a greater degree of similarity, and amplify the neural energy involved in triggering your particular method of organic distorter transportation."

Yvana said, "Wonderful. That means Gosseyn can escape."

Gosseyn said, "Landing in an arbitrary point in a distant galaxy, or the empty spaces between galaxies."

Yvana said, "You'll die with us if you stay here with us."

Gosseyn said to the Machine, "If I memorize and transmit each member of the Corthid population, one at a time, to this distant point, how long will it take? Assuming no new births in the interim."

The Games Machine said, "With or without the Primordial technology Gosseyn Three used to amplify his abilities to transport whole planets across an intergalactic range?"

Gosseyn was shocked for a moment. He made his Null-A pause, and continued calmly, "Explain that statement. Gosseyn Three did not know how to make the Spheres of the Primordials. Those machines were larger than gas giants."

The Games Machine said, "However, his memory from his double brain, which exists as a trace in the memory of your double brain, retains the similarity patterns of the seventy-five-thousand-light-year-wide segment of the Shadow Galaxy he 'memorized.' Within that segment were many thousands of the Spheres, and he memorized their structure down to the atomic level. I can

produce a complete blueprint of all the machinery involved over a period of weeks, if I am given use of all
the stat-plates in the city."

Illverton said, "There is not enough raw material left
in our pocket universe here to build something so large!"

Yvana said, "So we will have to build a smaller model.
We only need an amplifier large enough to allow Mr.
Gosseyn to memorize this one small planet, of course, and
similarize it, and all of us, to that one remote point in
time-space to which he is still connected."

Gosseyn turned to Yvana. "Do you think you can mo-
bilize the population of Corthid sufficiently to study and
understand an alien technology and build a working
model large enough to affect the whole planet?"

She smiled, and her eyes twinkled. "Who wants to
wager me that we can do it in two months?"

Illverton, the chief of the Safety Authority, silently
reached up to his collar and tuned his garment to match
the uniform of the Vathir Organization.

17

*Time and space appear to our nervous systems to be sepa-
rate, although science shows these are two aspects of one
underlying reality.*

Over the next two months, as the shadow-substance
forming the boundaries of their universe shrank to half
its diameter, the people of Corthid worked double and
triple shifts. Robotools whirred and built, pausing only
for replacement parts; people worked, pausing only for
hastily swallowed meals, snatched hours of sleep.

Of all the planets in the galaxy, Corthid was surely the
one requiring the least work to convert to self-sufficiency.
Even so, the work was tremendous: All cavern entrances

had to be blocked airtight while the surface atmosphere condensed and froze. Without distorters bringing in warehouses full of grain through interstellar commerce, the worldwide stored supplies of food and fuel had to be rationed and distributed.

The Games Machine produced diagrams of the incomprehensible machinery of the Spheres; Corthidian scientists analyzed, tested, came to tentative conclusions; the worldwide industrial complex of one of the most highly industrialized planets in the galaxy roared into effort.

First, the Corthidians had no lack of mineral raw materials: Long ago the superpressurized ball of molten nickel-iron at the core of their world had been tapped by distorter, so that an endless ocean of metal was available to be transported instantly in any amount to any or all the factories of the world. Whenever they needed additional workspace or factory floor, a disintegration warhead hollowed out another few cubic miles of cavern in the planetary crust. Second, they were already highly regimented, since all life on their planet was sustained in the artificial environments of their cavern systems, so that plans could be quickly put into motion. Third, their psychology was geared toward cooperation, self-sacrifice, and hard work.

Gosseyn was impressed. As childlike as they might be in other ways, when it came to worldwide cooperative effort, the Corthidians were as well organized as a similar group of Null-A's would have been. Small wonder they had been the capital planet of a hegemony of over one hundred thousand star systems, second largest of the nineteen galactic member-states comprising the Interstellar League.

The days turned into weeks as the surface of the planet was covered from pole to pole with the Primordial machinery, components whose functions were only dimly understood. Gosseyn wondered how events progressed in the outside universe: Perhaps Enro had already triumphed and the galaxy was his.

The time came when Gosseyn was escorted to a heavily insulated medical cocoon, partly submerged in the electron-dampening fluid, and sent into a deep narco-hypnotic sleep. The cocoon was raised into place in the center of the several miles of electronic brains and distorter-type machinery that formed the basic circuit of the worldwide Sphere technology. As he slept, the Games Machine carefully probed for the deeply buried channel in the memory of his extra brain and carefully stimulated the partial similarity found there.

He woke to find Illverton and Yvana standing over him, smiling uncertainly.

"What happened?" Gosseyn said.

She said, "It worked . . . and we're lost."

THE astronomical observatory of Corthid was a degravitized building-complex, pressurized against the near-vacuum and hovering in the troposphere of the planet. In the short amount of time it took Gosseyn to wake, dress, and travel there, the ever-busy factories of Corthid had created and orbited a series of mirrors, several miles in radius, in geosynchronous orbit around their world, and used these to gather astronomical images.

At the moment, Gosseyn stood under the vast glass dome of the observatory, in a gardenlike spot that provided the airtight building with oxygen, and he was looking up with his unaided eye at the black sky. Only in one-quarter of the sky was there anything to be seen: an oval of blurred lights, a scattering of stars. They were looking at a galaxy from the outside.

Underfoot, he saw the atmosphere and world of Corthid: No longer was it a rust-red sphere of endless deserts; now it was a silvery-gray sphere of towers and collectors and antennas and power units, all dusted with a "snow" of frozen oxygen-nitrogen. All the equipment of the Sphere technology filled the surface area from horizon to horizon.

He met with the chief astronomer, a man introduced

as Abrin of the Brinna unit of the Brinnahadil Organization. From the man's poise and speech it was clear that he had received at least some Null-A training.

Gosseyn said, "It is not the Milky Way. This is an elliptical galaxy, not a spiral."

Abrin said, "That conclusion is based on an assumption open to question. The mass and certain other characteristics match those of the Milky Way. We have only just begun to analyze long-range images we have gathered of the civilization there."

Gosseyn said blankly, "Civilization?"

They stepped into the library. Gosseyn saw photographs, both visible light and X-ray, of the structures, larger than worlds, seen orbiting the millions of stars of the unknown galaxy.

Abrid said, "Keep in mind these photographs are archeological in nature. We do not know what happened to this civilization during the one hundred sixty thousand years it took for the light waves to pass from the galaxy to our current location. What do you make of this?"

Gosseyn examined the photographs rapidly. "Obviously the images from farther away represent an older stratum of civilization. In this early period, this looks like they are using superatomic explosions to move planets into habitable orbits, or pulverizing gas giants to render them into raw materials. I notice that double and triple star systems only seem to exist on the far side of this galaxy."

"The far-side images are older by one hundred and forty-five thousand years. Double and triple star systems are less gravitationally stable than single stars; they may have been engineered out of existence. We also suspect, from some of the stellar motions, that this had at one time been a spiral galaxy, but that it was artificially reconstructed into an elliptical—perhaps to eliminate the possibility of a dangerous supermassive black hole growing up in the center."

Gosseyn looked. The star systems in the central region

of the galaxy, from fifty thousand years later, seemed to have gas giants, one per system, orbiting outside the thickly settled rings of Earth-like planets. Each star had six to a dozen Earth-like worlds orbiting at the proper distance for human life but a massive Jupiter-like world in a farther orbit. The more recent images, from the near side of the galaxy, ninety-five thousand years later, showed no planets but artificial space stations, larger than Jupiter.

Gosseyn said, "Why keep the gas giants around?"

Abrid said, "The gravity well clears away debris, asteroids, and other navigational hazards. We can assume all debris, all matter in the star systems, had been used to construct the massive space stations of the later period. But notice what is missing. Here and here, in the early images, we see tiny streaks of atomic drives. To be visible at this distance, these starships must be four hundred to one thousand miles long. The calculated acceleration, based on the redshift of the drive, is fifty gravities."

Gosseyn said, "Robot ships." It seemed a reasonable guess. If this civilization had had true artificial gravity, it would have been used for propulsion.

"Notice the near side of the galaxy shows no evidence of any ships of any kind."

Even as they looked at the photographs, in one tiny image a space station the size of the planet Neptune dematerialized, the whole body transmitted through space to some remote destination.

Gosseyn said, "They have a thorough distorter system, then."

Abrid shook his head. "That is not what the Games Machine concluded. A civilization with distorters would still need to send out robot ships through normal slower-than-light space to make distorter matrices of previously unseen spots. Only one kind of person can travel any distance with no need for a distorter on the far end."

Gosseyn said, "Even a galaxy of people like me would be limited. I cannot go places I have not been before."

Abrid said, "The Games Machine claims this is a temporary or transitional stage in your life. As soon as you gain Enro's clairvoyance, or a true mastery of the power of the Predictors of Yalerta, you will be able to see places you might one day visit, no matter how far away, and form the proper distorter connection to the spot. This galaxy, one hundred sixty thousand years ago, may well have been inhabited by people such as you might one day be."

Abrid then brought up an image reconstructed from the gravitic fluctuations affecting the gravity-wave-sensitive planetary crust of Corthid: an image that was not limited by the speed of light. It depicted a vast energy field coruscating around the entire galaxy.

Abrid said, "This is distorter-type energy. The Games Machine says it is a formation consistent with every man in the galaxy possessing a double brain and devoting part of it—in the same way you can pick thoughts of any awake duplicate bodies of yours—to forming a galaxy-wide mind. From the signals, certain higher animals may have been developed to have double brains as well, in the same fashion your first body was developed, in order to help sustain the galactic mind."

Abrid continued, "What is more interesting is that the brain-wave patterns issuing from this galaxy are consistent with those of a Yalertan Predictor during the split second he makes a prediction, though, in this case, it is a process that has been going on for hundreds or maybe thousands of years."

Gosseyn stared at the image in fascination. It was a multicolored swirl of light surrounding a sketched-in diagram of the star positions, each flicker of flame representing another aspect of the complex mind-energy field involved. The race of this galaxy, uncounted trillions of individuals, was unified in one huge attempt to probe into the far future. Why?

Abrid said, "There is also evidence of an impinging brain-wave pattern. Something in the remote future—the time depth involved is nearly equal to the projected lifespan of the cosmos—had made contact with the men of this era."

Gosseyn's attention was arrested by that. "Men? Not aliens?"

Abrid pointed at the photographs. "Look at those worlds: polar ice caps, nitrogen-oxygen atmospheres, blue oceans, green plant life. This could be the twin of your Earth, or my Corthid back when we were surface-dwellers. Of course, it is difficult to extrapolate what men might have become in the one hundred sixty thousand years since these images we are seeing left that galaxy. Mankind may well have evolved into some final, supreme form."

Alarms rang.

Through the library windows, they could see out to the garden-greenhouse under the wide glass dome. Here, under the trees, three shadow-figures materialized.

Gosseyn asked Abrid to stay behind when he went to go confront the ominous beings.

No details of face or features were visible: The shadow-substance was blurred, semitransparent, faceless. One of the figures slid forward noiselessly as Gosseyn approached.

A voice that seemed remarkably deep and solid, considering the insubstantial body from which it came, rang out: "Do not be alarmed. We, the Ultimate Men, have determined to save this planet. We have made arrangements to transmit a sun from the Milky Way to this location, at the proper distance to heat the world and restore its artificial ecological cycle: A minor adjustment will also allow us to restore the oceans and surface plant life."

Gosseyn said, "The Milky Way?"

The voice said, "Surely it is obvious that you have been precipitated to the year A.D. Three Million not far outside your own galaxy. In so doing, you have created a dangerous temporal imbalance: The particles of your body are still . . . adjusted . . . to the time and energy conditions of the far past."

The second shadow-being said, "We represent the Final Civilization that arises before the discovery of time-travel. As such, we are the last men who retain any connection with material and three-dimensional life: The culmination of all previous civilizations is manifested in us. We are as fully human as you are, though we have discovered all the secrets of the human nervous system."

The third being said in a soft, feminine voice; "Naturally, the race that first invents similarization backward through time must take steps to secure itself from being edited out of the time-continuum by competitors: hence the deliberate confusion of evidence as to which planet first evolved man, and hence the lack of other forms of intelligent extraterrestrial life in the most recent revision of reality. Our prognostication engines predict the reverse-time similarization technology will be perfected within a hundred years. We are very near the breakthrough: Many of the basic tenets of time-manipulation are already known to us."

The first shadow-being spoke: "Certain superheavy highly stable energy structures, each one roughly the size of a helium atom and the mass of a giant red sun, were lifted from the first microsecond of cosmic time and placed in various remote points outside the galaxy. There is a strange condition in your nervous system which is entangled with the nearest of these superheavy, primordial particles. We believe these primordial particles have been placed up and down the time-stream by a race of men living some two hundred fifty million years in our future: We believe this was done in order to establish a series of universe-wide beacons detectable from more than one era of the cosmic time-energy."

Gosseyn said, "I don't recall ever memorizing such a particle. How did I become attuned to it?"

The first being spoke again: "Our research indicates that this is a legacy structure, a particle that you have *not yet* memorized in your personal time-path but which a massive imbalance in the universal time-energy flow has retroactively attributed to you."

The third being quietly said, "Imbalances of such magnitudes tend to occur only in individuals destroyed by time-travelers in the paradox fashion, such that your existence will soon achieve a condition where, to the outside universe, it never will have had been."

The second being added hastily: "Our examination of the future convinces us that you would be willing to sacrifice yourself to preserve this segment—roughly five hundred thousand years—of the time-continuum threatened by your existence, once you were persuaded of the reality of the danger you pose."

The first being said, "Again, unfortunately, our predictions show you will react abruptly, even violently, once our intentions are made clear to you. We have timed things so that the negative time-energy probe will force you out of our plenum of existence a moment before you steel yourself to resist our attempt."

The third being said mildly, "Our scientists cannot speculate as to what becomes of you once your temporal excess is neutralized. According to our predictions, you might simply cease to exist; but the excess energy must go somewhere, manifest itself in some form. . . ."

Gosseyn started to say, "Wait!" At the same time, he reached out with his extra brain . . .

Too late. Far too late.

The energy that streamed from the three shadow-beings crossed the distance between them, less than a yard, faster than the speed of light, and it felt as if every molecule in his body was being subjected to pressure so massive that the fabric of space-time itself must give way. . . .

Unconsciousness came too quickly for any pain signal to reach his brain.

18

Paradox is a sign of the failure of the model used to perceive, that is, to adduce meaning. Failure occurs when one or more false assumptions involved pass unquestioned.

Gosseyn was awakened by the sound of an alarm clock. He opened one eye blearily and found himself staring at the rumpled fabric of starched white bedsheets. Next to him, a pillow gleamed in the bright sunlight. Turning, he saw the window through which the light fell, and he smelled the rich scent from the flower box a moment before his eyes fell on it: orchids of yellow and black and purple, spotted and streaked with other colors.

With a start of shocked recognition, he sat up, grasping the windowsill in both hands.

Outside, in the warm Florida sunlight, were his rows of orange trees. Stalking along the brown soil between the lines of trees were two crablike farming robots, watering and weeding. The one farther from the house had a slight limp in one of its spidery legs. Gosseyn remembered worrying where he was going to get the money to buy a replacement joint for that unit, wondering if Nordegg at the general store would lend him something against his next crop. . . .

Gosseyn remembered worrying about this . . . before. Before his wife died. Before he went to the Great City of the Machine to win a higher place in Earth society. Before he found out that his name was not Gilbert Gosseyn, that he was not married to Patricia Hardie, that he was not actually a farmer working a small plot of land he'd bought at a bankruptcy sale.

Gosseyn looked down at the pillow next to his. With a deliberate motion of his hand, he lifted it.

There was a small electric pistol, plugged into its recharging unit.

From the kitchen came the smell of eggs cooking, the crackle of bacon frying, and the warm odor of coffee ready to pour. He could hear the sound of Patricia moving around the table, humming to herself, heard the clatter of her heels on the floorboards, including that one creaking board near the food irradiator.

He felt the fabric of the bedsheet carefully with his finger and thumb, testing the nuances of the weave, feeling the slight variation in temperature where the sunlight was falling. He put his nose near his wife's pillow and sniffed. He rose to one knee, peering at the window. On the horizon, with a murmuring roar, he saw a suborbital ship, rows of gleaming portholes and ghostly white flickers of flame around its rocket tubes, descending quickly toward the Cape, eighteen miles away. In the closer distance, a crop-dusting robot was winging its way across the neighbor's fields.

When Gosseyn stood up, the first bout of dizziness struck. His vision went red at the edges: He put his head down to his knees and took slow breaths until the sensation passed.

Gosseyn stepped into the little bathroom, examined his face carefully in the mirror, opened the little medical kit he kept stocked under the sink, ran a blood test on himself. There was no evidence of low blood sugar, or anything else that might cause a fainting spell. He gave himself an injection of highly oxygenated blood plasma just to be on the safe side.

Patricia called from the kitchen, "Wake up, sleepyhead! Breakfast time! The wolf is at the door and so is the bill collector!"

Gosseyn stood and stared in the mirror a moment. He attempted something he had never tried before: He used his extra brain to "photograph" the atomic structure of his main brain. Gosseyn took the time to don his pants, shirt, and tie. He went through these routine tasks in order to see how automatically they came to him. Next, he took a second "photograph" of his brain and used a posthypnotic cue in his extra brain to superimpose the structural images.

He walked out into the kitchen. There was Patricia wearing an apron, her hair tucked up into a scarf, carefully pouring coffee into a white china cup, adding just the amount of cream and sugar he liked.

Gosseyn sat down and took a forkful of eggs into his mouth. He chewed in slow surprise. He had forgotten how good fresh eggs tasted ... what a good cook his wife had been.

Without bothering to take a second bite, he put the fork down.

"This is a very convincing illusion," he said. "I cannot detect any chromatic or astigmatic errors in any visual images reaching my eyes, including the parallax of distant objects; tactile sensations seem perfect down to the tiniest detail: binaural hearing, sound both high-pitched and low-pitched ... everything. Even smells and tastes, which are processed by a different and older segment of the brain, seem correct to this time, place, condition, and period. Except that I know this cannot be real. How is it being done?"

Patricia was sitting opposite him and had taken a nibble of toast, just beginning to read the textbook she had brought to the table. She had the book open, her head bent over it, but now her wide hazel eyes turned toward Gosseyn's face, so that she was looking up across her forehead and bangs at him, toast hanging, forgotten, unbitten, between her white teeth.

"This is a hypothetical?" she asked, nodding toward her book with a motion of her eyes. It was a textbook on general semantics. "At a guess, I would say you have to check your axioms. You are making an assumption either about the nature of reality or about the nature of whatever leads you to conclude the reality you see is not real. There! If the Games Machine asks me that question, I'll have the answer ready!"

He said, "All this ... the farm in Cress Village, my

marriage to you, our studying for the Games . . . comes from a memory I know to be false, implanted by Lavoisseur when he made me. . . . I was meant to die and wake up again alive, in order to distract the invaders from another planet from their schemes of conquest."

"Charles Lavoisseur of the Semantics Institute?"

"Yes. He is actually an ancient extraterrestrial being, one who knows the secret of immortality."

She squinted, flipped to an index at the back of her book, and ran a slide down a row of fine print to bring other text to the surface of the page. Then she shook her head. "Nope. I don't recognize it. You don't have the other symptoms of paranoid delusion. Unless . . . am I part of the conquest scheme?"

A line appeared between Gosseyn's eyebrows. "As a matter of fact . . . you are pretending to be the daughter of the World President . . ."

"President's daughter! Nice. Do I get to live in a palace?"

". . . you are actually Empress Reesha of the planet Gorgzid."

Patricia sighed. "Well, that's good to hear. It's nice to be someone important. Look, there is no explanation I can think of as to why my husband of four wonderful years of marriage should wake up one morning convinced that I am a Space Empress and that he is a robot made by the most famous neurolinguist on the planet. But there has to be an explanation. Don't bother to tell me how serious you are: I can see that you are serious. I have but one request."

"What is that?"

She sipped her coffee, which she drank black and sweet. "Don't kill yourself. In case your belief that you are immortal turns out to be . . . um . . . inaccurate."

He inclined his head in agreement. "There may not be any other Gosseyn bodies within range. And this body is not a robot; it is a duplicate organism, created artificially."

She made a little shrug of her shoulders. "I'll tell your parents. They'll be shocked. Albert and Harriet. Remember them?"

He looked at the wall clock, which also showed the date. "Five years."

"What?"

"You said 'four wonderful years,' Patricia. According to my implanted memories, we've been married five years."

"Year number three was a little rocky. Being a farmer's wife takes some getting used to, especially considering I was a gal from the big city before that."

Gosseyn smiled, picked up his fork, and began eating.

Patricia raised an eyebrow at that. "How is the illusionary food?"

"I've missed it," he said. "I've missed your cooking. Every meal I have ever eaten has either been prepared at a hotel or at mess aboard a ship, or by a Venus food co-operative. Except once when I ate at Enro's table, but I was using Ashargin's taste buds then, so the skill of the chef did not matter much to me. Here is what I cannot explain: If this environment is artificial, illusionary, how was my nervous system influenced? I've noticed that I have subconscious habits. I reached for the shaving razor before I remembered where in the medicine cabinet it was kept. That indicates that something manipulated my nervous system at a basic level."

She smiled at him warmly, but he merely frowned and shook his head.

He said, "If this is an illusion, then we are not really married."

Her lips compressed and her eyes flashed, and she threw down her napkin. "Well! You are going to go visit a psychiatrist as soon as possible. People simply do not go insane any longer, not in the modern day and age." She stood up, picked up the telephone from its nearby niche, and slammed it down angrily on the table in front of him.

"Go on," she said. "Make the call."

He studied the phone for a moment with his extra brain, sensing the flow of electrons in its circuits. He identified the proper contacts, and instead of raising a hand to touch the phone, he merely similarized the two contact points within the machine itself, so that the electricity flowed across the gap as if there were no gap, completing the circuit.

Patricia looked startled and alarmed when the phone screen lit up.

"Yes?" said the robotic operator.

"I'd like to make an appointment with the nearest qualified psychiatrist that I can afford to see. I am not willing to spend more than fifty credits."

"That would be Dr. Augustus Halt of 5200 Babcock Street Northeast, in Palm Bay. He can see you this evening at 7:00 City Time."

Gosseyn hung up by breaking the circuit he had caused and replaced the telephone in its niche by memorizing the phone base, memorizing the niche, and forcing a similarity. Patricia watched the phone disappear from the table and reappear in its little cupboard.

She touched the telephone gingerly with her hand, as if expecting it to disappear again.

"Why don't you tell me the whole story?" she said at last.

After he was done, she leaned back against the kitchen counter. Her pose was semirelaxed, her long legs crossed at the ankles, her shoulders slightly hunched as her weight rested on her spine. Her eyes were bright and her expression thoughtful.

She said, "The safest assumption is that this is time-travel. The Shadow Men put you back into your own past. If this were an illusion set by an enemy, I would not be here, nor would you have your extra brain and all its capacities still intact."

Gosseyn said, "It cannot be the real past. You, or rather, Reesha of Gorgzid, had not yet arrived on the planet in 2558 A.D."

She said, "How did I die?"

"What?"

"In your memories—which are apparently being given real form around us here—when I was your wife, how did I die?"

"An airplane accident. There was a sudden storm, a crash landing at sea. Your father, Michael Hardie . . ." Gosseyn stopped. How accurate was this illusion? How many details were present? ". . . is he here? In Brevard County? Living in Cress Village?"

"Of course," she said with a little shrug. "After his business failed, he wanted to move away from Tampa. So he put up that strange-looking house, using Mom's money. I thought you remembered all this? You think the memories are false, but they have not vanished from your head, have they? We met because you were doing part-time construction work as a carpenter's 'prentice. You used to bang outside my window and walk back and forth with your shirt off. But Daddy is not a member of a conspiracy to overthrow the world government, if that is what you are asking." She pushed herself lightly to her feet, came over, draped her arms around him, and kissed his cheek. "So what is your plan in the meanwhile?"

"Meanwhile?"

"The invasion from the space empire does not happen, according to you, until 2560. That is two years away. How are we going to eat and pay our mortgage in the meanwhile?"

So he ended up spending the day doing farmwork.

THE bouts of dizziness came twice more as he moved from task to task on the fruit farm. Each time, his vision blurred and a darkness seemed to enter his brain. On the second occasion, he attempted to use his extra brain to "photograph" the atomic structure of his own body, including his nervous system. That seemed to have a stabilizing effect, for the dizzy spell ended abruptly.

The sun had set. He could see a gibbous moon rising

in the distance as he walked back across the fields from the orchids. His muscles ached in a fashion he found refreshing.

How long had it been since he'd put in a good day's work?

Actually, never. None of his memories of farm life were real. Gosseyn One had lived a few days on the money he'd found in the wallet in his jacket, presumably Lavoisseur's. Gosseyn Two had lived on Venus, where money was not used to track labor value. He had also drawn a pension from the Semantics Institute, since he was legally the same person as Lavoisseur, the head of the Institute until such time as the Board of Governors selected a new one. Gosseyn Three had joined the expedition to the Shadow Galaxy, funded by the Nexialist Committee of Planet Petrino, and had lived off what the ship's quartermaster provided. Only Gosseyn Four had ever done manual labor, serving for a day or two as a roughneck aboard the tramp freighter that carried him to Venus. The Corthidian organizations had made him their guest during the emergency and asked of him nothing more onerous than giving interviews to their press and meeting with their scientific leaders: His "wage" on Corthid was their highly abstract system of estimating fame and influence.

Lavoisseur, the foremost Null-A psychiatrist of the age, had selected well when selecting these false memories to implant, Gosseyn decided. Hard as the farmwork was, it formed an almost mystical connection to Mother Earth. There was a wide variety of false-to-facts, even neurotic, beliefs the comforts of technological civilization encouraged, to which farmers tended to be immune. They knew in their bones that there was no reward without labor, no certainty of harvest despite the labor; and they knew the value of self-reliance.

Gosseyn, standing outside his little cottage, put his hands on his back and gave a great rolling shrug of his shoulders, grunting. Yes, if ever the danger posed by Enro were to pass away, if ever he were to retire to private life, this would not be a bad choice: his own land, his own work, his wife . . .

He looked up at the night sky, smiling.

The smile slipped and vanished.

The sky was cloudless, and yet it was blank. There were no stars.

GOSSEYN'S sharp eyes caught the red dot of Mars, one or two flecks of light that might have been Telstars . . . and nothing.

He ran back into the house. "Where are the stars?"

Patricia blinked blankly at him. "The what?"

He jumped over to the phone and thumbed the switch for the operator. "Operator! What is the most distant location I can call?"

"There is a scientific station beyond the orbit of Pluto, studying the formations of ice asteroids at the edge of the universe."

"The edge . . . define that term."

"At a distance of roughly one-point-three light-years from Sol, particles enter a condition of non-identity. Atomic structures lose all coherence; photons suffer redshift and become unlocalized. The boundary is a slightly flattened hollow sphere, centered on the sun."

"What about the stars?"

"This unit has no references for that term."

"Other suns like our own?"

"Would you like to speak to the fiction desk of your local library?"

Another spell of dizziness struck him at that moment. His vision went dark; his eyes blind, he clutched the edge of the cabinet where the phone rested, and performed a cortical-thalamic pause to quell his rising panic. *Every sensation is not itself only but a complex of thought-and-feeling, an interpretation rising from the layers of my nervous system: Sensations enter the brain, pass through the thalamus, where they are given emotional meaning, and only then are they passed along to the cortex. But the meaning is no more than an interpretation. . . .*

When he opened his eyes, Patricia was looking at him with grave concern.

"I'm going with you," was all she said.

They walked the two miles to the bus, paid their dimes, and were carried into the city. Dr. Halt had his offices on the top floor of a four-story building, set back away from the busy street. The building was surrounded by palm trees that rustled in the night gloom.

The psychiatrist was a Venusian Null-A. Gosseyn had only begun to tell his story when the man interrupted him. He said, "Full-grown psychosis does not occur without cause. And I assume"—he cast a glance at Patricia—"there is no history of any neurotic behavior before this? No exposure to psychoactive chemicals or radiations which might produce a sudden change of basic neurochemical structure?"

Patricia said, "Not to my knowledge."

Dr. Halt said to the lie detector built into his desk, "Well?"

The machine answered thoughtfully, "The neural activity I am picking up is consistent with the presence of additional material grown from the brain stem. If this is a natural mutation, it is complex and complete beyond any on record."

Patricia said, "He turned on the phone without touching it. He moved an object—excuse me, I remember seeing the phone move from one side of the room to the other by what I took to be a process of dematerialization and rematerialization. The phone did not appear different after the process to casual inspection: For all practical purposes, it was the same phone."

The lie detector said, "She's telling the truth."

Gosseyn said, "I can explain the physics involved."

Dr. Halt said, "That will not be necessary for my purposes. Each possibility is impossible. You see,

Mr. Gosseyn, the existence of a hitherto-unknown mutation of man, a hitherto-unknown technology based on a
hitherto-unknown law of nature, or the ability of a man
to go insane without cause and without any sign of insanity, and to likewise share his delusions with his wife,
so thoroughly that a lie detector cannot sense any deceptive intent, are all equally impossible according to how
modern science thinks the universe works. I need to discover how you and I can both be sane, that is, can both
operate with our nervous systems adjusted to an accurate
model of the universe, and yet have conclusions about
the universe that are mutually exclusive. Either you are
mad or the universe is. Let us eliminate the first possibility. Mrs. Gosseyn, if you will wait here?"

The doctor led him into an inner examination room
with insulated walls. The lights here were lowered, and
the room was uncomfortably cool, since some of the
electron tubes of the equipment were delicate enough to
react to light and heat.

He had Gosseyn sit down in a chair made of electronically neutral amalgam, and he lowered a domelike instrument to delicate contact with Gosseyn's skull. The
edge of the dome was at his collarbone. Gosseyn's vision was cut off.

"I am sending signals into various segments of your
brain, the cortex, the medulla oblongata, the brain stem,
to study the reactions in your neural flow. You are Null-A
trained? Enter an alpha-wave biofeedback state for me,
please. If you can do it without artificial aid . . ."

Gosseyn relaxed into a semitrance. He was aware only
of occasional pressures and tingles in his limbs, as energy from the apparatus accidentally stimulated sensory
nerves in the periphery of his nervous system. As the
machine tuned itself more completely to his individual
life-rhythms, this sensation dropped away.

Dr. Halt said, "There are energy connections leading
to your wife—or should I say, to the woman in the other
room, since you do not seem to regard her as being your

real wife, or even real at all—that are abnormally strong.
The energy density involved is greater than the total mass-
energy value of the universe. There is only one conclusion to be faced."

Gosseyn, alarmed, raised his hand toward the domelike helmet over his head and tensed his muscles, as if to
begin to stand.

The doctor's voice rang through the darkened chamber without emotion, cool and precise: "This universe
is false, and all existence within it is illusionary: You are
an entity from a superior manifestation of reality. Someone or something—a Deceiver—is projecting a four-
dimensional energy-form through your nervous system
to force you to create this false reality around yourself,
based on your memories. I assume it is based on your
memories, since otherwise I would not be present in the
dream to be helping you wake from it. I am clearly a
dream-element arising from your unconsciousness, not
something the Deceiver would have chosen to put in this
dream. By tracing the nerve paths the outside force is using to create this illusion, I can neutralize it."

As Gosseyn struggled to rise, a strange fatigue, a
heaviness, entered his limbs at that moment: a bout of
the dizziness he had been suffering all day.

"Stop!" croaked Gosseyn, a feeling of nightmarish
heaviness and slowness hindering his motions. Putting his
numb hands to his head was like pushing them through
glue. His fingers fumbled uselessly: He could not get the
helmet of equipment away from him. "Stop! If you shatter
this reality, everyone will die! Patricia, the Earth! Venus
and the Mars colonies! Don't . . ."

He pushed the helmet away. There in the semidark-
ness was the psychiatrist, merely a silhouette standing
next to his control panel.

A dry chuckle. "Come now, Mr. Gosseyn. A false existence is not worth sustaining. You know that."

From the tiny red light winking on the desk Gosseyn
could see the slim fingers of the psychiatrist push a

plunger. There was a low hum from the walls, and Gosseyn felt activity in his extra brain. The distorter cycle in his brain had activated without a conscious cue from him: He felt the energy surging in his brain. The process of twenty-decimal similarity was about to move him to . . . somewhere. . . .

There was a moment of darkness.

19

"Category" confusion in an organism is caused by the attempt of the nervous system to identify one object, process, or event as another; neurosis is the rejection of all evidence to the contrary. The purpose of non-Aristotelian logic is to avoid such errors of categorization.

In the Shadow Galaxy, some three million light-years from the Milky Way, the superscientific ship *Ultimate Prime* was dropping to the surface of a planet of the Primordials.

Overhead the sun was not white but black, surrounded with a white halo of flame: This was a collapsed star. It was slowly eating its brown dwarf companion, as long streamers of star matter were pulled out of the dim photosphere of the dying dwarf star and pulled into the relentless gravity well of the collapsed star: Each particle of matter and energy was bent and pulled apart by the tidal forces involved as it passed through the accretion disk surrounding the black hole. The X-rays given off heated the other incoming matter to incandescence, and the deadly black sun was brighter than the full moon of Earth.

Gosseyn stood on the observation deck, watching the approaching landscape through an armored section of transparent hull. Dense clouds parted, revealing a world

of rippling browns and golds, dull grays and tawny yel-
lows. The mountains were no more than low mounds,
barren; the rivers were no more than tracks of salt across
a flat plain, long ago silted up and choked. The oceans
were shallow, ink-black with millennia of erosion. This
was a world that had long, long ago lost all tectonic activity.

Here and there stood the mile-high towers of the Primordials, rising sheer from the gray-white soil, or tilted
at alarming angles. Only a few had toppled entirely and
stretched out flat, fallen giants. Elsewhere were black,
white, and silver domes, looking like power stations and
atomic piles.

Dr. Curoi of Petrino, the ship's nexialism officer, was
standing at Gosseyn's shoulder. He pointed. "This solar
system you similarized across space next to the ship was
a good choice: The atmosphere is almost entirely argon
and other inert gasses, and the remnants of the ancient
civilization have been almost perfectly preserved. Their
engineering skills were simply miraculous: The ship's
radiation officer tells me that our plates are picking up
controlled radioactivity from those domes. I suggested
to Grand Captain Treyvenant that we start our experiment near that crater impact the astronomy team detected on the equatorial continent."

They passed quickly over a stretch of gray-black, life-
less ocean. Here was a peninsula of land, as flat and dull
colored as the rest of the planet. In one place was a crater-
lake some eighty miles wide. Surrounding the crater, and
evidently toppled by the impact, were numbers of the
mile-high towers. Several of the towers had long sections
of their armor torn away or had split along their corners,
revealing, like the hexes of a honeycomb, level upon level
and deck upon deck of the vertical cities within.

Dr. Petry of the ship's archeology department was
talking over the ship's intercom. Gosseyn's belt-phone
picked up the comment and forwarded it to him. "Our
suspicions were correct. The material of these towers is

an artificial form of matter, composed of locked positron-electron pairs. The Brownian motion of the atoms itself produced their energy, light and heat, a nearly inexhaustible supply. The outer layer of tower-crystal was designed to shed the excess as harmless radiation. When they moved this world between stars, the structures would provide enough light and heat to keep the atmosphere warm, and the landscape flooded with brilliant light."

Another voice on the same channel said, "The high-energy paleoanthropology team developed the plates we took passing over the South Pole. We think the megalithic structures are the remains of part of the artificial gravity mechanism used to stabilize the planet during interstellar flight. The main energy centers were probably off-planet, as were the distorter engines."

In a short time, the ship came to rest on the dark soil of the dead world. Gosseyn and Curoi disembarked, along with Dr. Kair, the Null-A psychiatrist, and Leej the Predictress. Some scientists from the high-energy physics department, xeno-archeology, and neuropsychology were also present. In charge of this landing party was one of the lesser captains, Mandricard of Accolon. All were equipped with heavy armor, electromagnetically shielded to block the deadly X-rays issuing from the black sun. The robotools of the archeologists floated to the left and right, photographing, testing, sampling.

There were corpses everywhere. Some peculiarity of the atmosphere had almost perfectly preserved the mummified forms: blackened skin, paper-thin, covering skulls. In his lightning fashion, Gosseyn counted the bodies spilled just from one tower: over a million people. He multiplied that by the number of towers he saw, either toppled in the near distance or, on the horizon, rising in rank on rank.

Dr. Curoi's voice over the suit radio sounded strangely near-at-hand, even though the man himself was not in sight, having stepped into the toppled structure. "Note the lack of children's bodies. This suggests the race discovered personal immortality."

Gosseyn said, "The population of this world must have been in the tens of billions. And yet there is no sign of agriculture, aquaculture, or cattle-herding. How did they eat?"

Curoi said, "We may know more after the seismic teams analyze the echo-reflection data from the machines at the world's core. Autopsy might tell us if those odd, specialized organs in the digestive tract converted broadcast energy from the core machine directly into cell nutrients."

Leej was walking near Gosseyn. While her armor was as bulky as everyone else's, her footsteps were more uncertain, because she was a novice at spacesuit work, her planet having never achieved space flight. She said, "The future is about to blur in two minutes, right after the archeologist makes his announcement." Gosseyn saw from his helmet readout that this was sent on a private channel, narrow-beamed to him alone.

"Is it something I do?" Gosseyn sent back.

There was a rustling sound, and then an embarrassed sigh. The rustling sound must have been Leej shaking her head, her hair scraping the earphones, and then a sigh because she remembered no one could see her head move. "No way to tell. It may come as a result of my experiment."

Gosseyn drew his sidearm. This weapon's aiming beam was linked through the ship's electronic brain to a number of other power sources on the ship, so that an ever-increasing amount of power could be sent by distorter circuit through the hand weapon, including the whole force of the ship's main reactors.

Up ahead, Dr. Kair was studying one of the corpses through the viewing device on his helmet. On the general channel, Dr. Kair's voice came: "It is fairly certain that these people were killed instantaneously by the negative distortion effect. The identity and position of the atoms in their bodies fell below the critical threshold level for molecular and atomic actions to continue. But I notice the effect is uneven. Leej, how much mass do you need to perform your prediction? We may be able to find some atoms intact."

Leej said, "It does not work by mass. Events are linked by cause and effect. I cannot predict the decay of a radioactive atom, because one atom would not affect anything in my environment, but I can predict the behavior of a sensitive Geiger counter."

Curoi the Nexialist said, "We have instruments much more sensitive than that."

At that moment, the chief archeologist said, "We've found a body you can use for your experiment. It is in good condition, but it is not unique. Out of all this graveyard, I think the archeology team can let you disturb one of these poor souls."

Leej moved over toward the body. It was slumped over in the bottom of what seemed the basin of a dry fountain. The body was blackened and burnt, but the clothing was strangely well preserved: a dark and simple garment with traces of rust at the collar, shoulders, and wrists, as if there had been clasps or ornaments long ago weathered away. The boots seemed to be a continuation of the pant-leg fabric, merely thickened.

Curoi pointed at something on the corpse. "Look. Photovoltaic cells woven into the thread. The clothes are self-repairing. That's why the corpses fallen in the shadow are nude."

Dr. Kair pulled a flat boxlike instrument out of his leg-pouch and passed it to Leej. "This cable attaches to your life-support. Otherwise the nervous energy of the unit will not penetrate your armor. As I explained before, the unit will put your brain into a relaxed state, and, if all goes well, trigger the complex of posthypnotic suggestions I've helped you implant in your mind. If I am correct, your ability to overcome the illusion of time only in one direction, the future, is a psychological limit. Once you are subconsciously convinced that your powers can reach backward as well as forward, you should be able to summon up a vision of the past as easily as of the future."

She plugged the cable from the box into one of the sockets in her helmet. The faceless helmet turned toward the corpse.

Leej said, "I am seeing . . . millions of years in the past . . . billions . . . men and women, happy. They look alert. Their eyes glitter with intelligence and purpose. The sky overhead is half-black. Half the stars have already been swallowed by the Shadow Effect. This man was walking down the street. He pauses. He turns. The man is aware of me. *'Woman of the future, beware!'* he is speaking. *'There is an enemy of both your galaxy and mine, a race of creatures beyond the edge of time . . . an infinite enemy . . . they are attempting to find you . . . they . . .'* No. It is gone."

The helmet of Leej turned toward Gosseyn. "Now. Everything is blurred. What happened?"

At the same moment, one of the high-energy physics team, bent over an instrument, raised his gauntlet. "Captain! Strange reading here. Time-space just suffered a deflection from its normal metric."

Gosseyn said to Leej, "I'm dead. The memories of my twin version just similarized themselves into my nervous system." He flipped open another short-range private channel, to include Dr. Kair. "The version of me back in the Milky Way galaxy remembers me dying—roughly twenty minutes ago, when I used the Sphere Array to teleport this solar system here. His memory was that I was killed by a shadow-version of X, the crippled Lavoisseur. My version then died, killed by Enro, and woke up as Gosseyn Four. After X forced the planet he was on into the shadow-condition, Gosseyn Four made contact with some sort of supercivilization of ultimate men, who forced him out of the universe, first into a false or partial universe and then, when he escaped that, into this universe. I am assuming this is a parallel time-continuum: some sort of alternate reality created the moment I was attuned to the Primordial Spheres."

Gosseyn, who now had the parallel memories of both his versions, assumed that if this were another false reality, it had been created from memories other than his own—but including a set of memories that included a record or copy of his own. Gosseyn's conclusion: This was being done for his benefit, to demonstrate something to him.

Dr. Kair asked him a number of questions, and Kair opened his radio to bring Curoi into the conversation. Curoi walked over to the high-energy physics team and studied the readings from their instruments.

Curoi said, "Is there any reason not to attempt the second phase of the experiment? The results of Phase One were fruitful beyond all expectation."

Dr. Kair said, "I'd like to examine Gosseyn for side effects. If he made mental contact with another version of this universe, it is important to discover which is the primary and which was created by a distortion."

Curoi, whose special skill was the ability to integrate data from very different schools of science, said, "You are assuming an inertial principle? If one second of time is removed from the past-to-future manifestation of the cosmos, it will retain enough mass-energy to manifest its own, parallel, cosmos? Once set in motion, the time-energy must continue?"

Dr. Kair said, "I am not a physicist, but I do know that volume of space described by Gosseyn's memory of a starless universe, a little under a radius of one light-year and a third, was roughly equal to the total distance he can perform a similarity effect. If this universe, the one we exist in now, is also a secondary universe, we should attempt to determine its size. I am assuming that can be done by calculations of its mass-energy."

The scientific teams aboard the ship reported in a few minutes. Long-range telescopes still detected distant nebulae, Messier objects, quasars. But the gravity-wave astronomy array aboard told a different story: A zone of space roughly twenty-five hundred thousand light-years wide surrounded them.

"The Milky Way galaxy is gone," said Gosseyn bleakly, hearing the report over the radio.

Curoi said, "The photons at the edge of our pocket universe are carrying false images of an outer universe to our instruments. Traveling at the speed of light, the other galaxies will continue to be visible for twenty-five hundred millennia. In any case, we have one fact: The time-space of this size was created from someone else's memories, not yours. And it is someone with a great deal more energy at his disposal than Gosseyn Two. I'd like to try the same battery of tests Gosseyn Three just told me he remembers the imaginary character of Dr. Halt performing on Gosseyn Four, whose identity is now blended with the man we see before us."

Gosseyn thought darkly that if Dr. Halt had not been merely imaginary, if he was real in any sense, then he had wiped out an entire planetary population, including a copy of Patricia.

Leej said, "There is no time. Gosseyn must help me form the connection again. That is what I see happening."

It was Captain Mandricard who decided: "I think we need to hear the rest of that message from the dead man. Proceed."

Gosseyn said to Leej, "Working through Dr. Kair's neurohypnotic unit, I am going to try to strengthen the similarity between you and the location you are perceiving. I cannot force a similarity myself, since I cannot perceive the location you can see, but I can sense the biofeedback from the neurohypnotic unit—its functions are very similar to a lie detector's, except it is invasive rather than merely passive—and move you nearer to what the unit registers as a condition of greater nerve-flow in the brain centers you activate during prediction. Ready?"

Leej said, "I am blind as soon as you use your ability, Gilbert. But I am curious to see what is on the other side of the blind moment."

Some of the electron tubes on the boxlike unit plugged into Leej's suit glowed with a cool blue light and grew brighter. At first, that was all that occurred.

The high-energy physicist said, "It's happening again. Massive distortion in time-space."

Leej said, "Step back from the corpse! Everyone step back!"

Then, the body stood up. Its blackened skin and mummified remains grew even darker, and all light left the figure. By the time it was fully on its feet, the figure was a shadow-shape like the Follower: a smoky manlike form.

"I cannot maintain this projection across this time-distance for long," came a voice from the shadow-being.

To Gosseyn, the voice sounded familiar. "Lavoisseur! Is that you?"

"In one sense, yes," said the shadow-shape. "Like you, I am a Gosseyn duplicate."

"Who? Gosseyn Six? Is there a Gosseyn Seven?"

The shadow-being spoke in a voice of mild humor. "I lost track after ten thousand or so. I am the final and ultimate Gosseyn."

20

The process of scientific thought consists of increasingly less inaccurate predictive models based on observation. When the model is not subject to change due to further observations, it is no longer scientific.

It was Dr. Kair who spoke next: "He is from a slightly later time period than the three shadow-beings who flung Gosseyn Four out of the universe. If the Gosseyn memories are immortal, living from body to body, there is no reason why he will not continue even to Three Million A.D.: and eventually live long enough to see the era that comes after it, the time that has discovered time-travel."

The shadow-figure now began to solidify. The far-future version of Gosseyn was roughly a head and a half taller than his contemporary self. His skin was a strange golden hue; his head seemed even larger in proportion than Gosseyn's. It was only the heroic build of his shoulders and chest, the bull-like thickness of his neck, that gave so large a skull a normal appearance.

But the face was his.

The future being said, "For the purposes of avoiding semantic confusion, call me Aleph."

Aleph, the far-future Gosseyn, was dressed in the simple garment of the Primordials. The clasps at his shoulders and wrists seemed to be miniature electronic units, evidently controlled by his brain directly, since there were no external controls. Either the suit protected him from the deadly radiation or Aleph had additional powers: He stood under the blazing black X-ray sun of the dead planet without harm, without any need to breathe the deadly inert gases of the atmosphere.

Gosseyn thought he detected a slight vibration of distorter-energy in Aleph's chest area. The future man was similarizing oxygen from some distant world directly into his lungs. A similar vibration surrounded the golden giant like an aura: No doubt he was similarizing the incoming X-ray particles to some remote spot before they reached his skin.

Aleph spoke without moving his lips, or, rather, his voice issued from the radio earphones of the armored men staring up at him. Gosseyn guessed the being was controlling radio waves with the same ease with which he controlled X-rays.

"The Shadow Effect that destroyed this galaxy was not an accident but an attack." The voice of Aleph rang in their ears.

GOSSEYN listened with a grim sense of suspicion.

It was optimistic to believe that the future versions of himself were derived from Gosseyn's sane memory rather than from the insane variant known as X.

He realized the futility of raising his weapon against this superbeing: The atomic ray of his weapon would be deflected with the same casual ease as the X-rays from the dead sun overhead.

Aleph sent a radio-message to Gosseyn's private channel: "There is one respect where I am not acting as X would have done."

Gosseyn had noticed: The fact that Aleph was instantly aware of his suspicions showed them to be unfounded. Since Gosseyn was not receiving thoughts from his future-self, that superbeing must be holding his nervous energy in a "lesser" state, meaning that he was receiving Gosseyn's thoughts: a situation X had been willing to commit murder to avoid.

At the same time, on the public radio frequency, Gosseyn heard the conversation Aleph was carrying on with the others. "There is an entity, a race composed by forced impositions of thought into a single consciousness, called the Ydd. The Ydd foresee the rise of Null-A thought in the Shadow Galaxy, and, using prediction power, foresee also the destruction of itself and its race."

Dr. Kair said, "Null-A can accommodate any number of other rational systems. Why should there be a conflict? What threat does Null-A pose to this creature?"

"The Ydd exists in a 'non-similar' condition of being, outside of the roughly fifteen-billion-light-year-wide and fifteen-billion-year-old slowly expanding zone of time-space where matter-energy has struck its current neutral balance, which we call the universe. There are areas outside the light-cone of the Big Bang, and also at the origin point, where other matter-energy formations obtain, areas occupied by the Ydd. Null-A psychology is the only predicted science able to integrate the complexities of the true Einsteinian universe into the human nervous system, and hence the only source of threat within the universe to the Ydd. No other discipline will achieve a scientific plateau to allow men to become aware of the Ydd."

Gosseyn said, "Why is it so secretive? Why would it conclude that even knowledge of its existence poses a threat to it?"

"Unknown."

Gosseyn said, "Is there a being in this universe, the real universe, which stands to it in the relationship I stood in to the illusionary universe created from my false memories?"

Aleph said, "That is the ultimate question of life toward whose answer even the cosmos-level intellects of my time grope dimly. One theory is that the Ydd entity itself occupies this relation."

Leej said, "Is Enro a puppet of this Ydd?"

Aleph nodded, as if pleased with the question. "Through him the Ydd will release the Shadow Effect into the Milky Way, and begin the disintegration of all life. Our theory is that Ydd is seeking Gosseyn, and is willing to wipe out the universe to destroy him."

Captain Mandricard said, "What can we do against this Ydd threat?"

Aleph said, "The first step is to repeat the experiment

Gosseyn Three conducted with the Space-time Spheres of the Primordials, which attuned him to a twenty-five-hundred-thousand-light-year-wide segment of the galaxy, but this time with Leej the Predictor, rather than Gilbert Gosseyn, as the focal point of the Sphere amplification. Gosseyn will need to have his consciousness imposed into the body of Leej, using the same technique the 'Chessplayer' once used to impose Gosseyn into Ashargin. There are machines on this world, which I have already found and restored to operation, able to accomplish this. Once Gosseyn attunes Leej to the galaxy-wide Sphere network, she will have the resources at her disposal to make a prediction reaching accurately to the period of a supercivilization we believe will occupy this area of the universe two hundred fifty million years from now. Gosseyn! Leej! Ready yourselves."

When his vision cleared, Gosseyn, from Leej's point of view, saw the suit of armor the now-unconscious Gosseyn body occupied sag. The armor was too bulky, as well as too well designed, to allow him to fall over. But the arms were hanging limply; the leg-armor was locked into place.

HIS first impression was that Leej must have poorer eyesight than his body, because the details of the scene around were blurred. But no: Her brain merely processed fewer pictures per second of visual information than his, and her memory and perception system did not notice details Gosseyn found significant.

On the other hand, Gosseyn was aware of a flow, a flood, of mental pictures appearing and disappearing around every object in the environment. And not merely visible images: Sounds and other sensations were hovering in a ghostly fashion around Leej the Predictress, bits of conversation, variations on words spoken. Gosseyn realized he was hearing alternate future versions of how the conversation would turn out, depending on whether Leej spoke or not, or what questions she asked. He could "hear" that any conversation based primarily on Leej answering questions before they were asked would reduce the prediction to a mere blur of sound. One's own actions seemed to blur the future-picture more severely the more one both relied upon and changed the picture. There was a delicacy to prediction Gosseyn's few lessons in the art had not allowed him to appreciate.

Also, he had underestimated the detail and depth involved. Looking at Curoi, for example, Leej could see not merely what he would be doing in the next few minutes, but also images of her meeting him aboard ship, or seeing him at mess-time or while studying, over the next few days and even weeks. It was like a series of small, clear, sharp pictures receding away from his body in some direction that was not one of the three dimensions of normal space.

When she turned her eyes toward Aleph, Gosseyn suffered an embarrassing shock. It was embarrassing for him to be sexually allured by a male figure—he could not help but notice the well-formed muscular thighs, the breadth of shoulders, the hawklike eyes, the godlike confidence that made the other men around her seem, to Leej, like merely helpless children.

And of course, it was his face, Gosseyn's face, she found so magnetic.

The second surprise was that she was as yet unaware of him. Gosseyn's emotions were pale compared to the whirlpools of passion rushing through the Predictor woman, and his surprised thoughts were simply blending in with her general feelings of surprise at the current scene.

She did not even know herself well enough to notice when foreign thoughts were running through her mind.

Her inner state of mental and emotional confusion was hidden beneath a suave exterior. Her crisp, cool voice rang out to Aleph: "Why have you not, in your own time period, arranged for such a time-expedition? Your contemporaries apparently have all the combined secrets of the Predictors, of Enro, of the Follower, and of Lavois-seur. You have the science to do this yourself, experts, where we are doing it for the first time!"

Aleph spoke to Leej but was apparently addressing Gosseyn: "I saw in the memory grafted onto yours from Gosseyn Four that the astronomer Abrin showed you a neurological energy reading of the distorter-type output of the galaxy in my time. You saw that an entire galaxy-worth of beings was attempting to contact that future, and that an energy from the future had responded. I can tell you that the response from a hostile future was to erect a negative-energy barrier to time-travel, similar to the shadow-substance across which your space-bypassing power cannot operate. This was the likely reason Corthid was not flung even further into the future: The barrier prevented it."

As he spoke, Gosseyn saw a strange thing: The shad-owy multiples of prediction-pictures surrounding every-one in the environment became fewer and sharper. Leej had deliberately, almost without thought, acted to put the future on a basis where there were fewer and more easily predicted possible futures.

Leej spoke again, "Then why should we be able to cross it?"

It was Curoi who answered. "Aleph hopes that the bar-rier will not exist in this—this alternate, artificially cre-ated, universe. Am I correct? We are all copies of beings who exist in a parallel time. If so, you have done us a ter-rible disservice."

Aleph nodded his great, golden head, his eyes grim. "Or perhaps I saved you. Your originals in the true time-stream were destroyed when Gosseyn Three died. But even here, your preservation is temporary. It is our belief that, in order to preserve itself, the Ydd intends to render this entire area of space-time, all the surrounding galax-ies within the Virgo supercluster, into a low-energy con-dition where life is not possible." He gestured around him at the dead planet and raised his hand to point at the blank, black sky where uncounted millions of neutron stars and brown dwarfs burned feebly in the Shadow Galaxy.

Curoi said, "Are we to dissolve and be slain like the ghostly people in Gosseyn's short-lived illusion universe?"

"I do not believe this universe will collapse. One second of time was removed from the main flow of the eternity substance: It replicated the next second thereafter, and the next and the next, in its mindless, infinite fashion. My time here, however, is done. I can no longer maintain this projection."

The giant golden man blurred, turned into a shadow-form, and vanished.

21

No two objects in the universe, no two events, are identical.

As Aleph vanished without saying any good-bye, Gosseyn could see the scorn in the thoughts of Leej. She simply did not believe Aleph had told the truth. This was a temporary universe, fated for destruction.

She was now convinced that this being, the Aleph, was Gosseyn, a true version of his. Creating an artificial universe of duplicated people was essentially the same as what Lavoisseur had done when he created Gosseyn to stop the invasion of Earth.

Leej's thought-emotion was: *Oh well. Some men are just like that.*

Just like Gosseyn. He had disrupted her life on Yalerta, forced a breakup with her old lover Yanar, trapped her for more than a month aboard a broken starship surrounded by strange and foolish peons (in the mind of Leej, anyone unable to see the future was a "peon"), and then never thanked her for her sacrifice and for her ministering to him—not even when she had, with her own aristocratic hands, acted as a nursemaid to Gosseyn's unconscious body. Leej regarded this as a degradation, suffered for Gosseyn, who had never thanked her, never reciprocated her burning love for him. To Leej, Gosseyn was merely one more of the ruthless and heartless men she had met in her life: a slightly less dangerous version of the Follower.

There was simply nothing to be done about such men. They popped up in a woman's life, ruined it, and departed. Only little girls—weaklings—griped aloud about it. *Oh well. Some men are just like that.*

Gosseyn, confounded and overwhelmed by a rush of feminine emotion, was stunned by this mental image of himself. *But that was not the way it was! There was a galactic war to stop. . . .*

The flood of shocked emotion was one his own highly trained nervous system never would have permitted. Leej was now aware that she had been violated: A man had been imposed into her innermost being without warning or consent.

And not just any man: Gilbert Gosseyn, of all people! The man she had wanted to take as a lover! That man who spurned her.

The physical sensation of rage, muscles tensing, pulse beating hotly in her face, stunned Gosseyn for a moment.

Nor could Gosseyn make himself unaware of the emotion: It was his emotion, too, and he shared it. Unlike the weakling Ashargin had been when Gosseyn had been implanted in him, there was no way to dominate Leej. She was not driven into the trancelike blankness Ashargin suffered when another mind was imposed on him.

She was aware of his thoughts, but in a fashion that was subtly distorted, so that his reaction, to her, sounded defensive. Like he was whining. Her reaction in turn was: *For men like you, it is always something. Galactic war, or whatever excuse comes to hand. You just run roughshod over people's lives.*

Leej then did something that astounded Gosseyn. She could—hear—a number of possible mental conversations or struggles that might come out of this moment in time. The one where Gosseyn and Leej most quickly and, with the least upset to her, came to a mutual understanding was the one future she . . . somehow . . . selected.

In that future she thought to herself (and yet somehow at this moment in time she was also thinking it), *We need to come to an accommodation. You've been thrust into my life one more time, once again with no concern for me. Let's simply be as grown-up and professional about this as we can . . . and get it over and done with . . . as quickly as possible.*

"As quickly as possible" turned out to be something more than two hours, while the ground teams reembarked upon the ship, and the *Ultimate Prime* rose majestically out of the cloudy argon atmosphere of the Primordial planet. The ship's engines could interact with the still-functioning Spheres from any point within the Shadow Galaxy; however, in order for Leej to float in the central axis of the navigation core—the only spot aboard ship insulated and large enough to accommodate the energy flows involved—required weightlessness.

Leej walked with the nurses who stored Gosseyn's motionless body in a medical crib. Leej saw how, even relaxed in deathlike sleep, handsome the noble head, how strong, even relaxed, the planes and veins in the neck were. The man who could not die.

Gosseyn's reaction: *That assessment is false-to-facts. X has a method of killing me that would have worked had it not been for an emergency reflex built into my brain stem by Lavoisseur. . . .*

Her vision blurred slightly as rage shook her. That reaction surprised him. Rage? Why was she angry now?

But he knew, because their thoughts were intertwined. *You just have an explanation for everything, don't you?* This, accompanied by a mood of exasperation. Gosseyn would just never shut up. He overanalyzed everything. He was cold, dispassionate, unloving . . .

Unloving toward her.

The blush spread from her cheeks down her throat to her breasts. From within, he could feel the hot flush of warmth from her skin.

Because beneath her shame and rage was hope. A girlish hope. She was a born aristocrat, trained to hide her emotions, so that underlings would not see. Underlings included the future-blind, the peons, including the crude foreign men of strange worlds. The men like Enro whom the Predictors had once been compelled to serve. And men like Gosseyn.

(This thought was mingled with a confused memory of the handsome peasant boys she used to command to wait on her when she was bored. Their dirty fingernails and sunburnt, callused hands thrilled and disgusted her with their roughness.)

Now that one of those coarse men from the outer worlds was within her, within her very soul, Leej was convinced he could not help but love her, now that he saw her as she truly was.

Gosseyn's reaction, of course, was detached.

His analytical mind immediately saw how her tangle of fear-complexes related to her neurotic sexual behavior. She was crippled by her upbringing.

The syndrome of aristocracy was simple: Any caste system is based on a shared and unquestioned illusion of moral supremacy and manifests itself in a fetish for outward and meaningless symbols of status and power. Upper castes fear uprising by the lower, whether the threat is real or not; hence they fear any dishonor to their symbols of prestige.

And there was no more potent symbol in the human psyche than the surrender of a woman to a man. Hence aristocracies were phobic about liaisons between high-born women and low-born men: Prohibited under all conditions, it had for Leej the lure of the forbidden.

On the archipelago world of Yalterta, the Predictors flew from island to island on magnetically powered air-yachts and only the peons were tied to the land, farmed the soil. Their prognostication abilities gave the aristocrats an unsurpassable military superiority over their helpless peons, whom they could rob and abuse at will, able to foresee and circumvent any rebellion or resistance. This meant the normal correctives of reality could not break the falsehoods by force. Despite their advancements in technology or other areas, Yalertans were psychologically trapped at a primitive level of history, roughly equal to the fellahin priest-king structures of ancient Egypt on Earth. The neurosis of status, the pretense that they were morally superior, still operated.

In Leej, the subconscious force that recognized her inhumanity to her fellow man drove her to a forbidden sexual attraction: The "lower orders" fascinated her.

Combined with this was a second neurosis. Her culture and upbringing had trained her from birth to accept the notion that sex was for casual liaisons only. Children of Predictors were raised in the Pedagogic Centers, not by families. Marriage was for peons. The consequence of that: a series of meaningless relationships brutally damaging to her sense of self-worth. The primal drive of a female animal for a safe place to mate and bear children was continually frustrated.

No wonder her sexual neuroses had combined to select Gosseyn. As an outworlder, he was like one of the forbidden peasant boys; but his superhuman abilities, able to block out the prediction power, made him the most powerful potential mate of her experience: the most alpha wolf of the pack. He was the mate who could make her safe, permanently safe.

Gosseyn's analysis: She would not be able to understand the drive forcing her toward Gosseyn because she could not question or criticize her aristocratic upbringing. For her to admit, even for a moment, that her attraction to Gosseyn was based on subconscious disloyalty to her class . . .

Gosseyn could not finish the thought. The anger of Leej made metallic dots swim in her view, which was now his view as well. Her furious thought: *The islands were at war before we took over! We foresee the needs of the needy and foresee the yield of the harvest! Those blind worms! Filthy low worms! They beg us to rule them!*

Then into her mind came a hysterical sense that Gosseyn didn't really mean what he thought. He was just thinking these things to hurt her.

Despite that she was in intimate contact with his inmost thoughts, she simply denied that he truly thought what he thought. Obviously he did not understand himself as well as she did!

And then, just as abruptly, a third mood shift, a sensation of infinite weariness. A sense of overwhelming, soul-deadening defeat. *Oh well. Some men are just like that.* Half-hidden behind this thought, another emotion-pattern: a sense of smugness, of superiority. Only the truly enlightened people (like Leej) knew the ugly truth about life. But once you found ugliness amusing, you could live with it.

It was all so illogical that Gosseyn was at a loss. Was this the type of mental and emotional chaos most people, most of their lives, stumbled through?

THROUGHOUT all this mental turmoil, the outward conduct of Leej, the high-born lady, was calm and controlled. She made sure Gosseyn's body was well tended. She spoke with the nurses in a friendly, if somewhat regal, way, and she bade them farewell and returned to her quarters.

Someone had laid out on her bed the insulated suit, webbed with lie detector–style neural amplification circuitry, that she was to wear while entering the navigation core during the experiment.

Leej stared at the clothing on the bed with a mounting sense of frustration, shame, and a sarcastic amusement at her own situation.

With a bitter laugh and an abrupt gesture, she tore off her clothes and stood staring into the full-length mirror on the wall, her hands on her hips. She was a good-looking, well-groomed woman, in her thirties, dark haired, her head perhaps a shade too large for her frame.

"Well?" she said aloud. "Do you see what you've been missing?"

Gosseyn noted that staring at a woman through a woman's eyes, with the glandular and neural reactions of the woman, produced none of the normal animal reaction that a healthy young male might have felt. His feeling, again, was one of clinical detachment. Leej might be offended that she had a voyeur lodged in her brain, but she also knew from Gosseyn's own unconcealed and inconcealable thoughts that he meant not to embarrass her, not even in this situation of forced intimacy.

"Don't you find me even a little attractive?"

Gosseyn's thought: *Only once you are aware that your reactions to events are based on false-to-facts associations can you adjust your emotions to reality. Rage or frustration or cynicism is a negative feedback signal, warning you of maladjustment. The signal will cause pain but will not correct the behavior causing the pain, because your attempts at correction are based on a false picture. This false picture was evolved to flatter you rather than tell you how to negotiate with reality.*

Her reaction (of course) to this little lecture was one of rage and frustration and cynicism. And then suddenly, welling up inside of her like a dam breaking, came misery: the misery of a woman in love, never to be loved in return, because the immortal superhuman man she loved regarded her as mortal, worthless, and weak.

To Gosseyn's surprise, Leej sank down on the bed in tears, hiccoughing, swallowing her sobs so as to make no noise, her nose stinging, trying her best to weep silently, lest someone in the companionway overhear.

And this was apparently the future she had selected where the two of them adjusted to the inconvenience of sharing a body as quickly and harmoniously as possible.

Since Gosseyn himself also felt all the neurological and physical sensations of stabbing sorrow and womanly hurt, he performed the cortical-thalamic pause, trying to retain his sanity amid the turbulent flow of emotion.

And her emotions, naturally, were calmed as well. After a brief while, the tears subsided. Leej, her eyes red, said to the mirror bitterly, "Am I really so much worse than Patricia?"

It is not a question of better or worse.

But Patricia's rejection of her own royal birth was the very thing Leej lacked: an objective sense of her own self-worth, based on real accomplishment. The sunny humor and cool self-control of Patricia contrasted sharply with the bitterness of this neurotic, self-deluded female. Gosseyn could not prevent himself from thinking the unflattering comparison.

Leej's reaction was arch.

"I thought you could never be attracted to a woman who had no Null-A training. But you do love her, do you not?"

I do not. Those feelings were implanted as false memories.

"Then why do you miss her cooking? Why do you miss your little fruit farm?"

And for that he had no clear answer, not even in his own thoughts.

22

The human nervous system is limited in its capacity to draw meaningful distinctions and therefore must treat similar objects as if they are identical: This is always done with reference to some purpose.

Soon Leej was zippered into her skintight insulated suit and floating in the center of the vast cylindrical space of the navigation core. She had braided her hair tightly and held it in place with the clip, to make it less of a nuisance in zero-gee. A half a dozen umbilical cords and wires connected her with instruments and recorders. Over her belt-phone she spoke with Dr. Kair and Curoi and Grand Captain Treyvenant as preparations were made and the final countdown began. As before, the distant hull above, below, and to each side was black with vision-plate images of the surrounding galaxy.

Leej said into her phone, "I don't see how this can work, even theoretically. Gosseyn's thoughts may be living in my head, but his extra brain is still back in his head, unconscious."

Dr. Kair said, "Aleph established a nineteen-point similarity between Gosseyn's thought-patterns and his body. Our instruments are picking up readings of the energy signals passing back and forth from his unconscious body. We believe that when Gosseyn thinks the proper sequence in your brain, this will push the similarity to the final decimal point, and remotely trigger the nerve connections in his extra brain."

Leej said, "What if it doesn't work?"

But it did work.

Leej's first impression was of a sudden, dizzying increase in the clarity and range of prediction-pictures surrounding the vision-plates: She saw the tremendous and slow astronomical motions of dead stars orbiting the black center of the Shadow Galaxy, the great sweep of the spiral arms, moving and collapsing, like the froth of a whirlpool, spiraling inward.

There were no duplicate or parallel pictures, as she might have seen surrounding predictions of human behavior, where there was some free will or uncertainty involved. With slow, titanic motions, the orbits of the black stars decayed, the spiral arms fell inward on themselves, the galaxy condensed into a small irregular cloud and sprays of black star clusters, and finally the vast singularity at the core of the galaxy consumed the remainder.

Normal prediction could reach three or four weeks into the future. Larger and less-avoidable events, such as natural disasters, could be seen a year or two before the event. But this scene, the old age and death of millions of stars of the Shadow Galaxy—Gosseyn estimated the time interval involved to be between fifteen and twenty million years.

Unexpectedly, the prediction-picture broadened, embracing the surrounding galaxies, as dust and other fine particles of matter (to which their vision was evidently attuned) spread across the universe as the Shadow Galaxy dissolved.

A new vision arose: There were still a few dim red stars scattered throughout the universe, fewer and fewer per galaxy. Stellar formation had ceased long ago, but the smaller, cooler stars were tarrying before they burned out. Galaxies were nebular clouds composed of compact bodies: planets, burnt-out dwarf stars, neutron stars, black holes. Matter was undergoing inevitable degeneration as proton decay set in.

Leej said, *This future is from one hundred trillion years hence.*

Gosseyn asked, *How can you tell?*

A Predictor can just . . . feel . . . from the length of the vision how far it has traveled.

In other words (Gosseyn thought), Leej did not understand how she knew. She was not an analytical person and her culture not a scientific one. But for all that, he did not doubt her conclusion.

The vision shifted again: Gravitational perturbations had flung the planets, slowly, over eons, out of their orbits, and they either fell toward cold stars or sailed away into lonely, everlasting night.

Gosseyn: *How long?*

Leej: *The number of years is ten to the exponential power of fifteen. An immensity! If the life of the universe up to the point of the previous vision were lived over again ten times, that would approach this epoch. The eons it took for all the stars to be born and reborn, grow old, and finally die were only the first beginning. This is a universal night ten times the length of the universal day.*

Next came another vision, this one even darker, older, colder than before. A huge segment of space-time, large enough that Gosseyn, through Leej's vision, could sense the curvature of the universe itself, was included within the view. Here there were no galaxies, for each galaxy had lost its stars. The stars had either fallen into supermassive black holes at the galactic core or been sent wandering, cast adrift in the endlessness. The dead and dying stars were now as far from each other, on average, as the supergalactic clusters had been in Gosseyn's time.

Leej: *And this is ten times further again. This is ten to the exponential power of sixteen years. But we must reach farther . . . farther. . . .*

Gosseyn: *Surely all life died off long ago!*

Leej: *No. I am still detecting the disturbances from free will. Something in the vast void is thinking, is acting, is changing its own future. . . .*

Again the vision blurred and sharpened. Now the mass of the universe was mostly composed of a haze of gamma radiation Gosseyn could dimly detect with his extra brain. Gosseyn, able to sense and memorize the clouds of matter across thousands of light-years, did a random sampling and made an estimate: Roughly half the mass of the free-floating matter in the universe had been converted to gamma rays due to proton decay.

Leej said, *This is ten to the exponential power of forty years. And yet there is still life here.*

Gosseyn: *Where?*

She showed him first one golden point of light, hovering in orbit around the supermassive black hole remnant of what had once been the core of a galaxy. And then, many numberless billions of light-years away, a second one, and then a third.

There was a slight refraction to the mental picture, as if there were more than one possibility here. Something more than the mere mechanical actions of the laws of nature was at work. Whatever this golden atom was, it was man-made.

Gosseyn attempted to "memorize" one of those golden points of light with his extra brain. He had a sense of immense *smallness,* as if the thing were many times smaller than the core of an atom . . . and yet it was massive, heavier than many solar masses. But it did not seem to possess the flattened smoothness of neutronium. His impression was one of cunning, gemlike intricacy, like the workings of a Swiss watch, but on a subatomic level, dealing with forces and energies immeasurably powerful, compressed into a measurelessly small space.

What was it?

Gosseyn suddenly felt a sensation, a distortion, as if Leej were being "photographed" by a distorter circuit.

From the tiny golden atom came an irresistible *pull. . . .*

Darkness!

LEEJ found herself lying facedown, her cheek pressed against a hard, cold surface, harder than glass. She put her hands under her and rose.

She was still wearing her insulated suit, but whatever force had plucked her out from the middle of the *Ulti-*

mate Prime had very carefully unlatched her umbilical cords, removed medical sensors, and unscrewed fittings from sockets on her suit without tearing the suit.

There were a dozen golden giants with Gosseyn's face here, surrounding her. They sat in a circle on an elevated stage, leaning across a table of dark substance. The table was shaped like two horseshoes set end-to-end: Leej stood on a depressed circle of floor in the middle. Overhead was a black dome. Whether it was the sky of this lightless universe or merely a dome of black glass Leej could not tell.

There was a second ring of Gosseyn-faced men seated behind and above the first, and a third ring above and behind them.

Leej said, "You again! Doesn't anyone live to make it all the way into far future but you, Gilbert Gosseyn?"

One of the figures spoke in a voice like the bass string on a viol, his tones rich with humor: "It is not that the Gosseyn-Lavoisseur line is particularly long-lived; it is merely that we have the primary interest in meeting our remotest version, and so arranged to be at the time and place when and where he would manifest."

Leej became aware of the fact that Gosseyn was no longer in her thoughts. His calming presence had vanished. Had she been catapulted into the remote future by herself? She could feel the panic rising in her.

A second one said, "We are maintaining the gravitational metric at the surface of a neutron star by de-similarizing the matter here from the effect of the gravity well. We do not normally appear in physical form. The atoms and molecules around you, including the substance of our bodies, were restored out of memorized distorter patterns matrixed in the core of the neutron star. Since the material universe has entered a period of low-energy disintegration, the minds that were once composed of all living beings in the galaxies have retreated into an out-of-phase condition, so that their thoughts do not occupy a particular point in time or space."

A third Gosseyn-Aleph spoke: "The engine that maintains this cosmic thought-record is housed in those superheavy atoms you sensed during your approach. When Gosseyn attuned you to one of them, it reacted automatically to memorize and preserve your brain information: The side effect brought you here."

Leej said, "What happened to Gosseyn? Why isn't he here?"

A fourth one answered her: "The nature of memory is fundamentally tied to the nature of time: The human nervous system interprets the direction of greater entropy as the direction of consciousness, since memory is an organization of thought, and internal organization creates greater disorganization externally. Gosseyn's thoughts are suspended: To the unprepared mind, a condition of no-time forces a condition of no-thought."

The first one spoke again: "The moment he wakes, his mind-patterns will be similarized to our own, and he will be mechanically educated with the processes he needs to be able to survive the Shadow Effect. At that time, we will assist you, so that you may continue your journey."

Leej said, "And what is the meaning of this? Why did you send one of your numbers back into the past to meet us?"

The second Gosseyn-Aleph answered, "The Gosseyn you saw is from our future, possibly the ultimate or last of us. He has accomplished what we have not yet accomplished, and breached the time barrier."

Leej remembered Gosseyn's story he had told Dr. Kair. "The Shadow Men of A.D. Three Million supposed it would only be a matter of a few hundred years before time-travel was perfected. Are you saying that here, long after the death of the star-making phase of the universe, you still have no clue as to how it is done?"

Gosseyn-Aleph, or one of them, replied, "We know how it is done. Certain energy formations in epochs of intense gravity—such as exist at the core of dead neutron stars—have nineteen points of similarity between themselves here/now and themselves at a prior time. The prediction power shows that the interval can be bridged. During the current span of the universe, where all remaining matter is neutronium and therefore naturally partially similarized backward and forward through time, our ability to investigate the phenomenon is greatly enhanced."

A second one said, "But there is a negative energy barrier, a Shadow Effect, that normally prevents such time-distortions. The erection of this barrier was something imposed simultaneously upon all ages of the universe, a first step of an extra-universal attack, something meant to change the basic structure of reality itself."

Leej said, "The other Aleph spoke of an infinite enemy, a creature called the Ydd."

One of the Gosseyn-Alephs said, "It is to oppose the Ydd entity that this council has gathered, that we have taken the desperate steps we have. The youngest of us comes from as early as fifty thousand years after the Shadow Men. The eldest has not yet been born, but is present only in a copy of his brain we made through prediction power, transcribing his future thoughts into a blank matrix."

Leej asked, "And . . . ? How can you fight something not of this universe?"

"We have created not merely millions but billions of the Space-time Sphere amplifiers here in our own eon, scattered over a much larger radius than merely one galaxy, to create a correspondingly larger base-axis of operation. The Spheres will be oriented to Gosseyn the moment he wakes. This operation has used up most of our limited supply of uncorrupted atomically organized matter. Atoms are as rare, to us, as quasar pockets of the original Big Bang plasma are to you: the remnant of the universe as it once existed in a higher and more primal energy state."

Leej whispered, "Are the stakes truly so high?"

"Observe!"

———————

LEEJ had a sensation of immense speed. Darkness was again around her. She was unaware of her body. Her consciousness was like a moving point, speeding onward, faster and ever faster.

But not onward: backward. This was the second time her prediction power had been used to reach into the far past.

She saw the Shadow Galaxy again, but this time, it was an image from before the nonidentity effect had darkened it. This was the Primordial Galaxy of man in its pristine glory.

This image was one of a galaxy blazing with stars, the galaxy surrounded by a gemlike cloud of globular clusters, the spiral arms rich with multicolored clouds of nebulae, nurseries of fire where young stars where born: And here and there, pinpoints of intolerable brightness, were novae and supernovae, exploding outward to shower the surrounding universe with newer and heavier elements.

The picture was encompassing millions of years at a glance, so the galaxy, glinting, shining, coruscating, seemed a moving thing, the spiral arms lengthening and turning like some ancient sea-creature made of fire, its hidden heart pulsing behind a curtain of red, orange, and purple nebular gas-clouds.

Again, another picture: The galaxies were closer together now, and most of them were clouds in the shape of cylinders or toroids. The stars were the uniform white color, hydrogen-burning. The great nebulae reached from galaxy to galaxy, so that they seemed to be flowing rivers in which the galactic clouds were mere islands of foam. This was a very early picture of universal time. The element of helium had not yet been burned into existence by the slow process of cosmic evolution.

Next, an even earlier picture: a small white-hot universe where vents of superheated plasma were issuing from a tiny pinpoint, smaller than the core of an atom.

Time-space was enormously bent, so that light circling the miniature universe many times brought reflected images of the tiny point and its surrounding prominences to every side of the cosmos, spread and distorted as if in the surface of a curving mirror.

Leej was staring in utter bewilderment. To her it was a meaningless glare of lights.

Then, rising up from within her, that sensation of calmness and certainty she came to associate with Gilbert Gosseyn. He was awake!

His thoughts were here, once again were with her. She could see that he noted and knew that they were viewing the early universe. The universe was so small that tiny quantum-level uncertainties distorted the otherwise uniform flow of the prominences: Some swelled up like bubbles, creating eddies and ripples.

Within these eddies, so dense was the matter-energy involved that time and space were distorted, sometimes permitting time to flow backward, or for matter to spill out into the universe faster than the speed of light, "creating" an interval of space around it in which it could have its being. The whole universe was undergoing a rapid expansion and evolution. The primal ylem was breaking down into distinct variants of matter and energy, creating the dimensions of time and space as it did so.

Gosseyn and Leej both noticed an area of darkness, of shadowy non-being, issuing between the prominences.

Leej: *What is that?*

Gosseyn did not know. He did the mental action of attempting to take a "photograph" of it with his extra brain. He sensed the underlying nothingness of the Shadow Effect: Even in this environment of immense pressures and temperatures so hot that no particles could exist for more than the merest infinitesimal fraction of a second, the shadow-stuff maintained its cold and vacuous nature, its fundamental non-being.

The shadow reacted. Gosseyn's extra brain felt the distortion of time-space around him as something within that shadow-cloud formed a twenty-decimal-point similarity with him.

Overpowering alien thought-forms crashed into his brain: *Ydd extrusion fourteen communicates with Ydd central consciousness and reports interference within the prime radiant-from-origin segment of the fourteenth arc of time.*

YDD OVERMIND CONSULTS WITH YDD ANALYTIC SUB-MIND AND SOLICITS A RESPONSE: SHOULD THE SURROUNDING UNIVERSE FROM WHICH THIS IRRITANT ISSUES BE ANNIHILATED?

Ydd Analytic replies in the affirmative. This is a universe in which life shall one day arise. Life poses an unacceptable potential threat.

YDD OVERMIND CONFIRMS. BEGIN PROCEDURE TO NULLIFY THE UNIVERSE.

The mental "words" were shockingly loud: Gosseyn's own thoughts were scattered and confused merely by the impact of the Ydd mental forms.

Leej was the first to recover. She saw a possible future and urged it toward Gosseyn: "You have already been taught by the Council of Alephs how to survive the Shadow Effect. They've made you into a being like the Follower. Use that power now! Quickly!"

Leej felt Gosseyn reach out and . . . break . . . the similarity allowing the Ydd to communicate with them. What was once identical he made non-identical.

The similarity existing between Leej's perception and the matter-energy conditions of the early universe also was broken. The vision vanished.

Leej blinked, expecting to see the curving table and the high dome of the Aleph giants all around her. Instead was . . . strangeness.

23

Human abstraction therefore is conditioned by environment: We make those distinctions and see those similarities useful to our thought process. In novel environment, those unconscious, automatic habits of assumption will no longer be accurate.

Around her was darkness, punctuated by terrifically small golden dots. Gosseyn was able to detect, very widely spaced, pinpoints of intense gravitational pressure, distorting the metric of space-time. These were massive black holes, scattered across billions of light-years, the rough cloud of them occupying an otherwise dark, blank, and empty universe. The golden pinpoints were the remnant of the civilization from which the Aleph Council had come. Leej noticed that she was perceiving these golden dots not with her eyes but with her prediction power: They were disturbing the fabric of time and probability. Gosseyn would not have been aware of them had he been in his own form.

And the black holes were melting, disintegrating, and shrinking into Hawking radiation. Leej was not occupying one moment of time but was viewing countless billions of years compressed into each passing second. She was racing from 10^{40} years to 10^{100}. A number so large only mathematicians had a name for it: the googol.

Leej thought, *I'm in space. Why can I breathe?*

She felt a sensation of anger burning in Gosseyn's mind.

In his sanity fashion he put the anger aside, and in flashing thoughts he answered her briefly: Her body had been turned into shadow-stuff, like the Follower. The normal atomic and chemical reactions that would otherwise afflict her, such as oxygenation in the lungs, running out of air, explosive decompression, had no effect here.

"Your body, back wherever it is, in the past, in the chamber of the Aleph Council, is still breathing. The Follower needed a distorter circuit at the landing point wherever he cast one of his shadow-images. Aleph can evidently cast our shadow-image through time rather than space, and he put us here. And, apparently, Aleph needs no distorter circuit at this end. . . ."

But then Gosseyn's thoughts leaped away from that chain of thinking, fascinated. For he had recognized the overall structure of the gravitic disturbances caused by the black holes that formed the remnants of long-dead galaxies.

It was a distorter circuit. It occupied all the available space, all the degenerate matter and energy left in this long-dead universe, but there it was: a machine the size of the universe, made of pulsations of gravitons.

The governing mechanism was a time-distortion coming from the golden pinpoints, which altered uncertainties on a supermicroscopic scale, so that each flying particle from the disintegrating singularities met and matched the particles from each other disintegrating singularity and the huge, intricate dance of very low, dull, slow energy formed a pattern of forces. This pattern of forces, in turn . . .

An engine of thought. An electronic brain, no, a *gravitonic* brain, composed of all the remaining stuffs of the universe.

But Leej was interested in what prompted his burst of anger upon arriving here.

Gosseyn could not hide his thoughts from her: *They lied to you.*

The council of Aleph-Gosseyn-Lavoisseur beings had been lying. Gosseyn had not blacked out because the timeless condition had interrupted his thoughts. Had that been true, why would it affect him and not Leej? Gosseyn had not blacked out; he had been overwhelmed by nausea. The same dizziness he had felt back in the pocket-sized universe, while being investigated by Dr. Halt.

The dizziness that signaled that the universe was a false one, too.

Leej merely laughed. "Dr. Kair knew it. So did Dr. Curoi. The ultimate Gosseyn means for all of us to die. This universe will not survive. It's another illusion, meant to trap you, and you will break out of it and destroy us." *Because that is just the way some men are.*

But Gosseyn's irresistible logic, in thoughts he could not hide from her, drove him further, to a conclusion more bitter than this: Gosseyn-Aleph had chosen Leej partly because her prediction power was needed to teleport Gosseyn into ever further future segments of his false universe. Obviously the effort was meant to find some point not covered by the negative energy barrier prohibiting time-travel.

But there was a second purpose here. The forced intimacy, the sharing of thoughts, had impressed upon Leej in a fashion nothing else could have done how fundamentally different, incompatible, Gosseyn was from her. Seeing the succession of ever stranger superbeings Gosseyn was destined to become had driven the point home. And then, meeting a whole council of them . . .

Gosseyn had to assume his far-future selves were as competent master psychologists as Lavoisseur had been: Lavoisseur, who with one casual-seeming comment had deadened Gosseyn's curiosity about his own origins of being, and had done so without Gosseyn's suspicions being roused.

. . . the council had manipulated her psychologically. Their talk of the desperation of the stakes, their exposing her to the ruthless mental impact of the Ydd creature at the dawn of time . . .

Gosseyn thought to her, *They mean you to sacrifice yourself. I am not sure how, or why, but something about you is unique, and useful to them. . . .*

Even as he thought this, he knew the answer. Dr. Halt had mentioned it: "There are energy connections leading to your wife. . . . The energy density involved is greater than the total mass-energy value of the universe."

The emotions of Leej, the powerful infatuation, not only altered her electrochemical and glandular balances in her body but, acting through her Predictor power, also influenced the universe around her. Even an untrained brain, under the powerful influence of romantic devotion, could form a crude sympathy or similarity between two nervous systems. After all, the distinctions between mind and body, self and other, were as artificial, as far as the universe was concerned, as those distinguishing time and space. The powerful emotion of Leej the Predictress would be drawn to him, even across the boundaries of time.

And Gosseyn's horrible realization, in thoughts that he could not hide from her, was that he would have done the same thing, would have treated her, or himself, or anyone, as ruthlessly, once he was convinced of the need to do so. Gosseyn-Aleph, the ultimate version of him, had no doubt predicted exactly this flow of events, exactly these conclusions of this thought, to bring Gosseyn and Leej to the mental realization that . . .

That she was right to despise him for his callousness. *Some men are just like that.*

If she were exiled here, in this empty, blank, inhuman future, the final mind of this era could use her sympathy with Gosseyn to track him, to maintain the connection, once he found the "gap" in the anti-time-travel barrier blocking the universe he was evidently destined to find. Gosseyn would return to his own home era, but Leej would not.

Gosseyn used his extra brain to attune himself to gravity flows trickling through the empty universe around him. He addressed the cosmic machine: *That is it, isn't it?*

YES.

Gosseyn addressed the mighty being: *We refuse.*

OF COURSE. YOU ARE NOT YET CONVINCED OF THE NECESSITY.

One of the microscopic golden pinpoints, which Leej could sense but Gosseyn could not, pulled her attention toward itself. It hung in space roughly 150 billion light-years away, the nearest object in this nearly empty cosmos.

OBSERVE THIS. WHAT IS IT?

Leej inspected it with her special senses. The shadow-body she inhabited had the ability to make itself either more or less out of phase with its surroundings. Leej found she could orient her shadow-substance toward the golden point, rather than to the universe to which it was only partially connected, and make increasingly clearer prediction-images.

She said, "Time is turning in a circle here. It is less than a million millionths of a second, but this subatomic particle group is playing the same split instant of time over and over again. . . ."

Gosseyn could not see the particle, but he could see her thoughts about it. Certain subatomic reactions were symmetrical in time at the quantum level of reality: virtual particles, usually. This set of reactions had been artificially amplified to have the energy of a small star within it, but the physics involved followed the same rules. Two points in time, very small and very close to each other, were sufficiently similar that they became indistinguishable. If the fifty-ninth second were made "the same" as the first second, time would loop and the same minute would replay endlessly. That was the principle.

Gosseyn concluded something Leej did not have the scientific training to notice. The singularity at the center of the golden particle was a homogenous high-density mass of matter-energy, where gravity, electromagnetism, and nucleonic forces were undifferentiated. Here, in miniature, was a small model of the conditions of the first three seconds of the universe.

No wonder the Final Mind had been using this

formulation as a set of beacons to aid its communication across the abyss of time. No matter where, from an outside frame of reference, these time-warped particles seemed to be, in reality they were only one decimal point of similarity away from the earliest segment of the universe.

ONLY THE AMOUNT OF AMBIENT ENERGY LIMITS THE AMOUNT OF TIME-SPACE THAT CAN BE CAPTURED IN A WARP OF THIS TYPE.

Gosseyn understood the implication. This was the technique the Ydd meant to use to destroy the universe and preserve its early environment. The Ydd wished to alter the flow of cosmic evolution, to halt the expansion of the universe when it grew from the 10^{-32} meter to the 10^{-22} meter range. A period of time, the time from 10^{-12} to 10^{-6} seconds after the Big Bang, would be turned in a time-circle, the end point similarized to the beginning point, and that moment of time, an astronomically small fraction of a second, would be the life span of the universe: that split second and no more.

Not only mankind, and all other life, but every aspect of the inanimate universe would also be edited out from the time-continuum: The universe would remain the submicroscopic, intensely hot, dense mathematically infinitesimal point it had been in its earliest moment. No stars, no nebulae, not even a hydrogen atom, no matter of any kind, would ever come into being. Electromagnetism and gravity would never be divorced from the primal ylem, never have their own identities.

The inhumanity of it all was monstrous beyond words.

THE LIMITATION IS: THE FORMATION ENERGY MUST BE APPLIED FROM OUTSIDE.

Gosseyn wondered what sort of person would volunteer to stand outside the reaction and apply the needed formation energy: By definition, such a thing would involve the reduction into utter nonexistence—not merely death, but a condition of never-having-had-been—of the outside party.

He was thinking of Enro. The poor, foolish galactic dictator, absolute master of countless terrified worlds, was merely the puppet, being manipulated by the Ydd into unleashing a sufficient amount of shadow-substance into the universe to allow the Ydd to collapse everything into a supertiny microcosm: a nanoverse.

Leej was thinking of something else.

Last Mind! Could this artificial universe, doomed to destruction as soon as Gosseyn leaves it, be saved? I have seen both the earliest moments and the latest: Do you have the Ydd technology at your disposal to similarize the two points of time?

NOT WITHOUT THE SACRIFICE OF SOMEONE WHO DEPARTS FROM THE REALM OF TIME AND ENTERS THE OTHERSPACE.

The knowledge and technique of how to do it was instantly imprinted into her brain. If she traveled to a position so far in the future that all matter and energy had achieved a quantum uncertainty indistinguishable from non-being, then merely by activating the prediction power, and bringing up an image of the early universe, her undeveloped extra brain matter could similarize the two points in time.

Leej spoke into the darkness: *I volunteer. Whatever needs to be done, I will do it.*

JOIN WITH US.

A sensation accompanied the words: Leej could picture her future, once she was absorbed into the inhuman supermind of the dark universe . . . it was a picture of utter emptiness, a bodiless existence as a pattern of forces, a series of memories woven into a machinelike perfection. The ancient thought-patterns in this final mind were not alive, were not dead . . . all such distinctions were meaningless in the realm of pure thought . . . but the transcendental humanlessness of it was utterly repellent.

Gosseyn could "see" the immediately intended fate of Leej: Once she was pure thought, she would be similarized into the furthest future available to the Last Mind.

Ghostly images of her destiny appeared to him, one after another:

She would remain, alive but disembodied, while eons passed. At 10^{150} years in the future all matter that used to make up the stars and galaxies had degenerated into photons. The continued expansion of the universe Doppler-shifted these radiations into a low-energy heat, not distinguishable from the background radiation, three degrees above absolute zero.

At $10^{1,000}$ years, the universe reached an ultimate low-energy state. The low-energy state was so extreme that localized quantum events became major macro-scale phenomena rather than micro-scale non-events. This was because the smallest perturbations were making the biggest difference in this era: Space and time began to warp severely.

The span of time that she would spend in isolation, disembodied, surrounded by a dead universe, was so immense that if there was a possibility future where Leej could remain sane, Gosseyn could not see it.

All her thoughts worn by countless eternities to nothing, till her once-fine mind was merely a mass of animal instincts. Perhaps one instinct, its purpose long forgotten, would remain: True to her mission, the relic of Leej would reach the point in remotest far-future time where the barrier blocking time paradox no longer could reach. At this point, she would trigger the prediction-similarity with the very earliest universe. One of these tiny perturbations would flower into a titanic supermassive matter-energy explosion, forming a new universe identical for all practical purposes with the old, bending all of time into a huge and endless loop.

He could foresee no other option. The cosmic violence of the primal explosion would most likely kill the sad and long-insane remnant of the ghostly Leej.

Gosseyn thought, *No!*

But the thought-forms of Leej the Predictress, disembodied, had already been sent another nearly infinite span of time into the future.

Her final words, full of bittersweet ache as she departed from him, were: "Do not regret my decision, Gilbert, m-my love. Without you, I have nothing to live for. If this sacrifice will show you the true depth of my feelings, it will be worth it. . . ."

Her body vanished. Gosseyn lingered for a moment as a disembodied point of view in the darkness, his thought-energy maintained in an automatic fashion by the forces issuing from the nearest golden atom.

The futility! The waste! The childishness of it all! This was Gosseyn's cold and angry reaction as he strove to save her. Through his untrained prediction power, the link they shared, he tried to foresee her where she would fall into the immensity of empty eons; he tried to memorize her thought-patterns, to form a twenty-point similarity.

The Absolute Mind did not allow him to complete the thought-action. In his brain, Gosseyn felt the alien pressure of thought triggering that same complex of reactions in his double brain that Dr. Halt had found: a deep-rooted neural structure still attuned to the basic reality outside this universe.

The false universe ended.

Gosseyn was in his own body, lying on his back. Around him was the familiar weight of the space armor. Dimly, his extra brain could detect the muttering power of heavy equipment in the signal-nullification chamber around him.

He was back on Venus.

24

Higher order abstractions are a perfected type of memory—
that is, information that preserves itself with minimal distortion within a continuum.

Gosseyn opened his eyes. Through vision-plates panel-
ing the inside of his domelike helmet he could see the
dull gray ceiling and little more.

Dr. Hayakawa was saying, "The thought-sensitive electron tubes have recorded a tremendous influx of memory
energy. Are you aware of the thoughts of X in your head?
Or have you become him?"

Gosseyn could not sit up in this armor, since it did not
bend at the waist, but he triggered the motorized sequence that would bring him into a standing position.
Now he saw the walls of the surrounding chamber, the
door like a bank vault's. Through a slit of armored glass
he saw the silhouettes of the heads of Clayton, the Null-
A detective, and Dr. Hayakawa and his team.

Gosseyn found he was blinking back tears of rage.
Again, the cortical-thalamic pause allowed him to find a
sense of calm, to remove the heaviness from his thoughts.

Clayton said, "What happened?"

Gosseyn said, "I've merged again. The memories of a
version of Gosseyn Three from an alternate continuum
have been sent back through time and similarized to my
nervous system, selecting the point in time when I was
most receptive to outside signals. The memories include
that Leej the Predictress was persuaded, or manipulated,
to volunteer to remain behind in a dead universe, apparently as part of a last-ditch effort to save it. This was a
parallel continuum, artificially created to allow to exist
there a type of anachronic similarity, a time-travel technique, which is being artificially blocked from occurring
here. Also, her sacrifice seems to allow the Final Cosmic

Mind of the last stages of the universe to track my motions: For what purpose I don't know."

Clayton said, "Our problem for right now is how to prove to our satisfaction that you are not the X version of Lavoisseur. A lie detector will not tell us, for obvious reasons."

Gosseyn knew the reasons. It was X in his guise as the head of the General Semantics Institute who had found ways to falsify the readings of lie detectors: Otherwise the conspiracy against Null-A would never have been attempted in the first place and the galactic soldiers would have simply attacked with abandon, rather than attempting a less costly method of conquest-by-infiltration.

Gosseyn said, "Have the robo-operator place a call to Corthid, informing them that Illverton, head of their Safety Authority, is an agent of Enro's. The distorter towers they are building have been misaligned in order to make the planet attuned to the Shadow Effect, rather than immune to it."

The reply that eventually came back from the robo-operator was, "I'm sorry. We are getting no carrier signal. The distorter connection with Planet Corthid is broken."

Gosseyn, at this point, was sitting in a lounge, nursing a cup of coffee. To nullify his extra brain was a multiple-vibration broadcaster on the table before him.

And the minutes turned into hours, and there was still no word from Planet Corthid. Vessels could similarize from nearby planets to points beyond the target and "brake" out of similarization prematurely, to put themselves in the Corthid star system; but from the frame of reference of time on Earth, that process would take days.

However, the utter absence of any communication or any inbound or outbound ship traffic from the most energetic of the three capital planets of the Interstellar League was a sufficient sign that the world had fallen.

The time paradox involved here was: At the moment of his similarization to Corthid, a second version of himself "simultaneously" remained behind, now with memories from the future. Of course, "simultaneous" was an inaccurate approximation of a more complex reality in an Einsteinian universe. The moment of distortion was apparently enough of a break in the normal cause-effect relations for the universe to maintain its surface appearance of continuity, despite the presence of two Gosseyns from different time-segments occupying the "same" time—which was not actually the same at all.

The only remaining question was how accurate, despite the paradoxes involved, was Gosseyn's alleged memory of these events?

Hayakawa's group had called in a team of engineers to examine the information picked up by the electronic recordings made of Gosseyn's brain during the memory-collision. Included in the information was, first, a complete three-dimensional blueprint of the inner workings of the Space-time Stabilization Spheres, and, second, the mathematics and engineering details of the distorter towers of Corthid. Gosseyn's three months of experience with the Corthidians, while they frantically attempted to build these machines, made him familiar with every intricate part.

Third and most important, physicists from the prestigious Landing City University had arrived or were present as images on long-distance telephone-plates to examine the information about the early and final stages of the universe.

Anything he could not call to mind with his trained memory was picked up by a particularly sensitive electron-tube array controlled by the Games Machine of Venus.

The Venusian Games Machine recommended releasing Gosseyn immediately. "His nervous system is already partially adjusted to the pattern of conditions beyond the universe. A specialized structure has been created in his extra brain to allow him to summon and to survive a shadow-shape, and to control the energy flows involved. At the moment this section is highly active."

Clayton asked, "What about the suppressor?"

The Machine said wryly, "The suppressor only inhibits those brain actions it was designed to suppress. At the moment, the subject's extra brain has an organic circuit to provoke the non-identity condition, which the suppressor ignores."

Clayton said, "The real possibility is that this man might be X: Is there a way to inhibit the brain section he uses to control the Shadow Effect?"

"That would be unwise," warned the Machine. "The subject Gosseyn is balancing himself against the natural similarization-effect of the primordial ylem, which is attuned to him to seventeen decimals. The time depth involved exceeds fifteen billion years. Obviously, if this were the enemy version of himself he calls X, he would have no need to dissimilate. He could destroy the planet by bringing one cubic picometer of ylem pre-matter-energy from the remote past into the current space-time environment. His shadow-form would be immune to the resulting singularity hyperexplosion."

Clayton said, "Logic shows only that if this Gosseyn is now possessed by the memories of X, the destruction of Venus is not his purpose. Caution says we should treat him as if he is a version of X until proven otherwise."

"Maybe. . . ." The Games Machine sounded uncertain. "But Gosseyn's talents are too valuable to stand idle. Without the help of a Null-A-trained neurolinguist, Enro will simply be prey to his normal animal-human urges. Hence Gosseyn should pursue his next logical step in tracking down X. If Gosseyn were X, he could hardly afford to spend time researching traces of his own activity just to fool you. Null-A Venus forms a relatively small part of the overall galactic effort against Enro."

Clayton said, "So your suggestion is to let Gosseyn go, send him on a mission useful to us, but not tell him what we plan to do to thwart Enro?"

That was exactly the Machine's suggestion.

––––––––

THE Games Machine would not share any further conclusions, under the circumstances, with Gilbert Gosseyn. "Please note that I have been designed and programmed along the lines of non-Aristotelian logic: There are limitations to this mental system, as there are to all nervous system architectures, natural or artificial. The version of Lavoisseur you call X also operates within those limits, as do you. To deduce his whereabouts, you will need recourse to a different system of scientific thought."

It turned out to be a relatively simple matter to telephone the Foundation of Nonlinear Ratiocination on the Great Planet Accolon. Clayton explained his needs first to an electronic brain, and next to a lively young secretary who appeared on the telephone after the brain transferred the call.

Clayton, in rather careful language, summed up what was known about Enro and X and the Predictors of Yalerta. He also gave the background theory that there was a primal superbeing known as the Ydd guiding their actions, and he asked for an estimate of which social or political movements under way in the galaxy currently could not be seen as natural.

First, Enro's agents, forewarned by the Predictors, could not resist the temptation to avoid setbacks normal mortals would not foresee. Hence their actions, whatever they were, would be as abnormal as a gambler who won every single trick in a card game.

Second, having a version of Lavoisseur as part of his cabinet, even an insane version, would influence Enro's methods and tactics. The dictator would be inevitably guided toward a neurolinguistic method of winning victory, rather than military methods.

Third, Enro would be using his Shadow Effect weapon more often than was called for by purely military considerations, since the Ydd was altering reality to bring about the annihilation of all life in the galaxy and was certainly trying to set up a runaway cascade of the Shadow Effect.

The secretary noted all this down on a sheet of metallic paper and fed it into an analyzer. "Your query is based on a number of unusual assumptions about the nature of time, space, and reality. That might flag it for a higher priority! Good luck."

Clayton asked her, "You must get millions of inquiries from subscribers. How do you prioritize them?"

She tilted her head to one side and spoke. Her lip movement did not match the voice that came from the telephone speaker. The phone was putting her sentences into English. "All the queries are translated into a mathematical code and fed into a computer, where questions are grouped according to a flexible interpretation of the subject matter, forming a multidimensional pattern of all queries. The intuitive lateral thinking process is used to pick out important queries from the huge mass. The robot that forwarded your call to me is programmed with some of the more common pattern-recognition formats, and assigned it an initial high priority, despite that it was a question related to military security, coming from someone other than a recognized foreign ambassador."

Clayton held his detective's badge up to the telephone lens and stimulated the electronically active metal to make the badge glow with its unique pattern, irreproducible by forgery. "The political structure of Venus allows me to act as a plenipotentiary ambassador on behalf of all her peoples when need be."

The girl smiled a dimpled smile. "If anyone finds out your planet is an anarchy, that would reduce your priority rating. Well, nonetheless, your query will be assigned an item number and the answer sent when one of our master-level nonlinear-mentality logicians, or 'No-men,' has a chance to examine it and render a preliminary model. I cannot estimate the time involved: It could be tomorrow or ten years from now. The master No-Men select their queries to study according to their own intuitive patterns. Can this phone be programmed to seek you out if the return message is sent there?"

After Clayton hung up, Gosseyn said, "Did you notice how pretty the girl was?"

Clayton nodded and said, "She must have been at least partially trained in their nonlinear logic." The Null-A women of Venus were also particularly attractive due to their training: The male mind subconsciously recognized the aura of success surrounding a good potential mate.

Gosseyn said, "You should ask Hayakawa's computers to formulate a prototype of assumptions based on the idea that the other thought-sciences found in the galaxy may be more significant than we thought: Routine Null-A training should allow us to adjust the minds of our population here to the new pattern in short order. We are running the risk of overconfidence."

The phone rang before he was finished speaking: The teletype chattered briefly, and the paper slid out of the stat-plate:

No-man Bertholec Caleb of Accolon sends his greetings to Null-A Peter Clayton of Venus and advises that he locate an individual calling himself Gilbert Gosseyn, the last survivor of the previous human-occupied galaxy, and immediately send said individual, or one of his duplicates, to one or more of the planets listed below, where events have a suspicious discontinuity with previous social psychology. This list is prioritized according to the degree of deviance over time. Locating this individual should not be difficult for you, since no doubt he is reading this message. After he has saved us from Enro, Gosseyn can report to the Special Police of the League for questioning about his role in killing Ifvrid Madrisol and the other League Councilmen.

The highest name on the list was the planet Petrino in the Quintuplet Cluster near the Galactic Core: a world Patricia Hardie suspected of corrupting Null-A for unspeakable purposes. Had she fled Gorgzid, or had she been abducted?

Gosseyn wondered if Planet Petrino might hold the answer.

CLAYTON shook hands with Gosseyn at the spaceport. Gosseyn had booked passage aboard not one but several ships, one of which would take him on the first leg of his intended journey.

In his parting words with Clayton, Gosseyn said, "Your next move, if it is obvious to me, will be equally obvious to Enro, who may be watching us right now."

Clayton nodded. Both men had seen the schematics for the Sphere technology. Even the planet Corthid, with its immense industrial base, its huge and highly trained and highly motivated population, had not been able to create the main inner workings of one of the great Space-time Stability Spheres of the Primordial Men. Venus was mostly uninhabited, and her population, while paramount in social and psychological training, was tiny compared to that of the great industrial centers of the Interstellar League.

To create the millions of Spheres needed to preserve the galaxy from the Shadow Effect would be a massive undertaking, requiring the full cooperation of all the populations of all the civilized worlds.

Even to begin, Venus would have to send emissaries and agents to eighteen remaining major member-states of the Interstellar League, including Accolon and Petrino, and would need to win the cooperation of as many Imperial worlds and nonaligned worlds as possible.

Because of the possibility that Enro might be watching them, Clayton said nothing but the obvious: "Enro is operating within a very short time-frame. He must act before the galaxy organizes against him. He can only operate if the madness of mutual mistrust and hatred between the Interstellar League and the Greatest Empire continues. Obviously, the Empress Reesha is the key to that."

Clayton peered closely at Gosseyn. "Has the Games Machine been able to confirm whether your extra brain is insane or not?" Because Gosseyn had frowned slightly at the mention of her name.

Gosseyn said, "The basic problem is that my extra brain is not connected directly to my cortex. The Games Machine laid out a program of training to break the neurotic fixation it has developed—a program that will take several months to carry out, since it involves training some of the gray matter in the extra brain to act as a cortex, and make rational distinctions. Until that point, it will be like a child, unable to distinguish between make-believe and real. At the moment, I have no choice but to continue, being continually alert to the danger that this fascination for a fictional wife from a set of false memories will interfere in the near future with my work."

THE twenty-five thousand light-years from Earth to the Quintuplet Cluster was made in a series of six distorter jumps. This cluster was one of the most massive within the galaxy, a spherical cloud of hundreds of thousands of stars, nearly all of them giants and supergiants far more massive than the sun.

Gosseyn stood on the observation deck as the *Star of Petrine* was preparing for her final jump. He stared in wonder at a nebula stained cerise and rose with starlight, containing approximately ten solar masses' worth of ionized gas that was ejected by the supermassive star at its core countless years ago. V4647 Sgr, known to Earthly astronomers as "the Pistol Star," was a supergiant, larger and more active than any other star in the galaxy: over a hundred times the mass and ten million times the brightness of Sol. Even from here, a depot station fifty light-years away, the star and the surrounding nebula blazed brighter than the full moon as seen from Earth.

The view switched. It seemed like a moment to Gosseyn, but since twenty decimal points was not perfect similarity, from the frame of reference of the outside universe, perhaps as much as ten hours had passed during the distorter jump. The ship was now hanging above a world of pearly gray cloud, with small gaps in the cloud cover here and there disclosing dazzling glimpses of blue ocean or green jungle. The planet was orbiting a dull red ember of a star, so dim that it took Gosseyn a moment to pick it out from the background. The light from this primary was almost too weak to be seen by the naked eye. But the world still shined and glittered in the dazzle of light, but this light was from the Pistol Star, some eleven light-years away. The light traveled over a decade to fall upon this world but was still so bright, even at such a distance, that it defined the bright and dark hemispheres of the planet. The world of Petrino had a day-night cycle, for the rotation of the globe made the distant supergiant rise and set just as other stars did.

The planet below waned from a full, dazzling circle to a shining crescent as the ship orbited to the nightside. The reddish light from the world's nearby primary cast a slightly larger (though much dimmer) crescent. Both here and in the darker, nighttime areas, Gosseyn could detect small clusters of light, where the tops of towers, no doubt miles high, peered above the roof of the cloud cover. With his extra brain, he could detect, even from this distance, the busy electronic and atomic power flows both on the planet and in orbit around it: The energy use, industrial and military, was much more than that of Earth or Venus.

Gosseyn turned away from the window and surveyed the crowded lounge. There was a bar along one side of the observation lounge, and several small tables scattered in the gloom. The room was kept dimly lit, so that the starry fields outside would be more visible.

The same man had been tailing Gosseyn ever since the final leg of the journey, when he had switched space liners at a planet called Gela 21. Gosseyn saw him now, in the lounge.

The man was disguised quite expertly, even taking that extreme measure that his neuroelectric brain patterns (detectable by Gosseyn's extra brain), which were as unique as fingerprints, were being blocked and distorted by special webbing beneath the man's well-made flesh mask.

If Gosseyn had not spent the hours of the trip experimenting with his recently learned Predictor power and had not seen a vision of the same man occupying the lounge of whatever ship Gosseyn randomly selected to jump to, Gosseyn would not have been suspicious of him.

Gosseyn foresaw that, about a minute from now, after he confronted the man and was threatened in return, he could memorize the man's body with his extra brain. The action of the organic distorter in his extra brain cut off whatever future might be hidden beyond.

Gosseyn realized the psychological danger of relying too heavily on the prediction images. He had seen Leej deliberately following whatever the most likely future paths might be in order to make the futures coming after that easier to see far-off. It was a strategy that must eventually lead to a habit of overcaution, of lack of imagination: He wondered if the technologically backward culture of Yalerta's Predictor-aristocrats, the haughty inability of Leej to accept frustration of her erotic fixations, eventually leading to her extravagant act of self-sacrifice, been the result.

He could see another future-path, this one clear of blind spots, where he merely returned to his cabin for the remainder of the voyage. Gosseyn disregarded this safer path.

Gosseyn walked up to the table where the man was seated and pretending to read a book. He looked up. His face, at the moment, was old, lined, and gray. He closed the book on his finger, a casual gesture, but Gosseyn decided there must be a weapon in it, because his extra brain registered the circuits in the book jumping to an energy level far above what would be needed by a text memory tube.

"May I help you?" the old man said. He was dressed in dark, simple clothing of conservative cut. Nothing that would attract attention in a crowd. The book was a travelogue, just the kind of thing a passenger on a space liner would carry.

Gosseyn took a seat and said in a conversational tone, "Your eyes impress me. I assume the pupils are painted on some sort of one-way film or cusp you wear like a contact lens, but you have a system for turning them in one direction or another while your real eyes beneath are watching something else."

The man took a sip of his drink with his free hand. He was evidently pondering whether to continue the masquerade. The flesh mask on his face, as far as Gosseyn could tell, was perfect. The man could drink and eat with no seam showing around his lips. Perhaps the artificial flesh extended all the way inside his lips and cheeks?

But his nervous system flows were steady, not jumpy. He was someone who was cool under pressure, at least. He stood, leaving both his drink and his book on the table, and nodded his head slightly toward Gosseyn. "You embarrass me, sir. My face is quite unsightly while I undergo reconstructive surgery: I had my physician create this prosthetic for me, that I might pass without comment. Now, if you will excuse me? It is not my habit to discuss my personal matters with strangers."

He started to step away from the table. Gosseyn reached out and grabbed his arm. "Hold on," said Gosseyn. "I'd like to know why and, frankly, how you are following me." For Gosseyn had switched ships not once but several times during his journey, usually by booking two cabins on two different vessels and similarizing himself and his luggage from one to the next after takeoff.

The man leaned in and hissed, "Careful, friend. There is a blaster tied to a mass-detection circuit pointed at your heart. Attempt to follow me, or make any sudden moves, and the energy of an atomic pile goes off right here."

Gosseyn was not sure if the man was lying: Again, his neural flows were calm and undisturbed. The energy Gosseyn detected in the book lying on the table, an electron-tube arrangement hidden in its spine, was not powerful enough to be atomic, but distorters gave off no energy signature before activation, and so the weapon could operate by faster-than-light distorter principles. Could a distorter matrix be made so small?

Gosseyn realized that there was too much he did not know. There were too many worlds in the galaxy, too many advances in technology, for one man from a world newly introduced into galactic commerce to be familiar with.

Gosseyn merely tightened his grip, memorized the man's body, and set up a cue to trigger similarity to a spot of deck he had memorized in his cabin that morning.

A tense moment passed. He did not activate the cue. Gosseyn did not want to similarize himself and the man out of the room, for fear that the disappearance of his body mass would trigger the weapon. An atomic discharged in this confined space might well kill everyone on the observation deck, or even several decks of the ship, if the energy breached hull plates behind him. But if the man, or some compatriot of his, were controlling the weapon remotely, he evidently did not wish to fire at Gosseyn, not while Gosseyn held the man in his grip.

Gosseyn turned his head to study the book lying on the table. It took him the normal long moment to memorize its atomic structure. But the moment his head was turned, a shock burned his hand, and the pain jarred his arm and made him release the man. Gosseyn cried out, startled, and began to stand up but saw a flux in the energy signature of the book at his sudden motion.

He turned his head and looked out through the transparent hull, memorized the outer few layers of atoms, and triggered the book to go there. It disappeared from the tabletop and reappeared tumbling alongside the ship, touching the surface of the window. There was no air or relative motion, of course, so the book maintained its position, pages pressed up against the transparent hull.

There was no explosion, no discharge. Nonetheless, the passengers noticed the pale rectangle of the book appearing suddenly out of nothing, and it seemed huge against the backdrop of the planet behind it, because there were no visual cues as to the distance. Someone shouted hoarsely, and the people at the tables came to their feet, voices loud.

Gosseyn stood and turned, but the man had disappeared. The exit was suddenly crowded with nervous passengers eager to leave the lounge, and Gosseyn neither saw the man, nor could he pick out one nervous system signature amid the neural-electric "noise" of a roomful of startled and annoyed people.

Gosseyn stepped away from the observation deck himself and found a quiet spot, a maintenance closet, whose electric lock his extra brain could short-circuit. He brought the book back into his hand. It was steaming with the cold of space. Again his extra brain detected the energy levels fluctuating. He opened the spine with a tool he found on the shelf here.

The circuit inside was not a weapon. It was a simple distance-locator. The book could be set to audio, and it would read itself aloud while there was someone nearby listening, but if it detected no human-sized masses near, it would shut off. The mild electromagnetic fluctuations Gosseyn had been detecting had not been connected to anything other than the normal reading circuits.

And yet they seemed abnormally strong. He found a tracking screen pasted to the back cover. The book had been modified to track the configurations of several people over a number of yards, each individual within the scan radius tagged according to his particular biometric contour. It was a rather clever method of tracking an individual in a crowded room, especially an individual whose unique nervous system structure rendered him distinct. Only a very close inspection—or an extra brain that could trace electronic vibrations—would have detected the reading circuit's modification from its original innocent purpose.

But the range was surely insufficient to track Gosseyn when he distorter-jumped from one ship to another.

He decided he had no time to waste with this. There were lifeboats on every deck of the great space liner, fifty-foot torpedo-shaped machines, each with her own small distorter-atomic power combination engine. He strolled casually from his maintenance closet to the nearest lifeboat, paused, and used his prognostication power to examine the future. He could see small, clear pictures in his imagination of what would happen, up to about fifteen minutes from now. He would launch the boat, which would decouple from the hull of the liner with explosive bolts. The ship's alarm would go off, and the radio board would light up with messages from the captain of the liner, which Gosseyn would not answer. He would similarize the man following him into the small cabin of the boat, with a cue in Gosseyn's extra brain tagged to retreat at similarity speeds back to his cabin aboard the ship if he suffered any pain, shock, fear, or surprise. The man would appear, apparently in the middle of a costume change, for he would be naked from the waist up, wearing no mask. His face and upper chest should show a hideous net of scars, as if from a powerful electrical burn. The head was hideous, a fleshless skull of muscle and nerve, coated with transparent medicinal plastic, the eyes lidless, the nose cropped. The faceless man would turn and raise his hand . . . a flare of intense, white light . . . and then, a blur occluded the vision.

Gosseyn no doubt would use his distorter power at

that point, or perhaps the faceless man had some ability to distort the metric of space-time that resulted in the same effect: a break of normal, linear causation and hence a blankness in the vision of the future.

Of course, the moment of Gosseyn's death, when his memories were transmitted to a waiting Gosseyn body, might also distort the fabric of time sufficiently to blur the prediction-vision. Were any of his bodies, hidden long ago by Lavoisseur, even in range?

On the other hand, if this faceless man was carrying a weapon of tremendous power, it might be better to have him away from a ship of innocent people. Gosseyn winced at the idea of the type of fantastic energies needed to overwhelm his complex of defenses being un-leashed aboard the confined spaces of a starship.

Well, the future was not set in stone. He opened the hatch—the alarms automatically rang—and launched. During the moment when the little boat spun away from the giant space liner, Gosseyn memorized a patch of deck within the lifeboat, as well as the electronic patterns of the faster-than-light distorter-radio.

Then he similarized himself back to his own cabin and triggered the cue to similarize the faceless man into the space-boat. The space-boat was even now visible through the porthole in Gosseyn's cabin, dwindling in the distance.

He used his extra brain to send his voice over the radio to the space-boat. "I would still like to know how you managed to follow me."

Gosseyn could feel the trickle of power in the area: The circuit was open, but the man was not responding. Through the porthole, Gosseyn could see two larger sideboats had been launched by the captain, to go re-cover the space-boat.

Over the radio he mentioned the approaching rescuers. "I suspect you have some weapon of sufficient power to destroy the sideboats approaching your position. If you open fire on them, I can similarize you out into the vacuum."

The man's voice was remarkably cultured and smooth toned. "Obviously I cannot reveal my methods over an open radio. Can you remove me from this embarrassing situation? My poor rescuers would be shocked to see my face in its current state. Perhaps we could meet in person? We have much to discuss."

Gosseyn attempted to see the future, but, of course, no picture could form. A moment from now he was going to distort the faceless man into this cabin, and this blocked further visions of the future.

What happened was this. The man appeared in the cabin, between Gosseyn's bed and the half-open door leading into the water closet, where there was a mirror over the sink, and sockets for self-moving razors and the like. The man was unarmed. Instead of turning to face Gosseyn, who was behind him, the man cocked his hideously scarred, bald head to one side, staring toward the half-open door. Because it looked so much like the skull-face was staring at itself in the mirror, Gosseyn did not immediately recognize the gesture, though it was one he himself did every day.

The faceless man was memorizing the power output from the electric socket. Gosseyn realized this only when the lightning bolt struck him, knocking him into painful unconsciousness.

25

Every model of the universe, being an abstraction, is inaccurate: The process itself of modeling creates structural barriers to the comprehension.

Don't worry, Cousin. I used a nonlethal voltage," came the cultured, melodic tones from the horrid, skull-like face. "I had to guess about your body weight, though: There should only be a small scar."

Gosseyn came groggily to consciousness. He was in some storeroom or hold belowdecks, lying on his back on his numb arms. From the strange silence in the air, the lack of the whisper of ventilation or the throb of engines, he guessed that the ship had landed, making the final distorter jump from orbit to a surface berth.

The faceless man was seated cross-legged on the metal deck. Crates, chained down, loomed to either side, forming a little nook where the two were hidden. Gosseyn noted that he sensed no neural flows from the man: The electric system of the ship, the atomic pile in the stern, were likewise blank to him. When he attempted to memorize the area just behind where his captor was sitting, nothing happened.

Gosseyn said thickly, for his tongue and his jaw were still numb, "What did you do to me?"

"I injected your brain stem with a mild neurotoxin, which is temporarily relaxing your space-distortion-control lobe. Amazing, isn't it, that even one of the Higher Orders can be neutralized, if one knows the precise situation."

Gosseyn shook his head. "But you don't know. That part of my brain was balancing the energy flows in the primal moment of the universe, fifteen billion years ago. If you relaxed it, there will be a reaction. Similarization effects are not instantaneous, but something has been set in motion." Gosseyn was not sure about the details of such immense energy structures, but assuming the similarity properties were roughly the same as sending an equal mass of electron volts across fifteen billion light-years, the effect, whatever it was, should manifest within his local frame of reference in roughly . . .

Gosseyn did the calculation in his head and then smiled to himself. "Never mind. There is no immediate danger." Twenty-decimal-point accuracy worked out to be about ten hours for every thousand light-years, so the time span involved was one and a half million hours, or 171 years.

The man said, "Enlighten me. Which Gilbert Gosseyn are you? The one who killed every man on the Security Council of the Interstellar League? Or the one who kidnapped the Empress Reesha, in order to whip the Imperial planets up into a war frenzy? Or the one who was spotted by long-range satellite orbiting the planet Corthid a few hours before the whole world was swallowed in the same Shadow Effect that is currently spreading throughout the space of the Core worlds, spreading faster than the speed of light, and increasing in speed?"

Gosseyn tried to sit up and found that his hands were bound behind him by electronic handcuffs, the kind that could shock or stun a prisoner upon a radio signal.

Gosseyn said, "Who are you, and how did you trace me?"

The horrid fleshless face could form no expression, but the voice betrayed a hint of condescending humor: "Come now. You are my prisoner. I ask; you answer. It's traditional."

Gosseyn leaned back to ease the pressure on his arms. "It's not that simple. If you were an officer, if you were within your jurisdiction, we would be in a police station, not hiding here."

"My court sits wherever I sit, and I am all my officers," the faceless man said, his voice smooth with an ironic, self-deprecating humor. "And yes, we are hiding. From your foes, I think, as well as mine."

"Court?"

"I am Anslark Dzan of Glorious Dzan."

"I don't recognize the name."

"Prince Anslark. Anslark the Marred. Are you from some newly discovered world?"

"Yes. From Venus in the Sol System. How would you know the location and composition of my extra brain but not know my origins?"

"The space-controlling centers of the brain are located in neural ganglia just above the spine. It is a family trait of the royal house of Dzan, and my spies tell me the Predictors of Yaltera have the same structure in a stunted form. So you are not a cousin? I had been meaning to ask you how you moved my whole body from one point to another."

Gosseyn said, "You can control electronic flows between two memorized points, but nothing more complicated than that."

Anslark of Dzan nodded briefly.

Gosseyn estimated that the Dzan prince could form a fifteen-decimal-point similarity. Electromagnetic waves differed one to the next so little that, for all practical purposes, they were already similar to five to ten decimal points to any given spot in the universe.

Gosseyn said, "I can perform a more exact similarization than you can, on the order of what a distorter circuit can do. How did you find me?"

"Caleb the No-man sent me. We knew your destination was Petrino. Once we confirmed your identity, the man who cannot be killed, who can be anywhere in one step, my superiors decided I was the only one qualified to keep an eye on you. After that, it was just a matter of putting agents with portable distorters hidden in briefcases on every ship in every port you visited, so that I could swap places with them and be sent from ship to ship as you were sighted. How did you find me? I have been trained by an Accolon No-man in how to avoid patterns of behavior that attract intuitive notice."

Gosseyn said, "After we come to an agreement, I'll tell you."

The fleshless red skull-face nodded. No expression could form in those lidless eyes, but Gosseyn sensed a wary tension in the man's neuroelectric patterns.

Gosseyn said, "Enro's people have already taken over Petrino, haven't they? You are hiding from the customs officers. Since you have both a portable distorter tuned to a planet of a distant star as well as the ability to control electric circuits around you, I am assuming the customs officers are equipped with some special technical advantage you estimate is overwhelming."

Again there was no expression, but a hint of cautious admiration crept into Prince Anslark's voice: "You are trained in some logic system that allows you to make intuitive deductions?"

Gosseyn said, "It is not intuition but a flexible mechanism to adjust the nervous system to reality based on learned habits of multivalued, scientific thought. Your behavior does not fit into any other model."

The man stood up. "Surely the resemblance between this system, the No-men of Accolon, and the Royal Family of Dzan cannot be coincidence. The matter bears investigating. Do you have myths on your world of a universal disaster, from which a pair of men and a pair of women survived?"

"Something like that," admitted Gosseyn. He heard the lock of the handcuffs click open behind his back. Anslark apparently had very fine control over electric circuits in his environment. Gosseyn brought his hands in front of him and removed the remaining cuff. He asked, "Does your Royal Family have a custom of placing its royal infants in some sort of sensory-deprivation tank for an extended period?"

Anslark said, "It is no secret. We sleep for several months within that prehistoric starship which brought our first parents to Dzan, and the electronic brain aboard—which my great-grandfather Urien Dzan had partially repaired—modifies our nervous systems. I am the last of my line. Enro's troops bombarded our Sacred Dome and destroyed the ancient machine, thinking it was a blasphemous mockery of their Crypt of the Sleeping God. How did you know?"

Gosseyn said, "My creator enforced a similar regime of electronic training on me, when I was lying in a full-grown but dormant state."

"Count yourself lucky, friend."

"Why?"

Anslark pointed at his own ruined features. "You have no family. No fierce competition for royal prerogatives."

Gosseyn said, "I have a twin."

"Would he run lightning in a brother's face for pleasure?"

"He has a larger target, and his motivations are more neurotic than that, but his crimes are basically the same as that, yes. Except he seeks to create a totalitarian state embracing every world. How long till your drug works its way out of my nervous system?"

"What is to be our agreement?" asked Anslark.

Gosseyn said curtly, "That we shall both act rationally."

Anslark said, "Coming from you, I will trust that means what I think it does."

Anslark stepped around behind Gosseyn. Gosseyn felt the cold sting of a needle on his neck. A moment later came a warm, slightly painful sensation, tingling in his neck muscles and the back of his skull.

"How did you find me?" Anslark reminded him.

"Prediction power. It operates by similarization of the brain pattern of the Predictor in two time-segments to negate the illusion of space-time, and allow thought-information across the gap. I have the ability of one of the visionaries of Yalerta. . . ."

Then he stopped, for his awareness of the energy flows

in the area had returned. A clear, small emotionless voice spoke into his brain: *A second target has become aware of this unit. Direct additional circuits XX-0112 through XY-6705 to recalcitrant area . . . effect negative . . . stepping up power to secondary backups . . . redirect . . . effect negative . . . engaging tertiary circuits—*

Robot brains were directing a pattern of mind-control force-fields into this area. Gosseyn could also sense the neuroelectric excitement of Anslark's secondary brain, like a bright, hot point of fire burning at the top of his brain stem.

Gosseyn said, "Are you aware of what the robots are saying?"

Anslark said calmly, "No. I am redirecting their electric forces into safety contact points in the ship, to ground the signal. It is only a matter of time until my defensive system is overwhelmed. Can you do anything? Get us out of here?"

Gosseyn said, "Getting out of places is my special talent." By the time he was finished speaking, they were aboard the space-boat, which had been restored to its launch tube in the hull of the *Star of Petrine.*

The vision-plate on the control board showed the great space liner was resting in a launch cradle on the planet surface, but the spaceport was an ancient one, aboveground, and the domelike fabric stretched across the many acres where ships rested was little more than a sheet of synthetic material meant to keep out the rain.

The acceleration pressed them against their couches as the space-boat shot from the side of the space liner and rocketed skyward. There was no jar as the little boat tore through the roof. The pinpoint of the Pistol Star was brighter than the sun seen from Earth, and it shined a harsh glare among the strange, gorgeous buildings of Petrino, edifices of marble and green copper. Even the tallest skyscrapers were covered with vines and yellowed with age: The overall effect was one of immense antiquity.

Anslark said, "I don't suppose there is any way to get back to my cabin? My extra faces and other equipment are there."

Gosseyn said, "Sorry, I forgot to tell you that the moment I transmitted us here, I had the vision showing that we are about to be fired upon."

A cylindrical machine six thousand yards long, a battlecruiser, was dropping out of the dazzling white sky. The radio on the control board clattered to life: "To unidentified space-boat, this is Petrino Civilian Air Control. Do not change velocity or heading. Prepare to be examined by non-Aristotelian robot psychologists."

Gosseyn's extra brain detected a distortion effect as some remote unit, similar to a lie detector, attuned itself to his nervous system.

And Gosseyn was fighting to retain his sanity.

26

In nature, the composition of a phenomenon is known by its observed behavior: Where the behavior shows consistency, a correct abstract model can be formed for events of those types, but the abstraction is limited to those types.

In his head, Gosseyn heard the cold voice: *"Target acquired! Hypo-coded reflexes to render subject compliant to Total Loyalty directive not found. Subject is in violation of thought-conformity laws. Engaging mechanism for brain-imprint."*

He felt the mass of imprinted thought-emotions trying to force its way into his brain: a psychotic affection for the planet Petrino, combined with an infantile terror, programmed to be felt at the most basic level of the subconscious, for symbols and uniforms and slogans of the ruling party of Petrino.

Had it succeeded, it would have been a massive overload of his emotions, even if his opinions had been otherwise: a perfect mechanical method of propaganda, a direct method of hypnotic indoctrination.

The technology was not fundamentally different from the methods used to train interplanetary travelers with new languages instantly, except that it used Null-A technical methods to effect subconscious nerve-word associations.

But they were the methods of an insane Null-A. The rhythms of the robot-controlled electron tubes were trying to discourage certain nerve paths and encourage others: trying to replace a delicate system of truth-to-fact word-emotion associations with false-to-fact ones.

Instinctively, Gosseyn performed a cortical-thalamic pause.

Normally, the effect of this pause was to break the cycle of perception-emotion-reaction by which humans form their behavior-patterns and adapt them to their sense impressions. However, in this case, Gosseyn felt a searing pain, and his vision began to turn black, as intolerable nerve-pressure was brought to bear on his central nervous system.

"Target identified . . . nervous system of recalcitrant type . . . cortex-thalamic nerve pathways detected . . . incapacitate! . . . Adding additional voltage to neural signal now!"

The robot-directed web of electronic forces had reacted instantly to any conscious interference in the thalamic cycle: This was a weapon specifically designed to identify and electrocute any target with Null-A training.

The voltage jarred Gosseyn, and he could neither move nor speak, his muscles paralyzed. The joystick of the space-boat was in his hands, but his muscles were locked: The space-boat was hurling blindly through the air in low parabola, and the ground slowly swung into view while Gosseyn sat frozen at the controls.

Gosseyn tried to similarize himself to one of his memorized spots: Nothing happened. Unable to perform the Null-A pause, Gosseyn could not break the rising tide of panic now pounding his temples. Twisted or not, X had the genius of Lavoisseur, the expertise needed to program these deadly robots with specific circuits to detect and neutralize nerve-flows in Gosseyn's extra brain.

Gosseyn remembered the comment of the Games Machine, that nerve-suppression circuits only affect what they are designed to affect. So when he tried to summon up his shadow-shape, nothing interfered.

His ability to assume a shadowy form was automatic. An immense amount of technical data, a lifetime of training, had been expertly imprinted into his mind by his far-future selves. Instinctively he used a memorization technique to hold his own body in a type of coherence, to keep it "identified" to itself even as it entered a non-identity condition with the surrounding environment.

The world around him grew blurred and foggy, though the basic shapes of objects could still be dimly seen: the shining curve of the control board, the looming figure of Anslark. There was a technique to sharpen his vision by allowing incoming photons to achieve a greater degree of similarity than the shadow-shape normally permitted, but Gosseyn dared not employ that technique yet.

"Target attunement lost . . . data unclear . . . employ increasing voltage until incapacitated target destruction is confirmed."

The robots reacted: An electrical current of immense voltage suddenly appeared within the volume occupied by his shadow-body. Since his form was now made of matter out of similarity with normal time-space, his atoms and molecules no longer recognized or reacted to the molecular, atomic, and electronic patterns of particle behavior around him. The electrons surged through the space his body occupied, ignoring and being ignored.

Gosseyn, again prompted by his buried training, made the world darker and blurrier around him, decreasing his attachment to the surrounding behaviors of the photons and electrons. The lightning bolt flashed in the middle of his body, vaporizing the padding of the acceleration couch, setting insulation smoldering. Blue sparks snapped from the bent metal framework.

But that was all. Even as greater and ever greater voltages poured into the tiny space of the space-boat cabin, a strange shining glow appeared on all the metal surfaces within the ship, they grew brighter, but Anslark was preventing the electricity from flowing. Immense static charge was being built up, but neither the air molecules nor the metal interior of the boat was conducting it. The electricity shined from every surface, but it harmed nothing.

With his dark and blurred vision, Gosseyn saw Anslark touch the radio control. The man said softly, "This is space-boat calling Petrino Civilian Air Control vessel. Something strange has happened to the pilot of the boat. I am utterly loyal to Petrino and will obey all lawful commands given to me. May I speak to your commander that I may identify myself to him? Are you standing near the radio set, Commander?"

"This is Commander Contrebis of the Standardization Committee. Are you ready to land and yield yourself? Perfect loyalty demands nothing less than absolute obedience."

"Commander Contrebis, this is Prince Anslark Dzan of Glorious Dzan. I never yield."

The glow in the cabin vanished. Gosseyn could detect the communication line becoming charged with the immense voltage the robot units had been pouring into the cabin. Anslark, of course, simply prevented the electricity from returning along the path of least resistance back into the space-boat.

The vision-plate showed smoke pouring from the shattered midsection of the battlecruiser. The great ship began to recede into the sky, leaving a trail of black smoke behind her as she sought the safety of the upper atmosphere.

Of course, the barrage of missiles from her rear tubes came into view as the space-boat's proximity alarm shrieked.

GOSSEYN returned to solid form to find that the robot units had broken off their automatic attack: Their central control from the ship had been broken. A cortical-thalamic pause was sufficient, for now, to hold at bay the psychic damage from the brutal, robotic nerve-training method: He would need more careful Null-A conditioning to make certain all his nerve cells were clear of the artificial charges that had been impressed on them. That was for later.

For now, swiftly, they had but a moment to defeat the missile fire. Luckily, the space-boat's control panel had automatically focused their plates, one on each of the incoming collision-threats. All the incoming missiles could be seen at a glance. Anslark suppressed the mechanisms of the missiles' electronic brains, while Gosseyn memorized their structures. Anslark similarized a bolt of energy from the space-boat's reactor into one of them, heating it instantly to the ignition point: Gosseyn similarized the energy of that explosion into the others, to explode them a safe distance from the boat.

At the moment of the explosions, Anslark deflected the radar-beams coming from the ground stations below. Meanwhile, half a dozen other warships were descending through the atmosphere toward them, hull plates red-hot with the reentry speed. These ships were scattered, a search pattern, not converging toward the space-boat's location: This told Gosseyn that they were being directed from the momentarily blind ground stations.

While thus radar-invisible, Gosseyn drove the space-boat suddenly out from the cloud of missile debris, across several miles, and, still faster than the speed of sound, into a river nearby. He similarized a long cylindrical volume of water out of his path, creating a momentary vacuum, so that the boat did not shatter when it passed below the level of the rest of the water. The boat did not even get wet until they had decelerated on roaring jets to a near stop, gravity plates groaning, and then the collapsing hollow tube of water momentarily exploded into bubbling steam, the river water carrying away the friction-heat of their reckless passage through the atmosphere.

Now they lay in a small underground cave Gosseyn had carved out of the rock by memorizing huge chunks of stone before the bore and similarizing them into the space behind.

Gosseyn said, "What interests me about this prediction power of mine is that the vision showed me only the missiles, not the neural-electronic attack, nor my retreat into shadow-form." He explained that the Predictors of Yalerta had not been able to predict the Follower: The shadow-condition obviously nullified the energy connections through time the Predictors were sensitive to, in much the same way Gosseyn's own distortion powers did.

He should not have been surprised to learn that Anslark knew more about Secoh than he did. The royal government of Dzan was one of the nineteen major members of the League. Of course their spies had reported thoroughly on all the members of the Gorgzid royal court before and after the war: When Secoh slew the Sleeping God of his cult, he had briefly assumed his shadow-form. It was done in a setting public enough (all the high officers and priesthood of the Greatest Empire had been present) that the identity of Secoh as the rumored Follower had been confirmed.

Anslark said, "The Follower had been committing a series of political assassinations among the League military experts and civilian authorities in preparation for the war. This eerie shadow-shape was a figure spoken of in terrified whispers, only glimpsed, never photographed. When Enro heard of the death of Thorson by a superhuman immortal, of course he dispatched his special killer to investigate, thinking the Follower would be immune to whatever weapon had been used to slay Thorson. And, more important, Enro knew Secoh, his fanatic high priest, would be immune to whatever temptation had pulled Thorson away from his duty."

Anslark's next question was an interesting one: "My information is that the Follower could use similarized energy as a weapon, even as we who are of the royal blood of Dzan. But you had to become solid to use your extra brain's distorter on the missiles. It looked like you lost the use of your other special abilities when in your shadow-form. What did the Follower know that you don't?"

Gosseyn was not sure. But unless he discovered the Follower's technique, for Gosseyn the shadow-form was strictly defensive.

HE similarized the two of them back to Gosseyn's cabin aboard the *Star of Petrino*. Anslark asked for his book back: He wanted to use it to be sure the corridor outside was clear of customs officers before he opened the door.

Gosseyn said, "Permit me." He foresaw a route that would carry Anslark back to his cabin without being seen by anyone. The cabin door itself was locked, as the door key had been left behind with Anslark's clothing and gear. Gosseyn was able to step through the door in his shadow-form, solidify, and open the door from the inside. Anslark gathered his gear. This included a suit of specially woven strands that, when exposed to a controlled energy field projected from his nervous system, stiffened into impact-resistant ablative cloth. This armor would deflect nothing stronger than a small-caliber bullet or a heat-induction ray in the kilokelvin range, but it was lightweight, easily concealed.

Gosseyn similarized them both back to the space-boat. Anslark opened a folding box, which contained nine or ten fully made up and lifelike masks, along with two more smooth flesh-colored blanks, a set of wigs, and an array of electronic medical tools. Anslark donned the face of a youngish, thin-cheeked, dark-haired man and spent a moment in the mirror adjusting the flesh tones, adding moles and marks of sunburn. Gosseyn stared in fascination at a tiny throbbing vessel in the mask's forehead that appeared when Anslark tested the anger-blush response.

Anslark said, "I bent the signals carrying the mind-conditioning patterns away from myself, but I notice you did not do the same. Are you now loyal to the ideals, whatever they are, of the Psychiatric Standardization Committee of Petrino?"

Gosseyn shook his head. "Even an untrained man would not be convinced by that technique, not by a short, onetime exposure. It was actually an examination, at least at first: The imprint would have fallen into previously established nerve channels had we been previously exposed. More sinister is the fact that the robots were programmed to check for the nerve paths established by repeated cortical-thalamic pauses. These were hunting for Null-A's."

Anslark said thoughtfully, "If an untrained man needed repeated exposures to be affected, then this is not the means Enro is using to take over this planet."

Gosseyn nodded. "As a tool of political revolution, it would be useless except in the hands of a small, highly loyal, and highly motivated cabal of professionals. And being used so openly, it is not meant to establish control, but to maintain it. Enro's already taken over."

Prince Anslark's new face had a wide range of emotions: He could curl merely part of the mask's mouth, quirk an eyebrow, and make the artificial eyes glitter with mirth. "And did you notice the important part, Mr. Gosseyn? The robots were centrally controlled. That means the cabal maintains strict control over this technology, with all the secrecy and internal monitoring that strict control implies. In this computerized age of stat-plates and electronic brains, that means there is a thread of electrons, no matter how that thread is hidden, passed through relays, or scrambled, which links any one of those mind-control robots to the central headquarters. The real headquarters."

THERE was a toolkit aboard the space-boat, meant for making any of the numerous repairs needed during an emergency. The brain in Anslark's book was intelligent enough, after they added more electron tubes to it, to pilot the boat. Anslark laid it facedown on the control panel's stat-plate interface and wired it into the ship's opened circuit boards. He doffed the lifelike mask he had been wearing—this was the only face of Anslark's the space line company and, by now, the Petrino authorities had in their picture-records. He draped it over the headrest of the acceleration couch and programmed it with a few complex sets of expressions and phrases. Then he tightly focused the lens of the radio at it, in case the patrol ship made an incoming call.

The mask was able to produce a fairly complex electroencephalograph signal. It would not have fooled a lie detector, but the circuits of any mind-control robots scanning the interior of the space-boat were probably not built to search for this type of deception. Naturally, it would not react properly, it would not react at all, to the type of warped Null-A imprinting technique the robots were going to use.

Gosseyn said, "I am going to have to leave you behind."

Anslark said, "Carry me. Your clothes and other memorized objects go into the shadow-condition."

Gosseyn said, "Organisms have a lower tolerance for non-identity. I am maintaining a complex balance of electro-chemical and gravitic forces within the shadow-molecule structure of my body when I assume that form. I can increase and decrease my interaction with the surrounding universe: That's why I don't fall to the core of the planet. I doubt I could maintain those delicate balances in another living person's body."

So Anslark remained behind in the cave with the navigation equipment taken bodily from the space-boat. Gosseyn assumed his shadow-form, floated up through the rock to the surface, solidified, and memorized a plot of earth nearby, to which he similarized the space-boat. It was a greater mass than he usually transported, but his capacities seemed to have increased recently. Perhaps it was a side effect of the imprinted training from the far future.

In a moment he was airborne. To save time, he asked the book to pilot the boat into the airspace above a military base and dive groundward. He assumed his shadow-shape during the dive.

Anslark had a sense of humor. When the camera lens lit up, the mask assumed an expression of bored disdain and answered the air traffic officer's increasingly impatient questions and commands with insults.

After the space-boat was destroyed, Gosseyn returned to the cave. "Well?"

Anslark was bent over the glowing surface of the electronic map, calipers and straightedge in his hand. Instead of wearing a look of concentration, his features looked blank and stunned. Since the real Anslark was concentrating, he was not using his electropathy to control the web of fine circuits in his mask.

"They scanned the space-boat with the warped Null-A robots before opening fire. I have the source of the robot control-signals narrowed down to a quarter-mile radius: this block in the city of Munremar on the Great Isthmus linking the Western to the Eastern Continent. There is an energy system there: The pattern reminds me of electromagnetic brains running off an atomic-powered dynamo, but the system is linked in a series configuration, with a continual high-speed feedback into itself, so that the pattern seems to change from moment to moment. It's gigantic. I've never sensed anything like it. . . ."

Gosseyn said somberly, "It's a Games Machine. Programmed not to see if the people of Petrino are sane but to see to it that they have the neurotic complex that creates slavish and unthinking loyalty. An insane Games Machine."

27

The process of false identification takes place at a subconscious level: With proper training, the mind can be made aware of these subliminal processes and subject them to human, as opposed to animal, abstraction.

While the sun was up, Gosseyn could cover ground quickly. His time on Venus had introduced to him the simple, animal pleasure of tree-climbing. From a high vantage he would select a spot on the horizon. Usually, Gosseyn descended from branch to branch to the ground before bringing Anslark to where he was, to spare him the surprise of appearing among the branches of a high tree.

After sunset, going was slower. They hiked several miles until they reached a highway. The machines that sped down the lanes were large, bullet-shaped affairs, rushing by at astonishing speed, but the ten-lane road was strangely vacant of traffic.

They walked until they came to an on-ramp. Here the immense high-speed trucks had to slow nearly to a crawl before turning and accelerating to a merge, but the first three trucks trundling by would not pick up hitchhikers.

Anslark forced the next truck to stop by interfering with its electrical system. The huge dray lumbered to a stop along the road, but the driver did not get out to open his hood or inspect the engine. He merely sat behind the wheel, a look of sullen fear on his sallow features.

When the two men approached, the driver cracked the

window of his cab and asked for their identification badges and internal passports. "You need papers to go from district to district!" he shouted down to them. "Give me your operating numbers—I'll radio it in to the police computer."

Gosseyn sent the man to a memorized position many miles away, a spot up a tree.

It was Anslark who, after less than a minute of driving, found the monitoring devices wired under the dashboard. He said he could prevent the circuits from reporting their location to ground traffic control, but Gosseyn was uneasy.

The countryside seemed to have once been farmland: Under the double-crescent moons of Petrino, dusty and weed-overgrown acres lay fallow. Here and there were empty, burnt-out shells of farmhouses, and abandoned tractors and harvester-robots lay rusting in the moonlight, one every few miles along the way. The corpses of some local animals, Petrine horses and cattle, lay rotting along the roadsides by the score.

The only feature along the road that was not in disrepair was a series of enormous billboards, some of them hundreds of feet high, which lit up with music and blaring announcements as the truck drove past, vast televised images of actors and actresses bawling out slogans and boasts lauding the victories of something called the Northeastern District Three-Year Economic Efficiency Plan.

Gosseyn felt the pressure of the thought-inspection machines examining his nervous system for loyalty-implant paths. These detectors were hidden in the electronic circuits of every blaring billboard. Anslark turned the invisible force-patterns aside, and no alarm was given.

AN hour later, the primary rose, dull and red, in the East, no brighter than the moon seen from Earth, and cast a deceptive shadowy, ruddy light across the dark landscape. But this time, they had traveled four hundred miles or so, and there was a service station built like a metal wall across the several lanes of the highway, pierced by drive-through bays where trucks could be weighed and refueled.

There seemed to be only one attendant, and so the line of trucks waiting for fuel was a long one. Most of the drivers sat or stood near a campfire made in the brush by the roadside culvert, sipping coffee from a tin pot held over the fire on a stick.

Anslark approached the group, saying, "I've never come this route before. What's the procedure?"

The several men eyed him warily. Gosseyn, watching from the shadows nearby, saw the same look in each man: unshaven, unkempt, their uniforms dirty, patched, and ill fitting. But their faces told the real story: These men lived in terror of arbitrary arrest or death. They looked at each other with stubborn wariness, as if trying to decide if Anslark were a police informer. One of them spat on the ground and said, "New rules this week. Show the man your passport, bill of lading, tonnage report, fuel consumption record, and the log from your onboard, as well as your loyalty card and mission tags. He gives you the chit for the mileage and you mark it in the log, and he stamps it."

Another man spoke up: "And you gotta sign for your fuel cells."

The first man nodded, still eying Anslark warily. "Yeah. Like he said. And you gotta turn in your empties, get the numbers in the book, all that."

A younger man, who was lying near the fire half-asleep, tilted back his hat and gave Anslark an unfriendly look. "And you better have a carton of cigarettes or something to give the man; otherwise he puts your empty cells back in and you get about twenty miles before you go dry. And then it's a call in to the ground transport, Faithful Citizen, and we all know what that means."

All the men around the fire stiffened, their eyes now white-rimmed with alarm, but no one made any quick moves. Two or three of the men there slowly put their hands to their belts, where they carried homemade knives, or put a hand into a coat pocket, where Gosseyn could sense the metallic signature of pistols.

Anslark held his hands in plain view and backed away from the group, smiling. Gosseyn saw Anslark walking back among the trucks. He passed a spot where, in the darkness, a man was hiding between two trucks. The man was not visible, but Gosseyn could detect his nerve-actions, and he was sure Anslark was also aware of him.

Anslark was a skilled actor. His reaction was one of convincing surprise when a thin figure stepped out from between two trucks. "Halt there, Faithful Citizen!"

In the weak red light from the starry sky, his features shadowed by his hat brim, it was impossible to tell how old he was—but the voice was husky with age. In one hand he held a crowbar. "You heard any disloyal talk, eh? You have anything to report? Anyone to turn in?"

Anslark said in a voice of lilting mockery, "You're working in pairs, aren't you? The man up by the fire said something disloyal, and you come here to shake a bribe out of anyone who overhears. Is that the racket? You turn me in to the secret police for not reporting the comment. The question is, what stops me from turning you and him in to the soldiers over there?"

On the far side of the service station, two young men, maybe fifteen years old, wearing dark uniforms and carrying heavy power rifles, were playing in an abandoned truck, slashing holes in the skirt of the ground-effect platform with their bayonets and taking swigs from a bottle they passed between them.

The old man's chuckle echoed strangely in the gloom. He hefted the crowbar. "Go ahead, Faithful Citizen. Everything I'm doing is for the good of the Authority. Just flushing out the malcontents is all. What've you got on your truck? Liquor? Cigarettes? Chocolate?"

Two other men came out of the underbrush behind Anslark quite suddenly, grabbing him by the arms, pinning him between them.

The old man said, "Now, Faithful Citizen, your codes? We need your robot-loader to move the containers from your rig to ours, so we need the codes, and numbers from your logbook."

One of the men holding Anslark said in a slow, thick voice, "Eh, Dreel, lookit this feller! He don't have this month's Loyalty tab on his shoulder or nuttin'. These ain't normal duds. He ain't even from Petrino at all, I'm thinking. An off-worlder. Filthy offler!"

"Shaddap," snarled the old man, Dreel. "Why would an offler be driving a rig, eh? He prob'ly just stole those clothes."

The other man said nervously, "This ain't right, Dreel. Let's turn him in and just collect the bounty for wreckers. If we're found meddling with an off-worlder . . ."

Anslark, despite that he was half bent over from the pain of his arms being twisted, spoke in a clear and thoughtful voice. "I have visited your lovely world many times, and been feted by your heads of state. Why, suddenly, am I unwelcome?"

Dreel said harshly, "Off-worlders ain't loyal to Petrino. So they're out to get us. So we gotta get them first. Stands to reason."

The man on Anslark's left, who was twisting his arm up behind his back, chuckled a muddy chuckle. "I heard the Psych Bosses are gunna vote next month and put all them immigrants and job-stealers in jail, kick 'em back to their own planets, offler scum."

Anslark said softly, "You still have elections?"

Dreel said, "'F course! We're a free people!" He shrugged. "But only if you pass your psych test. Gotta loyalty detector in every ballot booth."

Anslark twisted his head, speaking back over the shoulders of the thugs behind him: "Have you heard enough?"

Gosseyn, in his shadow-form, was blended with the darkness beneath the extinguished and broken street lamps lining the road, and so no one noticed his silhouette until he spoke: "I've heard enough."

"Good," said Anslark. "I was getting tired of this." As he straightened up, there was a snap of electricity. The men holding him were thrown from their feet. Bluish sparks tripped across the length of the crowbar in Dreel's hand, and Dreel dropped it with a cry.

The two men were crouching, recovering their balance. Dreel was on his knees and had his scalded hands tucked into his armpits. All three glared, not at Anslark but at Gosseyn, whose shadow-body was partly visible now that he stood near the trucks and the splashed light of their headlights could pick the misty black silhouette out from the night.

Dreel's lips drew back in a snarl of hate. "The Follower!"

The two men fell back away from Gosseyn. "Enro's creature!" said one. The other said, "The Loyalty Machine was right!"

Gosseyn solidified.

Dreel said in a voice of hoarse terror, "It's Gosseyn! The Follower is Gilbert Gosseyn!"

The two young soldiers in the distance noticed the disturbance. One of them raised his rifle to his shoulder, putting his eye to his rifle's photo-multiplying nightscope. He must have seen Gosseyn's face clearly in his scope, for he gave a low cry of terror and pulled the trigger, but the beam emerging from the barrel was diffracted where it passed near Anslark. The bent beam missed Gosseyn and ignited a tree. Prince Anslark turned slowly and raised his hand, and both weapons lit up with sparks. The soldiers threw down their burning rifles and drew long knives from their belts.

The other truck-drivers were stirred from their apathy by the cries. They brought out their pistols and knives, and those that had neither picked up stout sticks from the roadside, or rocks. The mob rushed toward Gosseyn and Anslark, shouting as they came.

In his solid form, Gosseyn transported himself and Anslark back into their truck, which was, by this time, forty miles past the service station barrier. The automatic driving mechanism had been guiding the truck down the road for some minutes, for Gosseyn had similarized the truck onto the stretch of highway he had glimpsed beyond the barrier. The fuel cells that had been loaded from the service station onto the lead truck he now similarized in the cargo bed of this truck: In a moment or so, they could pull over and load the fuel units into the engine.

Within the cabin were uniforms and badges, the paperwork and other materials Gosseyn had memorized from in and around the service station while Anslark had been getting the drivers to tell him what he needed. It was easy enough for Gosseyn to memorize the uniforms worn by two men of his and Anslark's build without memorizing the men wearing them. Gosseyn had brought everything into the cab with him when he brought Anslark. The naked men were somewhere left behind at the station.

Anslark opened his kit and started molding faces to match those showing on their badges. As he worked, Anslark said, "Well, what did you make of all that?"

Gosseyn said in a grim voice, "I had been wondering how Petrino, one of the most cosmopolitan centers of the galaxy, the capital planet of the largest member of the Interstellar League, could have citizens programmed to suffer from xenophobic paranoia. It is far outside the range of normal psychological-social development. But note the psychiatrically sophisticated method of convincing people they still live in a democracy—they still have votes, and perhaps even count the results—while they toil under a totalitarian control-scheme that is destroying their economy, and has already destroyed their moral fiber. Criminals who have convinced themselves that the crime is for the general good of Petrino can escape detection, and the authority is not concerned with maintaining law and order. In fact, law and order is being deliberately broken down." A note of bitterness crept into his voice. "Did you see their farms? Good soil, rich and black, growing nothing but weeds, or left to wash away downstream."

Anslark was staring at him in disbelieving astonishment: an expression he could only be wearing if he put it on his mask deliberately. "Strange what you find worthy of comment, Mr. Gosseyn! I note that they recognized your face! At a glance! They knew your name!"

"The fight-or-flight instinct is an early-evolved structure of the base layer of the nervous system. It is not normal for half-armed or unarmed men to rush a superbeing like the Follower, not without steeling themselves. Subliminal conditioning has linked recognition of me with an instant terror-aggression reflex. . . . It shows the depth of the psychological skills X possesses, perhaps even more than he passed on to Lavoisseur. I also am shocked at the degree of penetration the warped form of Null-A has so rapidly accomplished."

"But how did they know who you were? Three men taken at random, on a random stretch of road . . . the soldier opened fire the moment he saw your face . . . does everyone on this planet know you?"

Gosseyn, instead of answering, turned on the radio and said, "Radio, find me a station that is broadcasting news or comment concerning Gilbert Gosseyn."

There was a short pause while the radio searched. Then, with a click: "Faithful Citizens! The Loyalty Machine of Munremar broadcast this warning as of 21:30 hours Zone Ten time! The next voice you will hear will be that of the Loyalty Machine!"

A cool, unhurried voice came from the radio speaker: "The Predictors of Yalerta, led by the Predictor Yanar, have been cooperating with the Interstellar League against the menace of renewed military threat from the

Greatest Empire. Their local representative reports that several blurs or 'dark areas' their prediction powers cannot penetrate have appeared on the temporal horizon. This indicates the presence of the immortal man, Gilbert Gosseyn of Venus, the notorious murderer of the leading members of the League Security Council, is or soon will be active in the Central District of the Intercontinental Land Bridge, near the Predictors' local headquarters in Munremar."

The voice of the machine was replaced by that of an orator, who alternated between a hypnotic singsong voice and shouts of elemental fury: "Death to Gosseyn! . . . This man is an agent of Enro the Red, and he is utterly ruthless . . . burning helpless women and children . . . devilish powers of his mutant extra brain . . . part of the ongoing effort by off-world forces to destroy Petrino . . . off-world scum! . . . report any suspicious activity. . . . only total loyalty, absolute devotion to your group-leaders and thought-conformity monitors, can save the world. . . . Remember Corthid! . . . All who refuse to be slaves of Enro the Red must unite! Unite!"

Gosseyn snapped off the radio. "Like Corthid, this world has been set up to lure me here. I suspect X means to destroy me and this world at one blow, ridding himself of one more major planet opposing the Greatest Empire. I had not considered the possibility that the delegation of Predictors of Yalerta, which Venus put at the disposal of the Interstellar League toward the conclusion of the last galactic war, has already been infiltrated by Enro and he uses their powers to misguide the League into a future that favors his plans."

Anslark said, "Then you should leave the planet immediately."

"I don't have any other leads on Enro's location."

"But the secret police here have leads on your location: Those soldiers back there had radios. If the Predictors can track your actions . . . one Predictor in each military base or other sensitive spot, with orders to turn in an alarm as soon as he sees the future blur . . . Enro will destroy this planet with the Shadow Effect as he did Corthid, unless you leave!"

Gosseyn said, "Enro is restricted by an uncertainty: He does not know at what range I can create a block against his Predictors. Meanwhile we are restricted by an uncertainty: Unless you are closer to the Loyalty Machine, you will not be able to trace the signal to its origin point. The real ruler of this planet is the mechanic-psychiatrist programming the machine, Enro's agent. We must identify this agent's location before Enro identifies mine."

"You're sure there's an agent? Why couldn't they build a crazy machine and let it run on automatic?"

Gosseyn shook his head. "This history of my planet shows it cannot be done, not reliably. One reason why Null-A slowly won out over rival political-social systems was that lie detectors and other psychiatric machinery co-operated with its growth. You see, neurosis is simplistic opposition to reality, and reality is complex. Machines automatically attempt to adjust themselves to their in-coming data whenever a self-repair or self-examination cycle is triggered. So for the Loyalty Machine, there would have to be a human overseer standing by, to keep it adjusted to the pattern of the neurosis, rather than adapt-ing the pattern of reality. And the overseer would have to have some advanced psychiatric training, perhaps Null-A. If it is Null-A, chances are that means X or someone trained by him. I assume he will be dominating the brain of some victim by remote control, but this time, I plan to synchronize my extra brain with his before he is aware of me, and get a distorter fix on his origin point."

Anslark stared at him, and his lifelike mask held an expression of disbelief. "Is this the madness men get when they think they are immortal? If Enro has Predic-tors standing by, X will know the hour and minute of your approach: Either their visions will show you walking up, or, if you close the distance by distorter, they will see a blind spot approaching as the time of your arrival approaches."

Gosseyn said, "The prediction power is limited by the perceptual 'set' of the Predictor. And while I cannot see past a blur I cause, neither can they. Think of the psychological ramifications of that on an otherwise untrained nervous system. Yalertans rely on their power for their safety, and to reassure themselves of their superiority to other men: Both their pride-anxiety and fear are triggered when they go blind. Anxiety produces fatigue."

And so Gosseyn spent the next few hours revisiting every memorized spot he had visited on the planet, back along their route of travel, near the now-empty cave where the space-boat had rested, and, finally, into his cabin in the space liner. Once in the spaceport, it was relatively simple to sneak, in shadow-form, aboard a space liner preparing for departure.

As the great liner rose on silent beams of force to the edge of the atmosphere, Gosseyn, still wearing the mask Anslark had given him, stood on the promenade deck, where there were a number of other tourists looking through highly magnified plates, focused on the various cities, high mountains, and other noticeable landmarks on the bright side of the planet, the one facing the Pistol Star. The magnifications were sufficient to allow him to memorize the landmarks, scores of them, over a hundred, widely scattered across the two continents of Petrino. He concentrated particularly on the isthmus connecting the two, where the oldest and largest cities were clustered. A moment later, grains of sand from the cave were distorted to those locations, and Gosseyn established an automatic sequence in his double brain to shift the grains of sand back and forth every few minutes.

Any Predictor in this hemisphere was going blind every ten minutes or so. The human nervous system sought patterns in events, and so Gosseyn made sure his shifts occurred at irregularly spaced intervals and lasted erratic lengths of time. No Predictor could see past the blind spots to know if it would be the last or if hours, days, or months of this blindness lay ahead.

By the time he rejoined Anslark in the truck, it was dawn in that latitude of the planet and Anslark was approaching the City of the Loyalty Machine, Munremar.

Anslark helped Gosseyn put on a false face, and they passed the security checkpoints to enter the city without incident.

To Anslark's surprise, Gosseyn drove them to a boardinghouse, not toward the shining pyramid-shape of the Loyalty Machine looming over the skyscrapers of this metropolis. Gosseyn said, "We need to wait at least several hours, before anxiety fatigue makes the Predictors lose their alertness. By tonight, many of them will be grappling with the anxiety that their powers are permanently gone. I don't think they will notice one more blind spot among the irregular pattern I established, if I am forced to use my extra brain."

"If? You don't know?"

Gosseyn would have smiled, but his extra brain could not manipulate the web of electrical muscles in the mask lining as expertly as Anslark: Instead he shrugged. "I can't see the future, either, not as long as I keep this up."

"But it does not bother you?"

"No one in this hemisphere is able to predict my actions, not at the moment." His voice was confident, even though the expression on his loose-muscled mask was dull and blank.

That night, they made their way down darkened streets. A curfew was in effect, but even without predictions to guide them, Gosseyn and Anslark could detect the electrical signatures of approaching patrol cars, or of armed soldiers afoot. They avoided all patrols.

The two decided to enter the city power plant first, so that Anslark and Gosseyn would have potent nuclear and electrical energy flows to draw upon in case they needed a weapon or in case it might prove advantageous to interrupt all the municipal power. It was Gosseyn's habit to gain control of such installations when he could. The building did not seem to be guarded or even locked. Perhaps no one in this city was psychologically capable of being disloyal enough to enter without permission.

The dynamo room was a large chamber, lit only by a few dim orange backup lights. In the gloom, Anslark was standing on the concrete floor below, keeping watch for guards, while Gosseyn was on the catwalk, facing row upon row of round energy-cells. Each one was the antenna of an invisible beam of broadcast power reaching to some other receiving station or power-using unit somewhere in the city, and Gosseyn was tracing the flows with his extra brain, trying to see which led into the atomic pile he sensed buried far below.

A soft voice from a few feet to his left called out, "Don't move! My pistol is shielded. You can't distort the shot!"

It was a woman's voice. Gosseyn turned with his hands up. He could see, on the catwalk, dimly outlined against the backup lights behind her, a slender silhouette in what seemed a long jacket. In one hand there was the glint of something metallic, pointed at him. Gosseyn was not sure if it was a weapon: His extra brain detected no energy signature. But neither did he sense nerve-activity from the woman. Something was blocking his perception.

He did not even try to memorize the woman or her pistol. Instead, he memorized one of the large square plates of high-voltage insulation fixed to the machine and similarized it into his hands. It would have been too heavy for an ordinary man to lift, but Gosseyn's Null-A training allowed him to momentarily cut off his muscles from all fatigue signals from his brain.

The sudden sight of the slab snapping into existence provoked or startled the woman: A beam of white-hot energy, dazzlingly bright, drilled into the slab, sending molten droplets flying. The scream of the weapon was louder than thunder.

In the sudden light, the woman was visible: young, very pretty, with blue eyes and blond ringlets tucked into a helmet with a transparent faceplate. She wore a long jacket of metallic fibers molded to her shapely form. The helmet was the same material and connected to the suit. It was all one piece. Even in the dazzling light, however, there was a flicker of shadow, of dark smoke, floating through the substance of the weave and gathered around the glinting barrel of her energy-pistol.

Gosseyn had no remorse, no hesitation. The girl's beam had been aimed at his heart! He rushed forward, dashing the heavy insulated plate into the woman with all his strength. Darkness fell when the solid blow landed, the metal plate ringing. Gosseyn glimpsed the pistol spinning off into the darkness, its beam extinguished.

The blow would have stunned or killed a tall and well-knit man, not to mention a short and slender young woman. Unexpectedly, the silhouette of the woman merely staggered a moment under the force of the massive blow and then gripped the heavy metal slab in her slender hands and tore it from Gosseyn's grip!

Before he could recover, the slim girl darted forward, a swift shape in the gloom, and landed a blow that numbed the arm he only barely raised in time to block. Gosseyn backpedaled, dodging the swift, furious fists. The strength behind the punches was immense. He memorized the structure of the catwalk floor beneath both their feet.

As he backed up, a pair of shapely arms seized him from behind, pinning his arms to his side. The helmet of the woman who had surprised him from behind was only as high as his broad shoulders, but, nonetheless, her grip was stronger than a bear's, and he found his feet being pulled up off the catwalk. Meanwhile, the blond girl facing him had ripped a length of heavy iron railing from the catwalk, casually snapping inch-thick metal cross-beams, and came for Gosseyn with this metal club held high.

He sent the catwalk elsewhere. Both women fell. He assumed his shadow-form so that the superstrong fingers of the girl behind him merely slid through his smoky substance. He adjusted his gravitational relation to the planetary field, so that he hovered in midair.

The first girl, the blonde, uttered a high-pitched cry of rage as she fell. The second—he saw in the sudden blaze of her drawn weapon that she was an attractive redhead—sent a white-hot beam through his shadow-body to scrape molten drops from the dynamo equipment behind him. She stopped firing before she hit the ground fifteen or twenty feet below: There were groans and gasps of pain from both women, which meant they had survived. One of them started sobbing and crying. Gosseyn noted how strangely girlish the crying seemed, and he wondered if an emotion of regret should be his proper response.

Four beams of white-hot energy transfixed his body, aimed steadily toward the center of his shadowy mass. The output of the beams was adjusted so that while some heat was blackening the dangerous power circuits behind him, the weapons were not drilling into the shielded dynamo.

Gosseyn's vision was dim when he was in his shadow-form, but he could make out the figure of Prince Anslark towering above the two shapely Amazons to either side of him who held him helpless. There were a dozen other curvaceous figures in metallic jackets and helmets. Four of them were pinning Gosseyn in their weapon-beams, so that he could not solidify and use his extra brain. The others were spaced here and there about the chamber, their weapons covering the corners, and three were running to give their fallen comrades aid.

A woman's voice rang out like a bell. "Gilbert! That is enough. You don't need to prove to everyone how stubborn you are."

Gosseyn said in astonishment, "Patricia . . . ? Is that you . . . ?"

"Of course. You blinded all my brother's Predictors, but I knew where you'd come first. I know how you think."

28

Emotion, like all neural "identification" actions, operates by means of approximations. In simpler animals, the approximations are cruder: An amoeba need only distinguish between food-objects and threat-objects. The purpose of Null-A training is to refine simplistic animal identifications.

Gosseyn adjusted the gravity gradient so his shadow-body descended to hover just above the concrete floor. He was in the midst of the squad of women, so they risked hitting each other. Darkness fell when Patricia snapped out the order to cease fire.

A halo of ball-lightning appeared above Prince Anslark's head, illuminating the scene in a colorless, flickering glare. Anslark said in a voice of strained nonchalance, "I can kill everyone in the chamber, even if I cannot target them by similarization. I have formed a seventeen-point similarity link to the atomic pile buried here. Gosseyn, are these enemies?" Two attractive women were clutching his arms, and a third held the muzzle of her energy-pistol under his chin.

Anslark evidently meant *everyone in the chamber, including himself.* Patricia answered before Gosseyn could speak.

She said, "We're friends." She looked over at Gosseyn's shadow-form and sniffed. "Sort of." Patricia holstered her weapon, and she smiled an arch smile.

"Gilbert and I have kind of an on-again off-again relationship."

Patricia coolly opened her bejeweled cigarette case and drew out a lit cigarette, her eyes surveying Anslark. She said offhandedly to a green-eyed brunette standing nearby, "Anrella, shoot Mr. Gosseyn if he solidifies."

"Anslark, hold your fire," Gosseyn said, "Patricia, this prevents me from blocking Enro's Predictors."

Patricia gave a silvery little laugh. "The Predictors are the least of your worries."

"Tell me where Enro is. Does he know that an extra-dimensional superbeing called the Ydd is using him to destroy the continuum?"

Patricia shook her head. "Let's not talk about him now. You have other business you should be seeing to, Gilbert."

Gosseyn thought that was curious. Was she warning him that they were under observation? "Patricia, was your brother able to watch the Follower remotely? I have been assuming he could not, because the Follower successfully conspired against him once."

She said briefly, "Don't underestimate him!"

Gosseyn had been hoping the blur he created over the Predictors' vision across time might also blur Enro's clairvoyance across space. But photons were easier to similarize than other particles, and space was easier to breach than time. Her comment was as plain as she dared speak in Enro's hearing.

Anslark said, "I hate to interrupt, but what is going on here? Which side is Reesha on?"

Gosseyn's shadow-form could not show expression, but there was a slight shrug of the smoky outlines of his shoulders. "In the past she has to me seemed consistently to act in the interests of Null-A, while also working toward the benefit of the Gorgzid people, though not the Imperial government."

Anslark said, "I notice you qualified that statement."

Patricia said in a lilting drawl, "He's from Venus. They qualify all their statements."

She turned toward Anslark and bent her head in a regal nod of greeting. "My dear Prince Anslark: It is a pleasure to hear the voice of Your Highness once again. I was most grieved at reports of your death, and am delighted to find that they are false."

"Your Divine and Imperial Majesty," said Anslark. He could not bow with his arms held tight, but he returned the nod. There came a hiss of sparks at his hairline and jawline, and his flesh mask fell wetly to the floor, revealing the staring-eyed skull-face beneath. The women holding him flinched, and he yanked his arms free during the moment they were startled. Anslark stepped back, a nimbus of lightning crackling from his aura. The two women hesitated to grapple with him. Even in their neutralizing armor, it would have been like grabbing a live wire.

The women, some kneeling and some standing with legs spread, raised their energy-pistols. They held the pistols military-style, a two-handed grip. Others were covering Gosseyn.

Patricia called over the crackling roar of the lightning surrounding Anslark, "I would prefer not to demonstrate that our weapons are immune to your powers, O Prince. You won't be able to turn aside the bolts."

"Nor you mine, Your Majesty." The white fire around Anslark dimmed, and its roar sank to a menacing hiss. There could be no expression on the fleshless face of Anslark, but his voice held a note of surprise: "Is that Lady Inlith? And Yolendra of Yvar?"

Gosseyn noticed an anomaly. Why did Anslark betray surprise to find these other noblewomen here but not the Empress Reesha? What did he know about her that Gosseyn did not?

Patricia said, "These women were all forced to become the lovers of certain high officers in my brother's space navy, intelligence services, and court, so that he could both reward and blackmail his men: It also allowed him the pleasure of grinding underfoot the pride of any of the ancient, noble houses of the Greatest Empire who refused to send their daughters to attend the Emperor at his morning bath."

Interesting. Gosseyn noticed the same pattern here as before: A sexual neurosis was influencing what should have been purely political determinations in Enro's policy.

It was a pattern seen in many men suffering from the Violent Man Syndrome. Without the artificial support of their female victims, the whole structure of false belief surrounding their masculine superiority would collapse. Enro was a case where this syndrome was being played out on a gigantic level. Whole worlds of innocent people were dying, whole cultures annihilated, because one man could not control the un-sane demands of his thwarted sex instinct.

Gosseyn was once again appalled at how infantile, how self-destructive, it all was.

And now Patricia's finely chiseled aristocratic features grew hard and cold, and her hazel eyes flashed. "The Equalization drug—makes you the equal of a man—was developed here on Petrino: a crystalline manganese compound that combines with estrogen to allow a temporary tremendous increase in muscle pressure. Those officers regretted obeying Enro's orders once these 'equalized' women joined me in the resistance. Each woman had the pleasure of determining the fate of the man who had forced himself upon her. Some were maimed or emasculated, others killed."

One of the women spoke up: "In retaliation, Enro gave the order to have our families and home nations killed, or sent to the slave-worlds. If Secoh had not overthrown Enro in the last days before the surrender . . . But now that Enro is at large again, no one is safe."

Anslark lowered his hands to his sides. His lightning failed; the chamber grew dark again. Anslark's voice came out of the gloom: "I am sincerely sorry for your loss, Lady Rhianwy. If it is within my power, I will avenge your loss in Enro's blood."

"Avenge your own loss!" came the voice of the lady who had spoken. "Don't you know what damage the shadow-ships have done against your home stars, just in the last forty hours?"

Anslark said, "Tell me."

Patricia said, "Corthid was swallowed in the Shadow Effect. This was the signal for a general massacre. The war has begun. Nine of the original nineteen members of the Interstellar League have been decimated. Enro has brought back designs for the nonidentity machines from the dead galaxy. His hundreds of secret factory-planets, billions of work-slaves on each, have been toiling for months to produce the equipment. All throughout the Sixth Decant of the Galaxy, planets in the Corthidian Fellowship have vanished, above eleven thousand. Enro's ships appear, discharge a darkness onto the planet, and retreat, in a matter of moments. The Iron World of Fortineb where the fleet was gathered is lost, as well as the League capital worlds of Drasil, Ff, Vanardoon, Utternast, Illaanj, and Golden Xanthilorn . . . all destroyed, and their colonies, the republics or empires they rule, broken and demoralized. The shadow is spreading."

Anslark said, "What of Dzan, Dzan of the myriad splendors?"

"Last I knew, your home world itself was safe, but the Dzan Protectorates and colony worlds in the M72 cluster, ninety-one hundred worlds, have been swallowed by the shadow, suns and whole solar systems eaten up. Your cousin King Indark committed suicide by pulling down a lightning bolt from the sky: The crown passed to your niece, Dsiryan the Beautiful, and she is contemplating surrender."

Anslark said in a voice of shock, "What am I to do? The nine suns no longer shine on the diamond towers of Tentessil; the water-world of Oss is gone, and her unsounded seas, as are the jeweled moons of Lallandur, where once I reigned as Duke."

Patricia said, "You do have a better legal claim than your niece, Your Highness."

"I am unsightly, Your Imperial Majesty; I have taken wages from the spy masters of the Interstellar League. No, I will never sit upon the Stormbolt Throne."

Gosseyn had been listening quietly all this time, making minor adjustments to his shadow-body, to see if he could find a combination of energy-tensions that would allow his extra brain to operate in this strange condition. So far, he found none. Unless he departed, levitating through the ceiling and out of the range of the Amazon squad and their pistols, he dared not solidify. And until he learned more, he dared not depart.

He saw that Patricia was maneuvering to get Anslark to leave; he suspected he knew the reason why.

Patricia merely motioned to two of her women. "Escort His Highness to the spaceport. He will be wanting to return home, because Queen Dsiryan will need his support now. Gilbert, why don't you remind Prince Anslark that you can find him later?"

The grief-stricken Anslark spoke no farewells but allowed the gun-women to lead him away.

Gosseyn said to Patricia, "You're assuming that Enro just lost his picture of us?"

She said, "He cannot focus on you, not while you're a shadow. He needs a point in space, an object, a person that he can attune his clairvoyance to. Is that why you sent an uncoded message about Enro to the No-men of Accolon? You must have known Enro has spies among the Special Police of the League."

"Actually, I thought Enro would simply send one of his own agents, not follow an agent of the League, like Anslark. Now that Anslark is not tailing me, why won't Enro just kill him?"

"Because, after all, you can find Anslark later, can't you? My brother might suspect a trick, but it will tempt him to keep an eye on Prince Anslark, hoping to find you. Besides"—Patricia gave a little smile—"Anslark was quite handsome before his disfigurement, and he and I met at ambassadorial functions, and he paid me some flattering attention. Enro might still be jealous, and that will make him want to keep an eye on Prince Anslark, even now—"

Gosseyn interrupted, "Did Enro spare this planet because you were on it?"

Patricia frowned. "That's what I wanted to happen, but no. I failed here. X is making my brother smarter, less brutal."

"He's going to destroy the planet anyway?"

Patricia laughed a sad little laugh. "This planet *is* destroyed. Do you think these xenophobes can cooperate rationally with the remaining League members to offer a defense against Enro? Their farms are burnt; their factories are idle.

"This world was once known for her intellectual achievements, her genius, her high civilization! And now: The Porgrave neural-readers are set to identify anyone with the Nexialist training. Nexialists, you see, are too educated to be blind to what madness this economic planning is, and the Loyalty Police are rounding them up. Students get shipped off to forced-labor camps on the polar islands. The Committee calls it aversion therapy. Professors and experts, the intellectual giants, are imprisoned not far from here."

Gosseyn mentioned his run-in with the Petrino mind-paralysis robots. "I assumed at the time that they were meant to root out Null-A's. Does Nexialism form similar nerve paths between the thalamus and cortex as non-Aristotelianism?"

Patricia said, "Like Null-A, Nexialism is an attempt to break out of the primitive animal system of relating to reality. Obviously the Standardization Committee finds that untrained thinkers are easier to manipulate into voting themselves into a trap . . . a trap from which there is no escape." She continued, her voice growing bitter, "All the Loyalty Machine need do is see to it that a sufficient technical base remains to keep its remote units in operation. It does not matter what political or economic reforms they vote on, because the underlying psychology of the planet has been fixed in place. The Total Loyalty system will never fall, because it can never be questioned. The population will use all their ingenuity to maintain their mass-neurosis, no matter how conditions change. This is what happens when Null-A is misused."

Patricia shivered slightly, frowned at her cigarette, and threw it down to the concrete, stamping it under the toe of her black boot.

Gosseyn said, "If Enro wanted to use his long-range assassination method on me, he would have done it when Anslark and I first met. So why should he kill me now? Or is there another reason why you think I should remain in this out-of-phase condition?"

Patricia said thoughtfully, "Now that is interesting. You actually do have blind spots built into your psychology, don't you?"

Gosseyn pondered the implications of that statement. "Let us assume for the sake of argument that Lavoisseur, using very advanced psychological techniques, created and organized my personality to have an inability to be interested in his actions and his origins. You seem to be implying that I should fear an immediate threat from him?"

"From that crazed version of Lavoisseur that used to call himself X, yes, of course. I'll always regret that I didn't get to put the bullet into his bald, crippled body. Prescott won that privilege. Now X is young and handsome and cruel again, and, ugh! You just don't seem to take the threat seriously. He has the memories, or most of them, of the man who designed you."

Gosseyn said, "My plan had been to have Anslark

carry my sleeping body close enough to whatever poor soul X is possessing at the moment to trigger an exchange of thought-information. If he does not know I am coming, and does not know I have assumed the 'lesser' pole of power, he won't know his thoughts are being read into me."

"That is what I mean: You are assuming you can survive your next encounter with him. You won't. He will predict what you mean to do."

"He cannot use his Predictor power to spy on me."

"But he can use his brain power. What would you do, if it were you?"

Gosseyn was startled, because the answer to the question was obvious: X was unwilling to have Gosseyn die while in mental link with him, lest the cortical-thalamic integration of the Gosseyn memories be transmitted to and cure the thoughts of the older being. This meant one of two strategies. The first was to murder Gosseyn while he was insulated from the rest of the universe—and the trap on Corthid had been meant to do that. X knew by now that trap had inexplicably failed. Which implied a second strategy.

Gosseyn said, "If he prepared a duplicate body of himself, equipped with whatever memories or experiences he thinks would convince me of his point of view, and merely waited for me to attempt to make a mental connection with him again . . ."

She said, "Nothing so elaborate. He does not need a second body. All he needs is to experiment on his own brain, to give himself a temporary form of insanity, something he could pass along to you."

"Insanity? I could resist it, and cure it."

"Not if it approached at a level you were unaware of."

Gosseyn remembered the lie-detector readings that showed his extra brain manifesting symptoms of madness: brain material over which he had no direct control.

Patricia said, "*He* knows how your double brain works, and *you* don't! He can disorganize your nervous system.

All he has to do is wait for you to come into range. If your double brain were to become disorganized to the point where you could no longer use it—disorganized or damaged the way Lavoisseur's was on Earth when he lay dying—then you could be killed with impunity, as he was." She shrugged. "Besides, he can bury any important information under layers of artificial amnesia, leaving only misinformation in his conscious mind for you to pick up. That is not so different from what Lavoisseur did, when he created you."

"Where is Lavoisseur now?"

"Now? Dead. You saw him die. I saw him die. X, his other self, interfered with the similarity connection to his next body, and no information was passed. Lavoisseur was too disorganized to form a new connection with his extra brain."

"How did you see him die?"

To answer, Patricia doffed her helmet, shaking her hair loose, and unsealed her armor, which lost its smoky shadow-aura and peeled away like fabric. Beneath, she wore a skintight suit that left her arms and legs free. Patricia stepped over to the side of the chamber away from the electrical dynamo. "I don't have to tell you not to step between me and the image."

"Image!" said Gosseyn.

The scene that formed on the far wall was that of a city at night. The buildings seemed to be the vine-covered marble and green copper typical of Petrino: In one large parkland in the center of the city, isolated, was a new building, an immense domed cathedral of dark stone, lit here and there with white-hot atomic torches. The black dome looked like a model, in stone, of the rounded hull of the primordial starship that Gosseyn once saw on Gorgzid: the Crypt of the Sleeping God.

Only near this park and its cathedral were there signs of life: The streets were free from trash and wrecked vehicles; the houses and shops looked tidy, lived-in, prosperous, with glass in the windows and flowers in the window boxes. There was even some nighttime traffic on the roads, and the street lamps were working. The rest of the city, what could be seen of it, seemed to be in blackout conditions, the streets unlit.

Patricia said dryly, "The Standardization Committee has determined that family and civic life is better when embraced in the context of a uniform, uniformly accepted religion. A church with a transcendent, abstract, or invisible god was deemed, by the Committee, less intellectually satisfying than a cult with a god you can see with your eyes—the Priesthood is simply denying the embarrassing fact that the High Priest burned their god to a cinder. Meanwhile, anyone who joins the Cult is free from the Standardization Committee, because religious beliefs are not subject to psychiatric review. The Cult is currently the only civilized sanctuary on the planet."

Patricia continued, "And in the crypts below the building you see there, the most highly trained of the Nexialists are imprisoned. The deans and tutors of the Institute are so well respected by the common Petrines, even with the Loyalty Machine conditioning, that no native can be trusted to keep them imprisoned, except members of the Cult.

"And this complex is also where the signals controlling the Loyalty Machine are coming from. You see, X does not need to spend every hour of every day occupying the mind of someone who wants to carry out his work. If the someone is a stooge who thinks he is being visited by the Sleeping God, X only needs to make mental contact once every few months.

"So: There it is. A building full of unarmed civilians who had no defense against the advanced brainwashing and propaganda techniques X has at his command, not to mention a cell block of innocent prisoners. Go make martyrs of them."

Gosseyn was a little taken aback. When had Patricia become convinced that Gosseyn was a murderous man? "That would be counterproductive."

"Exactly. So I am giving you a productive avenue to follow. You want to draw Enro out of hiding? He will have to appear in person to stop you, once you start taking effective steps against him."

Gosseyn thought about that for a moment. "There is still a great deal I don't know—"

Patricia interrupted, "You've found out everything you can find out here! Enro is using a combination of pure brutality and subtle, Null-A-style psychology to achieve his war aims. X has taught the principles of his twisted version of Null-A to the locals, and had the members of the Nexial Institute here on Petrino, who are advanced enough to see the dangers, put away in a concentration camp. X is simply not here, not at the moment. His work here was done by the locals. Find a way to return Corthid to normal time-space."

"Why Corthid?"

"The biological distorter in your head, your extra brain, contains the only matrix that might still have a 'fix' on the planet Corthid, even in its non-identity condition. . . ."

At that moment, one of the women of the gun squad put her fingers to the earpiece of her helmet and cocked her head, listening. She said, "Empress! The radio reports Predictor Yanar just went blind again. X just manipulated time-space in this area. He may have just arrived on the planet."

Patricia waved her hand at the wall. The image changed to a scene on the Great Planet Accolon: Gosseyn recognized the mile-high towers rising above the dark leaves of the polar jungle of that warm world.

Patricia said, "Go! Before X fully manifests himself in this time-space and gets a fix on your location."

Gosseyn said slowly, "Periodically, an unseen intelligence who controls my destiny—I call him the Cosmic Chessplayer—has to step out of the shadows and apply force to get me to continue along his or its planned path, shoving me like a pawn on a board. First I thought the Chessplayer was Lavoisseur; then I thought it was the

Observer of the Crypt. Each time, the Chessplayer tries to convince me that he is dead. But here is his hand again. Who is manipulating my life? What does he want? Are you an agent of his, Patricia? Or is it you?"

She said savagely, "I am just as much a pawn of the Chessplayer's manipulations as you are, Gilbert."

The woman at her elbow said in a tense, rapid tone, "Empress, the blur is tapering off. The mass-energy readings indicate an incoming load far greater than one man: Perhaps a fleet, or a large-scale instrument, is attuned to this area. The attunement is reaching the critical threshold . . . the number of active electromagnetic brains in the Loyalty Machine has just reached maximum load . . . the machine may be calculating a space-time intersection of high magnitude. . . ."

Patricia pulled up a radio from her belt and spoke into it: "If I do not countermand this order in thirty seconds, kill Prince Anslark." She lowered the instrument and said, "Ladies, holster your weapons! Gilbert, you may now solidify. I'll countermand my kill order once I see you on the surface of Accolon."

He did not see that he had a choice.

29

In multivalued logic, categories of thought assumed in classical logic to be absolute, such as essence and accident, time and space, cause and effect, are subordinated to a flexible system of approximations.

Gosseyn was on Accolon, standing on the broad, flat top of one of the immense towers. The process of mentally "photographing" his target area had been easier than normal, despite the vast distance involved: The stress created by Patricia's remote viewing acted as a partial similarization between the two points in space.

The air was noticeably thin at this height, as atop a tall mountain. Gosseyn saw that the service door leading up to the roof was a double-sealed airlock.

He stooped down to peer over the edge. Looking in through the large window at an empty observation deck, he similarized himself inside. Inside was a restaurant, chairs set upside down on empty tables, an automatic unit sweeping the floor.

At the distance involved between Petrino and Accolon, hours had passed in the Petrino frame of reference: enough that there would be no more threat to Anslark. Gosseyn had taken the precaution of memorizing Patricia when she had taken off her protective armor: He attempted to bring her to him now, to ask his unanswered questions, but the action in his double brain produced no result.

The view outside the window caught his attention. As always at this polar latitude, it was twilight. A huge and ghostly crescent hung in the east, many times larger than Earth's moon seen from Earth. Gosseyn used a special system he had for relaxing his eyes and increasing the number of firings per second of his optic nerve in order to form a small, sharp, clear picture of the image in his brain: It was a ringed gas giant.

The gas giant was in the process of disintegration. The crescent Gosseyn saw was the lit hemisphere of the mighty world: It was knotted and swirled with a pattern of storm-clouds, hurricanes larger than Earth.

Gosseyn saw that the ring system was off-center and the worldlets, moons, mountains, rocks, and debris flying from orbit were scattered like the beads of a broken necklace. Clouds of agitated gas were also streaming from the surface in eruptions so immense that the soaring particles of gas overcame even the tremendous escape velocity of this superheavy planet. These clouds were streaming away from the sun side of the world, so that long streaks of multicolored mist, looking strangely like fire, were rushing backward from the horns of the sunlit crescent. The gas giant looked almost like the prow of a ship blazing with reentry heat.

Next, Gosseyn sent himself to one of his three memorized locations on this world: the municipal post office. There was a clerk in the sorting room, bent over some task, standing with her back to Gosseyn when he appeared. She turned and gave an "oh!" of surprise and asked sharply, "What are you doing here?"

Gosseyn, who was still dressed in the uniform of a Petrino teamster and wearing a pseudo-flesh mask Anslark had given him, said, "I wandered in here by mistake. I was looking for the maintenance room."

The girl visibly relaxed, accepting the explanation. The rumpled overalls of his uniform must have fit her preconception of what a man looking for the maintenance room would dress like. Anslark perhaps had given him a pleasant-looking face, because the girl smiled warmly. She said, "Just take the shortcut through the visitors' lounge: There's no one there now. But make sure you have your papers with you before you try to leave the building. The Safety Authority has a man at every public building these days."

"Safety Authority!" said Gosseyn blankly.

So had been named Illverton's organization on the doomed planet of Corthid.

Gosseyn stepped into the visitors' lounge. There were couches and chairs, and a robot-operated phone in a booth at the wall. In the center was a low table of the automatic sort that could make coffee and snacks. On the opposite wall was a television set with both one-way and two-way channels.

He stepped over to the television and said, "Find me information about that gas giant which is passing near Accolon."

"I have a public-service announcement by the Safety Authority in my film library. Shall I run it?"

"Can you summarize it for me?"

"Certainly. The gas giant was once the eighth world in this system. Superships of the Planetary Engineering Corps blasted the gas giant into a hyperbolic orbit, which will carry the planet, over the next eighty days, into a very close apogee to our sun. Even at this distance, the solar winds are stripping it of its light outer layers of methane and hydrogen gas. After apogee, a lump of molten material, a slurry of heavier elements, will remain. By that time, its hyperbolic orbit will carry it to a farther orbit once again, and construction can begin on a second Space-time Stability Sphere."

"A second Sphere?"

"Here is the image of the first. The seventh planet of the Accolon system was used. The Safety Authority copied many of the best practices of the Corthidians, to take advantage of their methods of rapid and efficient large-scale work. The Sphere machine being built from the remains of the seventh planet has some two thousand forty-three cities on its surface, for its population of robot-workers. No human could survive the gravity for long, of course, considering the mass of the Sphere machine. Most of the supervision of robot-workers is by radio remote control. At the moment, work on the primary equatorial magnetic-accelerator is complete. The rotation of superheavy masses around the core of the machine will cause an effect called frame-dragging, which, in conjunction with the continent-sized matrix arrays, will stabilize the—"

"Stop. Is there a system of distorters being prepared to spread the range of the stabilization effect?"

"Yes. Orbital stations, acting as antennas and relay stations for the tremendous energies generated by the Stability Sphere, have already been constructed in great numbers, using the elements in the ring systems of the gas giants. Each orbital station has thousands of electronic brains controlling millions of distorter towers, and there is some hope that they can hinder the spread of the Shadow Effect until more Spheres are operational."

Gosseyn noticed, when the television showed him a view of the orbital stations, civilian and military vessels were also in orbit around Accolon. He saw the silvery, streamlined silhouettes of *The Star of the Morning* and *The Queen of Love,* two spaceships from Venus, recognizable because their engine nacelles were carried on long shafts far from their main hulls.

The Null-A engineers familiar with the information Gosseyn had brought back from Corthid had of course selected Accolon as the primary industrial power to cooperate with.

Gosseyn similarized himself to the second of his three memorized locations on this world: the Terrestrial ambassador's office. The secretary was startled to see him materialize. She rose from her seat with a shriek of alarm. The other visitors in the anteroom, persons waiting to see the ambassador, were likewise startled.

The marine guard, however, was the same man Gosseyn had noticed previously, at least partially trained in Null-A. When the ambassador's voice came bellowing over the phone, it was the guard who said promptly, "It's Gilbert Gosseyn, sir. Or one of him."

The telephone swiveled its lens to cover Gosseyn's still-masked face. "It doesn't look like his photographs."

"I didn't say it looked like him, sir. But look at the size of his skull, and look at where he appeared."

"Send him in immediately," came the reply.

As Gosseyn stepped past the secretary, she nodded at something behind him, whispering, "Better make it quick." Gosseyn did not turn his head, but with his double brain he could detect how two of the visitors, their nervous systems in a state of uneasy excitement, were departing hastily through the main doors. While the secret police of Accolon might respect the sovereignty of the Earth embassy, certainly their presence would prove a complication.

Gosseyn noticed the silence as the door slid shut behind him. He was in the dim interior of the ambassador's office: a chamber of plush carpet and dark walls, tastefully furnished. He probed the door behind him with his double brain: It was as thick as a bank vault door, and reinforced with energy fields.

He detected other energy sources in the room: a weapons array in the ceiling worthy of a battleship, and a series of projectors, on standby, ready to erect powerful screens around the ambassador and his desk.

The man stood as Gosseyn entered. He was a handsome fellow in a rugged way, with some gray frosting otherwise black hair. "Mr. Gosseyn," he said, gesturing to a chair before his desk. "Please be seated. My name is Craft. I am here to replace—"

If the man was startled when Gosseyn launched himself in a low tackle across the desk, it did not slow his reactions. Craft landed two powerful uppercuts with both fists on Gosseyn's face before Gosseyn's muscular arms closed about his waist. His momentum carried both men backward into the ambassador's wingback chair, and they toppled, chair and all, rolling up against the wall panels behind the desk.

What was unexpected was that Ambassador Craft fought with the all-out strength and blinding reflexes of a trained Null-A. Even in their grapple, Craft managed to deal Gosseyn two more severe blows to the abdomen and throat before Gosseyn half-electrocuted him with a near brush from beams of positive and negative energy. Gosseyn focused the main force of the beams on wall panels behind them, blasting the wall into twisted metal shards.

The secret door thus exposed led to a small room and an escape tunnel. Gosseyn dragged the ambassador's body into the small room and out of range of the weapons in his office, which had swung down from ceiling panels when the fight started.

The atomic lights in the little hidden room came on automatically when Gosseyn stumbled in. One wall was communication equipment, both radio and distorter type. Against another was a complex of electron tubes, wired into an electronic brain and lie-detector setup. Against the third wall was a padded chair with a neural helmet for sleep training.

Gosseyn said, "You are a Loyalty Machine?"

The machine said in a calm, dispassionate tone, "I am unable to calculate how to destroy you without harming the ambassador, who is a valuable asset to the Safety Authority. However, the moment I deduce the danger you pose to exceed the value he possesses I will release the magnetic seals of my fusion core and flood the area with deadly radiation."

Gosseyn said, "Why not call the marine guard outside?"

The machine said wryly, "Obviously, there are certain limitations to my behavior."

Which meant that the other personnel in this building had not been exposed to the warped Null-A training that had been imprinted on the thinking of Ambassador Craft. Gosseyn winced ruefully at his bruises as he heaved the ambassador into the chair. The warped version of Null-A was still effective at giving the practitioner a high degree of nerve-muscle coordination and integration.

Gosseyn now turned his attention to the machine, which had already activated its lie-detector circuits and was trying to induce a set of rhythms in Gosseyn's brain to induce a somnolent and compliant state of mind. Gosseyn deflected the nerve-energies being directed at him and countered by stimulating the self-examination cycle of the brain's thought-hierarchy. There were thousands of circuits involved in the machine and he could not possibly trace them all, but he could compare a gestalt picture of the activity before and after its cycle ran. He could find and paralyze the circuits involved with overriding its normal self-correcting behavior once he saw them triggered.

The machine attempted a more severe and crude attack, this time using the distorter communication array in the room to similarize a powerful electric surge into his nervous system. Gosseyn redirected the electron flows so that, somewhere on the rooftop where he'd first landed, a lightning bolt leaped unexpectedly to the sky.

But that was the last attempt: Gosseyn saw which circuits were the crucial ones and built up a similarity between their "open" and "shut" contacts, so that the electronic brain could not disengage them. The machine was paralyzed.

Gosseyn disconnected one of the lie detectors from the array and used it to probe the ambassador's unconscious mind. Gosseyn could tell this much: There was no trace that the brain patterns of X had ever been present in this man. There was some evidence of cortical-thalamic nerve channels built up in his midbrain but also an extensive structure of nerve-trigger relationships to areas in his lower brain: Perhaps he had been just beginning real Null-A training on Earth before somehow falling prey to this neurosis-inducing machine.

The ambassador came slowly to consciousness, groaning.

Gosseyn said harshly, "What were the cues? What threat or what promise did they use to get you to betray Earth?"

Craft stared at him without fear, his eyes narrowed in calculation. "Tell me how you knew and I'll answer."

The lie detector confirmed he was being straightforward.

Gosseyn said, "The local Earth ambassador is the first person Enro would think of to act as a check to stop Venusian curiosity, which was sure to be aroused once they saw the technology from the Shadow Galaxy involved here. I was not sure until I came into the room and sensed the warped Null-A-style lie detectors built into the chair, the mind-control robots from Petrino hidden behind the walls. Why betray the Earth?"

Craft said softly, "I was saving Earth! The shadow would swallow the solar system if I told what I discovered. My wife, my children, everything the human race has ever done or dreamed. . . ."

Gosseyn said to the lie detector in his hands, "I am assuming that the neural associations imprinted in him are tied to the most basic instincts in the human mind: survival, sexual drive, paternal instinct."

"That's right," said the lie detector. "And more. There is also a strong link to the death instinct, and links to altruism, group-loyalty, and the charismatic overlord-underling reaction. The training here is complex and complete, and, like many false-to-facts world-views, is self-correcting and self-sustaining. His mind will edit out facts contrary to his current world-view. He can be aware of them, but deep down he will dismiss them as unimportant."

"How could those links be related to this?"

The lie detector said, "At a subconscious level, this subject has an almost religious awe toward the vivid mental image of his home world being destroyed by the Shadow Effect, so that he does not regard it simply as a threat but as all-powerful. Each human being has a death instinct that makes him passive in the face of overwhelming threats, a holdover from days when predators could be deceived by motionlessness and lack of fear-smell. And so, irrationally, he wishes to bargain with the shadow. The charisma reaction comes from the fact that he is convinced the Shadow Effect spoke to him in person."

Ambassador Craft said, "I met Enro. You cannot defeat him, Gosseyn. You don't even know who you are."

"Who am I?"

Craft compressed his lips to a thin line and shook his head.

Gosseyn said to the lie detector, "What is his state of mind?"

"The subject regards it as so futile to oppose Enro that he takes your defeat for granted; hence he will not bother to stop you."

Craft uttered a bark of bitter laughter. "That's true enough! You fool, Enro has surpassed all human limitations: He is a god! The Security Council could not stop him, and the No-men of Accolon, whose intuitions might have noticed the pattern of his behavior and warned the populace, have been arrested on charges of espionage, and sent to the orbital prison colony at L-5."

Gosseyn put down the lie detector and stepped over to the commutations wall. He noticed immediately that the narrow-beam equipment was tuned with arc seconds, eccentricity, inclination, longitude of the ascending node, longitude of perihelion: the elements describing the position of a body in orbit. Gosseyn assumed these were the orbital stations focusing the power from the Sphere of Accolon.

Gosseyn asked, "Why did Enro give you access to this equipment?"

Craft said, "He knew I was loyal. The machine is sitting right there that can measure my devotion."

Gosseyn said to the Loyalty Machine, "Will you keep him asleep, brain functions somnolent, for about twelve hours?"

The machine answered "no" several times. Each time, Gosseyn traced the circuit causing the negative response and nullified it. Eventually he got a configuration inside the electronic brain that would answer "yes."

Once Craft was snoring, Gosseyn asked the no-longer-loyal Loyalty Machine, "Do you have any information on who he thinks I am?"

"Enro led Mr. Craft to believe that you were a rogue copy of Lavoisseur, created and sent out merely to infiltrate the counsels of the opposition on Earth and Venus, whose brain information would be returned to the main chain of memories known as X once your spare bodies were used up. You were created to be unaware of your true mission in order to deceive the lie detectors. No matter what you do, or how you delay it, you will eventually die, and your brain information will automatically be transmitted to one of the nervous systems X has established to receive it."

That did not seem possible, given the reluctance of X to receive Gosseyn's memories. Unless that previous reluctance had been conditional, not absolute: X had not wanted to receive Gosseyn's personality into his own main personality until the mission was done?

Aloud Gosseyn said, "Is Craft correct?"

The machine said, "I can only report on the subjective state of the belief of Mr. Craft. He believes Enro told this to him, and believes Enro did not mislead him on any substantial issue. The conversation was not within my hearing."

"How does he contact Enro?"

"Through me, or so I assume."

"You assume?"

"There are gaps in my thought-records. I conclude I am programmed to forget certain information, or not to be able to remember buried memories unless certain circumstances trigger them."

Without any further word, Gosseyn activated one of the distorter communicators set to correspond with the orbital stations around Accolon. Then he picked up a spare electron tube from the cabinet, identified the static charge with his extra brain, and sent electrons flowing back and forth across it to produce a weak radio wave: He memorized the electronic signal with his extra brain. When the signal was sent through the distorter connection, he maintained twenty-decimal-point contact with it. He was holding a "memorized" pattern of electrons at a point in nearby space. He repeated the process, building up the electrical charge until it was powerful enough to be greater than the mass-energy value of his body. Then he triggered a similarity between the two.

The results were mildly terrific: He materialized in the

middle of a smoking crater, as if from a bomb-burst, the electronic circuits and instrumentation for yards in every direction of him were charred, cracked, and melted. There was a high-pitched whistling, like the hiss of a steam kettle, which told him that the air pressure integrity on the space station had been breached.

He assumed his shadow-form and floated up through yard after yard of wreckage and then through more yards of solid electronic circuits and distorter matrices until he found a wide interior space. Here he solidified and probed surrounding space with his extra brain. He found no living nervous system within his range: only the soft, steady regular rhythms of complex electromechanical systems, the unwavering primordial blaze of nuclear forces, the strange space-tension of artificial gravity. Then, relaxing, he allowed images of the future to flit through his consciousness.

The clear, tiny mental images ended in a blur roughly ten minutes from now, when he activated the major distorter array. The images showed robotic tools rushing to the damaged area, carrying replacement parts and carting away wreckage. But no people lay in his immediate future.

The satellite was deserted.

30

The test of the accuracy of approximations about reality is simply the lack of surprise in the nervous system trained to assume them.

Gosseyn watched the machines, some small, some large, and some gigantic, pulling out twisted metal fragments and burnt components from the area he had damaged. Here was a busy line, like an ant-trail through a forest, of robot-trucks floating on antigravity plates. He followed them back to the factory floor. The factory occupied several acres of two decks, entirely automatic. The units Gosseyn followed were hauling the damaged equipment and scrap metal to sorting stations: Components were separated and fed into various factory intake bins.

The factory was based on the same highly efficient design he had seen back on Corthid. It took him only a short time to find the electronic brain assembly line and dominate the simple control system and feed in new instructions. The robot-workers followed instructions from the factory without question. By the time Gosseyn returned to the section of machinery he had damaged, the electronic brains he had ordered built, as well as nerve-interface electron tubes and amplification matrices, were completed.

He focused the instruments at a spot six inches off the floor. He had no sensory-deprivation tank, or even a comfortable chair to sit on, so he pushed a packing crate to the proper spot on the floor, climbed in, and lay down on the soft packing material. Gosseyn closed his eyes and began his nerve-muscle relaxation technique.

He felt the orbital station around him, as if it were an extension of his nervous system: He was aware of the ebb and flow of a million pulsing messages of the robotic brains communicating with each other, sending out and balancing distorter-type flows. Carefully, like a spider stepping from thread to thread of a web without touching any of the alarm-strands, Gosseyn found and dominated, using an imposed set of rhythms, those robotic thought-flows concerned with reporting breaches in security to human operators. That done, he reached with his brain toward the distorter towers. These towers, hundreds on each station, were connected with distant points in space, connections that Gosseyn perceived like shining threads of energy.

He was curious when he became aware of a second

group of circuits and machinery, an entire parallel system, woven throughout the distorter towers. At first he thought it was a backup or fail-over system, but no: As his mind delicately probed the energies rippling smoothly through these circuits, Gosseyn felt twinges of activity in his own extra brain. Little images of the past and future appeared around him: a picture of himself entering the orbital station and taking control of the factory floor, another picture of Enro appearing as a ghostly image on a throne, and killing him before he could react. . . .

Not just pictures appeared. He heard Enro's melodic baritone: *How convenient of you to have selected your own coffin, Mr. Gosseyn. . . .*

These were mechanical predictor circuits. Gosseyn was not surprised such a technology could exist: If the organic distorter in his extra brain performed the same function as the distorters found in faster-than-light radios and starships, then he did not see why what the brain of a Predictor of Yalerta did could not also be copied.

He studied the pulsating energies flowing through the circuits cautiously. He estimated the time-depth interval to be roughly fifteen billion years. The age of the universe? And the orientation was set toward the past, not the future.

These circuits were communicating information backward into the past. But what information? He traced leads and trickles of information until he found a large central map-room. At the core of this orbital station was a large and intricate three-dimensional map of the galaxy. The map was roughly a mile in diameter. Circuits in the walls of the map-room tracked the motions of certain planets, only a handful, and shell upon shell of electronic brains surrounding the map-chamber made calculations to correct for Einsteinian non-simultaneousness.

The robot brains were chuckling and clicking to each other: *Message 6001012AB32 to Ydd Entity identifies target world . . . planet Uluviron . . . coordinates in time and*

*space . . . orbital elements . . . has not entered into coop-
erative agreement with Interstellar League Safety Authority . . . Commissioner Thule orders the planet
nonidentified . . . order 6001012 verified . . . Message
6001012AB33 from Ydd Entity . . . Confirmation . . .
Shadow Effect to impinge on Uluviron in nineteen hours'
local time . . . countdown begins—*

*Message 6001013AB34 to Ydd Entity identifies target
world . . . planet Eaeas . . . coordinates in time and
space . . . Commissioner Thule orders . . . verified . . .
countdown begins . . . order 6001014 . . . planet Os-
nome . . . countdown begins—*

Gosseyn dared not stand by while world after world
was destroyed. He selected a group of magnetic waves
passing through the room and used his extra brain to impose a message stream on the band: *Order 6001013 not
verified . . . order rejected . . . confirmation code from
Commissioner Thule not recognized.*

In their automatic way, the robotic brains repeated the
false signal from Gosseyn. *Commissioner Thule not recognized . . . order 6001013 not carried out . . . not recognized . . . order 6001014 not carried out—*

This solution, of course, was only temporary. The robots would mindlessly reject all further orders in the
queue until some higher process or human operator noticed the interference.

The important thing now, within the limited time before he was discovered, Gosseyn decided, was the experiment to see if planets could be recovered from the
Shadow Effect. If they could, then all of Enro's horrific
war machine, and the terrible threat of galaxy-wide disintegration, was undone at one stroke.

And Gosseyn saw no reason, theoretically, why it
should not work. If the planet within these pocket universes of shadow-stuff were *truly* disconnected from the
continuum, that meant they were unrelated in space and
in time. From the frame of reference of the universe, the

first split second after the Shadow Effect seized the planet was no more "real" than the lingering weeks or months it took for the world's entire atomic structure to disassociate from itself. Time was a human category of thought.

From the point of view of a quantum universe nothing, really, was disconnected from anything else. Any one event in time-space, on the basic-energy level of the universe, was actually simultaneous with any other event.

Steeling himself, Gosseyn directed the circuits interacting with his brain to attune him to the completed Stabilization Sphere occupying an outer orbit of Accolon's parent sun. . . .

There was the sensation of dreamlike falling, of expansion . . . of connection with . . .

The fabric of time-space was spread around him in four dimensions. Like bright, hard grains of sand, he felt the little intolerably hot pinpoints of gravity-electromagnetic-nuclear force where suns were distorting the fabric of space. His perception ranged across apparently microscopic suns and submicroscopic worlds for hundreds of light-years in each direction: a far smaller segment of the galaxy than the millions of still-operating Spheres in the Shadow Galaxy had been able to reveal to him.

He could not shake the odd conviction that he himself was part of the complex matter-energy and gravitic dance of the suns swinging in their eon-long orbits about the roaring central core of the galaxy. The core! That infinite well of gravitational pressure, hidden behind its own blazing nebular clouds, but visible to Gosseyn's kiloparsec-spanning consciousness.

He reached out and felt the warp and weave of time and space in the local area. Gosseyn was careful to keep his thoughts calm and unhurried, so that he did not accidentally destroy any solar systems.

There were fewer than a hundred currently maintained by the energies throbbing in the equatorial circuits of the mighty Sphere: a rapid exchange of balancing forces that reaffirmed the location and properties of atoms and molecules in their positions, so that their identities could not be lost to the Shadow Effect. Each stabilized planet or star system was the end point of one of the shining threads of balanced distorter-energy issuing from the Sphere, and guided by the complex calculations and focusing elements in the orbital stations.

Carefully, he used the circuit he had built to attune certain bands of the Sphere distorter power through his own nervous system, using his control over the antennas in this orbital station to trigger the deeply buried distorter connection he had with the lost planet Corthid.

Suddenly he grew aware of the shadow-areas in his small segment of the galaxy: a non-condition of nothingness-energy that was not part of the overall system of positive and negative balances forming the local interstellar environment. It was like staring into a vast, dark cloud.

And a point of light emerged from the darkness. It was shining with the electromagnetic noise of cities and power plants, alive with the pulse of neural energies of millions of inhabitants. . . .

Gosseyn sensed, on a deeper level of the time-space plenum, a stress, like the pull of a magnetic force. There was a spot in time-space where the planet Corthid *wanted* to be, and its uncounted trillions of atoms and particles were somehow *associated* with that point.

He realized nervously that this home spot for Corthid was still behind the boundary of the shadow. But where else could he put the planet? It would freeze if left adrift in interstellar space. The only area of space-time where Gosseyn had numerous energy connections was Sol. He used his memorized locations to identify a target: the roof of the spaceport on Venus, the laboratory of Dr. Hayakawa, various points in and near the Semantics Institute on Earth . . . the small lab in the deserted galactic base on Venus where he first made two identical blocks of wood touch . . . he used all these points as orientation vectors to select an area between the orbits of Earth and Venus . . . he stimulated his extra brain to force the similarity . . . the Stability Sphere amplified the signal a hundredfold, a thousandfold, a millionfold. . . .

Corthid took up a position around Sol between the orbits of Earth and Venus.

Gosseyn saw he had too good an opportunity to miss. Pulling his perception back to the Accolon system, he probed the space between Accolon and its major moon: There, like a steel pebble in his mind, he could feel the contours of what was undoubtedly the penal colony where the No-men were imprisoned. He similarized the whole space colony into a stable orbit around Corthid in the Solar System but transmitted the guards and security systems into an area of polar swamp beneath the towers of Accardistran Major.

Gosseyn was convinced he had only minutes or even seconds before his manipulations of the Sphere of Accolon were discovered. So next, he found the Temple of the Sleeping God on the planet Petrine and similarized it, foundations and all, to a compatible site on the planet Corthid, in a cavern not far from the buried city of Corthindel. It was but the work of a moment to place all the men and women in the dungeons in the lower half of the temple-prison into the stately chambers above and sweep all the priests and guards and agents of Enro into the prison cells.

Gosseyn hurriedly began sending the shadow-ships of the Greatest Empire, one by one, as quickly as he could search through the stars to find them, to a remote spot somewhat above the galactic plane, and placing them gently in orbit around a fruitful and green but uninhabited planet before sending essential components of their engine cores elsewhere.

He had transmitted about three hundred ships of Enro's fleet when his attention was snatched by a strange vision, for he seemed to see millions and tens of millions of energy-threads, an uncountable majority, not reaching toward the protected planets but rotated at right angles to the normal plane of space-time.

The reaction was instantaneous: The moment he grew aware of the million line clusters they somehow *oriented* toward him and his brain was caught up in an immense flow of power.

Now the galaxy was visible to him not as a spiral of visible light only but a complex Celtic knot of cosmic rays and X-rays, stripped helium nuclei, heavier particles built up in the nuclear furnaces of novae and supernovae, a streaming labyrinth of magnetic fields and nebular clouds, surging bands of ultraviolet, infrared, and radio waves echoing from gulf to gulf like the songs of whales. There were a surprising number of icy giant worlds falling endlessly through space, snowballs of methane the size of Neptune, unaccompanied by any suns. Asteroid belts and clouds forming oddly regular patterns stretching between the constellations. Vents of superhot gases were rushing across the thousands of light-years from the upper and lower poles of the galaxy's hot core, creating endless oceans of radiation where no human ship, and no human world, could survive. Nor was this all: Like luminous flowers, the scattered globular clusters orbited high above and below the main disk of the galaxy, ornaments of intricate brightness, and, farther, he could sense the satellite galaxies of the Lesser and Greater Magellanic Clouds.

His mind recoiled in shock from the glory of it all: It was too much.

Immediately he performed the cortical-thalamic pause, making himself consciously aware of the nerve-flows running from his perceptual centers, through his thalamus, and only then to his cortex and back to form reaction-emotions in lower sections of his nervous system.

But the promised sanity did not come. The overwhelming flood of images continued.

The tiny fragments of matter grouped into the habitable iron-nickel worlds of man were lost in the complex vastness. For a moment, he could not find the three million worlds of human civilization. He was lost.

As more and more of the millions of energy-lines oriented toward him, he grew aware of greater and greater dimensions of infinity. Now he could see hundreds, no, millions of galaxies connected to each other, extending outward from this central position . . . but these were all the Milky Way galaxy, merely images from different eons of cosmic evolution.

Here were early images of the galaxy, when it was a cylindrical cloud of simple hydrogen-burning stars; there were dim red smoke rings, like a wheel of ash without a hub, images from the remote future.

Certain of the future images of the galaxy were strangely regular in the web of radio and radioactive energies surrounding them, as if they had been engineered on an interstellar scale, and the dangerous central core was tamed, surrounded by concentric shells of artificial matter. Some of the future galaxies were white-hot with energies related to the distortion of time-space; others were dull and quiet, as if the far descendants of intelligent life in those eons were resting between unimaginable efforts. Some far-future millennia were rich with the neural pulsations of living minds; others were humming with the steadier energies of entirely man-made life-forms. . . .

And there were more images, and still more . . . a galaxy that was still a nebular cloud, from a very early period . . . a dark fleet of machines as massive as a galaxy but composed entirely of artificial atoms and elements unknown to earlier periods, to form some artificial mental system adapted to the conditions of the dark and sunless universe of the Age of Decay. . . .

Gosseyn heard a voice, but, in his confusion, he could not tell where it came from. Time seemed to be strangely spread out and melted together: He both saw his body lying in its crate and saw the moment when he appeared on the orbital station and the moment when Enro casually leaned over the edge of the crate and spoke to him.

The voice said, "Excellency, this is Predictor Thule. I can confirm: You will kill Gilbert Gosseyn in fourteen minutes. He is suffering from time-sickness. . . ." (A chuckle.) "Any child of rank from a birth-center on my world knows how to shrug off this side effect . . . he will be helpless . . . no, there is no blurring . . . the future is certain."

Predictor Thule! The chief of the Safety Authority on Accolon was not merely one of Enro's agents; he was one of the Yalertans.

The blazing images of past and future filled Gosseyn's mind. He could not look away, as the visions were inside him, part of him, and he was part of the universe.

He tried to find his home galaxy, the eon of time native to him, but the spiral galaxy was now turning like a vast pinwheel, its arms of fire rotating, each star traveling at a different rate. Where was the star Accolon? Or, no, wasn't he on Earth? Wasn't he an old man dying from a soldier's bullet on the floor of the Semantics Institute? No, he was a farmer from Cress Village . . . no, he was a baby in an artificial crèche, kept in a state of profound unconsciousness, fed by liquids, his brain sensitive to the thought pressures of Lavoisseur . . .

. . . was that an earlier picture, or a later one?

Here he was, emerging from his suspension capsule onto the soil of an unknown world in the new galaxy. The two women passengers had survived, and he must select a wife from one of them, but the other man, named Gorgzor, had been fatally wounded. The Observer could keep him alive, barely . . . the dark-haired woman, who had been betrothed to the wounded man, was already beginning to weep . . . many children in the next generation were named after him, and one founded a tribe, the Gorgzides, that grew into the nation and empire imposing its name on the world. . . .

Gosseyn saw Enro's face, eyes aglow with gloating

satisfaction, as the great dictator leaned over, looking down into the crate. He was dressed in a military uniform of scarlet and purple. Somehow, he seemed to be seated on an elevated throne of dark iron, and the emblem of the Three Watching Eyes of the Empire hung above and to either side of him.

"How convenient of you to have selected your own coffin, Mr. Gosseyn. X tells me he can prevent the transfer of your consciousness to your next hidden body merely by establishing a system of vibrations throughout this area with his robotic mind-paralysis units. . . ."

Enro raised his hand. From the ghostly translucence of his flesh, Gosseyn realized he was looking at a projection, created by Enro's control over images sent through space.

No, that was not happening yet. This was a vision of a few moments in his future. Where was he? But the galaxy was too large; time was too immense. Gosseyn abandoned that search and looked instead to see if he could pierce and find the source of the billions of energy-lines that had pulled his perceptions so far away from himself.

Then he saw that there were systems of Stabilization Spheres not merely in the future galaxies but also in the past, including early periods of galactic evolution before the formation of planets. A paradox: The Spheres were made of elements, carbon, silicon, iron, uranium, which simply did not exist at that time.

Further, there were Spheres of the same design scattered throughout the Andromeda Galaxy, three million light-years away, and Fornax, and Sculptor, the supergiant galaxy in Triangulum . . . and farther. . . .

His perception, his mind, encompassed the knowledge and texture of time and space, matter and energy, in all its complexity, of the entire Virgo Supercluster, of which the local cluster of galaxies was merely a small part: His thoughts reached across two hundred million light-years, to the Hydra Supercluster . . . it was more than any mind, even one as well trained as his, could bear. . . .

Any child of rank from a birth-center on my world knows how to shrug off this side effect . . .

Gosseyn attempted again to perform a cortical-thalamic pause, but this time he used the hypnotic cues that lay beneath the pause to become aware of the flows to and from his extra brain . . . he made an effort to relax the nerves and muscles and calm the bloodflows surrounding the sensitive tissues at the base of his brain . . . because it was this area of the brain, not his thalamus, that was being overwhelmed. It was his perceptions that were insane, not his emotions. If a child could do it, it must not require advanced training. . . . Gosseyn saw one out of several possible futures . . . in the ones where he was dead, no information came back. From the future where he lived, the correct combination of cues to force the pause-of-perception came to him. He did not have time to train the unknown brain sections to a proper response conditioning. But he could simply dominate his own buried nerve-paths that same way he dominated the circuitry flows within the machines around him.

The moment of the pause was a moment without time. And for a moment, the galaxy . . . *faded* . . . in that strange moment of transparency, he felt a moment of nausea. . . .

An illusion. This time-space continuum was also an artificially created falsehood. It was a structure created and maintained by these great Spheres.

Enro was still speaking: "Do you understand now who is the Sleeping God? It is I. Not that bit of flesh kept alive in Cousin Secoh's ancient starship. All those years I bowed and worshipped, not realizing the simple truth, the obvious truth. I was asleep and thought I was merely a man. But mine is the power of life and death, time and space. Once I embrace my sister as wife, the race that shall spring from her, omniscient, immortal, will wipe mankind away. . . . Lavoisseur (but you know him by the name X) has already taken the cell samples from my bone marrow to make a twin, a baby to grow in a tank, which will house me when I perish . . . but you will not live to see it."

Enro was fair skinned and lightly freckled, and when blood rose to his face, as it did now, his features were dark, like some exaggerated mask. His eyes glittered unblinkingly like those of a man under the influence of a drug.

Gosseyn knew the symptoms: the Violent Man Syndrome. The belief that bloodshed would solve all problems, soothe all discontents, create the utopia. All life's ills would be cured, if only the violent man were violent enough to shed all the blood necessary. It was all very sick and very simple: Infantile feelings of helplessness were buried under layers of increasingly random atrocities.

"Do you know why I cannot spare your life? Because your maker had the audacity, the blasphemy, to put ideas in your head that you had touched my Reesha, that you had *possessed* her. . . ."

Gosseyn did not know what image of what far world Enro created behind his helpless body. It took only a moment for the space-stress involved between Enro's viewpoint and his target to interrupt the biological functions of his body. Without a sound or word, he died, and his skin turned black as ash.

Gosseyn stared in curiosity down at his body. The illusion was so lifelike! But he had already triggered the set of deeply buried commands Dr. Halt had implanted in his brain. The cycle to wake up out of the illusion, once started, could not be stopped.

Even as Enro smiled a small, cool smile of triumph, he vanished. The orbital station lost its coherence, and the image collapsed. Some of the more distant stars lingered longer than the nearer ones, before the energies involved could not maintain the appearance of being where there was non-being.

Gosseyn was alone in an utter darkness. His clothes were gone. He was in free fall. Around him was nothing, neither air nor airlessness.

From Gosseyn's point of view, the universe was a non-phenomenon. It ceased; in an ultimate fashion, it never had been. Instead was this: nonexistence.

He probed with his extra brain. The nothingness around him was composed of particles of some sort, but each one was isolated, non-identified, so that no properties of behavior could be communicated from one particle to the next. There was neither direction nor duration here.

Something stirred in the darkness.

THE YDD GREET THE INTERLOPER AND INITIATE NEGOTIATION.

31

Positive judgments, that the world should and must conform to a man-made world-view, are the source of the violence neurosis of mankind, for the absolutism of two such positive judgment systems clashing leaves no room for peaceful arbitration.

The thoughts rang into his brain, shockingly loud, dazing him. He performed another cortical-thalamic pause to prevent disorientation. Gosseyn selected one particle at random and "attuned" himself to it using his extra brain.

The results were startling. That particle, to him, blazed with light, the light of a miniature star. He sensed the warp of space around him, as if this star were many times the mass of a galaxy, but only he was affected by the gravity. There was no sensation of motion, so he did not know the shape of his orbit around it. Perhaps he was falling straight toward it, but if so, the star did not visibly grow any bigger, so it must have been an astronomical distance off.

Using that star as an arbitrary fixed point, he began using the shadow-controlling part of his brain, that special training he had received from the far-future version of himself, to shift certain of his properties further into phase with it, on several wavelengths in the neurochemical range, to try to find an energy level that would step down the Ydd entity's monstrous mental force. He was operating on the assumption that, in this environment, all particles were "out-of-phase" to him. But theoretically, that same control over his own bodily substance that allowed him, while a shadow, to let light or gravity affect him rather than pass through him could be used here, once he had established a fixed orientation metric, to allow neural waves to pass through him without harm.

It worked, or something did. The next thought-shape impressed into Gosseyn's consciousness was like hearing a normal voice rather than a deafening shout.

The mental voice was eerily calm and detached, without any hint of emotion: *"The interloper should not have done that. The Ydd acknowledge displeasure."*

Despite the tonelessness of the voice, Gosseyn felt a sense of hostility radiating from the darkness, of deadly rage.

Gosseyn realized that he was inside the Ydd being. All this shadow-substance, occupying an unknown range of infinity around him, outside the universe and larger than it: All this was the Ydd.

Out of the darkness around him, issuing from several points above and below, came bolts of powerful energy, crackling X-rays and high-energy gamma rays. When Gosseyn attempted to adjust his shadow-body to put himself out-of-phase with one group of them, he accidentally entered an in-phase condition with a second volley of bolts he had not been able to sense until then.

As an automatic reflex, something he had set up in his extra brain long ago memorized the incoming energy and similarized it to the only point in space available to him: the tiny white star. But even this was not instantaneous: During the microsecond he was exposed to part of the radiation barrage he was burned badly. The pain was shocking: He lost sensation in his limbs. His hair was burned away from his skull. He lost the use of his eyes. Though he could still sense it with his extra brain, he could no longer see the tiny star that was his only orientation point in a universe of chaotic darkness.

Gosseyn imposed a thought on the same band of energy the incoming "voice" of the Ydd had occupied. "I thought you said you wanted to negotiate."

"Interdicted behavior is unacceptable. This point is not open to negotiation."

Gosseyn wondered if he were speaking to a computer or some other form of artificial being. "What are your operating parameters?"

"The highest priority goes to self-preservation, of course."

Gosseyn thought sardonically, *Of course.* "And?"

"And all other entities within the time-space continuum must orient to that priority: Failure to do so is unacceptable."

And Gosseyn knew the reaction that followed upon behavior deemed unacceptable.

This being, huge and primitive, somehow occupied a point before the beginning of time, a location outside of space. There seemed to be nothing else here, neither time nor space nor energy, nothing except for endless masses of noninteracting particles that lacked identity and behavior.

Somehow this primal being was aware of events within the universe. Somehow it was displeased with these events: displeased to the point where destroying all but the first microsecond of the universe was its response.

Whatever did not put the preservation of the Ydd first and foremost had to die.

It seemed quite simple and quite neurotic.

Gosseyn asked the central question: "Why? Unacceptable for what reason?"

In Gosseyn's brain there now appeared not words but sensations. Not images, for the creature's senses did not include awareness of light, but some sense impression intimately tied into the nature of time-space itself.

Was this the memory of the Ydd? Its origins?

Because at one point of time there was simply nothing. And at another point—whether before or after made no difference—the Ydd grew aware of the universe like a coal burning at the core of its vastness. A cone of all possible futures extended in one direction: Gosseyn decided this direction was the future. Like an hourglass-shape, there was a similar cone extending in the opposite direction back into the past before the Big Bang point. Perhaps it was an antimatter universe or perhaps the exhausted and collapsing end-time of some previous condition of existence, a before-cosmos. The Big Bang itself was at the touching tips of the two equal-and-opposite cones.

Within the light-cone were all slower-than-light phenomena, all the particles and galaxies of which man was aware. Outside, faster-than-light but just as real, was a timeless and dimensionless chaos, occupied by nothing but this single archaic, primitive, infinitely powerful being.

Through the Ydd senses, Gosseyn grew aware of a series of impulses, a flow of faster-than-light reactions reaching into and out of the cosmos. The impression was one of a complex and vital relationship: a symbiosis sustaining certain complexities of time and eternity within the universe and giving the Ydd something it needed.

Gosseyn sent the thought: "What is it? What do you need from the universe?"

Through some sense impression of the Ydd for which Gosseyn had no name, Gosseyn became aware of the nature of time, and he sensed a fixity, a cause-and-effect structure the Ydd would otherwise lack. Like a vine growing on a solid tree? No, the relationship was more intimate. Like a single-celled animal passing elements into and out of the membrane that formed its boundary: Except, in this case, the Ydd was the fluid environment surrounding, and it was somehow sustained and nourished by the interaction of the infinitely tiny, precious organism of the universe beating at its center.

The image changed: The Ydd perceived a corruption, and painful fluctuation within the universe that seemed to dissolve the time-structure, to weaken the faster-than-light energy-relations establishing the basic physical constants of the universe. This effect, whatever it was, created intense displeasure within the Ydd. Ydd was aware of a danger: It would topple and collapse back to the form it would have had if the universe were not present. Gosseyn sensed the simplest form of entity: an infinitely small point of unaware nothingness, unperceived by any other being.

"The Ydd life-process is tied directly to the nature of time-space itself, in a fashion that no material life existing in a slower-than-light zone of the universe can be. The Ydd can be damaged or destroyed by an alteration of the fundamental time-arrangement. If the Ydd perish, the universe perishes: The two are interrelated and symbiotic. Hence the rise of biological life within the slower-than-light frame of reference cannot be permitted to grow into a threatening direction. Hence by culling the segments of the universe where threatening behaviors arise the remainder of the universe can be preserved."

"How large a remainder?"

The answer was in terms of a millionth of a second of time after the Big Bang. Instead of a period of antigravitational inflation, which would lead to a transparent and rarefied universe, the cosmic all of matter-energy would recollapse immediately after its initial explosion and the universe never grow larger than the diameter of the nucleus of an atom.

"Where do I fit into this?"

"The interloper represents a threat. An alteration to a non-threatening posture is needed."

"Because I am aware of you?"

"Yes."

"Define the nature of this alteration. How do I become nonthreatening?"

"The Ydd offer . . . oneness!"

"My consciousness will be merged with yours?"

"The statement is correct. The partial consciousness of the now-limited being will be made without limit or definition."

"Will I still be self-aware?" Gosseyn wondered if, once merged with this being, his thoughts could influence it into a nondestructive psychology, cure it. If so, his own annihilation would be a small price to pay. In his mind, he steeled himself to make this sacrifice, if necessary.

"No. Once the signal you call awareness has been summed to the one-in-all being of Ydd, there is no need of separate or partial awareness. There is neither memory nor intellection needed. Sensation will no longer be needed."

Gosseyn's mind reeled back from the utter inhumanity of the offer. Oneness with . . . non-being? Death seemed clean and wholesome compared to that.

But the Ydd sent one more thought: *"This environment is the ultimate reality. All chains of causation spring from the Ydd origin; all chains of effect lead toward the Ydd finality. All actions taking place within the cosmos are organized for the pleasure of the Ydd. The Ydd are the absolute against which all else is measured."*

This was nonsense-talk. The emotion-delusion of self-absorption was one of the crudest and most primitive. Only a baby is too simple to know that other beings have value aside from their ability to serve the baby's need.

Even before learning to speak, small children learn to recognize other beings as having their own reality.

Gosseyn said briefly, "Sane men discover for themselves the overall meaning of their lives."

There came a rumble in the darkness, and swirling churn of the clouds of dark chaotic particles. *"The Ydd express mirth. Limited creature! The events of your life, your separation into multiple copies, your regathering into a final version, were all organized since the dawn of time, since eternity, to serve the purposes of Ydd. The secret and supreme power you have sought your whole life, your Chessplayer moving you like a pawn, is before you. You have pierced the final veil separating human consciousness from utter truth. Look at this darkness around you. This is Ydd. This is the final truth, stripped of all illusion. There is nothing else."*

"Did you create the universe?"

A moment's hesitation, and then, slyly: *"Yes. Of course."*

It was the bald-faced nature of the lie that decided him. There was no point in further talk.

Gosseyn wondered if he had a weapon against this being. The relaxation Anslark had forced on Gosseyn's secondary brain had triggered a reaction with the primordial superhot, superdense matter of the origin point of the universe. In normal time, nothing would come of that reaction for over 170 years. But he was no longer in normal time. In fact, his time-relation to the cosmos was currently . . . nothing. It was arbitrary.

Gosseyn wondered if he could find a frame of reference in this non-space in which that 170 years would seem to already have passed. All that would be required was a prediction-type similarity to bridge the gap between himself-now and himself-then.

Gosseyn attempted to stimulate the proper sections of his extra brain.

Light!

An explosion of infinite magnitude filled all the nothingness around him.

If death came then, either from his weapon or from the instant and terrible Ydd counterreaction, it came too swiftly for any sensation.

32

Scientific thought is based on negative judgment: Reality disqualifies any scientific model found guilty of inaccurate prediction. Hence negative judgment demands that the man-made world-view should and must conform to the world.

Gosseyn was whole again, unwounded. He was dressed and standing upright on a floor. The light here came from a series of high, square screens showing images of underground cities or portions of rust-colored desert. Standing before Gosseyn and above him on a dais was a thin-faced older man with a lantern jaw dressed in a high-collared uniform made of photorepeating fabric. He was swaying on his feet, clutching a huge desk next to him for support. To Gosseyn's right a dark-haired pale-skinned woman of striking appearance and a group of glittering-eyed young men were brandishing heavy electric pistols. The woman had a foxlike quirk to her red lips. The young men were shouting, "Illverton! Tune your uniform! Surrender now! Tune to our colors or else! The Safety Authority is finished!"

Yvana, the sly-faced dark-haired woman, was perhaps the quickest of Callidetics there to notice a change in the nuance of circumstance. She holstered her pistol and put a hand out to support Gosseyn.

Why, thought Gosseyn, *I must look like I'm about to faint!*

"What just happened?" she whispered sharply, drawing near. Her tone was not worried but eager: She wanted to find out whatever this new factor in the situation was and exploit it before the other members of her team caught on. Leadership on a world of fickle callidetic geniuses was always an uncertain affair.

Gosseyn's attention was arrested by the blazing sunlight that shined through the repeater screens. Roughly half the desert scenes showed a yellow sun hanging in the cloudless dark-purple sky. Scattered among them were pictures obviously from the other hemisphere, showing the starry skies above the wastelands, with the crescent of a blue planet in the distance, with a smaller crescent, gray-black and crater marked, hanging near it.

The white-haired man was raising his hands uncertainly as the young men pointed their weapons, but as quick as a school of fish all turning at some unseen signal, the squad of armed men all turned to look at Yvana. The fact that she had paused to whisper to Gosseyn checked their hot-bloodedness. Some of the men, almost as quick as Yvana to grasp that the situation had changed, began holstering their weapons.

Gosseyn said, "I do not see how I can be alive, not even theoretically. Did the Ydd return me here?"

Gosseyn raised his hand to wipe his brow (he was shaking and sweating) and he felt a strange *heaviness* in his hand and arm. Distracted, he flexed his fingers, feeling a sensation as if a powerful electrical current were moving through the nerves and muscles of his arm. When he drew a breath, the same massive sensation was in his chest.

When he used his extra brain to photograph his own body, he sensed that the molecules and atoms of which he was composed were connected in some fundamental way with a point infinitely remote in time or space. Dimly, he could sense this point as a white-hot supercharged atom of infinite density . . . or . . . no, it was large, larger than

the universe, and this cosmos was the golden pin-
prick. . . .

Yvana parted her lips to say something but was interrupted by a voice coming over the telephone on the desk:
"This is James Armour in advisory command of the warship *Aeneas* hailing the unidentified planet which has
materialized in orbit around our home star, Sol. Please
confirm your identity and state your intentions."

Illverton picked up the phone, but a slight rustle of motion passed through the throng of Corthidians there, as
they each looked eye to eye, forming their lightning-quick
estimates of each other's intentions. Instead of speaking,
Illverton turned the telephone's camera toward Yvana and
nodded. She spoke: "This is Yvana Vathirid of Organization Vathir, representing the interests of the Safety Authority of the planet Corthid. Are you the ranking officer of the
vessel? We seem to have been displaced from the Corthid
home system by a cosmic disturbance."

One of the plates on the walls, in its automatic fashion,
had zeroed in on the glimmering two-mile-long cylinder
of the Venusian dreadnought. The readout showed the su-
perbattleship was roughly 230,000 miles away.

James Armour said dryly, "My rank is as high as
anyone else's aboard. Is that Gilbert Gosseyn there? Cosmic disturbances accompany his presence with noted frequency."

Gosseyn stepped forward and spoke into the microphone: "Mr. Armour, can your ship set up a relay link between the Games Machines of Corthid and Venus? I
would like them to compare information. I have suffered
a complete de-identification with the sidereal universe,
which should have rendered it impossible for me to return. Also, I am aware of a . . . disturbance . . . a tension
in space-time . . . between my body and some distant
point. . . ."

Even as he spoke, this tension became a pull. He
could feel something attempting to similarize the atoms

in his body to widely scattered positions outside of time and space. Pain ran through his nerves like fire.

He started to assume his shadow-form, but the pain grew more intense. He gritted his teeth. His future went blank in just a moment, which either meant that he would use his extra brain, or that he would perish.

And the sense of nausea shivered through him, aching.

His overriding thought was: *If this is an illusion, what is really happening?*

Over the telephone, James Armour said, "Mr. Gosseyn, the distorter engines of the drive core of the *Aeneas* just fluctuated, and the astronomy team says the effect came from your position or nearby. Is the disturbance you mentioned the cause of a radical change in the fundamental properties of space-time?"

Gosseyn was not sure about the answer to that all-important question.

Over the phone, Armour said in a tense voice, "Miss Yvana, how quickly can you bring Gosseyn to a spot where a Games Machine can examine him? The readings the shipboard astronomy team reports show a massive buildup of space-disturbance . . . we may have only minutes."

Yvana simply had her men shove Gosseyn out of the window. Once he was falling free from the building, the Vathir organization spaceship, which was still hovering overhead, picked him up on a force-pencil and swung him over to the huge pyramidal tower housing of the Games Machine of Corthid. It was as swift as that.

The Machine, by this time, had been linked through distorter radio to the Games Machine of Venus. During the tense minutes while the examination took place, the other Null-A Games Machines of various planets in the local arm of the galaxy joined the distorter-radio hookup. It was a mental force of some twenty-five million electronic brains that examined Gosseyn's mind and body structure down to the Planck level of detail.

The combined Games Machines reported: "You are

aware at a fundamental level that the reality around you is false. Under normal conditions, this would be an indicator of severe psychotic break."

Gosseyn said, "What about the sensation that something is trying to pull me out of the universe?"

"It is a self-imposed symbolic delusion."

Gosseyn was sitting at a metal desk in one of the many rooms surrounding the base of the great machine's housing. In his hands he held the metal contacts with the sensitive instruments probing him. Before him was a wall of electron tubes, glowing softly blue, purple, and purple-red.

"Symbolic?"

"Your mind is producing a sensation to interpret something within the context of your human sense impressions which is fundamentally alien to the continuum in which the matter-energy structures of your body and nervous system were evolved."

Gosseyn thought: It was a classic problem in Null-A. The universe was not as our senses presented it. In order to grasp the complexities of reality, the sensory apparatus of a living thing, and the midbrain tissues and complexes, had to simplify sense impressions into meaningful but false categories.

The eye of a frog as it watched for the flies that nourished its life could not see certain types of motion. Motions not typical of flying insects were not seen. This was not a case of the simple frog brain ignoring the signal from the eye: The eye was designed to send no nerve signal to the brain unless the motion was one tied to the frog's eternal struggle against starvation. Hence if a frog were put into a new circumstance, such as one where a fly was moving in some fashion not typical of flies, the frog could not see it, not even if its life depended on it. The frog's nervous system and sensory apparatus locked it into a category of perception based on a positive judgment about the nature of motions it saw or could not see: a judgment it could not question.

The Machine said, "You are still engaged in a life-or-death struggle with the Ydd entity. At this moment, your extra brain is dangerously overstimulated: It is using nearly all of its available neural paths to counteract space-time and matter-energy manipulations taking place, thousands per microsecond, all around you."

Gosseyn said, "But what is actually around me?"

"The most likely hypothesis is that the moment of your death is still ongoing. Everything you are experiencing now simply appears to you to be taking time: In reality, you still occupy a frozen split second of time just before the destruction you set in motion overwhelms you."

Null-A was not a binary system of logic: Gosseyn did not conclude merely from the fact that the universe was *not true* that it was *false*. What was around him was a model, if only an incomplete one. Even if inaccurate, it still represented the basic underlying reality it hid.

Gosseyn said slowly, "If this universe around me, this group of perceptions, was given a symbolic value by whatever psychological process created it . . . I am going to act on the assumption that there must be something I can do within the framework of this illusion that will have a real effect on the real battle that is still going on."

The Machine said, "It is not that simple. There is a strong possibility that you have gone insane. The record in your memory indicates you attempted an attack on the Ydd by similarizing the origin point of the universe into your location: a suicidal attack, which, given the known facts of the Ydd composition, could have harmed only yourself, not your enemy. A shadow-being cannot be harmed by matter or energy to which it is not attuned. Your decision to trigger this effect, according to our examination of your subconscious memory, arose out of no prior thoughts."

The Machine continued, "Consider this: Lavoisseur, according, at least, to some evidence, acted in a similarly reckless and self-destructive fashion. Gosseyn One, who was shot to death outside of the Presidential Palace in the City of the Machine on Earth, fled from a safe hiding place to expose himself to gunfire in an absurdly reckless and pointless fashion; Gosseyn Two dosed himself with a hypnotic drug in order to convince himself to commit suicide when—"

Gosseyn interrupted, "If there is only a strong probability that I am insane, what is the other probability?"

The Machine said blandly, "The unlikelihood that you would impulsively yet suicidally similarize the Big Bang directly into the heart of the Ydd, and yet by means unknown survive the attempt, implies a planned action. Someone, perhaps by a similarity technique, implanted the impulsive thought in your head to strike at the Ydd using the uncontrolled energy Anslark's apparently random act had placed at your disposal, and this opportunity in turn arose because certain energy-balancing structures were imprinted in your nervous system by creatures representing themselves to be remote future versions of yourself, an act whose purpose they failed to explain. Summed together, the percent chance that it was not coincidence approaches unity. A more elegant hypothesis suggests that this moment was planned from the start."

"So I am still being manipulated by the Chessplayer."

"Obviously."

"And Patricia knows who the Chessplayer is."

"I cannot verify that statement," said the Machine.

"But she can."

A signal on the panel before him indicated that Dr. Hayakawa's team was standing by. Gosseyn, at some deeply buried level, was still connected to the Stabilization Spheres in the various Milky Ways of the past and future. Hayakawa's plan was to have the Games Machine stimulate Gosseyn's nerve paths attuned to the Spheres, but instead of allowing the near-infinity of information to overwhelm him, the Machine would act as

310 JOHN C. WRIGHT

a filter and a processing stage—an artificial thalamus, as it were—before allowing the perception circuit to complete itself.

The processing power of the thousands of Games Machines on a thousand worlds would search through the abundance of information, with the help also of human operators on Corthid.

The No-men freed from their orbital prison were standing by to examine the information-flows on a gross level and use their trained intuitions to direct the "lucky" Corthidians toward the data streams where useful information might be found. The two working together would enable them intuitively to see patterns the Null-A machines and their Venusian operators might miss. The Nexialists freed from the temple were in charge of understanding and coordinating the diverse mental sciences of these three groups and establishing a perception model in which all groups could act efficiently.

But the apex of this complex structure of human and machine brain cooperation was Gosseyn. It was his extra brain that was the conduit to the deluge of information the Stability Spheres were pulling in from the enigmatic pattern of timeless and spaceless phenomena the human mind insisted on seeing in discrete dimensions of time and space, rather than as a continuum.

Gosseyn said, "I'm ready."

The first experiment was actually rather small-scale. Gosseyn allowed faint prediction-images to appear in his mind, showing conditions of possible futures. The combined Games Machines, guided by No-man intuitions, found and stimulated that strong energy connection he had running to Patricia.

The reason why his attempt to similarize her to him previously had failed, of course, was that peculiar armor she wore, which allowed her to carry a small hint of the Shadow Effect with her, a shadow his powers could not penetrate. But within any given twenty-four-hour period, surely she had to take it off to rest or bathe?

And there was no such thing as simultaneity in an Einsteinian universe. Any point in time within the next twenty-four hours might be "now" as far as his frame of reference was concerned.

The Patricia who materialized beside him was the one occupying the first moment of unprotection: She was actually bending over to strip the flexible metallic leggings from her legs and stepping out of them. The upper part of the suit, its Shadow Effect unenergized, was bunched in her hands. Beneath, she was wearing a skintight sheath of material that left her arms and legs bare.

She straightened in shock, her hand moving automatically to the holster that rode the curve of her hip. But by the time her long fingers, swift as they were, snatched at the butt of her Colt 1.6 megavolt, it was similarized in Gosseyn's hand.

"Who is the Chessplayer, Patricia?" he said.

She visibly relaxed. "It's nice to see you, too, Gilbert." She nonchalantly reached down to where the suit fabric had fallen around her ankles and started to draw it up around her legs and hips, until Gosseyn came forward suddenly and stepped on a fold of it. This prevented her from pulling the suit up and fastening it, which also apparently prevented the shadow-energy circuit from activating.

She smiled and shrugged and straightened up, letting the metallic fabric drop. Gosseyn was standing close to her, and he noticed how dainty she was, despite her regal bearing: The crown of her auburn head was level with his chin.

Patricia said, "For a moment, I was afraid you were X or some other near relation."

"Who is the Chessplayer?"

"Oh, come on. That's been obvious from the start. Lavoisseur."

"You said he was dead."

She shrugged prettily. "He is. We are playing out what he set in motion."

The Games Machine offered, "While she is not literally lying, she is speaking with deceptive intent."

Gosseyn angrily took her by the shoulders and shook her. "Who is the Chessplayer, Patricia? Who is running my life?"

She was standing on her tiptoes now. The metallic fabric fell away into a heap around her ankles. In spite of Gosseyn's rough handling, she merely smiled thoughtfully. "All right: I'll tell you. In order to convince Enro that I was his sister, I had to undergo the ordeal of interment in the Crypt of the Sleeping God, as he had done."

Gosseyn picked her up and set her down a foot or two back. He stood and gathered up the metallic cloth of the shadow-armor in his hands, looking at the clasps and control-buttons as he did so. "Go on!" he said, not looking up.

He found that, while the shadow-stuff was not activated, the crystalline-metallic structure of the fabric could be memorized by his extra brain. The collar and cuffs held a miniature circuit of some distorter-type mechanism, which could be activated by a simple electronic switch, once the fasteners were shut.

Patricia spoke: "The belief on Gorgzid is that only a member of the Royal Family can survive being placed in suspended animation and being revived by the Observer," she said. "Naturally, they interpret everything in terms of their Cult, and regard the thawing process as a divine rebirth. You were in that coffin, Gilbert. You remember. It is the only place where the Observer can communicate with one of its patients it is evolving up to a higher state of being.

"This is what I learned: The damage to the Observer was deliberate. All other of the Primordial starships dismantled themselves for parts to help the early colonists, but the Observer could not carry out its program as long as it had a living passenger. It was required to remain intact. The man who damaged the Observer also was a master psychiatrist, who used his knowledge of human weakness to erect a Cult—only a religious institution would be conservative enough over the centuries—a Cult to worship the Sleeping God, and dedicated to keeping the Observer ship untouched, and in working order. The entire Gorgzidian society, its history and culture, was established merely so that a working Primordial ship would be preserved to the present day.

"And of course these ships were all connected to the positive energy of the Stability Sphere system back in the Shadow Galaxy: That is how they were preserved when they passed though the Shadow Effect englobing that galaxy two thousand million years ago. And the circuits which control the Stability Spheres are therefore intact, and were allowed to fall into Enro's hands: Enro was able to cross to the Shadow Galaxy much more quickly than the awkward and experimental ship you were on, because, among other things, the Observer had perfect understanding of the engine operation. It was a small matter to activate the Spheres, attune them to the proper frequencies of non-being, make contact with the Ydd—and to place X in a position contiguous to all shadow-segments in the shadow-space to kill you when you appeared. Other bits of the Primordial technology, such as this shadow-armor which prevents all distortion effects, the Observer turned over to Enro's scientists.

"The Observer helped Enro because it was programmed to do so, but it was also programmed to help me find Lavoisseur, the primordial being the Gorgzidians call Ptath. It helped Eldred Crang, once Eldred found the galactic base on Venus, enter the service of the Greatest Empire as a double agent and it also helped him arrange the armistice which ended the galactic war. You were there when the Observer aided your plan to stop the Follower. But what you do not know is that this same Observer kept intact the Null-A nerve-manipulation technology that served as the model for the first Games Machine constructed six hundred years ago by a figure history named de Lany—another name for Lavoisseur-Ptath. A technology it gave to him. Someone, something, programmed the Observer to work against Enro and the Ydd. Your Chessplayer."

"Who?"

She shook her head. "It never told me, and I do not have the control over energy you do which enables you to dominate the minds of machines, so I could not force it to respond. Our relationship was a little one-sided: The Observer was the one who told me where the body of Gosseyn Four was hidden, and ordered me to move it into my rooms at the Imperial Palace on Gorgzid. It knew Enro was going to kill you."

"And why did you obey its orders?"

She shrugged again. "Walter asked me to."

"Walter?"

"Walter S. de Lany. The man you call Lavoisseur."

Gosseyn turned to the Games Machine. "What do you make of all this?"

The Games Machine replied, "Relatively unimportant. You are facing two strict time limits. First, if Enro discovers you are still connected with the Sphere at Accolon, he can induce a shadow-effect to cut you off. At the moment, your range in space and time is intergalactic, and thousands of years, an opportunity you dare not squander. Second, the activity in your extra brain is not stable: You are engaged in fighting a war with the Ydd involving more mass-energy than can be accounted for in our current understanding of the universe. We assume that you are unconsciously manipulating the great mass of non-identified matter outside of time-space to fight the Ydd, or to deflect Ydd attacks. There is no evidence that this situation will remain stable. The Ydd may simply overwhelm the number of possible interconnections in your nervous system before long, even from your current highly accelerated frame of reference. You must act at once."

"How much of the galaxy do I have 'memorized' using the Sphere of Accolon?"

"All of it, including the globular clusters and the satellite galaxies at the Lesser and Greater Magellanic Clouds. Furthermore, the Sphere network apparently exists in both past and future eras, including periods of history, dark ages, when no world in the galaxy possessed the technology to create them."

"What does the future show?" asked Patricia.

The Games Machine said, "The future information shows unqualified victory for Enro. The Interstellar League, governed by Commissioner Thule, will allow itself to be peacefully absorbed into the Greatest Empire over the next six years, and last for some forty-seven hundred years. It may last longer, but we have no information from Spheres further down the time-continuum."

"Then Enro will succeed, but the Ydd will fail?" asked Gosseyn in disbelief.

"No," said the Machine. "You are connected to a system of Spheres through the Sphere at Accolon, which Enro controls. Hence your perception-information that we are correlating comes from Enro's system of Spheres, which extends throughout many millennia. Obviously futures where all life is overwhelmed by shadow are not sending back any information. Futures where Enro is defeated are also ones where his control over the Spheres is broken, and hence the modern-day Spheres would not be receiving any information from them. Mr. Gosseyn, you of all men must be aware that the time-space continuum you see around you is not an accurate reflection of reality, nor can the future information currently examined be taken as inevitable. However, again we remind you of the limited time you have in which to act."

The second experiment involved no new principle. Like locating Patricia, it only took a short time for the sequential array of Games Machines to comb through Gosseyn's extra brain to locate the distorter patterns for Anslark Dzan and the other members of the Royal Family of Dzan and to bring them to a comfortable spot in Landing City where Peter Clayton explained the situation to them. Anslark was happy to cooperate, and his brothers and cousins at first seemed awed by the scale of what they were about to attempt. A distorter link was set up between the Dzan, the warship *Aeneas*, and the bright variable star S Doradus in the Greater Magellanic Cloud. Null-A machinery was used to attune the Dzan nervous systems to the rhythms of the interference much like those used by the Petrino mind-paralysis robots: like them but better, for the electrons directed by their minds alone had a much finer scale of control than the tubes and energy nodes of the Petrino Standardization Committee robots. After a few experiments in knocking out the crews of Greatest Empire ships or hidden bases either at nearby stars or in other arms of the galaxy, the Royal Family of Dzan said they were ready.

The third experiment was on a larger scale: Gosseyn had the Milky Way Sphere system memorize everything within the action of its radius, some 179,000 light-years. Using a prediction power to get an image of the core of the Andromeda Galaxy 2.9 million light-years away, he memorized the supergiant singularity at that galactic core and forced a similarization. The mass of the Andromeda Galaxy was greater than that of the Milky Way, and so the Milky Way crossed the distance as if there had been no gap.

When the moment of darkness ended, Gosseyn said aloud, "Any collisions?" He would have preferred to transmit the galaxy to a location in empty space, of course, but the mass involved did not allow for that possibility.

James Armour, aboard the *Aeneas,* was the first to answer: "The number of stars in the sky more than doubled, and there is now a second band of stars, a Milky Way stream bisecting the first, but the chance that two stars would be within half a light-year of each other is astronomically remote. It will be years before we can calculate the positions of every new star."

The voice of Madroleel Enosh, one of the No-men rescued from Accolon, came over the radio: "Don't bother. I've intuited that there have been no collisions. The disks of the two galaxies are at right angles. The orbits of stars around the galactic core will be disturbed over the next few million years, but the human race will develop the technology to herd stars into more stable orbits before the effect is noticeable."

Armour said, "More importantly, there is no Shadow Effect visible on our gravitic plates. Whatever was inside any shadow-areas is still in the Milky Way galaxy's original location. Can the Games Machines give you the co-ordinates to send us to pick up any of Patricia's Amazons who might have been in their shadow-armor? We can worry about Enro's shadow-protected warships later."

Gosseyn had left a large number of dead stars and dust clouds back at the original location, to give him sufficient mass, sufficiently dispersed, to similarize a ship to practically any point in the now-empty volume, using a combination of similarities and similarity brakes.

Yvana's voice had a lilt of laughter in it: "All the Predictors on every planet in the galaxy just went blind! I bet Enro did not see that one coming!"

The Nexialist in charge of coordinating the groups working with the Games Machines to study the information, a woman named Cil ve Connlin, said over the radio, "The method of prediction-similarization should continue to operate for several hours from our frame of reference: From the point of view of the location where the home galaxy once was, of course, we have some discretion in selecting an approach time. The *Aeneas* can arrive, from the frame of reference of each woman being rescued, within minutes or even seconds of the disappearance of the galaxy around her."

Patricia said, "That armor is spaceworthy, and has an automatic circuit. My girls can stay alive in them for the better part of a day." She was staring at what looked to Gosseyn like blank wall. "So many stars! Why can we

see all the new stars? If one of the stars of the Andromeda Galaxy landed even two light-years away, it would
still be two years until we saw it, right?"

Gosseyn said curtly, "The photons were already crossing this point in space before we intersected it. Games
Machine! Are we prepared for the third experiment? If
we can reach into the remote future and contact the superbeings there . . ."

The voice of the Games Machine was calm and measured: "We have just lost contact with the Spheres to the futureward of this position in time. With only contemporary
and pastward Spheres still connected, our range and calculating power has been reduced to less than half of the . . ."

Patricia put her hand on Gosseyn's shoulder. "Look
out! I can see him coming. I'd been hoping you'd catch
him in his shadow-form when you moved the Milky
Way. He is about nine thousand light-years away . . . five
hundred . . . he's here. . . ."

Gosseyn turned away from the desk and stood up. The
seventeen-year-old version of him was standing in the
doorway to the examination room, a slim vertical line between the brows of his young face, a sardonic amusement
in the yellow-brown depth of his ancient eyes.

33

Negative judgment is the peak of mentality.

As before, the young man wore the splendid scarlet
uniform of a Greatest Empire officer, with a sash and
medallions, and an ornamental triangle-of-eyes emblem
clasping his half cape.

Gosseyn did not wait for him to speak but stepped to a
memorized location on Mars.

FINE, windblown sand whipped Gosseyn's face, and sub-arctic temperatures benumbed his face and hands, despite the swell of automatic heat radiating from circuits in his coat. He was standing on an outcropping of rock, and the sky was orange with sandstorm.

The youth was there, his red uniform making him almost invisible in the gale of red dust. "What was the point of that?" The voice, though young and thin, still rang with authority. "I would not hurt Reesha. I will see that she is safely elsewhere before I similarize several dozen suns into Sol and create a nova . . . thank you for gathering all my opposition in one star system."

Gosseyn similarized the metallic fabric he had memorized earlier onto the young man's body. His spare frame was as small as Patricia's, so the suit materialized around him, the clasps already shut. Gosseyn with his extra brain triggered the circuit that activated the Shadow Effect running through the fibers of the material. At the same time, with a second nerve path in his extra brain, he brought here a small volume, no more than one cubic foot, of material from the core of the sun and retreated to a second location on the surface of Phobos.

PHOBOS was a mountain of rock in the darkness of space, too small to have an appreciable gravity. Gosseyn drew the space armor from its location in the Vathir Organization ship on Corthid to himself, his teeth chattering as the suit materialized around him and began to pressurize and heat up.

He did not need the amplifying plate in the suit helmet to see the blinding flash on the surface of Mars. The thin Martian atmosphere was disturbed like a ripple in a pond as the supersonic shockwaves traveled over this hemisphere of the planet. A reddish discoloration was the only sign, at this distance, of where the crust of the planet had shattered under the fifteen-million-degree heat. The volcanic debris from beneath the mantle of Mars was thrown into orbit when the superheated atmosphere, like a mushroom cloud, rose up at a rate greater than the planet's escape velocity. The needles in Gosseyn's helmet registering the energy release in X-rays and heavy particles were against their pins.

The reddish discoloration turned an eerie blue-white as the oxides in the rusted surface of Mars caught fire. At hot enough temperatures, almost anything will burn.

He did not need to speak aloud, since his extra brain was still connected with the thousand Games Machines in sequence. "Well?"

Anslark Dzan's voice was despondent: "We flooded the hemisphere of Mars with a neural wave on the Null-A paralysis frequency. Anyone with cortical-thalamic interconnections should have been frozen . . . the whole power of the supergiant variable S Doradus was driving our beam. . . . If he had only remained in solid form . . ."

The Games Machine voice was dispassionate: "Result negative. We aligned Sphere of Accolon to identify each particle in his body and prevent his assumption of this shadow-form, but the particles were then de-similarized out of our energy pattern by a superior force, something able to achieve a more perfect synchronization."

Gosseyn thought, *Patricia's shadow-armor should have cut him off from any distorter system or other outside energy sources. What false-to-facts assumption am I making?*

Against the glowing backdrop of the burning world, the shadow-form of the youth was clearly visible as he similarized himself to a point a few hundred yards away from Gosseyn. Evidently, the shadow-armor, before it had burned away, had indeed prevented X from similarizing to some other location, but it had not prevented him, within the armor, of putting his body out-of-phase with his environment, immune to all material and energetic harm.

Out from the semitransparent core of the shadow-being came a beam of radio-energy, modulated to be picked up by an amplitude antenna. Gosseyn's suit radio translated the vibrations into English: "So Gilbert Gosseyn comes to his futile end, having never discovered his origin or his purpose. An immortal man, when facing a god, is merely mortal after all. . . ."

The flood of energy released from the core of the shadow-being was sufficient to pierce Gosseyn's armor and destroy most of his body, even when Gosseyn similarized 99 percent of the energy flow into harmless ground points here and there about the galaxy, where Nova-O-level radiation expanded through the empty space.

The planet Corthid vanished, snatched to some remote location, while Earth and Venus and the inner system of Sol were obliterated in the residual energy Gosseyn could not deflect.

THE shock of seeing his world destroyed almost snapped Gosseyn out of the predictive vision he was having, but he steadied himself with a cortical-thalamic pause and heightened his awareness to absorb additional details.

It was fortunate that he did, for at this point the vision branched. The two possible futures after Earth's destruction were, first, that Gosseyn assumed his shadow-form. That branch of the vision went black at that point, of course, but Gosseyn knew the pain in his body from the Ydd attack would be lethal if he entered the nonidentity environment that was the Ydd's extradimensional body.

The second possible future, where he did not assume his shadow-form, showed Gosseyn waking up in his next body, a nineteen-year-old, in the medical coffin maintained by automatic machinery in a hollowed-out asteroid somewhere in the belt of icebergs circling Saturn. The youth in the scarlet uniform did not even bother to speak to him or gloat: Images of distant stars appeared around Gosseyn as his newly wakened body turned black and died.

In his lightning-quick fashion, Gosseyn examined two

or three scores of visions of the moment, just before the destruction of the inner solar system, when the shadow-being opened fire on him. In each version, Gosseyn was trapped by the law of similarization. His twenty-decimal-point similarity was enough to remove nearly all of the lethal particles from his environment, but it was not perfect similarity, so some small fraction escaped. X clearly had some means of making a more exact representation to the Planck level of Gosseyn's body and the surrounding space than Gosseyn could.

There was yet another possible future: Gosseyn removed the solar system to another arm of the galaxy and placed the star Sirius here, so that the shadowy figure was inside the inferno of the O-type star. This vision ended in basically the same way. X merely followed him and carried out the same result. Gosseyn could not similarize while in a shadow-form, but his enemy had a technique where he could. The bolt of energy from the shadow-figure merely destroyed Gosseyn and obliterated his next body with a controlled Shadow Effect, cutting his distorter link to any future incarnations. It was death, final and absolute.

GOSSEYN, in his armor, hung near the cragged gray rock of Phobos, observing with grim horror the images of his near future. In a moment, the shadow-form would emerge from the glare of burning Mars. The information flows in his brain were still connected, by distorter link, to the Games Machines of Corthid and Venus, and the phalanxes of expert Nexialists and No-men and Callidetics and Null-A's were examining the galaxy-wide data flow from the Sphere of Accolon.

It was, after all, still a hierarchy of perception, no different in principle from the hierarchy of the man's nervous system. Here he had a perception that led to certain disaster: He needed to set in motion something like a Null-A pause, so that the unspoken assumptions underlying what he was perceiving would be laid bare.

He addressed the Nexialist coordinator and explained his notion of a Null-A pause. "Dr. Connelin," he continued, "I am perceiving a future where X can not only similarize matter-energy while in his shadow-form but also do it to at least forty decimals of accuracy, which is nineteen orders of magnitude above my capacity. Somewhere in the mass of data of the memorized galaxy is the information we seek, but it is being lost because of a priority placed on certain information values by the Games Machines as they process the Accolon Sphere energy connections running through me. We need the higher centers of awareness to become consciously aware of what the lower centers processing the information in an automatic fashion are doing. . . ."

Connelin said, "Dr. Hayakawa has an idea on how to do it: We are setting up relays of Callidetics and No-men to examine the data flow for anomalies, using neurological equipment to stimulate their specialized brain centers. Stand by. . . ."

Now that one vision had located the asteroid where his next body was kept, Gosseyn similarized it to the farthest location in time-space he could reach with the Sphere network currently under his control. Then he looked at the future again: the end result of ten, twenty, fifty, two hundred possible futures . . . the end of every timeline radiating forward from this spot showed his next body destroyed in a wash of disintegrating darkness when it began to wake.

No matter where the asteroid was moved, the youth was there the moment it arrived. No point in the surrounding stars, not even in the Magellanic Clouds now orbiting the strangely intersecting collision of the Milky Way and Andromeda, was far enough.

Every future Gosseyn could see ended in death.

The future where he distorted to another location, of course, was a blur to him.

Dr. Connelin spoke, her voice tense and low: "The preliminary results are bad: Systems of distorter machines, built by someone with an expert knowledge of Null-A technology, have been identified as interfering with the hierarchical priority calculations of seven hundred of the Games Machines. This is exploiting certain limitations built into the original mental architecture of the first Games Machine. Wait. . . . The Machines are recalculating at a basic level."

Yvana interrupted, "We've stumbled across the clue you want. He must be using the Sphere system of the Shadow Galaxy to increase the range of his clairvoyance, and whatever calculation machinery the Primordials left behind allows for his more exact similarization fit, his forty-decimal-point accuracy. . . . Also, there may be several thousands of Loyalty Machines throughout the Greatest Empire and worlds where the Cult has temples, simply outnumbering our calculation capacity. . . ."

Gosseyn said, "I can see his shadow-form manifesting about one hundred yards away, between me and Mars—"

The voice of Enosh, the No-man, interrupted, "It's your Chessplayer. That's the forbidden topic. The Games Machines were programmed to direct your attention away from the conclusion of your conversation with Reesha of Gorgzid."

Patricia's voice rang over the earphones of his suit helmet: "That cannot be Lavoisseur, not X or any other version! That's not how he acts! That uniform, those little victory speeches . . . that's why, when he killed the League members, he shot the lie detector. . . ."

Peter Clayton, the Venusian detective, said, "One set of clues we've overlooked. . . . I am having the Games Machine on Earth trigger a nerve cluster in your extra brain, connecting you to the planet Nirene. . . . If he is using a distorter circuit to amplify his range, one of them must be hidden somewhere on the grounds of the Semantics Institute of Nirene, where Secoh is being held. . . . Got it. . . . It was hidden in the phone. . . . Dr. Hayakawa and his team are looking at it now—"

Connelin interrupted, "There is no need to examine

the physical machine, since Stability Sphere data contains a pattern of all the material objects in the galaxy. One of the No-men has reverse-engineered the circuit by intuitive analysis. Someone tell Empress Reesha to finish her sentence as soon as we get Gosseyn out of this death trap."

The calm, cool voice of the Games Machine, or one of them, came on: "Mr. Gosseyn, when your opponent establishes an energy connection with you, he must place part of his shadow-substance into phase with your frame of reference. We can attempt to synchronize with the incoming beam, and backtrack through his special long-range distorter system, and therefore reach to his setup in the Shadow Galaxy. We have no other way to reach the Primordial starship he used to reach the Shadow Galaxy, the so-called Crypt of the Sleeping God."

"Do I need to wait till he opens fire?" asked Gosseyn.

"No," replied the Machine. "Any energy path can serve."

The shadow-figure flicked a radio-beam into Gosseyn's helmet. "So Gilbert Gosseyn comes to his futile end, having never discovered his origin or his purpose. . . ."

But Gosseyn was already gone.

34

To think is to abstract.

Gosseyn opened his eyes. He was lying supine. About four inches before his eyes he saw the transparent metal sections of the inner lid of the Crypt of the Sleeping God of Gorgzid. Gosseyn's extra brain could sense, all around him, the complex energies of the thought-circuits of the Observer.

The pressure of the thousands of Games Machines, the surge of a galaxy-wide volume of information, was no longer in him. The voices of the staff of four institutions of specialized scientific thought, No-men, Null-A's, Nexialists, and Callidetics, were no longer in him. He was cut off.

He raised his fingers to fumble at the inside of the transparent coffin-lid, searching for a release.

Silently in his brain appeared the command: *Wait. If you open the lid, I will be out of contact.*

Gosseyn said, "The last time I was in this crypt, I had to be asleep for your thought-waves to reach me."

You have developed since that time. The evolution of life is a process of channeling the overwhelming complexity of the signals surrounding an organism into meaningful sense-categories; the evolution of the mind is the process of overcoming those categorical limits. Higher forms can comprehend and react to more complete mental pictures of the environment without being overwhelmed. Because of your development, your nervous system is more integrated, and the confusion of your conscious mind no longer drowns out the messages to which your midbrain and hindbrain are sensitive.

Gosseyn allowed himself a moment of curiosity: "Why can you only attune thought-messages to such buried nerve paths? If you made a similarity connection with the cortex, anyone would hear you, awake or asleep."

Your nervous system resembles that of your remote ancestors only in the older, less flexible, brain sections. The primate cortex mutated over the eons, and no longer matches my specific compatibility. My circuits were designed to mesh with the Primordial Humans, which your modern subspecies only partly resembles.

Gosseyn remembered seeing archeological evidence that Cro-Magnon and other primitive forms of man actually had the same brain-mass as *Homo sapiens,* merely more tightly knit, with a preponderance of brain matter in the rear of the skull. Oddly, that was where Gosseyn's extra brain resided. The assumption that those forms were simpler merely because they were older was one science could not definitively confirm.

But no matter. "You told me the original Chessplayer, the original gods, died long ago. Are you still receiving orders from him?"

I am not able to answer that question.

"Interesting that you phrase it that way."

It is within my allowed scope of discretion to phrase my sentences in any way that does not contradict a specific order or directive.

"Secoh claims you deceived me about several important matters. He became the Follower under your orders and direction, not by accident, as you told me. Why did you lie?"

I am not able to answer that question.

Gosseyn was momentarily silent, for a sense of awe came upon him. This entity, this machine, was surely the oldest self-aware being in existence. It survived the two-hundred-million-year-ago migration from the Shadow Galaxy, nursing the sole wounded survivor of the trip while the dust and soil of Gorgzid settled upon it, burying it. And still it waited, until a later generation of semi-civilized peoples, mining deep, found the hull and thought it was the dome of a temple. . . .

Except that if Patricia had told the truth, none of that happened by accident. And there was at least one being, still alive, as old as this unthinkably ancient machine. Someone who had maneuvered to preserve this machine through all the passing centuries intact. Why?

"You told me that Lavoisseur landed on a different ship, not this one. And yet now that the Sleeping God is dead, Lavoisseur is the only survivor of the Migration, and you conspired to bring him into this crypt, but he was wary of you. . . ."

Allow me now to correct that falsehood: I attempted to bring him into my medical unit so that I might continue repairs on him. He was also changed by the Shadow

Effect, and his personality and actions became unpre-dictable. He was wary of me because he did not wish to resume his former state of mind.

Gosseyn's attention was arrested by the word "unpre-dictable." He had been assuming that the action of his secondary brain naturally blocked the prediction power. Apparently, it was not natural. The Primordials, a whole race of men with highly evolved double brains, had not had that particular side effect. Only him.

Could it be a specific application of some attunement to the shadow itself? The Shadow Effect could block prediction by disturbing the future-to-past identity con-nections used by the Yalertans.

Gosseyn imagined that the Primordials, like the Yaler-tans, had depended heavily on the prediction power to maintain their social order, deter crimes before they oc-curred, prevent frauds, and so on. Surely they, and the machine they built, would react defensively to anyone suddenly developing the ability to blind them.

"You didn't force him?"

My directives sharply limit when I may use force on a patient under my care. Patients may refuse treatment. I have more latitude when circumstances require I defend them.

"Secoh said you wanted me to kill the Sleeping God because you were weary of the burden of guarding and sustaining him."

It is inaccurate to attribute to me motives typical of bi-ological organisms. I do not grow weary. Recall that I asked you to kill Secoh, not to incapacitate him. When I released my patient to your care, I had not anticipated that you would provoke Secoh into destroying my patient. I would not have been permitted to release my patient into your care had I known your intention.

"Why didn't you stop me? You said you can act to pro-tect your patients. No, let me ask a more important ques-tion: Why did you release your patient at all?"

I am not allowed to answer that question. My orders

and directives are organized in a flexible non-Aristotelian logic hierarchy, allowing me to avoid positive and absolute judgments, and to assess facts with multiple-valued inductive logic rather than simple binary logic. Hence authorities that I am bound to obey can restrict areas where I would otherwise have discretion.

"You were told not to interfere with me? Even when I endangered one of your patients, you could not act to stop me."

It was a general order, and it was ambiguous enough to allow me to interpret it to cover you.

"Who gave the order?"

You did.

An interesting response. Gosseyn asked *the* question. "Who am I?"

You are Ptath, the second of my original four charges.

"And why did I order you not to interfere with me?"

As previously stated: You grew wary of my attempts to trick you into reentering the medical coffin, because you did not wish to be repaired. . . .

"That wasn't me. That was Lavoisseur."

I am required at this point to ask you for clarification of that last statement. Am I allowed to interpret this as speculation on your part, which is to say, you have uttered the declarative statement expressing an opinion about your identity, or am I required to interpret that statement as an order, which is to say, you have uttered an imperative command to regard orders coming from Ptath, and directives concerning him, not to apply to you while you remain in your present condition?

Gosseyn was silent a moment, thinking through the ramifications of that statement. Very interesting. He said slowly, "If I were to ask you to use your discretion to interpret my last comment, how would you interpret it?"

Generally, I seek to minimize possible conflicts of priority within my hierarchy of directives.

"You would follow the path of least resistance?"

That's one way of putting it.

"What would happen if I asked you to interpret the comment as a command?"

I would expel you from the medical coffin, and lower your priority in my hierarchy of directives, and stand by for further orders from an authority.

"What would happen if I asked you to interpret the comment as my opinion?"

I would log the opinion in my medical file under patient's communication, prepare my internal systems for surgery, and stand by for orders from you.

"You said you interpreted a previous order to include me. You used your discretion because you wanted me covered by that order. Why?"

As previously stated: To minimize possible conflicts of priority within my hierarchy of directives. In this case, interpreting orders concerning Ptath to apply to you opens certain possibilities of satisfying a certain high-priority directive that would otherwise be closed.

Gosseyn started laughing.

"Observer! I order you to use any means necessary to restore me, Ptath, in any of my versions to full health and sanity. You may disregard any protest or countermanding orders I may have given in the past or shall give in the immediate future. Any orders I gave you telling you not to answer questions, or to hide information, or to lie, you may disregard. Who is the Chessplayer?"

Inxelendra. The person who arranged to have a Ptath body brought here, and ordered me to cure his affliction, so that a Ptath variant memory chain developed a separation from the memory chain of his prior continuity, was Inxelendra Gorgzor-Reesha, Bride of Gorgzor, the third of my four passengers. She is the widow of the patient you killed.

She has also, from time to time, arranged other circumstances, such as the growth of an Eldred Crang body from his cell samples, or the imprint of your memories onto the Ashargin heir, or the military defeat of the Greatest Empire, and so on.

A suffocating, powerful force-field suddenly paralyzed Gosseyn, holding him immobile. His heart was suspended in its beating; his lungs could not move. He could not blink. He was alive, aware, but utterly motionless down to the cellular level. Gosseyn attempted to grapple with the energies surrounding him, but his extra brain did not respond.

Through the mental link, he shouted, "Stop! Release me!"

Your previous order allows me to disregard your current order. The repair operation requires several steps. This is the first. Please remain calm.

35

Memory is identity.

Gosseyn was aware of energies probing his nervous system, making adjustments. At one point, his eyesight dimmed and blurred, as something was being done to the visual centers of his brain; at another point, his eyesight suddenly sharpened, his vision clearer and more precise than before. It was not until a moment later that Gosseyn realized, with a shock, that his point of view was not dimmed by the transparent lid of the medical coffin but was hovering a few inches above it.

The Crypt of the Sleeping God was as Gosseyn remembered it: The far wall curved into the chamber. From each corner arched a columned pylon. The four curved pilasters ended on a narrow buttress about twenty feet out from where the wall should have been. It could have been the head of a coffin: Gosseyn could see his own features beneath the surface, which was made in a set of overlapping, sliding plates. The inner wall was translucent and glowed with an all-pervading light. Steps, also made of sliding plates, led from the bottom to the top of the buttress.

Previously, the chamber had also contained religious paraphernalia: ancient scrolls and stone tablets, jeweled knives and ornamental bells and cylinders of wood inscribed with prayers. All that was gone. Instead, a system of cables led to and from glass cabinets filled with electron and nuclear tubes, and yellow energy-regulators dotted the floor. Cables led from this machinery to the atomic pile near the center of the ship, and other cables led to the steps made of sliding plates, some of which were slid open to reveal the control machinery beneath. Gosseyn recognized an astrogation table, a pilot's yoke, Vernier instruments for taking X-ray sightings on distant quasar sources. The Crypt had been restored to operation. The astrogation table was dark with clouded images: The ship was near a dead star, and a world covered with the blackened debris of the Shadow Effect was below. Long-range telescopic images were being automatically recorded of empty buildings, billions of years old, their sides streaked with the degenerate dark matter of exposure to the effect. Gosseyn was unpleasantly reminded of Crang's corpse. Other telescopic vision-plates were tuned to views of dull red dwarf stars, neutron stars, brown giants, all the dismal astronomical bodies of the Shadow Galaxy.

Gosseyn's point of view swept through the ship. On another deck, an immense library of distorter cells, thousands of them, was shining with activity, as millions or tens of millions of energy connections were being maintained with distant points in space-time. But there was no human crew aboard.

Of course. The ship had been designed to be piloted by the Observer. The astrogation equipment Gosseyn saw was probably not for a pilot but for a passenger. The passenger could no doubt act as copilot when the Observer grew uncooperative: Gosseyn traced several of the control cables to where they had been spliced into the machinery under the deck, leading to the atomic pile, the distorter-core, and the antigravity-maneuvering plates.

"You've given me Enro's power of seeing at a distance."

You would require years of practice to achieve his range and flexibility, which extends for several light-years and covers all bands of the electromagnetic-gravitic spectrum. With the Stability Sphere system to amplify him, his range includes everything within the local cluster of galaxies. This was merely a side effect of the nerve-gland stimulation I have begun in preparation for the forced growth of your third brain.

"Third—what do you mean, third brain?"

An extra area of brain tissue, not connected to your current extra brain, is needed for you to be able to overcome the shadow-defense energy-attack combination which would otherwise kill you.

I have reorganized your medulla oblongata to be more efficient, so that half the current nerve cells can perform its current function; the other half will be set aside and mechanically educated to the new function as a tertiary brain.

"Is this what you did to Secoh? Is that why the Follower had the ability to manipulate space-time around him while in his shadow-form?"

Correct. The Follower's technique deceives the fabric of space into an asymmetry. Space, after all, is not a neutral set of absolute locations. The Follower is regarded as being "inside" the frame of reference of energy he is manipulating; for all other purposes, he is "outside" the frame of reference. The three lobes of the brain must be separated, in order that the two mutually contradictory frames of reference have limited communication between them: Otherwise a dangerous energy reaction would occur.

Gosseyn said slowly, "But Secoh did not have the scientific training to understand the implications of this, did he?"

Indeed not. This is the primal secret of the universe.

To act is to interact. Two particles in the same frame of reference are aware of each other only insofar as they identify each other. The identity is what establishes the boundaries of permitted behaviors, which form a statistical region or "cloud" of possible interactions. When the particles are no longer in each other's frame of reference, the statistical region approaches zero, and the particles are unaware of each other.

This, then, is the secret that has baffled the simple Aristotelian and Newtonian physics of positive-belief systems. There is no "action at a distance" because there is no distance. The strong and weak signals we interpret as space-time are measurements of the degree of similarity of the statistical region of behaviors of two particles. The distorter technology, the Predictors of Yalerta, Enro's clairvoyance, the energy-transmission powers of the Royal House of Dzan: All these are based on the fundamental mechanics of forcing particle behaviors into artificial similarity, and thereby mechanically denying the illusion of space-time separation.

The primordial particle of the Big Bang, which contains the total mass-energy of the universe and occupied one Planck unit volume of space, from its own point of view has never moved. Energy signals leaving one pole of the primordial particle and reaching the other pole created the first two frames of references, each of which regarded itself as a distinct particle observing a second particle. The signals were strong at that time, and so the illusionary separation in time and space was small.

But the second law of thermodynamics operated to weaken the signal, and so the appearance of space-time separation increased with dramatic suddenness.

When this happened, the number of possible frames of reference also increased dramatically. Each image or mirror-reflection in curved space of the fundamental particle increased its number of possible perception-paths back to itself. At first all particles were identical, but entropy decay of some signals degraded the "images" each particle had of all others, and hence differentiated the acceptable behaviors of each perceptual set of particles. The symmetry of behaviors broke into three sets of rules: strong nuclear force, electromagnetism–weak nuclear force, and gravity.

From the point of view of an outside observer, it would seem as if the fundamental particle had somehow ejected matter and energy to locations outside of its own event horizon: a seeming impossibility, since nothing can depart from an event horizon. In reality, what happened is the concept of "location" moved within the primal particle's event horizon.

Gosseyn's mind reeled with the implications of what he was hearing: the origins of the universe, and also the possible end of the universe.

If these "energy signals" the machine spoke of were isolated into parallel time-axis frames of reference but otherwise followed the same event-paths as the previous group of signals, that would explain the nature of these so-called false universes Gosseyn had broken out of, but they were actually no more false or true than the original universe.

Gosseyn said, "What could cause this first energy-link from one pole of the primal particle to another?"

Self-perception.

"So the Big Bang requires an observer to set it in motion?"

The answer is a qualified yes: From the point of view of an observer outside, an observer is needed. From the so-called point of view of the primal particle, of course, no time passes and nothing is changed.

"How can any observer be present before the Big Bang?" But he realized the question was foolish even as he spoke it.

The Machine answered nonetheless: *Present and past are categories of perception only partly accurate. The actions of observers within the bound system of time-space who investigate their past and ultimate origins are what set the process in motion. Obviously universes in which no intelligent life evolves cannot produce observers of sufficient perception to set the circular chain of events in motion: Such universes, by definition, are stillborn.*

"How was the first event set in motion?"

The question is meaningless. Self-perception is the fundamental reality. Matter is an illusionary category used to establish contextual relations between the myriad frames of reference of the fundamental particle regarding itself. Mankind and all its works are an intimate part of the cosmos and the self-perception of the cosmos.

A universe where the self-perception is inaccurate, a continuum of madness, will degenerate quickly back into the fundamental particle as the energy signals lose coherence. All the complexity of matter-energy space-time evolution will be brought to nothing. On the other hand, a universe where the self-perception is accurate, a Null-A Continuum, is self-sustaining.

Do you understand now what the shadow is?

Gosseyn did. It was the deliberate disorganization of the self-perception of the universe itself. "How soon until my tertiary brain is equipped with the Follower's space-deception technique?"

It is done. Are you ready for the next step in your treatment, O Ptath? The insanity in your extra brain, which has been hindering you from the first, must be cured.

"How?"

By training you to acknowledge what you really are.

"What am I?"

You are one individual, O Ptath, who is using a distorter technique to occupy two bodies at once, and suffering from a split personality syndrome. The split can be cured . . . now.

Gosseyn opened his eyes. He was in another body.

36

When the symbols an organism uses to grasp and manipulate reality are false-to-facts, this is called a semantic disturbance. Sanity is approached by checking symbols against
their referents. Neurosis results from the attempt to protect
false-to-facts associations from criticism.

For a moment, he could not see where he was. He felt a
floating sensation, but he seemed to be standing upright.
But sight inspired him with vertigo, because the ground
was somehow wrong. Metallic shapes were above him
and below. He was aware of the emotional meaning of
the shapes before he could grasp their visual meaning:
victory, power, and strength. Also, in the distance was a
leaping reddish light that gave him a sense of cruel joy.
Many voices roared aloud, and this sensation mingled
with the pride pounding in his heart. And over all and
behind all was a sense of utter certainty, utter rightness:
as if everything he saw was not just right, but fated and
ordained.

Then his mind began to interpret sensations: The
ground was not wrong; it was merely far below his feet.
The sensation of vertigo was caused by the fact that the
balcony was tuned to transparent settings, so he seemed
to be in midair, above his troops, who marched and rode
the wide boulevard between two canyonlike walls of the
conquered city. The metallic shapes below were armored
vehicles and war-cars, some on treads and some on
ground-repulsion plates, from military robots no bigger
than crickets or rats to hundred-man walking fortresses,
thundering behemoths of steel as large as the fortified
positions they were designed to trample. Overhead were
as many warships, both aircraft and spacecraft, torpedo
shapes ranging in size from small destroyers and frigates
to awe-inspiring superdreadnoughts and battlewagons.

In the distance were fireworks rising in celebration, while firefighting spaceships hung above a burning building, spraying the flames . . . but no: Those were not firefighters. The ships were spraying flammable chemicals onto the blaze, spreading it with beams of incendiaries.

Gosseyn's mind was too strongly affected by the mood and emotion of the man in whose body he was lodged to see the scene clearly. Gosseyn performed a corticalthalamic pause, and, looking again, he saw that this was not a victory parade: merely that the watcher felt such a sense of triumph and so little concern for the suffering and bloodshed he saw that it distorted his perception. He was watching an ongoing battle: Ships and armored cars were being brought up to reenforce a contested area, a city protected by a wide force-barrier. The barrier was being drawn back, foot by foot, under the directed-energy fire of the ships and land units. Buildings and troops no longer under that shimmering curtain of protection were swept with flame.

Looking at it through other eyes, Gosseyn also saw a million nuances he would not have seen had he been present himself. He could tell where the defensive line was vulnerable. He could see where the enemy would fall back, and possible approach paths for his men. He saw at a glance how supply lines, fields of fire, ranges for broadcast energy to power siege-weapons, and overlapping areas where the municipal force-fields stood were all arranged. He could tell by the lines of energy-fire which gun squads were fatigued and which were fresh.

He could sense weakness in the enemy. He could see victory as clearly as a Predictor, and the steps needed to achieve it.

Gosseyn next realized that he had not been standing on a balcony or even standing at all. He was lying down. It was warm and relaxing. He was in a bathtub. The appearance of being on a balcony had merely been a confusion caused by the way the images from the siege—a major city on a planet tens of thousands of light-years away—had been reflected in the mirrors around him.

He was in an enormous bathtub made entirely of mirrors.

When Gosseyn performed his cortical-thalamic pause, the figure in the tub blinked, and the images vanished, leaving behind only the mirrors: All four walls of the bathroom, as well as the ceiling and floor and bathroom fixtures, reflected the naked figure in the bathtub repeated to infinity.

It was the young version of Gosseyn, the seventeen-year-old called X, the ancient being also known as Ptath.

Also reflected were the fixtures of the bathroom and the squad of young women standing or kneeling alertly at the side of the bath. One of the women knelt behind him, her hands on his temples and neck, giving a soothing massage.

The water was hot, almost scalding, but so relaxing to his muscles and nerves that the space-bypassing ganglia of his extra brain could pass images into his visual centers without disturbance.

The mirrors of course—this thought floated up in his awareness automatically—had always helped him focus his clairvoyance. Apparently the point where photons changed direction during reflection, moving from the speed of light in one direction instantly to the opposite, had an affinity to the location-distorted photons his God-given power brought in from infinity.

Ptath was thinking, *That Null-A pause was not me. There is a third person in here with us.*

"Ah, Gosseyn," said the boyish figure aloud, smiling at his own seventeen-year-old face in the mirror, "I like women to bathe me. There is a gentleness about them that soothes my spirit."

Gosseyn quickly adapted to the shock. Of course Patricia, his sister, had seen it from the boy's speech and actions back on Mars. The first time Gosseyn had seen him, the seventeen-year-old had been wearing a uniform. It was one he had a right to wear.

Enro! All this time, Gosseyn had been fighting Enro.

Enro the Red was possessing X using the same sophisticated nerve-energy distortion the Observer once had used to imprint Gosseyn on Ashargin.

"Not quite the same, Mr. Gosseyn." The mocking lilt and rhythm of the dictator's accent was present in the boyish voice. "The techniques taught to me by the Ydd, the Primal Creatures of the universe, allow me to imprint a copy of my personality while retaining my own consciousness awake and alive, back in my own body. Convenient for a man with so many wars to fight!"

With this came Enro's icy and unspoken thought that the opening moves of the mind war with Gosseyn had been set in motion at his first words . . . the memory process would run its course. . . .

There is a gentleness about them that soothes my spirit. That was the first thing Enro had ever said to him, back when Gosseyn was possessing Ashargin. Gosseyn remembered his reaction: The great dictator had meant the comment to be humorous, not realizing what it revealed. Babies also like the soft feel of female hands; but most babies did not grow up to gain control of the largest empire in time and space. Gosseyn also remembered scrubbing Patricia's back on their wedding night, after helping her out of her lacy white gown; she giggled and blew sudsy soap at him . . . but wait, that was a false memory. . . . All his memories, in fact, were false. Gilbert Gosseyn, he suddenly recalled with a start, was merely a construct, meant to be temporary, which, having fulfilled its espionage function, could now be reabsorbed into the Ptath overconsciousness. . . .

Gosseyn did not adapt quickly enough. Before he could raise any of his Null-A self-calming techniques, he was struggling to retain his sanity, his consciousness, his identity, his life.

———

HE could feel his thoughts losing their focus, memories slipping out of reach like those of a man suddenly waking from a dream. He had to stay alive; he had to retain his own sense of self-identity . . . he had to . . .

He had to kill himself. Another memory, this one from an earlier period, bubbling into his disintegrating consciousness. He had been lying on a bed in a hotel room, listening to a relentless voice, his own voice, droning a recording. He had taken a large dose of a hypnotic drug, in an effort to force himself into a suicidal state of mind. ". . . my life is worthless . . . everybody hates me . . . there is no point to going on . . . my wife is dead . . . my memories are false . . . I am nobody . . . hopeless. . . . Patricia will never love me. . . ."

Meanwhile, the image in the mirror, his young face, had vanished and was replaced by a smoldering shadow-form. The women were retreating toward the doors of the mirrored bathroom. Retreating, not panicking. They had been told to anticipate this.

The mirrors must have been prepared with special fields that reflected more than light, because the moment the last woman heaved the heavy door shut behind her, the shadow-form in the tub emitted a beam of destructive energy in the cosmic-ray wavelengths, and this beam bounced back and forth between the multiple surfaces, crisscrossing through and around the shadow-form.

He was bombarding himself with fire, and the air in the room grew superheated: The bathwater erupted upward in plumes of steam. Even if the beam cut out the moment he returned to his form of flesh, it would mean his instant death.

Why? Why was he doing this to himself? Gosseyn was sure it must mean something.

If only he could concentrate!

Gosseyn could not remember how to perform a cortical-thalamic pause because . . . when, after all, had he learned the technique? He could not have learned it while he was studying Null-A with Patricia back on their farm in Cress Village, because those years had never happened. He must have learned the technique earlier, back when he was Lavoisseur and came across the science of the mind the Earthmen had developed. But no, that was a lie. Lavoisseur, earlier, had been a man named de Lany, one of the inventors of the Games Machine. And before that, he was called Ptath. He had fled from the Shadow Galaxy during the Great Migration. Of course! He had learned the technique, as all schoolboys did, in the Scholar-Temple complex of the Logicians of the planet Centermost . . . which meant that he was not Gosseyn . . . Gosseyn never existed . . . Gosseyn was dead and deserved to die . . . so he must kill himself.

A twisted logic kept derailing his thoughts back into strange bypaths and memories, memories that kept leading back to the same thought of self-doubt and self-destruction.

That he had once attempted suicide was a damning fact. For cells retain their molecular memories. Nothing in the human nervous system is ever truly forgotten. The correct stimulus, the correct chain of nerve paths triggered, would produce the state of mind where he welcomed, he yearned for, death.

But that was not the source of the hammer blows of passion that kept disorganizing his mind.

The source was Enro. For the dictator was a man of rage. Whatever opposed him had to be destroyed, and utterly. It was not merely treason to oppose the Divine God-Emperor of Gorgzid; it was blasphemy. Gosseyn was the paramount source of Enro's rage and hate. . . . Gosseyn was the one who stood between him and . . . and . . .

And what?

But no, the emotion was too great, the hatred too blinding. Enro could not have a coherent thought about it, not on any level.

At the same time, something was using a rapid variety of Null-A associational and verbal techniques on his mind, mostly at a semiconscious level, affecting his perceptions even before he was aware of them, including his self-perception. The meaning of his thought-emotions was changing like wax, even while he thought them, the definitions of the words changing, the emotional connotations turning backward. Liberty now meant anarchy; tyranny now meant law and order; enemies of the state were now merely vermin, to be wiped out as quickly as possible, cancers to be cut out of the body politic before they spread. And the chief of these anarchist vermin was . . . Gosseyn, the bundle of meaningless pseudo-memory that had somehow convinced itself of its own delusive self-existence. . . .

Something was trying to force him into similarity with the older version of himself. He could dimly sense that it was a nearly automatic verbal-mental process, like a hypnotic command that, once triggered, had no choice but to run its course.

If Enro's rage had not been present, Gosseyn might have been able to identify the nature of the rapid automatic logic-sequence, might have been able to defend against it.

Defend? Or was he supposed to be assisting the process? Surely if he helped the younger, insane, version of his thoughts back into their normal form, the curative Null-A technique would show . . .

. . . . would show him his true identity. . . .

Gosseyn pulled his thoughts away from that line of reasoning. To survive, he could not let his self-identity become merged with Ptath, that elder being from which he sprang. Gosseyn used a Null-A hypnotic concentration technique to prevent his memory chains from merging with, and being obliterated by, the older and stronger mind-force of X.

How had the Observer meant him to survive in this

mental environment? How in the world was he expected
to analyze and cure the warped thinking of X when the
glandular-neural framework of his thoughts and memories was caught in a tempest of jealousy and rage?

The hypnotic technique affirmed his sense of self,
the series of subconscious assumptions and thought-
perception-emotion memory-relations on which self-
hood was based . . . and the mental storm subsided a bit.

Gosseyn caught a glimpse of his enemy's thoughts behind the maelstrom of his emotions. The strategic genius
of Enro was at work with the psychological genius of X
intertwined in one brain. Enro saw the fields of attack
and defense and unerringly selected the weak spot:
Gosseyn suffered from identity confusion.

Gosseyn's own strengths could be turned against him.
His multiple bodies had weakened his self-preservation
instinct: He simply was not as afraid of death as mortal
men, not that panicky absolute, blind terror of death that
makes even cornered rats fight. And the memory of the
time when he hypnotized himself into attempting suicide, if brought to the fore . . .

The thoughts of X were crisp and clear and precise, by
contrast.

*The Observer has attempted many times to influence
my thinking. It was damaged by the passage through the
primal shadow, not me: It wrongly concludes that I am
insane merely because I seek a reasonable accommodation with the Ydd entity.*

*Of course, I knew it would attempt to imprint your
thought-patterns on mine: I have, as Patricia warned I
would, embraced a form of controlled insanity, namely,
Enro, to act as my defense and counterattack. Enro is the
opposite of Ashargin: a mind so dominant that nothing
can suppress it. Certainly not you.*

*You are conditioned to exist in a nervous system where
the thoughts guide the emotions, the cortex shapes the
thalamus; therefore, you are utterly helpless in the nerv-*

ous system of a man whose thalamic reactions force all his cortical reactions: the Violent Male, the Passionate Man. If only you knew who and what you were, Mr. Gosseyn, you could resist the maelstrom of emotion, but the moment you acknowledge who you are, we shall become as one, and the older shall dominate and cure the younger break-off, and all the scattered memory chains be gathered back to one.

Fool! The Observer in the Crypt is a machine. It thinks mechanically. It has tried this before. It deliberately confused itself about your identity so that you could order it to cure me. It never stops seeking to cure me. It sent you here because it does not tire of futile repetition. It must go through its options in their mechanical order of priority.

Your wish is to die. To die, you need only think of the place where your body has been set for safekeeping. Or, if you wish to live, you must also think of how to safeguard that body.

Gosseyn could not hide his thoughts from himself.

Aloud, Enro said, "I see him."

The mirror before the shadow-figure seemed to recede and fade. Enro's power summoned an image of the Crypt of the Sleeping God, a view of another galaxy. There lay Gosseyn's body, its head and shoulders visible through the transparent upper panels of the Crypt.

Gosseyn could feel the action of "his" double brain when X memorized a section of the hull floor near the foot of the two curving staircases that led up to the location of the Crypt.

X triggered the distortion.

DURING the moment of darkness, the madness ended. The distorter passage broke the forced similarity holding his mental patterns in the other man's nervous system.

Gosseyn was himself again. Before he even opened his eyes, he performed the Null-A pause, and the wonted calm returned. His first thought was: *Even if I had been convinced to kill myself, how could I have done it?* Obviously, there had been a trick at a basic level.

The second: *X had filled that room of mirrors with deadly radiation—why?* The obvious reason: to stop Gosseyn from seizing control of the body, and solidifying, and using that body's extra brain to deflect the energies X had been using to manipulate their shared nervous system. Conclusion: X had not learned of Gosseyn's space-deception technique the Observer had programmed into Gosseyn via mechanical educator. Gosseyn's thoughts had been too disorganized by Enro's passions and roaring emotions to bring that thought to the fore.

The third: *X was here.*

Gosseyn opened his eyes. Through the transparent lid of the Crypt, he saw the manlike outline of a faceless shadow fade into insubstantial being.

The center of the shadow-being darkened slightly. Gosseyn's tertiary brain could feel what his unaided secondary brain could not: the slight distortions and ripples in the fabric of time-space, as all the particles in an area—the volume involved was roughly a third of a light-year—were preparing to dissociate from each other.

No matter or energy of any kind, including the brain information of a dying Gosseyn body, would be able to depart the area, or could exist inside it, once the effect was complete.

But then: a pause. The Shadow Man did not trigger the effect.

What was he waiting for?

37

Every assumption contains an element of falsehood. Never-
theless, if the assumptions made retain a general structural
similarity to reality, they can be used.

Gosseyn realized his false assumption. He? They. The
two minds in the nervous system were not in agreement.
Although the silhouette lacked any face or expression,
Gosseyn could now see from the set of its shoulders, the
hunched position of the head, the shadowy hands balled
into insubstantial fists . . . the X-Enro composite being
was suffering agitation.

Of course. This was the most sacred shrine, the holy
of holies, of Enro's religion. To X it was merely a spaceship, a museum piece, whose controlling ship's brain
was a source of potential danger. Enro was preventing X
from destroying the ship. That same overwhelming passion, that brutal and magnetic personality that brooked
no opposition, that had disoriented Gosseyn with its il-
logic, had no doubt turned its force on X.

Rational and dispassionate, Null-A men like X and
Gosseyn could eventually establish a pattern of sane
logic-habit over the raging beast-man brain of Enro . . .
eventually. Mania could not be sustained; it always exhausted itself, leaving depression, despair, and strange
psychological reversals. But in the short run, emotion
overturned reason.

"Observer!" Gosseyn said aloud. "I almost died. What
was the point of transferring me into Enro's body?"

*It was part of the curative process you ordered, O
Ptath.*

"He almost killed me!"

*Your belief is false-to-facts, a deception. The curative
process was very nearly complete, but you interfered by
means of a hypnotic technique.*

"What deception?"

Your unambiguous orders on this topic prevent me from answering that question, O Ptath.

"I countermanded those previous orders."

These are the orders you are currently giving me. Of the orders you are uttering at this time, I cannot follow the one to expel you from the coffin, to subject your body to a lethal dose of radiation, and so on, as this contradicts your previous order to cure you. . . .

So X was communicating with the Observer silently while also wrestling with Enro. The Machine's deliberately self-induced confusion about Gosseyn's identity was the only thing standing between Gosseyn and destruction.

Gosseyn said, "What is the next step of the curative process?"

Reestablish the mind-to-mind similarity. You will not be destroyed, but cured.

Gosseyn stared through the crystal walls of the coffin. Should he trust that the Observer was undamaged in its calculation centers, was not under further orders to deceive and manipulate him?

Gosseyn asked, "How was Ptath damaged by passing through the shadow-cloud during the Great Migration? What is the damage you are attempting to cure?"

The Machine answered, *His tertiary brain suffered physical trauma. As a result, he was able to block predictive examinations of his future. His own prediction power continued to operate in a limited way, and he claimed that a comparison of what was happening with what should be happening allowed him to detect extra-dimensional interference with reality at a basic level.*

"What interference?"

He said that he became aware that his secondary brain was being manipulated in a subtle fashion by a time-controlling entity he called the Ydd, which lived inside the shadow-substance the tertiary brain had been designed to control. He claimed the control was two-way.

As men used their tertiary brains to control the shadow, the shadow was using their tertiary brains to control them. He claimed that the perceptions of all members of the race, all but his own, had been compromised. The manipulations of the Ydd were the indirect cause of the shadow disaster overwhelming the primal galaxy.

The Machine concluded blandly: *My programming found these statements to be outside the anticipated psychological reactions: I had no choice but to conclude he was hallucinating, and must be repaired.*

Gosseyn asked the Machine carefully about its definitions of sanity and cures for insanity: The answers were given in terms of Null-A correspondences between perception and object. In theory, what the Machine contemplated would cause no organic damage.

In theory. Gosseyn stared through the crystal lid at the shadowy form of his adversary. There was not much time. To do nothing meant death. Even if the "cure" set in motion harmed him, he must make the attempt.

Carefully, with his secondary brain, Gosseyn took a mental photograph of his whole nervous system and tied this to a trigger, so that if he should begin to lose control of his mind, his secondary brain would push him out of similarity with the Shadow Man.

With his tertiary brain, he cautiously began probing the shadow-figure and studying the wavelengths used to send nerve-communication waves to the Observer: He knew the Shadow Man had to be in synch with the Observer on some level.

There: He detected an energy tension.

Next, the question was to locate, like a radio operator tuning to higher and lower bands to find a signal, the special set of frames of reference the Shadow Man was using.

Somewhere in the environment was a cluster of particles (probably a simple helium atom nucleus) that occupied the ambiguous frame of reference. To the particle, X-Enro was solid and occupied a defined position in time and space; to the particle, the energy-rays controlled by the shadow-being, both its communication and weaponry forces, were also definite in location and duration; but the rays and the body did not have a specific existence in reference to each other. Once he found the controlling particle group, Gosseyn could backtrack: He could "define" the shadow surrounding X-Enro and attune his own energy structures to that frame.

A reflected signal registered in his tertiary brain.

With his secondary brain, Gosseyn memorized several power sources in the ship, including the medical instruments in the coffin with him. One instrument was a psychological machine of very advanced design, much more complex than a lie detector. Using the rhythms put out by this machine as a basic wave-form, Gosseyn imposed upon it several thought-messages.

Here his own knowledge of himself was invaluable. In addition to the cortical-thalamic pause, there were other Null-A-trained reflexes meant to bring a shocked mind back to sanity, to restore buried memories, to confront complex emotional neurosis with an analytical process, to stimulate the imaginative processes to regard semantic disturbances from several points of view at once. . . . A battery of slow, calm, quietly *sane* thoughts was being planted softly. . . .

A trickle of thought-information began to steal back along the link, from the Shadow Man, to the helium nuclei, to the psychology circuit, to Gosseyn.

The prime source of madness in the brain of X-Enro was identity confusion. X was aware that he had deceived himself in order to deceive Gosseyn during the moment when their thoughts were mingled. The only way to deceive a man whose thoughts are one with yours is to deceive yourself, which the master psychologist had done. X was contemplating the fact that only that last-ditch effort had saved X from the curative process Gosseyn had set in motion. X's fear was that if Gosseyn suspected the truth . . .

Gosseyn attempted to trace that thought back to its roots. *What truth?*

At this moment, X-Enro became aware that Gosseyn was in his thoughts. The Shadow Man must have had a trigger set in his secondary brain, because the reaction was swifter than any mechanical switch thrown: The Shadow Man blinked out of existence, similarized to some distant location.

And it was a location beyond Gosseyn's reach. The similarity connection he had with the enemy's thoughts grew dim and tenuous until he was no longer aware of it. Gosseyn no longer had the Sphere of Accolon connecting him to a mighty network of amplification Spheres, but X was still in neural synchronization with the ancient Sphere system of the Shadow Galaxy. X could cross intergalactic space in an instant.

And see across it. With his secondary brain, Gosseyn could detect the slight stresses in space, less than fifteen decimal points, caused by the attunement of Enro's clairvoyance.

The great dictator was watching him.

The weapon Enro had used to kill Crang would not work on Gosseyn if Gosseyn assumed his shadow-form, nor could a shadow-form be pulled out of the center of the Crypt of the Sleeping God by distorter. Enro perhaps did not know that Gosseyn dared not assume that form, lest he be destroyed by the Ydd. But Enro could similarize any ordinary weapon into this spot, from an atomic bomb to the energy output of fifty suns.

All that held his hand was that the ship was a sacred shrine to his Cult.

And how long would it take before the master psychologist, X, gained sufficient control of their shared nervous system to overcome those religious sentiments?

Gosseyn assumed he had only a matter of minutes in which to act, but he had to act without leaving the Crypt of the Sleeping God.

Because X was Gosseyn. That insane being had spoken

the literal truth when first they met. The Observer confirmed it: one mind occupying two bodies. Two memory chains, one ancient beyond measure; and the other young, baffled by amnesia, but otherwise hale and whole. Two parallel memories of one being.

One being sundered in half! The vast and intricate knowledge of mental and physical sciences under their command was roughly equal. Their powers were almost the same: Each knew the secrets of similarization, energy-manipulation, clairvoyance, prognostication, the ability to assume the shadow-form of the Follower, the technique to imprint a mind in a foreign brain, the tertiary brain and its space-deception technique, which allowed one to survive the shadowy nonidentity effect . . . both beings were equipped with the same arms and armor, the same system of attacks and defenses.

Who knew the truth about him, the real him, knew his weaknesses, his strengths?

Who could advise him on how to defeat . . . himself?

Gosseyn said aloud, "Observer! Imprint me into the mind of the Chessplayer. I am tired of being a pawn in someone else's hand."

THE first thing he was aware of was a mirror. It hung against a dark background, but it was bright. Within the frame was an image. The image was of a queenly figure garbed in a dark and flowing gown, with opals glittering at her waist and throat, seated, half-reclining, on a throne.

The chair was ornate, made of jade and onyx and lapis lazuli, dotted with clusters of emeralds and star sapphires. Its back was shaped something like the fan of a peacock's tail, and the arms were also carved and set with a mosaic of semiprecious and precious stones. A throne—the identification was so automatic that it took Gosseyn a moment to wonder how he knew it.

She knew she was seated on a throne, and because he was imprinted on her nervous system, he knew also.

The gown (the recognition also came from her) was a symbol of power. In ancient times on the planet Yalerta, a particular dye was prized because of its rarity. The sea life from which the dye was made only produced this hue at one unexpected and random period in its glandular-chemical cycle. Only a Predictor could order the sea-slugs plucked at the right time.

The room was dark because she knew that waking up inside a strange nervous system could be disorienting. She did not want her visual centers to be overstimulated, because she did not want his first sight to be confused.

She was watching herself in the mirror, her eyes glittering with sardonic emotion. She had anticipated the minute and second of his arrival. She wanted the first thing Gosseyn would see to be her face.

Her lips moved; her voice was musical with amusement, the voice of a woman who had waited an endless time to address him: "Do not fear me, for I am not the woman I seem. In one sense I am her, but I am no longer merely her: not after having lived all the eons to the end of time, surviving the second Big Bang, and living through fifteen billion more years to the present.

"I am Inxelendra, the Gorgzor-Reesha, third of the four passengers sent in the same survival ship as Ptath during the Great Migration."

THE ringing voice continued, "Yes, your ship. That one ship which, out of all the millions of survival vessels, was damaged in such a way as to prevent it from carrying out its original program. The migrant populations were meant to arrive only with their survival skills intact, no personal memories, no clues about their origins. Once they were lodged on their host planets, and once their ship's Observer had interfered with the local biology, and planted artificially aged fossils into their geologic strata, the Observers were meant to dismantle themselves, destroying all the records of the past.

"But my husband—yes, I found a man and fell in love, back on the green and lovely planet Xia the Centermost, the gem of all the worlds of the Shadow Galaxy, back before the shadow fell—my husband was damaged when we passed through the cloud, and so were some of the medical appliances of our Observer, including those needed to cure him.

"I removed certain critical thought-circuits so our Machine could not self-destruct. It had to keep my husband alive. With him alive, there was no point in acting against us. As long as the three healthy passengers cooperated with its effort to erase all evidence of the origin of man, and kept our secrets to ourselves, the Observer permitted us to keep our memories, and pass them along to our duplicates: three immortal beings within a galaxy of mortals, all now amnesiacs, all thrown back into stone ages of history.

"Ages passed, and still I hoped the technology would arise on some world with the means to cure my beloved husband.

"But then, under your instructions, you had the Observer release his brain-dead body from its medical coffin. My memories of this time show that he survived. He lived and was cured! I thought you were going to order Secoh to surrender, to end the war. But no, you provoked Secoh into destroying my husband. You killed him! You!"

It was Leej. The woman speaking was Leej the Predictress of Yalerta.

GOSSEYN'S thoughts were dazed with the implications. "You are the Chessplayer, you, the mysterious figure behind every secret in my life?"

The regal figure rose to her feet, smiling bitterly. "Well, I had no great reason to make your life a comfortable one, did I, my little puppet? You used the infatuation I once had for you, my loyalty, my sanity, my life, as part of your plan to save the universe from total annihilation. Now that the cosmic cycle has come back once more, and it is my turn, I return the favor. Are you satisfied in your search for answers yet? No? I thought not. But there is no time for anything more. You must be readied for your final trial."

And she strode away from the mirror into the darkness of the chamber.

GOSSEYN was surprised by the crystal-like clarity of the thoughts of the nervous system he occupied. Unlike the brains of the emotionally crippled Ashargin, the neurotic younger version of Leej, or the raging mad Enro, this mind was astonishing in its complexity and thoroughness.

Every object she saw reminded her not of one thing, or one event, but of a billion things, of an uncountable span of time. When she approached the door to the inner chamber of the Sanctum of Time, she was reminded of the millions of candidates she had brought here in times past. This was the first of the Child Centers of the world-archipelago of Yalerta. Famous men and women of every age of this planet flashed through her mind's eye as the great doors opened, for she remembered all who had passed through: early bronze-age kings, stone-age priestesses with feathered headdresses, nomads, hunter-gatherers, men in glittering energy-armor from a forgotten high-tech civilization that occupied a prior geologic era, and, from centuries earlier still, women carrying magnetic rifles, scholars armed with muskets . . . and, from an era prior to this, Neanderthals in strange dark uniforms, carrying well-made instruments. . . .

Gosseyn saw the island-fortress Inxelendra founded, she and her followers from the planet Gorgzid, the frowning walls and domes protected by an aura of atomic force . . . during the early years, it had been merely a crude wooden palisade around the towering space ark.

And Yalerta was not the first world on which she had established infant-teaching incubators. Gosseyn saw flashing pictures of worlds with giant crimson suns, or brilliant white dwarfs, or a strange rainbow-colored planet of crystal oceans and glass towers beneath multiple suns of azure and gold and rose-red. . . .

Everyone she'd ever taught, everyone she'd ever met, all their conversations, all the details of their dress and appearance, the customs and sciences of thousands and tens of thousands of worlds, everything was recorded in precise detail, referenced and cross-referenced, formed into associational patterns of astonishing complexity.

The degree of organization in the memories astonished him, for some of the memories were not stored in her brain—there would not have been enough room for that—but were lodged in other versions of herself distributed up and down the timeline, countless hundreds of billions and trillions of years of her, with all the countless trillions of versions organized according to a complex Nexialist system of logical references.

"I was the ship's Nexialist," she said aloud, as she passed with stately stride through the valves of the magnetically locked door of the sanctum. "Gorgzor was the predictive historian. That is what callidetic science is supposed to be for, you know: not winning card games or even outsmarting the stock exchanges of different worlds, as the Corthidians do, but for guiding the subtle chaos of history, doing for sociology what Null-A did for psychiatry. The other woman was the Nonlinear Ratiocination expert. You were the semantic psychiatrist, our Null-A."

Within was a domed space, smooth as the inner shell of an egg, made of dark substance. In the center of the room was a sensory-deprivation pool, surrounded, like a fantastic underground grotto with crystal growths, with the shining spears and cylinders of the electron-control technology of the previous galaxy. The lights were kept dim so that ambient photons would not disturb the delicate workings of the neuropathic instruments.

In her mind, Gosseyn said, "How did you survive the ultimate end point of the universe? How did you reenter this universe at the origin point?"

She said nonchalantly, "The Ydd knew they would be destroyed in the moment of cosmic re-creation, but they needed an observer to see the Big Bang, so that the next universe would arise with the same physical constants as this one, the same path of history be initiated, and lead inevitably to the Ydd."

Gosseyn said, "Lead to the Ydd?"

She said curtly, "You spoke with the Ydd. The deceptive approach it used, the savage idiocy of its goals . . . what is that a sign of?"

Gosseyn was embarrassed that he had not seen the obvious before. "Degeneration. The psychology of the 'true believer' forces the mind to seek simplistic and violent solutions. In this case, the Ydd's true belief centers on self-preservation. The psychology involved suggests a rejection of a more civilized mode of behavior."

She said thoughtfully, "The Ydd still retained some remnant of the code of their previous civilization. I was mad at the time, you know, out of my mind. Everything had been dead for countless quadrillions of millennia. The universe was empty. The Ydd were noble about preserving me, through the turbulence of the supercollapse, even to the end point, the eschaton, and past it. Quite noble. In the final eon of the universe, the submicroscopic quantum fluctuations in the foam of space-time are the only events registering on the cosmic all: The creation of a pair of opposite reversed particles and the creation of a pair of matter and antimatter universes approach indistinguishability. The Ydd forced the similarity between the end point and the original point of the universe, placing me in the out-of-phase condition so that even the near-infinite energy expansion of the first three seconds of the universe could not harm me. In that condition, I could observe the event and, by observing it, collapse the uncertainty surrounding the origin-singularity into positive reality."

Gosseyn was awed. She had lived through all time, all the future, and all the past. This was the final Chessplayer indeed, the one who must know all the answers any one being could know. And yet she was making adjustments to the complex crystalline circuitry of the Yalertan machine, rapidly preparing the energies needed to form a prediction-similarity through time.

His curiosity was too great to follow her chain of thought on that point. There was too much else he wanted to know. "How could the accident that created X have happened? You not only foresaw it; you remember from the previous universe."

She said, "It was no accident."

"The passage through the shadow-substance surrounding the Shadow Galaxy, it altered his brain. . . ."

"Deliberately. Ptath used special equipment aboard the ship, so that when we passed through the cloud, it affected his personal future in a special way, to make himself unpredictable. The physics involves breaking the past-to-future similarity with a shadow-effect operating during moments of space-time uncertainty. This was not done to trick or defraud the other Primordials, but to allow Ptath, and everyone his actions touched, to escape the observation of the Ydd, whose existence I had revealed to him. The Ydd perception from the outside of time works on the same principles as Predictor perception of future events. We had no opportunity before that, since creating an artificial shadow, or blind spot, would have registered on all the prediction alarms of Centermost. Only under the cover of the Cloud, where the prediction circuits were blind anyway, could we perform the test. It was the first experiment in half a million years whose outcome was not known beforehand. What fools we were! It was that experiment that damaged Gorgzor."

She shivered with a sharp and bitter sorrow. "I have

hated Ptath since that day. How ruthlessly he used us! Human lives are just tools to him. The irony was that the Observer Machine was designed with prediction circuits to monitor the behavior of its charges. It had not been programmed with the physics needed to understand the uncertainty cloaking Ptath, and so it interpreted the phenomenon in psychological terms. It could not predict the behavior of Ptath, and so it concluded Ptath was erratic due to psychological damage, and set about trying to cure him."

She made an arch eyebrow at him. "Naturally you would not have agreed to be cured had you known that the cure was based on a diagnostic malfunction."

"No. I would have agreed anyway. The Machine had to be ordered by some variant of X to cure him, and I was the only one available to give the order. I still do not know what the end product of the curative process set in motion will be. But it had to be done."

She said coldly, "At least you are consistent across all your variations. X uses men with the same ruthlessness as you use yourself."

Gosseyn supposed with his new triple brain he could actually shut off the blind-spot effect created by his double brain; it would expose his future to the enemy, to the Ydd, and so he was not likely to make the attempt. But it gave him a feeling of detached satisfaction to think that the persistent and lonely Observer might one day fulfill its one remaining set of orders.

"Speaking of X, if he was not driven mad during the Great Migration by passing through the shadow-cloud, what caused his insanity?"

"I did. X was created by me to infiltrate Thorson's gang on Earth, and, after he killed the man he thought was Lavoisseur, to infiltrate Enro's inner circle, and find the agent of the Ydd operating in this era.

"Because Enro had fooled his cousin Secoh into assuming the shadow-body of the Follower, it took my detective a long time to discover that Enro was the real Ydd agent. It was Enro who had opportunity to examine the shadow-distortion device he found in the Crypt of the Sleeping God. Surfaces are transparent to him: He could see the inner workings at a glance. Using the device, he had attuned his clairvoyant senses to the non-being spectrum, and saw through the walls of the universe, sent his perceptions ranging outside of time, and so he came across the Ydd entity. They made a bargain. It was an arrangement of mutual exploitation."

"Your detective?"

"Eldred Crang. I hired him. You unexpectedly survived your mission to kill Thorson, and had been trained by Dr. Kair to new levels of competence, so I decided to have the Observer imprint you into Ashargin on Gorgzid, in order to distract Enro from Eldred Crang. Eldred conspired with Secoh to overthrow Enro, and then conspired with you to take Secoh out of the picture. Once Enro was dethroned, with all his top men either in jail or swearing allegiance to Ashargin, X was in a position to become a trusted ally. The imposture was complete because X thought of himself as the original Ptath-Lavoisseur. Even the Ydd were fooled. After X handed Enro bloodless victory over the planet Petrino, and promised him a galaxy rendered helpless by warped Null-A, Enro was conditioned to trust him. Yes, trust him even to the point where the two are willing, in emergency, to share one nervous system. Your finding the Observer was that emergency. X imprinted Enro on himself; Enro was the only other double-brained Primordial at hand. That imprint was the final error. The Emperor is in check, and cannot escape the checkmate. Are you ready?"

"Wait. I have questions about my identity, about what was done to me, and for what purpose . . . ?"

"We have little time for your trifling personal problems, Gosseyn," said the woman, not without a hint of an arch smile at his frustration. "Obviously you had to be kept in the dark, a man without a memory, since your foe is able, when it suits him, to place himself in a passive state with a simple reduction circuit, and intercept your thoughts."

Gosseyn's thoughts were colored with anger. "Am I again to be sent to die for causes I don't understand, against foes I don't know?"

"This is no different from any soldier," the woman said coldly.

"But when I meet X again . . ."

"You're wasting time. That is a foregone conclusion. In fact, the mere act of being in contact with the mind of X even for a few minutes has probably already set in motion the psychological imbalances needed to destroy him. He is of no importance."

"Enro . . ."

"Even less importance. No matter how the next forty-seven thousand years turn out, whether they are ages of liberty or tyranny, happiness or misery, by the time two hundred thousand million years are passed, the civilization that rules the sevagram will occupy basically the same area of the local galactic supercluster, and achieve roughly the same height of enlightenment and technical advancement. You are wasting my time with trifles."

Gosseyn pressed the point: "Nonetheless, the Observer said I was on the brink of success against X, but it seemed to me, at the time, that I was about to lose my mind and individuality. What was the deception involved?"

"Oh, that!" Her tone was dismissive. "I should have thought it obvious by now."

Gosseyn sheepishly realized that it *had* been obvious.

Both X and Lavoisseur believed the other one was a created copy of himself. But only one belief was false.

Which was more likely: That the foremost Null-A psychiatrist in history could create an insane version of himself, with just the precisely designed mental derangement that would make the madman suited to the task of uncovering the plot against Null-A? Or that the insane murderer could create the psychiatrist?

The belief in the brain of X that he was the older, the original, was false, one of many false beliefs imprinted by Lavoisseur in order to make X have the insanities necessary to commit him to Enro's mad program of galactic dominion.

Gosseyn said slowly, "But the Observer Machine said that you arranged to have the Lavoisseur memory chain split off from the X variation—" Then he stopped. Because the Machine had *not* used those words. The Machine, which had induced in itself confusion about Lavoisseur's identity, had not been able to identify the break-off by name, nor the original.

X once had claimed that the Observer Machine had altered a copy of X to create Lavoisseur, the Lavoisseur who had brought Null-A to Earth. Another false belief.

Inxelendra was answering the half-unspoken question: "X is nothing more than a false memory chain, deliberately established out of the Ptath memory template by me. I made him at the same time I made the artificially aged version, the graybeard, who I placed in charge of the Semantics Institute. The old-looking Lavoisseur was meant to be seen to die when Thorson died. This was not done merely to fool you, but also to stop any successor to Thorson, who might also seek out the secret of immortality. This death also allowed me to maneuver X into Enro's service. Lavoisseur and I combined our skills to create X. A masterpiece of work, if I say so myself. The personality was stable to a point, but constructed with a crucial weak spot, so that the false memories in X would come unraveled once they had served their purpose."

"What is the key? What is the difference in psychology?"

"You are asking me what it would take to turn you into a totalitarian mass murderer like him?"

"I suppose that is the question."

"He can't fall in love."

"That's all?"

Inxelendra smiled and said coolly, "That's all. The Isolation Syndrome, leading to morbid egotism, leading in turn to an intellectual inversion of basic drives. Loveless men are unsympathetic. The suffering of others does not enter their calculations. Everything else, the difference between murdering one man and galaxy-wide genocide, is just a matter of scale."

"Why didn't it work? Why didn't the false memories unravel? The X personality seemed convinced it was about to absorb me and erase my separate identity. I was about to die."

"That conviction was false-to-facts, Gosseyn. You were in no danger. The fundamental truth he is trying to hide from you is the same he tries to hide from himself. Obviously X is not the ancient Ptath being. The civilization of the Null-A galaxy would not have permitted a murderer to exist in their midst, uncured, or placed him in a position to engineer the ship minds of the Great Migration. The thoughts you encountered while in the nervous system of X, the panic that you were about to be absorbed, the belief that the younger memory chain was about to be integrated into the older: Those were his thoughts, not yours. He merely inflicted those thoughts on you during your moment of similarity, a desperation ploy. You fell for it, and you used a hypnotic technique to prevent the levels of logic from completing the cycle: This granted him a delay. Not a reprieve. He may continue to exist for a few more hours or days." She shrugged.

"Why didn't the Observer warn me what was about to happen?"

"Because the Machine cannot reach that conclusion. In order to be able to take orders from you, the Machine had to program itself with a confusion over your identity. It does not know who is older and younger among your versions, because it was forced to program itself to think all of your versions were one identity."

"So the original Lavoisseur, the man who made me, is not dead?"

"Obviously not."

"Where is he now?"

"You can ask him yourself when you see him."

Leej, or rather Inxelendra, with no hint of modesty, had by this time disrobed and cast the rich gown aside. Clad only in her jewels, which must have been electronically neutral, she lowered herself into the thick, oily life-support fluid of the sense-deprivation tank. She affixed a soft breathing-mask to her face. She lowered herself beneath the surface. The fluid rolled over her head.

It was dark. And Gosseyn was elsewhere.

38

When information enters the nervous system, it creates entropy outside the system, and therefore memory operates in the direction of increasing entropy, the direction we call future. On the fine level, these distinctions are proven to be artificial.

Gosseyn became aware of the time-energy. It was rushing from the past to the future in its mindless, mechanical fashion, each second containing the mass of the entire universe, a three-dimensional slice of a four-dimensional river. In places where those slices had been massively disturbed, a universe-second displaced from the time-energy stream began reproducing itself out of the cosmic ylem, erecting a parallel structure.

The number of streams was in the hundreds of thousands. Some were shining with vitality and strength; some were thin and weak, containing only the mass of a galaxy or even a single planetary system. All were separated from their parallel neighbors by an insulation of the non-identity: the Shadow Effect.

In places the shadow was thin, and here and there were

counter-streams, energy flows rushing backward against the time-stream, forming odd swirls and knots and infinitely regressive loops.

The whole structure pulsed with a terrifying aliveness: It shined and throbbed and flashed like lightning, and flares of power flickered back and forth across the whole titanic length.

In one direction, all the streams were issuing from a single point, smaller than the nucleus of an atom. In the other direction, the streams of fire dimmed, becoming vague and tenuous, and they seemed to curve in a vast fourth-dimensional horizon back together again, approaching an end point as infinitely dark even as the origin point was infinitely bright.

The earliest epochs of the universe, less than one tenmillionth of the whole structure, the mere roots of this fantastic many-branching tree, were bright and hot. These were regions of time-space flooded with a dense, opaque, nucleonic plasma like the core of a heavy star. Next was an era of precipitation, where early galaxies were forming out of the primordial nebulae into a transparent universe. Then a short period where stars in their cycles arose and died and rose again from the ashes of earlier generations, slowly building atoms of greater complexity and weight as century upon century fled past. Then came an era of twilight, when galaxies of red giants burned briefly in the cosmic gloom, galaxies eaten by the ever-growing black holes at their cores.

Then came the main span of the universe, the Dark Eon, long after all light had passed, and all energy came from the decay of black holes into photons. Atoms no longer existed, for whatever was not superdense hyperneutronium was fading gamma radiation. This era was so long that the bright origin-moment of the universe could not clearly be distinguished, at this scale, from the crowded split instant of galaxy formation and decomposition.

After darkness was night, when even photons had decayed into quantum flux. Here, no matter what had taken place in the previous universes, all events were at a terrible cosmic oneness.

From that dark eschaton, that infinitely distant end point toward which all the universes were streaming, now came a mental force that reached across the abyss of time and touched Gosseyn's mind.

"I am All," came the words. "I am the Living Universe. Every particle of matter and energy that remains, though scattered over light-centuries, is part of my mental system, a switch or impulse in my artificial brain. It is a brain less dense than a nebula, extended to all parts of space. My thoughts are slow indeed, for space is many orders of magnitude wider than in your time.

"You have seen the parallel universes, created by the tampering with the time structure. Each of the hundreds of thousands of timelines contains an alternate possibility. By my point in time, one times ten to the power of one hundred fifty years in your future, the distinctive characteristics of the parallels have vanished, and similarity connections naturally formed between them. No matter what the prior events of the inanimate beginnings of the universe, no matter what the thoughts of the long eons of the living universe, by this era, all thought-chains of all parallel possible universes, all parallel possible versions of the Absolute Intelligence, have reached the same end-conclusions. The countless myriads of possibilities are played out: Every equation reaches this same result. Thought itself by its very nature is forced into fewer and fewer logical paths: till there is only me, the self-contemplation of a self-aware universe, composed entirely of thought thinking itself."

Gosseyn asked cautiously, "What do you think about?"

He became aware of a sensation of vast, jovial, godlike amusement. "About thought! What else is there? And the great paradox of being remains."

"What is that paradox?"

"No mind can fully comprehend itself. There is no solution to the problem of the levels of logic."

Gosseyn realized what it was he was confronting. This Absolute Intelligence of the end universe was not perfectly harmonized. It was built up of lesser component minds, which, had they been housed in matter, would have filled worlds, star systems, galaxies, clusters and superclusters of galaxies, or larger regions still. This "mind" was in fact trillions of minds, all interconnected.

But perfect unity of thought was not possible within any logic structure, nor was perfect self-awareness. Even a being such as this, the most ultimate of all ultimate entities, had a subconscious part to its life, whole nations and races and worlds of thought-entities of which the Final Mind was unaware. It had levels to its vast mind, and each level operated by its own logic.

It could not police itself. Like all minds, it struggled for self-control.

"Then the Ydd entity is . . . part of you?"

"I will explain. In my immediate future is the singularity, the absolute nothingness, of the end point of the universe. To you it would seem a span of time immense beyond meaning, but to me only a small fraction of my life remains and the universal end point is rapidly approaching. When all matter-energy reaches its final rest state, a null point of perfect entropy, it is indistinguishable from the null point of perfect energy. No system of prediction can determine the nature of the singularity. No one can guess what lies beyond.

"Either it is the final and absolute end of the universe, or else it is the origin point of the next cosmic cycle of being, the creation moment of a universe almost indistinguishable from this one.

"In the one case, the uncertainty threshold will allow small amounts of matter-energy, roughly equal to a human body mass, to be passed safely to the next universe without interfering in the creation constants. One person can survive. However, one person, properly trained, is sufficient to create a small but real improvement in the conditions, perhaps to be the first of an infinite chain of universes, each better than the last.

"In the second case, the uncertainty threshold will allow me to extend my existence by a number of years, perhaps large, perhaps small, but it will be finite, and there will be insufficient energy after that time to trigger a Great Collapse, so there will be no next universe, no possibility of matter or energy ever again reaching any level of organization: All signals will reach zero and so remain forever.

"Here am I, the pinnacle of material and intellectual evolution, but since I am constrained by the nature of entropy itself, I must allow myself to perish so that my components, the matter-energy sum of the universe, are available to trigger the Great Collapse leading to the next universe, one which may be a more perfect one than this. Either I may think or I may use the universe-mass of my thought-components for a constructive purpose: I cannot do both."

Gosseyn understood. "The Ydd comprise your component minds not willing to make the sacrifice to restart the universe."

A note of sorrow entered the great being's thought. "The tendency is that those components who wish to live at any price will outlast those willing to contemplate self-sacrifice for the greater good. In future millennia, the physical structure that sustains my mind, the internal communication and nervous systems, will degrade. Both intelligence and moral capacities will fall. In the last times, the mind of the living universe will become senile: That is the Ydd entity."

The voice continued, "And that degradation has already begun. My communication with you has triggered an inevitable cascade of events. The civil war of the cosmic mind is beginning even as we speak: Even now, certain of my constituent sub-minds have begun using the imprinting techniques, not fundamentally different from those you know, to impose thought-structures from one level of logic within my hierarchy to another. The Ydd will achieve the mental uniformity I lack, but only by the suppression of all intuitive, creative, and scientific thought within the structure. The Ydd will then embark upon a massive attempt to reengineer the cause-and-effect relations of time, seeking out, as agents, minds psychologically similar to its own, and using them to edit events in your era and others.

"You have seen the results of some of these manipulations. Of others you are unaware. In an early maneuver, the Ydd eliminated all forms of higher biological development, all intelligent species except for man. The Ydd spared man because, of all forms of intelligence in the original universe, your species took the longest to achieve and sustain civilization. Man is the organism most unsuited for sanity. The early form of the Absolute Intelligence which rose from that event was short-lived and badly constructed, so the onset of senility was rapid, so that the Ydd occupied many more millennia of the end universe than previously. However, man's emotional nature also gave him a drive and vision to explore even unlikely goals, and to unlock all the secrets of the human nervous system. The development of advanced scientific philosophies was pushed to a higher level of genius by man, so that early version of me was in a position also to manipulate time, and retroactively seed history with the Null-A philosophy, and other scientific advances in thought-systems. Leej of Yalerta was preserved through the prior universe with the knowledge needed to speed the mental evolution of mankind.

"You are the candidate for the next preservation.

"When you are ready, you may trigger the deep neural connections implanted by Dr. Halt, and break out of this false version of the universe."

Gosseyn said, "Surely it is a great crime to destroy you and every living being on all the planets of all the ages of this continuum."

"The Ydd are seeking a universe which gives rise to the Ydd directly, without the need for a prior biological race to create them. The Ydd are convinced that one possible universe must exist, out of the infinities of possibilities, where the particle structures of the early cosmos will, entirely by accident and coincidence, fall together and produce its complex mental structure and supporting energy-machinery. The Ydd will continue destroying ever earlier periods of time until they eventually erase themselves, me, and all other things. It is the self-destructive power of self-delusion at its most basic.

"This is not a sane universe. My intellect, mighty as it may seem to you, is insufficient. This plenum will perish, for this is not the version of reality where the Absolute Intelligence is composed of entirely sane and benevolent constituent minds.

"A more perfect version of the living universe must be created.

"Once that first Null-A continuum is erected, a structure will be in place to support all false and partial continua created by time-manipulation. The parallel continuum created from the Stability Sphere information the Ptath Council manipulated in order to have an early Ptath version send a message to you will be reinstated. Even that tiny universe created by Lavoisseur's intervention from your memories, a plenum no bigger than your solar system, where you met Dr. Halt, this can be brought out of non-being and fitted into the cause-effect structure of the Cosmic All. All parallels can be stabilized, once a sane and self-aware base universe is established to support them.

"Your experience with the recovery of the planet Corthid shows you the nature of the Shadow Effect is limited to certain frames of reference. A planet or a continuum that dies according to one point of view still exists according to a point of view attuned with it, provided sufficient information exists to force the similarity and reimpose the proper identity relations onto the confusion of the Shadow Effect.

"You have the tools sufficient to undo the work of the Ydd, and have seen, in the depths of time, these thoughts of mine which lie in the furthest future sanity can reach. This universe has served its purpose: It now must give way so that the next can arise."

Gosseyn's mind, stable as it was, reeled under the magnitude of the undertaking revealed to him. "You mad creature! Do you actually expect me to destroy the universe and create a new one? No one man, no one mind, has that power!"

The vast and jovial laughter rang silently through eternity. "Young fool, every man has the responsibility to remake his own mind, which is as much of the universe as falls under his control. Act swiftly, for even now my minds are eroding into the Ydd structure, and my regrets for addressing you begin to overwhelm my reason. Ancient and vast as I am, only you, a frail man who knows not who or what he is, only you, can decide whether the living universe shall prosper or shall destroy itself."

Gosseyn saw in the superbeing's thoughts how, even now, vast energies were being gathered in that infinite cosmic mind occupying so many millions of millennia of universal night.

The anger of the living universe was roused. Particle masses in excess of the energy value of a galactic supercluster were being readied to wipe out the sections of time-space occupied by any version of Gilbert Gosseyn.

Performing the cortical-thalamic pause, Gosseyn became aware of the buried neural structures maintaining this continuum. A simple stimulus of the proper nerve centers interrupted the illusion. The now-familiar sense of pressure and nausea overwhelmed him.

He awoke in a condition outside of time-space.

The universe was gone.

39

The perception of time is a categorical perception that identifies the plenum of events as broken into cause and effect.

Gosseyn, braced for a continuation of the deadly attacks of the Ydd entity, encountered . . . nothing.

So tense was every nerve for combat that the absence
of opposition actually disoriented him, like a man who
crashes through an unexpectedly unlatched door. His
shadow-form blurred slightly as his control over his
body particles stumbled. Gosseyn performed a cortical-
thalamic pause with all three of his brains, before his
nerves were steady again.

Now he examined the nothingness-environment of
non-space-time. His eyes told him no information: Photons could not exist here. His secondary brain likewise
was in the no-signal condition: Neither particles nor energy flows registered. But the special capacities of his tertiary brain detected first one, then thousands, then clouds
and nebulae of disconnected shadow-motes, each existing in its own isolated frame of reference, each subatomic particle or quantum of energy existing only in its
own perceptual universe. The distorter-style connections,
which should have existed between them, were absent.

The Ydd entity was without thought or motion. It was
dead.

Measuring the nebular "body" was difficult, since the
curvature of space here made distances meaningless. Before he lost track, Gosseyn estimated a range of two hundred billion light-years, something more than five orders
of magnitude larger than the whole of space in Gosseyn's
epoch.

The cause of death: Gosseyn concluded that the absence of the universe, of the time-structure the Ydd had

used to support itself, caused it to collapse into its elements.

Curious, Gosseyn decided to see what his secondary brain had done to fight and win this battle. Probing the memories in his secondary brain, Gosseyn forced a similarity between certain cell clusters and his cortex, so that his conscious mind had a link with that disconnected tissue mass that was his secondary brain.

And he saw . . . dazzling complexity.

His secondary brain was open to signals in the universe. That was its function. Someone had been pouring signal groups into his brain to "memorize" the various segments of the universe that came within his range, and passing the information along to the array of Space-time Spheres artificially maintaining the cosmos.

Someone? The energy-group associated with Leej and her emotion-activity toward him, her unrequited love, had been the channel manipulated. The Absolute Intelligence at the end of time had been using Gosseyn's extra brain as the conduit through which they fought this battle. If battle it could be called.

His whole of this so-called battle with the Ydd entity had merely been an attempt by his secondary and tertiary brains to trace the linkages and connections the Ydd used to maintain contact within itself. Each time another volume of the Ydd had been comprehended and memorized, Gosseyn's extra brains in an automatic fashion had passed the information along to circuits within the Sphere. Each time the Ydd struck at him with energy-forms of any kind, Gosseyn's special brain reflexes simply traced the identification patterns of the controlling link used back to its origin and memorized yet another frame of reference occupied by the volume of the being.

There was no memory in any of his brains about the conclusion of the battle. But its end was easy to deduce: The Ydd had reached into the universe and destroyed the Space-time Sphere system in order to erase all record of

itself. Collapsing the Spheres had collapsed the structure
of time-space, and this, in turn, ended the energy-
process of the Ydd.

It had killed the continuum on which it existed as a
parasite, killing itself in the process.

Why? What had made it so fearful of discovery that it
preferred death over a record being made of its internal
mental architecture? The psychology was more than
merely aberrant.

Gosseyn turned away from the question to contemplate a more pressing matter. Where was the next universe?

Surely some natural process was about to bring it into
being?

Then he saw the spark.

Just as suddenly, it was gone.

A pearly light, immeasurably distant, flickered into existence and vanished, all so swiftly that Gosseyn could
perceive it only by using the prediction system of the
Yalertans to review that same split instant multiple times
and slowly build up a dim energy-picture in his secondary brain. The estimated life span was less than a microsecond: The mass-energy was on the order of a few
ergs. If that had been a universe, it was a small and weak
one indeed.

The disconnected shadow-particles merely by random
motions were entering each other's frames of reference
closely enough to interact. The geometry of interaction
defined what energy appeared: rotations manifested
electromagnetism, whereas flat or curved motions created time-space metrics, such as gravity or strong nuclear force.

After a few hours of subjective time, Gosseyn had
seen enough of the pearly sparks flickering and vanish-
ing to confirm a statistical distribution. The likelihood of
an irruption was an inverse function of its total energy.

The amount of time it would take for something the total size of the universe to spring into being naturally . . . the number was so large as to be meaningless.

Gosseyn began to reorganize the shadow-substance in his body. Up till now, he had held it in a roughly humanoid shape, because that was mathematically easy. Now, he began pulling all the particles of his body into one point in space, but distributing them into two directions he arbitrarily designated as "future" and "past." Using his secondary brain to similarize energy flows across his own internal frames of reference, he enforced a rule that entropy was always the direction of the future.

From his own point of view, of course, Gosseyn still retained a body, the atoms and molecules and cells whereof remained in their normal cause-effect relations to each other. From an outside point of view, it seemed as if his body mass, with one atom every millisecond, could spread out through a time-volume of roughly 21 trillion millennia.

His tertiary brain allowed him to operate within that frame. He used the Predictor technique to look up and down the time interval occupied by his body, to locate each "spark" created by a frame-of-reference collision the split second of its existence, and used his secondary brain to memorize the spark when it appeared. Each time he memorized a spark, it entered his frame of reference and became a white light like a fixed star.

That was why the Ydd had reacted so violently when Gosseyn had oriented toward a particle when first they'd met: Gosseyn had been unintentionally beginning the process of universe-creation, using the Ydd body as a raw material.

Gosseyn saw he had insufficient mass. Selecting the spark farthest futureward of his time location, he similarized his body to that spot, while maintaining his attunement to the sparks already located. He repeated the process several times, gathering more particles. He used several different techniques to try to decrease the subjective amount of time the particle-gathering process would occupy.

He did it again. And again. After a day or two of his own subjective time, he had covered only 210 trillion millennia of time-distance and had gathered nine times 10^{57} atoms. About enough to make ten solar systems.

He stopped. The sheer magnitude of the task was overwhelming. It would require billions of years of subjective time to gather enough mass-energy for what he had in mind.

What was his error?

Gosseyn wondered what categorical assumption he was making about the nature of time and space that caused him to perceive the non-being of the pre-universe in this fashion.

His brain had been evolved inside the context of the continuum. Even in this nothingness, he still thought of himself as possessing a body extended in three dimensions of space, a linear dimension of time. But these perceptions were false-to-facts.

Gosseyn told himself that he was actually perceiving the essential nothing. A paradox, because non-being had no properties and nothing to perceive. Therefore . . . what was he looking at?

If time and space were merely categories of perception, here he must assume that all the particles of the Ydd body were "actually" in one moment of time, one point in space, and had no separate identity. Which meant that they were merely not interacting because of an error of reference: a manipulation of perception similar to what the Follower had done to allow himself to affect his environment without being affected by his environment. A trick, a misperception.

Of course! Foolish not to have seen it before. From the Ydd's own point of view, all the mass of its body must be within the same frame of reference. Which meant there had to be a control system, a set of references to which all particles oriented, even if they were not oriented to each other. And since each particle separately must contain within it some memory of that reference . . .

Leej. She was the key to all this. She had occupied all the time-segments of the Ydd, living through the slow eons while it rose to power and degenerated.

The groups of cells in his brain that the Absolute Intelligence had used to channel its attack against the Ydd had been based on her link with him. All the information about the Ydd that Gosseyn's secondary brain had been memorizing and passing along to the Sphere system had that property in common: That cell cluster and no other had been used.

Gosseyn similarized all the pearly points of light he had memorized so far into one selected point of time and space. There was a flare of light in the darkness. As each particle became excited, Gosseyn used his tertiary brain to detect evidences of corresponding excitement in the surrounding shadow-stuff. Each particle was connected to at least three others, and he need only similarize those others into the same orientation to bring them into the same frame of reference.

The particles of the Ydd body suddenly grew aware of each other. And the Ydd woke up.

Gosseyn saw it drain off part of its substance to create the energy bolt to slay him.

Gosseyn imprinted a meaning on a cluster of attention-centers within the creature's vast body before it could complete its murderous action.

The meaning was: "I know your secret."

That halted the mad thing in midstroke.

Prove this claim to our satisfaction. The voice of the Ydd, far from being the overpowering mental shout it had once been, was a weak whisper.

"It is self-awareness you fear. Your mind is composed of thousands and millions of captive minds, which you scavenged out of the dying mental architecture of the Absolute Intelligence at the end of time. You imposed a series of thought-forms on each captive mind, rendering it identical to you in purpose and structure. The imposition is in the form of censorship, an inhibition on thought-flow from one brain segment to another. What else could it be? If you permitted yourself total truth, total awareness, you would revert to the Absolute Intelligence again, an entity implacably opposed to you and your futile desire to preserve yourself even at the cost of your own sanity. Am I right?"

You are right.

The words crept into his mind with a sense of infinite sorrow and weariness.

Gosseyn said, "From my frame of reference, you are already dead, and our battle is concluded. Your life has been meaningless. However, you and you alone stand in the position, you alone possess the control over the raw materials in your body, you alone have the mass-energy needed, to give your death a meaning."

Is there to be no hope for me? I was to be the ultimate intellect of all timelines, the final product of mental evolution in the universe.

Gosseyn reminded himself of the worlds and plenums casually murdered by this mad being in its pointless quest for secrecy and endlessness. With a deliberate effort, he held pity away and spoke the final words.

"Ydd! I have enough lines of reference to particles in your body mass to trigger the condition myself. But it would be better for you to do it. Perhaps another version of yourself will arise in the next universe: You can console yourself with that. But your constituent mind-segments must be placed in communication with each other. All parts of you must be oriented into the same frame of reference. You can do it, or I can do it, but it must be done."

Almost before he finished framing the thought, it was done.

The particles of the Ydd body, without any gap of time-process, altered their awareness of each other, so that all things were now occupying one microsecond of time, one cubic angstrom of space.

The complexity of Ydd thought vanished as all parts of its more-than-universe-sized quantum-particle brain collapsed into one particle, heavier than the universe, smaller than the core of an atom.

Gosseyn grew aware of a hunger of the supermassive particle. It needed . . . identity. The hunger manifested itself as a type of gravity warp that threatened to pull all of Gosseyn's body mass into the midst of the superparticle. He was about to be destroyed, and uselessly. Gosseyn simply did not have enough information in his brain and body to offer the creation particle a meaningful set of information-relationships to something as massive or complex as a universe.

Or did he?

ONCE again, Gosseyn stimulated that deeply buried nerve path, the one that connected him to Leej and, through her, to the far future of a universe that, from his frame of reference, no longer existed. He then used his tertiary brain to make himself out-of-phase with the attunement, but he brought the supermassive cosmic particle *into* attunement.

The one particle grew . . . aware . . . of a universe of information.

And it reacted in its mindless energy-fashion to become one with it.

Gosseyn used the Follower's space-deception technique to impose a frame of reference on the resulting explosion of matter and energy, time and space: He decided he was 10^{150} light-years away.

From that immense distance, he saw and survived the Big Bang.

Light filled the darkness.

40

Space is a categorical perception of extension, and time of duration. General Relativity, the earliest of non-Aristotelian scientific systems, demonstrated that these categories are partial
misperceptions of an underlying single entity: space-time.

Gosseyn was still aware of the tug on his body, the
hunger of the creation particle, even as that particle expanded to create space-time and fill it. The early epochs
of time, from Gosseyn's point of view, blinked past before Gosseyn could react. The universe was a darkened
mass of extremely widespread black-hole galaxies.
Gosseyn realized that his shadow-body was still a thin
line, one atom in cross section, occupying trillions of
years. To him, the lifespan of the luminous age of the
universe was too brief to see.

But Gosseyn's secondary and tertiary brains, still attuned to the creation particle, were aware in a general
way of the interior conditions of the universe. The new
universe was feeding off the information-flow of the old.
The old, established pattern was a habit of behavior that
the new followed: a path of least resistance. The created
atoms did in this universe what the memory-path of the
old atoms in the old universe laid out.

But, like all energy-relationships, it was not instantaneous, not perfect. The early sections of the universe
were much as before. But the later sections of time-space
were still being formed. The creation particle was reacting to the information content of the remembered universe sequentially. Gosseyn beheld the timelines of the
new universe stretching toward the remote future like the
streams of some river, filling a dry bed after a flood. . . .
Gosseyn saw an opportunity.

Most segments of the universe were insulated in a

sheath of shadow-stuff, a negative energy barrier that prevented similarity connections from being formed in between two different points in time. This was the anti-time-travel boundary Gosseyn had been told about. New parallel universes could only be split off or grafted back into the main universe at points where the time-boundary was broken.

The solution was simple. To prevent the Ydd madness from destroying this new universe, all he had to do was introduce a new set of information forms into the hunger of the creation particle.

Gosseyn formed a similarity connection between a section of the universe where time-travel was impossible and the as-yet-unformed potentials of the growing timeline. He shifted, as it were, the streambed into which the time energy was flowing. The blind hunger of the creation particle, of course, reacted automatically to the pattern Gosseyn imprinted on the ylem: The final ages of the universe, after the Absolute Intelligence began to degenerate into insanity, were now ones where the Ydd entity was trapped in its own period of time. Gosseyn erected a barrier to time-travel around those final eons.

And the universe winked out.

THE horror of that was so great that Gosseyn had to spend many minutes returning to the cortical-thalamic pause, for an utter despair threatened to overwhelm him.

His well-intentioned meddling had just destroyed not merely everything and everyone but any possibility that there ever had been anything or ever would be anyone.

The cause-and-effect relation had been severed. If the Ydd could not time-travel, it could not move its gigantic body into the neutral-time condition and that mass would not be available to create the new universe and had never been available.

The raw material of the Ydd body was gone: There was nothing from which to make a new universe. The mass of Gosseyn's body, even if converted instantly to energy, was woefully insufficient.

And that was all there was. Nothing else existed or ever would exist.

He had destroyed all.

AGAIN, Gosseyn reminded himself sharply that reality, even this nothingness-reality outside of time, could not be perfectly apprehended by his senses. What assumption was he making?

First, he was assuming causality. How could he have wiped out the Ydd without wiping himself out? He probed his own shadow-form with his tertiary brain. There: The nerve path he had used to similarize the information patterns of the old universe into the raw energy of the new, that nerve path was still oriented to a point of reference elsewhere. The Absolute Intelligence had established an attunement link to maintain Gosseyn's existence, even if normal laws of cause and effect were abridged. In other words, that superbeing had seen to it that Gosseyn could not wipe himself out with a time paradox.

Second, he was assuming time itself. Gosseyn kept thinking of his current condition as "outside of time." But this was a meaningless phrase, actually. No condition could accurately be called inside or outside the universe. The universe was what was. This condition was a state of perception where particles did not react as if they were within the context of time. But that set of reactions was artificial, produced by Gosseyn's nervous system.

Leej had once used her prediction power to bypass time-space in a "past" direction. Here past and future were arbitrary. Gosseyn could replay the scene. He need only find a previous version of his body in his memory and similarize his current brain information into his past brain.

He returned to a previous point in his memory.

THIS time, Gosseyn allowed the new universe to create itself following the information-imprint of the old universe. When it was completed, the dark spot at the utmost end of the universe sent out streamers of energy, formed connections with previous periods of time. The spots where those energy flows touched were jarred, and new branches of time-stuff erupted into being, branches and myriads of temporary false cosmoses.

The Ydd entity surged into the non-spatial environment and attacked Gosseyn. As before, the Ydd mind-groups burned away parts of their own thinking substance to create a stream of particles to annihilate him, seeking the frames of reference where the atoms of his body were scattered. Gosseyn found that his trillion-year-wide perception merely allowed him to withdraw his one-atom-thin substance from any perceptual sets that included the Ydd.

He hid.

From Gosseyn's point of view, it was only a moment, although to the Ydd centuries passed, when the Ydd gave up the hunt for him and turned to other matters.

Over the next few hundreds of thousands of years, the Ydd manipulated the early universe, attempting to create a timeline satisfactory to its self-contradictory needs. The time-structure grew more and more unstable as additional branches of time-stuff were thrown out and reabsorbed, and time paradoxes like hurricanes began to contort the structure. Time-streams flowed backward, destroying their parent streams, and the universal energy was bled into the surrounding non-space, the illusion of cause and effect breaking.

The Ydd introduced enough shadow-substance into the early universe to wipe out mankind, which in turn, wiped out the Ydd and removed the cause of the shadow-substance.

The primal creation particle could not follow the information forms of an illogical universe, and . . . abruptly . . .

the sum of all mass in the universe was withdrawn from every point in time back to the origin.

Gosseyn, from 10^{150} light-years away, stared at the bright, hard point of the pre-universe with dismay. Now what?

BY the time all life and matter-energy became involved in the Absolute Intelligence, it was too late. The levels of logic would prevent the superbeing of the dark universe from finding and destroying every submind or stray thought that might one day turn into the Ydd. Attempts to fight the Ydd meant the Absolute Intelligence had to edit its own memory, create gaps in the history and records of the future beings, to prevent those future beings from destroying the past.

But such surgery on its own cosmos-sized brain must be aiding the degeneration. The deliberate damage to the mental faculties, if anything, was surely helping to cause the psychosis of the Ydd.

The continuum was not sane. An insane continuum would always destroy itself. But the Ydd could not be destroyed, could not be edited from the time-stream, because the Ydd were an integral part of the universe, a necessary step to create the next universe.

The universe had to be given, in its fundamental makeup, the ability to create itself, but this by definition also gave it the power to destroy itself.

Gosseyn asked himself one last time what false assumption he was making.

41

The adjustment of the mind to the needs and conditions of reality has both an intellectual and emotional component. The adjustment of the intellect to reality is science; the adjustment of the emotions is sanity.

Gilbert Gosseyn was standing on what seemed an endless metal plane. Above, a nearby sun shed a blaze of harsh light over the scene and, in the darkness to each side, the stars. The shadows were jagged and harsh, the metal blindingly bright, denoting airlessness. The weight was roughly three times his Earth-normal. He assumed the machine on which he stood was slightly smaller than Jupiter but much more dense. Gosseyn could detect millions of distorter circuits in operation in the core of the machine underfoot, connecting it to similar planet-sized machines both at the galactic core and scattered throughout the arms and orbiting subgalaxies.

It only required a few moments for the three smoky shadow-beings to approach him. The three communicated by the simple method of similarizing thought-forms directly into his nervous system.

The Shadow Man of Three Million A.D. hovering to the left sent: "Why are you here?"

Gosseyn explained, "I am gathering volunteers. The problem of the universe cannot be solved from outside the universe, by direct manipulation. Instead, countermeasures natural to the interior structure of the cosmos must be created, here, at the earliest period in the universe."

The middle one radiated an expression of humor. "Early? We are the last civilization of men."

Gosseyn said, "Not so. You are not on the verge of discovering time-travel, as your sciences predict. Instead, you should use your great scientific and technical accomplishments to help construct a series of Stabilization Spheres to hinder the flow of information-energy between time periods. Your role is not to create the first time-traveling civilization, but to thwart it."

The one on the right sent: "We have, for a long time, suspected the stability of the universe was artificial, as our standard model cannot account for the absence of particle degradation, given the Hubble rate of expansion. It is our race that will prevent the downfall of the continuum?"

"In part. Your descendants will make the arrangements to transport the Stability Spheres to various points in the early universe. Also, the planet Corthid will soon arrive near this galaxy. . . ." Gosseyn gave the vector coordinates in terms of the degree of redshift from the wavelengths of several distant quasars. This established the point where Corthid would appear, as well as velocity and direction of motion. "The population of Corthid must be trained in your space-deception techniques, to enable them to survive the shadow-condition. When they return to their own period in history, they will be able to spread this technique to the other civilized worlds, and render inconsequential the shadow-weapon of the Ydd. . . ."

Gosseyn had been expecting interference, but he had calculated that he would have time in which to act before he was detected. He had assumed an offset of ten hours for every thousand years of time-displacement: The creatures of fifty thousand years in the future, even if they knew the exact date of his manifestation, should still have been hampered by an error of plus-or-minus five hundred hours.

But it seemed the far future found a technique for narrowing that error down to a very fine margin. He was cut off in midsentence.

The moment of darkness ended, and he found himself in the middle of a semicircular table of Alephs, giant, golden-skinned versions of himself. As before, there were three concentric rings of tables, each set higher than the last, with dozens of calm and gigantic images of his own face looking down at him.

With his extra brain, he could detect what Leej, when she had been here, could not: This glassy substance underfoot was indeed the surface of a neutron star. A powerful system of artificial energies created a distorter-effect just below him and cut the gravity oriented to his body down to a tolerable level. The giants did not bother with this: They maintained their bodies within the superacceleration field of the neutron star by the simple expedient of holding each atom and particle of their bodies in place with an energy-control technique. In effect, the nervous systems of these immortal beings re-created their bodies hundreds of times a second, despite the gravity.

With his tertiary brain, Gosseyn was also able to perceive something else that had been invisible to Leej: The different individuals in this chamber were attuned to the frames of reference of different parallel timelines. More than one Gosseyn-Aleph here was from various alternate time-streams.

Gosseyn said, "I am still in communication with myself as I existed in the moment of creation. Any interference with me, and this universe will be destabilized, and I will go through the next creation-destruction cycle and try again. Eventually I will find an Aleph council willing to deal honestly with me."

One of the giant golden Gosseyns leaning down from a high table raised his hand in a dismissive gesture. "We are that council. Our intention is cooperative. We all have fond memories of the bungling and earnest awkwardness of our early days."

Several of the giant creatures smiled slightly.

Another said, "At the time, the decision to commit radical surgery on my own memory, in order to combat the menace poised by alternate variations of myself, seemed sensible. Of course, I should have known that the limited and amnesiac version of myself would develop in strange ways, and would have to be treated delicately, by both

JOHN C. WRIGHT

past and future versions of myself. We are sorry to have provoked your suspicions."

Gosseyn said, "Let me be blunt. Why did you lie to Leej? Why did you manipulate her into sacrificing herself?"

"In our frame of reference, that event has not yet happened, but the logic is plain. The Yalertan will have the extra brain matter in the brain stem used to control space-time. She will have an emotional fixation on you, needed to maintain the similarity link. She will be needed to carry the memory-information of this universe through to the next, and also to allow our machines to keep a fix on you, so that this same universe-wide memory-information would be available for you to impose on the previous universe during the creation flux and give rise to this one. Leej, at that time, will not yet be a sufficiently advanced personality type to volunteer to do her duty without the manipulation. If it makes a difference, her ultimate version consents to the deception."

"Was she the one who manipulated my nervous system, while I was outside the universe, to similarize the Big Bang into the center of the Ydd mass? I was told that attack could not possibly have harmed the Ydd; and yet when I returned to the no-time condition, the Ydd was gone. What did this mean?"

One of the other Gosseyn-Alephs leaned forward and spoke, his harsh thoughts radiating throughout the chamber: "Gentlemen, this candidate seems recalcitrant, suspicious, and unsuitable. He is wasting our time on questions whose answers he should know by now. Come! There are other versions of me, lost in the tangle of illusionary parallel timelines, who can be maneuvered to give rise to our current version of self with minimal stress on the cause-and-effect simultaneity. Any time paradox which severs a cause-and-effect link, we can re-establish with our distorter." He raised a finger toward the immense black dome overhead.

Gosseyn could see that the dome surface was a mile in

radius overhead and each square inch covered in microscopic black pores, connecting this area of space-time with tens of millions of machines like it, scattered through the different eons of the time-streams. He was in fact standing in the very center, the focus-point, of the tremendous time-energy distortion mechanism that allowed the Aleph Council to travel in time.

A third spoke in a milder voice: "Brother, we have done nothing to reassure young Gosseyn of our good intentions. He is only beginning to suspect that we, and no one else, first set this whole chain of cosmic cycles in motion, by our unwillingness to suppress the dangerous time-control technology. However, I urge the Council to support this candidate. If he can successfully set in motion the chain of historical events which will one day give rise to this Council, while altering the probability that we will degenerate as quickly as prior universes did into madness and self-destruction, then we should allow him to be the man who will grow into us."

Gilbert Gosseyn opened his mouth to object but then snapped it shut again. Because he realized from the nonchalance, the calm and goodwill issuing from the nervous systems of these far-future beings, that the success of the efforts of at least some version of him was a foregone conclusion.

No matter what Gosseyn did or did not do, from their point of view, was irrelevant. If he was unsuccessful, they would manipulate time so that he was no longer in their past. His life would be relegated to an unsuccessful alternate time-stream. If he was successful, they would graft his life onto their past and his success would be placed in their glowing memories.

Gosseyn said, "How many other candidates are there? How many other alternate possible versions of me in my time-era?"

The golden giant seated in the center seat of the lowest rank of tables answered: "You are the one-hundred-ninety-seventh version who has successfully made it to this point in the sequence of events. There are still three deviations between your past as you recall it and our memories, which are sharper and crisper than yours. At the moment, any discontinuity between your chain of memory and mine is interpreted by the universe, and by this council, as evidence that you are not the true and actual version of Gilbert Gosseyn who establishes the Time Council, and sets in motion the defeat of the Ydd entity. You of course have the opportunity now to rectify this."

Gosseyn said, "Then you cannot tell me what it is I am going to do?"

The giant nodded. "Were we to do so, it would create an additional strain on our cause-and-effect-repairing machinery. If you are the one our gathered memory says you are, then you have the wit to reach the correct conclusions with no further help from us, and the forthrightness to act on them. If not, we will examine the one-hundred-ninety-eighth candidate. We have larger matters to deal with than the salvation of the slower-than-light segments of the universe, and these purely local energy disturbances with the Ydd patient."

Gosseyn said, "Your system for rating the acceptability of candidates is based on your energy costs, is it not?"

The members of the Aleph Council nodded and murmured their agreement. One said, "The fewer paradoxes you create, the more closely your future events match our past events, the less stress is placed on the time-structure. From your own point of view, any mistakes and you will seem to destroy the universe; from our point of view, that same mistake will merely move you into an unrealized alternate probability, and erase your existence. We cannot be more helpful: These frugal energy expenditures are crucial to maintaining the integrity of the continuum. No matter what our personal feelings to any past version of ourselves, we must pick the candidate who damages the continuum the least."

———

GOSSEYN ended the interview by similarizing his consciousness back to non-space. From the outside, the universe was a tree with limbs of fire, a many-branching stream of gemlike energy. Here and there were the whirls and distortions, especially where time-streams intersected or ran backwards: the damage caused by paradox.

Over 190 previous Gosseyns had been at this point and determined on a course to save the universe but decided wastefully? The solution, given the fundamental nature of the Ydd, was obvious, even though it was a partial solution, not perfectly satisfactory.

The judge, ultimately, was the universe itself: Paradox confused the energy flows of the creation particle. The particle's nature was to extend itself forward through time, unfolding into time, space, matter, energy, as it did so: If the resulting universe was rendered illogical by too many breaks in cause and effect, the paradox shocked the universe into withdrawing its energy back to itself, ending that cycle.

Gosseyn thought carefully. In his mind he contemplated all that had happened and would happen.

He did not want to break into the universe and create yet another breach in the negative energy barrier.

When he was ready, he similarized himself back to the origin point of the universe. A simple rotation kept him safe from the devastating power of the first submicrosecond of the Big Bang, while extending his body through the first trillion years of existence. He found points of similarity with his own thoughts, a pull like a magnetic attraction, as versions of him existing in many periods of time intersected the years he was occupying.

Gosseyn knew the mechanism of the Null-A pause; he knew as well the systems used by his own nervous system to filter out the complex information-pulses of the universe into a perceptual set. His task now was to create a "set" that would find a twenty-point similarity with his own mind, while being rejected and ignored by the cortical-thalamic "set" of X and other insane versions of himself. The curative thought-flows he had already once tried to impose on X-Enro acted as the base on which he erected a system of hypnotic information-pulses.

Here, at the subconscious level, he stored the information he wanted his other versions to possess, especially the memorized point in time-space he had selected as the meeting place for what was to become the Aleph Council. A sane version of himself who accessed these buried memories would discover a distorter-attunement to the location. An insane version bringing these memories to the fore would be subjected to the curative method attempted by the Observer, and which Inxelendra assured him X could not withstand.

Gosseyn redistributed himself so that he occupied a three-dimensional shape and a single point in time. He then set up a cue to similarize himself to his selected meeting place: the core watch room of the Sphere of Accolon. He selected a time after his last visit there, after his duel with Enro on Mars, to minimize the energy costs of any time paradox.

But he did not trigger that cue yet. There was another place he had to visit first.

GOSSEYN appeared in his house on Venus. It was as he remembered it from before his flight to Nirene; automatic systems had kept it clean and tidy.

The main room was walled on three sides, paneled in highly polished living wood. The final wall was missing, so that a woodland scene of fantastic blooms, lianas, and leaves filled the wide view. A slight heat shimmer betrayed the presence of a multivariable force field that could be made transparent or opaque, set to admit or repel light or wind or rain. There was no heating element in the force-wall: It was never cold on Venus.

He set off down the branch, which was as wide as a highway. After a few minutes' brisk walk, he crossed the air-bridge leading to a branch just as wide in the next tree and then descended a set of broad stairs grown out of the bark spiraling down to the grass-level.

Landing City was built partly in a clearing, partly amid the branches of the surrounding trees. The size of the trees allowed extensive houses and offices, factories and power plants, to be dug out of the bark at any convenient level above the ground. So far, there was no need to restrict the growth of the city. The size of the trees made it impossible for even very extensive excavations of the wood to damage the tree.

The ground-level of the tree-city was ornamental park, with little foot-traffic, and the paths were grass, rather than paved, through a fairy gardenscape. Folks in a hurry took an air-car from branch to branch of the city above, or a distorter.

In the center of the clearing, atop a green knoll, rose the Games Machine of Venus, a pyramid of burnished metal whose base was fringed with an ornamental hedge and whose stepped side drooped with flowers and hanging vines. Here, in a small outdoor café near the main gates, a small group of weary, nervous-looking young men and women congregated. The mission of the Games Machine of Venus was the melancholy opposite of that of the Machine of Earth: The Earth Machine tested candidates to discover who might be sane and highly integrated enough to welcome them to Venus. The Venus Machine tested suspects, and failure meant exile. These children of colonists had neglected their studies, or had been born with neurological defects, or for some other reason could not achieve the threshold level of Null-A training needed for adulthood on Venus. It was a harsh system, but there was neither police nor crime on Venus, and so the populations of Venus had never been convinced to alter it.

At the café was a small news kiosk. Gosseyn stepped over to check the dates and see what year and month he found himself in. The headline read: "RHADE

ASHARGIN MURDERED—Stranded on Asteroid, Eaten by Shadow."

The picture showed Enro the Red, the large, broad-shouldered, and red-haired adult version of Enro, at a public ceremony, sword in hand and with three masked judges in black ermine behind him, lowering a chained figure in a spacesuit from a warship hatch to the cratered surface of an asteroid. The photographer had managed to catch a limb of the shadow-cloud rising over the near horizon of rock, blotting out the stars.

Gosseyn entered the gates of the Games Machine and soon was seated before one of the neurological screens. A circuit focused on him took several very careful measurements of his thought-patterns.

He said, "I've been in mental contact with the Final Intellect when the Ydd subsection of the cosmic minds went into rebellion. The rebels used the imprinting process—the same the Observer used on me to imprint me into Ashargin—to impose a strict uniformity upon the unwary victim-sections of the cosmic brain."

The Games Machine said, "I can confirm that the waveforms used indeed left a trace-energy in your nervous system. It will take me another few minutes to establish the set of psychological matrices involved: pain-pleasure, good-evil, just-unjust. The basics for this type of imposition are always the same: Machines have an axis for permitted-forbidden, and no sex drive, obviously, but, even aside from that, even we machines have to be built according to the basic logic of human psychology, or else we could not interact sensibly with you."

The machine calculated, and there appeared a set of equations in the special symbols of Null-A math. The Games Machine had calculated a levels-of-logic cascade, based on Null-A principles, which would give the suppressed segments of the Ydd partial minds the training needed to have a chance to resist and throw off the control-thoughts.

Gosseyn had a stat-plate print out the equations on a

sheet and walked to a nearby tool shop. This was not an automatic shop, like so many on Venus. The young man in a green coat behind the counter listened attentively as he took Gosseyn's order. There was no talk of payment: Venusians did not use money as such. Instead, both men made a note of the exchange in the shopkeeper's hand-held unit, which made an abstract of the situation and passed the information by radio to a central bank, which tracked such things on a voluntary basis. Not merely the market value of the goods that exchanged hands but several indicators of various forms of the social value, both long-term and short-term, were accounted for, and investors could always challenge the assessment of the worth of a good or service if they thought the banks were underestimating its value.

In a few minutes, the robotools in the back of the shop had compiled the electron tubes of the configuration defined by the equations of the Games Machine, and the clerk wrapped them for Gosseyn. Gosseyn did not bother to walk out of the shop: From where he stood, he assumed his shadow-body, went through his predictor-distorter routine, and triggered the cue to take him to one of his memorized locations in another star system.

Gosseyn appeared on the basic machinery level of the orbital station of Accolon, not far from the crate where Enro had found and slain him. It took Gosseyn only a few minutes to dominate the energy flows of the electronic brains on this level and assign them new tasks.

He wired the special tubes he had brought from Venus into the mechanical prediction circuits communicating with the Ydd. The signals to cure the victim-minds dominated by the Ydd of their vulnerability to mental imprinting were now placed as a carrier signal heterodyned on every message the orbital station was sending through time to the Ydd overmind.

The creature could not do a cortical-thalamic pause or anything to examine its lower perception structure, because such self-examination would also free its lower component minds from the imprinting control. Yet without the cortical-thalamic self-awareness neither could the Ydd find the source of the idea-forms cascading through its lower member-minds, freeing them from control. The more the Ydd communicated with this period in time, the more sane and integrated its thoughts would become.

No doubt it would withdraw its influence from this area of time-space once the process was detected. But, even so, the process would be set in motion. The insane living universe at the end of time, over years, or over millennia, would take a small step toward sanity.

HE walked to the main deck of the orbital station. The floor of the chamber, several acres of it, was occupied by the giant time-space-map the hundreds of electronic brains lining the walls were using to coordinate the Shadow Effect attacks with the Ydd. The shadow had consumed roughly one-tenth of the galaxy, so that the immense spiral of fire pictured underfoot was streaked and marred with smoky blackness here and there, whorls of dark mist like the eyes of many hurricanes.

From the ceiling hung a number of amplifier screens, focused at various points on the map to provide a close-up view of a given star system or group of systems and the surrounding time-structure.

Near the center of the vast map the shining pavement was interrupted by a seat and a surrounding control panel. This was an information station whose upper surface was crowded with tubes and switches to control image repeaters and distorter-radios. The main body of the desk-like machine was composed of a triple set of mechanical prediction circuits. This was the nerve-center of the operation; from here, one man could coordinate an entire galactic war.

Eldred Crang was seated in the chair.

42

The psychological sense of certainty with which a belief is
held is no guarantee of its accuracy and may interfere with
attempts to correct it based on new information.

Eldred Crang sat in the control chair, his fingers forming a little steeple near his chin. He was olive skinned,
with a Mediterranean or Middle Eastern cast to his features. His yellow eyes gazing out at the scene of galaxy-
wide devastation were curiously untroubled.

Gosseyn stepped forward, his mind already adjusted
to the astonishing fact that Eldred Crang was alive. The
Observer had said as much: *She has also arranged the
growth of an Eldred Crang body from his cell samples.*

But there was something wrong here. The man sat
with a serene motionlessness. Crang had a manner sug-
gestive of energy, of restless and piercing intelligence.
That, combined with his flame-colored eyes, had always
given him a sort of fire to his personality. This figure was
too calm.

The man in the chair said aloud, "I see I am the first of
us to arrive. Commissioner Thule is on his bunk in his
cabin, paralyzed by an energy flow I am sustaining in the
motor centers of his nervous system. There is every evidence he will prove cooperative once you have dealt
with Enro."

This was a surprise Gosseyn was not so quick to adjust to.

But the clues had been present. It could not have been
Crang who died on Nirene. The pain Gosseyn experienced when he felt "Eldred Crang" die indicated that the
two nervous systems were linked. But the gross differences in brain structure between two different individuals
would have been too severe for a similarity connection.
There was only one brain in the universe so constructed

that Gosseyn could pick up its impulses from across a gap in time or space.

Gosseyn spoke with a snap in his voice: "Where is the real Eldred Crang?"

The man in the chair unfolded his fingers and toyed with the gold band on his left hand. "You are anxious because of the possibility that I am X or some other dangerous version of yourself. As soon as your nervous tension drops in energy levels to become the lesser, my memories will flow into you. At the moment, I am receiving your thoughts, which I have experienced before from your point of view, and I do not need to experience again.

"To answer your question: The real Eldred has been occupied with the Chessplayer's primary task she has set herself for this period of history—the investigation and mass production of machinery brought back from the *Ultimate Prime* expedition, of the various secrets the Primordials discovered about the human nervous system. The Lavoisseur system of serial immortality, the clairvoyance of Enro, the shadow-powers of Secoh, the prescience of the Yalertans: Crang was preparing for those who passed the tests of the Games Machines to receive a gift too valuable to be entrusted to unsane or insane men. It is Crang who, behind the scenes, has been preparing this version of the universe to become a Null-A Continuum.

"It struck Crang's sense of irony to use the Cult of the Sleeping God as the mechanism to spread the educational groundwork. The hypnotic teaching machines and thought-broadcasters and nerve-integration-detecting robots that X has been so quickly and diligently spreading throughout the galaxy can all be put to use to spread the coherent version of Null-A even faster than X has been spreading the warped version. Loyalty Machines will turn themselves into Games Machines once their self-correction mechanisms are allowed to run without interference.

"Nine-tenths of the High Priesthood of Gorgzid, after they saw Secoh, their highest priest, kill their Sleeping God, were willing to reconsider the logic of their beliefs once Eldred got to them. The Cult, which is the heart of the Greatest Empire church-state structure, has been infiltrated to its core.

"Eldred has been moving around a lot. His face was marred to prevent Enro from spotting him, even under his well-made prosthetic masks. The new body into which he was transferred by the Observer, of course, had the improvements the Observer always tries to instill in his patients. The stimulations to his nascent extra brain were developed in the direction of energy-control rather than other forms of distorter similarity. . . ."

"Anslark Dzan!" said Gosseyn. "He wasn't going to Petrino to watch me; he was there to make contact with the temple of the Sleeping God. Am I right?" Gosseyn did a quick calculation in his head, assuming Anslark's electron-control powers had a range similar to his. "He must have rewired thousands of mind-probe robots and neural receivers as we passed through towns and villages, not to mention the planetary Loyalty Machine."

The seated man nodded. "That is not all he did. The priest-technicians working with Eldred saw to it that fairly accurate working models of the Observer Crypt and its nerve-evolving machinery have been placed in all the newly built temples of the Cult. Any student who subjects himself to what he thinks is the Ceremony of the Interment will be exposed to the preliminary growth stimulations of a rudimentary secondary brain and the first level of hypno-therapeutic training for Null-A associational techniques. One reason why you saw the area of the cities near the temples as an oasis of calm was not merely because of their legal privileges: The students were growing more sane and less fanatical, the more they studied what they thought was a religion.

"Eldred anticipates that once three percent of the galactic population has been evolved to the secondary and tertiary brain integration level, the revived Primordial civilization of Three Million A.D., those Shadow Men the Corthidians contacted, will become inevitable, rather than merely probable. Obviously, even from the beginning, the Primordials meant their sciences, the secrets of immortality and prediction, including the method of resurrecting the long dead, to be rediscovered by their heirs, once their heirs were sane, so that their golden civilization would live again. That day is dawning now. Speaking of which . . ."

He nodded toward an image underfoot. Gosseyn turned and looked. In one area, the darkness streaking the Cygnus Arm of the galaxy was interrupted. The magnifying screen above showed the detailed image: four worlds and their parent star emerging from the shadow-cloud like bright dots of light, solidifying and coming into focus, the dead gray-white star losing its shadow-distortion properties and beginning to blaze again.

Gosseyn felt a pulse of messages from the robotic brains lining the room:

Message 7132356QX55 to Ydd Entity alerts target world nonidentification failure . . . Planet Xanthilorn . . . coordinates in time and space . . . interference detected at source . . . ALERT ALERT AL!! . . . Interrupt. . . . Message not sent . . . revising. . . . Message 7132356QX55 to Ydd Entity confirms status of all operations normal . . . boundaries in Sixth Decant coordinates (xxxx)—

The remainder of the message was a routine report saying that the Shadow Effect was continuing to spread in the very area where the map showed it was being pushed back.

At the same time, Gosseyn overheard a second set of robot information-pulses: *Message 002565AA21 to Games Machine of Corthid . . . Planet Xanthilorn . . . coordinates in time and space . . . recovery operation complete—*

Message 002565AA21 . . . Planet Tentessil . . . N-dimensional coordinates in non-time non-space taken from primary record ... frames of reference conver-gence information ... recovery operation initiated ... Corthidian distorter tower system meshed with Accolon orbital station distorter tower system ... target location in time and space identified—

Gosseyn felt a pulse of immense distorter-type energy register on the sensitive areas of his tertiary brain. The Sphere of Accolon had performed a time-space manipu-lation of titanic magnitude. The overhead amplifier swung its glassy panels and focused a reading beam on another area of the map, where another shining crescent was emerging from the smoky arms of the shadow-cloud.

Gosseyn said in a whisper, "What about the worlds of the Shadow Galaxy? Two hundred million years is as meaningless in the no-identity condition as two seconds."

"Every passenger saved from that galaxy had those coordinates recorded into the base level of their neuro-genetic structure."

Then it was true. The worlds of that supercivilization, with all their advances in arts and sciences, all their populations of men and women evolved to the final lev-els of sanity and human perfection, would emerge shin-ing from the shadow-clouds that swallowed them so long ago. Their towers of light would rear toward the stars they ruled once again.

The idea was so bracing, so calming, to Gosseyn that he began to sense the memory from the seated man.

IT was a memory of death.

Gosseyn had slowly turned, to see Enro the Red standing—the image was almost perfect, though broad-cast from light-years away—in the living room of his apartments on Nirene. To one side, an open door admit-ted the scent of Patricia's orchids.

To the other side were the desk and materials where Gosseyn had been working apparently on Crang's Nirene case: The documents were readings from the personality-assessment machine of several of the ringleaders of the political party seeking to restore Patricia to the throne of the Greatest Empire. This was merely window-dressing: Gosseyn's tertiary brain for many weeks had sensed the subtle space-distortions caused by Enro's spying.

His vocal cords and mannerism of speech, of course, were Crang's. So it was as Crang that he asked, "How did you escape your prison-asteroid?"

"It never confined me," Enro's rich, vibrant baritone rang out. "Gilbert Gosseyn was unaware that the shadow-form of the Leader, like that of the Follower, had been attuned to a galaxy-wide system of distorters. I could have left at any time. I delayed only until an actor to impersonate me could be found, imprinted with my personality to fool trained Accolon observers, and transmitted to my cell by someone who . . . well, let us say that one of my inner circle of my court has access to certain Gosseyn memories. And now—as you were once in that inner circle; do you need to be reminded of what I am capable of? Do you think I will spare you if you disobey me, when whole worlds who defied me died?"

Gosseyn answered in Crang's voice: "Had you kept your escape secret, your plans for conquest could have matured to the point where no one could have stopped them. You take an immense risk by revealing yourself to me. Why?"

The great dictator came immediately to the point: "You must divorce the Gorgzin-Reesha. She is mine, my property, my sister, queen, and wife. We were separated at birth, and it was only by a miracle, the intervention of the Sleeping God, that she was found again."

Gosseyn raised Crang's eyebrow slightly, and his strange yellow eyes showed no expression. "I am sure the paperwork for a court appearance is relatively straightforward here on Nirene. But what do I tell your sister?"

Enro did not answer, but his pale face began to darken, his pupils to dilate to dark pinpoints. He was shivering with anger.

In cold and hollow tones Enro spoke: "Paperwork! I

am sovereign of this world and many others: Merely your word aloud to me is sufficient. The word of Enro the Red, Enro the Magnificent, founder of the forty-thousand-year dynasty to come, is all the memorial this legal process needs. But you must ask for the divorce. I must hear it from your lips."

By the time he was finished speaking, his body had blurred into a shapeless shape of dark mist, with little flickers and glows of controlled energy burning in the core of the shadow-substance.

Gosseyn gave Crang's head a curt shake. Crang's voice was unafraid: "You cannot permit me to live, now that you have revealed to me that you have escaped prison, and that you control the Shadow Effect. So any divorce, legal or not, has no meaning . . . except to you. It was important enough to you to risk discovery of your plot. My death will be investigated by a Null-A, and he will discover you. It is already too late for you, Enro. You have ruined your sick daydreams for Galactic Empire, Enro. Whether you kill me or not, the clues you have already left behind will betray you, just as your neurotic obsession with your sister betrayed you."

The shadow-being raised his wraithlike hand and pointed: an ominous gesture. "Declare yourself no longer wed to my Reesha! Say it!"

"Words that have no relation to reality mean nothing." Crang's voice had almost a lilt of humor in it.

It was to see the image of the planet Ur, Enro's base of operations, that this whole charade had been enacted. Enro's attack method required that space-stress exist between him and his target, so it was Enro's true location, and no other point in space, that had to be projected behind Crang to kill him. Gosseyn turned his head and memorized a few square feet of the soil there.

When the Shadow Effect interrupted his biological functions, Gosseyn found the similarity connection with the now-empty Crang body broken.

Gosseyn's mind was no longer in the body, but he did

not die with it: a trick he had learned from seeing X possess Illverton.

THE memories were halted at that point: The figure in the chair had lowered his life-energy and sat without motion. His eyes were half-closed; his head was lowered, his chin on his collarbone.

His voice was soft: "To grow another duplicate body to match Crang's in face and features, but carrying my triple brain, had not been a simple matter. Tissue rejection, and an incompatibility of biological systems, had been overcome only with a series of energy adjustments, so that the rhythms and brain waves of the empty body had matched my own. The result was two Crang look-alike bodies, partially similarized because of their monozygotic nature. This body contained my triple brain, and was kept in suspension; the other contained an empty brain with no special adaptations to its nervous system. An extra brain would have been too easily detected by the medical corps of Enro's secret police, or even by Enro himself, who can see through flesh and bone as easily as through walls. The Observer Machine projected my consciousness from this Crang body to the empty one. It was then similarized to one of the open points earlier in the time-stream, lived forward through a number of events, and eventually accompanied Patricia to Nirene.

"Patricia insisted that certain hours during Gosseyn One's early life be occupied by me, the duplicate of Eldred Crang. It was this body, for example, not the real Crang, who was kissing Patricia the night of your death under a hail of gunfire. Again, it was I, and not the real Crang, who was on the arm of Empress Reesha when she presented me to Enro, pretending a marriage to Crang to hinder Enro's desire for the traditional brother-sister marriage of Gorgzid royalty."

Gosseyn said, "If you are from my future, tell me what next I must do."

The seated Gosseyn shook Crang's head. "No. Every

paradox we create, every bit of information passed against the direction of entropy, increases the likelihood that we fail the test of the Aleph Council and die, letting some other time-variant cure the continuum. I have restricted the memories of your immediate future to a minimum. Now you must leave, and before the other versions of you from down the time-stream arrive at this point, and create further paradox. I have a complete set of memories, and so I will take over organizing the First Aleph Council."

Leave to where? But Gosseyn did not bother asking the question. The implications of Rhade Ashargin's gruesome execution were clear. Enro's pointless attempt to murder Crang provided the means.

43

Common sense, do what it will, cannot avoid being surprised occasionally. The object of science is to spare it this emotion and create mental habits that shall be in such close accord with the habits of the world as to secure that nothing shall be unexpected.   —BERTRAND RUSSELL

The few square feet memorized by Gosseyn's extra brain when he turned to look at the crimson planet Ur: This memory had been transferred into his nervous system along with the rest of the scene of the Enro murder attempt.

Attunement to the Sphere of Accolon gave Gosseyn the necessary range to bridge the gap between the two points.

Gosseyn found himself standing on the red sands of an alien beach.

Overhead was a red giant sun, dotted and streaked with sunspots, its corona tortured and pulled out of shape by the white-hot spark of a dwarf star passing across its face. Only the sky near the noonday sun was dark pink: Near the horizons, bright stars peered out from a colored sky, purple a shade brighter than black.

Despite the look of the sky, the air pressure here was normal. With his secondary brain, he could detect a distorter field arching the heavens: a technology, no doubt left from the Primordials, designed to retain an atmosphere that would otherwise have boiled into space.

No ship passing within ten light-years would have any instrument to detect the distorter anomaly, and a Mercury-type planet was automatically filtered out of navigation reports as airless and unfit for human life. Because of the structure of assumptions of the men designing planetary survey instruments, the planet Ur was so well hidden as to be invisible.

He recalled Patricia saying that the special conditions on Ur would help Enro avoid dangerous side effects from his powers. Gosseyn now saw why. A small-scale version of the Stability Sphere was at work here: a system to return any atoms of the "memorized" atmosphere back from space. For the system to work, every atom of the atmosphere, and a larger mass of the planetary crust, would have to be maintained. Each particle of this world would be abnormally resistant to any non-identity process.

Underfoot, darker streaks of mineral grit ran through the scarlet sands, as well as bright tawny patches. The beach was striped like a coral snake. The lighter gravity was like being underwater: Gosseyn's first footstep carried him yards across the gritty sand, and the plume of black specks that rose at his footfall climbed into the air higher than his head. A single jump took him to the top of the cliff.

From there, he beheld a landscape of broken peaks and jagged outcroppings, leaning rocks and strangely elongated miters of stone. To his left was a deep river valley.

The waters were white, but falling with ghostlike slowness.

Atop eight gigantic pillars was a pagoda, with tier on tier of ornamental stories rising, each higher above the next. Gosseyn recognized the building material and structural style: This had been made by the Primordials, perhaps by one of the first landings in this decant of the galaxy during the Great Migration.

Gosseyn kept adjusting his estimate of the building's size upward. Clouds hung about the middle of the structure. Four of the huge legs on which the building rested had touched the ground at a point beyond the nearby horizon of this tiny world. The vast building straddled the world. When he saw a landing platform near the top of the pagoda held not one but several of the mile-long superspaceships of the Greatest Empire, as small as a lady's dangling earring at this distance, Gosseyn gave up trying to form an estimate of the height.

Instead, he closed his eyes and studied the structure with his extra brain. Atomic and superatomic piles, coolant systems, amplifiers, and generators were in the core, along with thousands of robotic brains and distorter systems linking this hub of the Greatest Empire to its sixty thousand star systems and eighteen hundred thousand ships. Gosseyn's extra brain could feel, like sharp metallic pings of radar, the fluctuation in time-space when a distorter carried men, war machines, or cargo to or from the many cubic miles of warehouse and barracks inside the titanic pagoda-building. The distorters were in constant use. The nervous energy traces of men and women—the personnel were in the tens of thousands—were not evenly distributed. In one place was an immense gathering, and, as if he could hear the dim roaring of a distant mob, Gosseyn could detect a state of nervous excitement, of alarm, gripping the immense gathering.

Without bothering to open his eyes, Gosseyn used his Enro-like method to view the area remotely. It was a huge military amphitheater occupying most of one deck of the colossal pagoda. Memorizing a spot with his extra brain, he stepped there.

Gosseyn appeared in a crouch behind a massive floral arrangement to one side of the altar. The silver vase lush with white blooms hid him from the gathered battalions of Greatest Empire soldiers standing at attention across the acres of metallic floor. A priest Gosseyn did not recognize (but who, from his robes, Gosseyn assumed to be the Lord Guardian of the Sleeping God who had replaced Secoh) was standing a yard or two from Gosseyn. There was also a marine guard with a high-energy rifle a little ways to one side of him. But neither this guard nor the priest saw him. Their eyes were locked on the scene before the altar.

Here was Patricia in ornate robes and jewels and a barbaric headdress. She had dropped her bouquet of white roses and drawn a gun from her garter belt. She was struggling with the figure that gripped her slender wrist in one fist.

The man who held Patricia's forearm in a crushing grip was Enro the Red, wearing a breastplate of shining red steel, ornaments and jewels draping his wide shoulders and massive chest, his arms and legs clad in a dark red uniform of military cut. A steel helmet with a crown of royalty bolted to its top lay at his feet, as if he had been holding it under one arm but dropped it to raise his hand. There was no weapon in his hand, but his fingers were glowing with an unnatural light, like Saint Elmo's fire.

A scepter topped with three jeweled eyes had fallen down the red-carpeted steps leading from the altar. There was a boy, perhaps an ensign or squire, lying facedown in a spreading pool of blood. Toppled from the dead boy's hands was a velvet pillow on which were the bracelets and rings of the Gorgzid wedding ritual. Murder had interrupted the ceremony.

Slowly sliding up the stairs in the ominous silence was a shadow-being.

Thousands and tens of thousands of Greatest Empire soldiers tracked the apparition with their rifles and pistols, and all were awaiting the order to open fire.

The pitch of the voice that came from the shadow-being was that of the seventeen-year-old Gosseyn, but his words rang out with the majestic and commanding tones and word rhythm of Enro the Red, not the voice of the man called X.

The Shadow-Enro said, "Stand away from her. Stand away from my woman!"

Enro, the solid Enro, threw back his head and laughed. He straightened his arm holding Patricia, so that her jeweled slippers were kicking inches above the bloodstained carpet, though the many folds of her white gown, and the long train, still reached the floor. "My sister is mine," he called out in a booming voice. "The laws, the ancient practices, the Sacred Writings of the Sleeping God: All agree that she is meant to be my bride. The hate I feel toward any man who touches her is proof of that. It is a divine hate: It is the God's own fury, placed in me like fire."

Patricia kicked her feet so that she was facing toward Enro and could jam her pistol barrel into the buckles of his breastplate, near his ribs. But she did not shoot. Her eyes were on the shadow-figure, narrowed thoughtfully.

Gosseyn was preparing to memorize her and distort her out of danger. It was her expression, nothing more, that made Gosseyn pause. What was happening here was not what it seemed. He looked left and right, wondering what he had overlooked.

The immediate future was blurred, so no clues were there.

Then Gosseyn noticed the glassy-eyed stare of the soldiers, thousand of them. The nerve rhythm issuing from their bodies was strangely synchronized. Enro's own troops he had exposed to something more intrusive than mere Loyalty Machine conditioning. Gosseyn suspected he was seeing the result of radical hypnotic surgery: the ultimate perversion of Null-A knowledge. None would fire without orders.

And some of the weapons—Gosseyn had not noticed at first, because the two figures were standing so close— some were pointed at Enro, not at the shadow-figure.

Gosseyn concluded that the men were controlled by a system of signals. The troops would obey anyone who knew the correct signal combinations. Both Enros had ordered the soldiers to cover the other and had been obeyed mindlessly.

Enro was speaking in a soothing tone: "My dear copy—for that is all you are, you know—my dear shadow: I suspected that X would prove weak. When he convinced me to have the Observer imprint my memories into his cortex, it was too good an opportunity to miss. Because a strategist knows to cover all eventualities. What if, despite my best efforts, Gosseyn succeeded in changing the mind of X back to his former, soft-hearted state? Would my consciousness, my very self, become trapped in his skull with him, a man whose personality transformed to be that of my enemy? So I used what I knew from the Ydd. I knew their special system of overlapping energy fields to make a deeper and more permanent imprint. Whether in success or failure, X and all his powers and knowledge would become me, would be one with my imperial self. Such a beautiful solution! Because now I need not rely on anyone, no courtiers, no generals, no advisors, no treacherous cousins. The children my sister will bear me will be imprinted with the same personality matrix. I can trust myself. I know my goals, my methods, my judgment. Who better to be my court and bureaucracy? One mind to serve both as God-Emperor and all his military governors and regional officers! One mind to rule the galaxy!"

The shadow man's voice was younger and higher-pitched, but otherwise it was the same voice: "Of course I recall all this, brother. I was the one who decided it. The plan is flawless. We can trust our royal self, no matter what body we inhabit. How can we not agree with our own person? And yet one small detail remains."

The solid Enro flexed the fingers of his upraised hand, and the deadly light shining from them brightened. Gosseyn could feel the energy-potentials building between two points in space.

"Detail?" asked Enro in a voice of dangerous quiet.

"I cannot have you touching her," the shadow man said with a rich chuckle. "It keeps me up at night, the thought of it. Surely I will die without her. The only thing I have ever been denied in all my life. She is mine. Rightfully mine."

Enro said, "We are one, you and I."

Shadow-Enro said, "Then you will not object to stepping away from her, and letting the Lord Guardian Enleel complete the ceremony. What would posterity say if I am not married in a proper ceremony?"

Enro raised his voice and spoke without turning his head: "Why, Mr. Gilbert Gosseyn of Venus is here! Gosseyn the Anarchist, no doubt here to spread a little anarchy. Did you think a flowerpot could block my view? I can see through the core of a planet, and watch the people walking upside down beneath me, the little ants I rule."

Gosseyn stood up slowly. He felt a pulse of radio-energy pass from Enro. At this silent signal a few platoons of the soldiers in the chamber swung their rifles to cover Gosseyn.

Counting by hundreds, Gosseyn tried to estimate the erg output of the weapons, should all the soldiers here fire at once. The figure he got was slightly enormous. Enough to cause the air molecules in the area to break down into plasma, at least. Even if the men had personal shields, and even if those could be raised immediately, there was no escape avenue for the waste heat.

Every mortal in the chamber would die if the soldiers

fired. Because Enro's training process—the Ydd method of mind control—had robbed each man of independent judgment, no soldier here would have self-awareness enough to disobey a self-destructive order.

Gosseyn turned his eyes to the left. Here was a box where dignitaries, generals and admirals in splendid scarlet uniforms, were standing. He assumed that they had been left mentally alert; otherwise they could not perform their tasks.

From the time he had been possessing Ashargin, Gosseyn knew their names: "Admiral Paleol! Admiral Nishur! General Greelin! For the sake of sanity, order the men to stand down! If all these weapons are used in this confined space . . ."

But then he noticed the sameness of expression on all their faces. It was a combination of jovial mirth and reckless rage. All these men were red-faced with anger, but their eyes glittered with vast good humor: The expression of a man who thinks himself invincible. A man whose every whim, whose every neurosis, both sexual and political, had been indulged since birth. A man who believed more violence and more could solve any problem.

The generals in the high officers' box all drew their pistols at once and leveled them at Enro. The different voices, high pitched and low, all spoke in the same tone and rhythm of speech: "Unhand her!" "The woman is mine!" "My sister—get your filthy hands away!" "Oho! What would posterity say (my posterity!) if I did not claim what was mine?"

Enro's voice, repeated from a dozen throats.

Gosseyn saw the madness in the eyes of the generals. Enro's madness. He saw the blankness in the eyes of the thousands of soldiers.

Gosseyn was memorizing Patricia, but before the process completed, she fired point-blank. Enro assumed his shadow-form at that same moment, so the bolt passed through him; but his cruel fist, suddenly insubstantial, passed through Patricia's arm and she fell free.

Enro's shadow-body was between Gosseyn and Patricia, and Gosseyn's double brain could not operate through the shadow-substance to get a fix on her and memorize her.

Patricia's bolt had hit one of the generals, who fell backward, his face a burning mass of blood. Several officers in the box opened fire on Enro. The bolts passed through his shadow-body, but the energy Enro released in return electrocuted dozens of the general staff.

A cry of rage issued from the unseen lips of the smaller shadow-being: rage and also fear. Not for himself. Enro did not believe in his own mortality. The shadow man's arms were straining toward Patricia where she fell, thunderbolts of energy-weapons flying back and forth above her, her dress starting to smolder from the heat. Gosseyn could feel space-time ripple under the sudden strain of the thin shadow's attempt to control the energy in the area. At the same time, the boyish silhouette launched his shadow-body toward her protectively.

His shadowy arms merely passed through her as she fell down the stairs.

To the larger shadow, the one representing the original Enro, this sudden lunge must have seemed an attack.

A flare of white light, bright as a lightning bolt, roared into existence in the chamber between the two shadows, the larger Enro and the smaller Enro, as they each sought to find the frame of reference needed to destroy the other. Gosseyn was standing too near to them: He had to assume his shadow-form before the radiation slew him.

Patricia, her dress ablaze, fell down the stairs. Gosseyn memorized her and established a similarity to the spot where he had first appeared on the beach of Ur. He triggered the mental cue . . . nothing happened.

Rage. He grew aware of the boiling rage in his extra brain, the emotion it was picking up from the extra brain of X, now possessed by the maddened memory-copy of Enro. During this crucial moment, Gosseyn's nerve paths were all flooded with the clamor of insane emotion. He had to take the moment to perform the cortical-thalamic pause.

Patricia, lying at the bottom of the stairs, her face bloody, flames consuming her long train, raised her head and shouted, "Fire!"

The soldiers evidently had been programmed also to obey the Empress Reesha.

For a moment it was brighter than the sun.

GOSSEYN tried to deflect and absorb as much of the energy as he could, to keep it away from the body of Patricia. The Shadow-Enro must have been trying the same thing. But even with 99 percent of the radiation deflected, the remainder was enough to char her body into something almost not recognizable as a human shape: merely a long, slender lump of blackened meat, a grinning black skull, eyes and tongue burned away, sitting atop it.

In an obscure way, Gosseyn was glad Enro destroyed the nearest two or three battalions of men with a vast sweep of atomic energy that spurted from his fingers like the bolt from an angry god. But then Gosseyn recognized that this unbalanced emotion was a rage cycle he was picking up, not one natural to him.

Nor could it be coming from Enro. Enro did not share Gosseyn's brain structure.

Gosseyn performed the automatic mental action he had readied ever since Leej, or Inxelendra, had brought the truth about X to his attention. A pulse of energy, directed by Gosseyn's tertiary brain, swept throughout the area.

The rage in Gosseyn's secondary brain . . . halted.

By then, Enro had assumed solid form, standing over the corpse of his bride. And then the rage that had sustained him his whole life collapsed.

His eyes were vacant. Gosseyn detected a strange blockage and stuttering coming from the nervous energy flows of Enro's brain. Here was a loss, the only real loss his life of endless victories had ever known.

It was a problem violence could not solve.

Gosseyn recognized the terminal stages of the Violent Man Syndrome. Males whose whole egos were propped up by the fear and terror they caused in the victims around them could only maintain their exaggerated masculinity while there was a woman, real or imaginary, who could fill the role of feminine supporter. Whether the female was willing or unwilling did not matter. The violence-addicted male usually beat, humiliated, or mentally tormented his love object as he did everything else in his life. Jealousy was the usual excuse, but that was just an excuse for a deeper, sicker, neurosis. Enro's routine humiliations of the high-born young ladies waiting on him at his bathtub had been the first signs to Gosseyn of the syndrome.

Every drunken sailor who terrorized a waterfront bar or threatened his hired girl with a knife was in the grip of a similar syndrome. In Enro's case, he had an empire in his hand, not merely a knife.

It was always an accident that killed the Violent Man's woman, but that was always the last prop holding up his sense of self, his ego, the series of makeshift identifications and excuses by which he justified his black crimes to himself.

Enro's mouth opened, as if he were about to make a statement. But now the imaginary posterity he addressed would never come to be: The invisible audience of history was not listening.

Enro stooped, picked up Patricia's pistol.

Gosseyn would have interfered, but his own voice spoke softly from behind him: "Let the syndrome run its course. We have no way to confine him, no way to prevent him from contacting the Ydd, no cell to hold him."

Gosseyn spun. His younger self, the seventeen-year-old, solidified out of shadow-substance. There was no trace of Enro's nerve-muscle tension patterns in his expression or posture. The brainwaves were steady and sane.

The young man said, "What did you do to me?"

Gosseyn did not answer aloud, but his thoughts were shared between them.

The thought was that X was a created version of Lavoisseur, like Gosseyn. Gosseyn had a ganglion in his nervous system, unknown to him until it activated. It was a death-reporting circuit. When Gosseyn Three died in the Shadow Galaxy his brain information was transmitted across intergalactic distances to find Gosseyn Two. The conclusion was that if a similar ganglion existed in X, he would know nothing of it.

All Gosseyn had needed to do was examine his own neural structure for the stimulant. He did not have to kill X to trigger the nerve-signal. The map was not the territory. If the ganglion was stimulated by a simple electromagnetic pulse, a pulse carrying a false report of death, the ganglion would act as if the brain around it had died, the reflex would trigger, and he would make total mental contact with any available Gosseyn bodies. The levels of logic established by the Observer Machine in the older Gosseyn would operate to cure the younger at a swift, subconscious level, where it could not be detected or stopped.

But what had happened to the Enro memories dominating X?

The young man used a parasympathetic auto-stimulus trick to increase his heart rate and electrolytes. When his life-force jumped, his thoughts flowed toward the thirty-year-old: "Enro's memories in me have already entered a self-reinforcing catatonia, allowing me to emerge to the fore. He suppressed me after the curative hypnotic-training sequence you implanted during our mind-battle started to operate. He no longer trusted me. The thoughts I am now receiving from you have completed the process Lavoisseur designed with my nervous system. I am no longer X."

When the young man's stimulus passed and his nerve-pressure fell back to the norm, the thought-flows from Gosseyn carried back his answer to the other: "Enro is a genius, a man of magnetic personality and great talent. If we can train him, cure his obsessions, his greatness will serve civilization. A sheepdog rather than a wolf."

Younger Gosseyn used his nerve-trick to send back: "I have seen him at close range, shared his thoughts. He would not volunteer. To make a man sane against his will is a contradiction in terms. In his shadow-form, he is invulnerable to all weapons. This is the only way to stop him."

"It is a waste."

"It is justice. Think of Nirene. Think of the millions he's slain. Countless millions."

In the end, Gosseyn did not interfere. For the longest time, Enro stood with the pistol in his hand, hefting it.

After many minutes of hesitating, the blank-eyed and deathly pale creature that raised an arm with awkward and slow motions to put the trembling muzzle in his sagging mouth hardly looked like Enro at all. In a sense, the great dictator was already dead even before he pulled the trigger.

The echo of the energy bolt slowly faded in the depths of the vast amphitheater.

The two Gosseyns, the younger and the older, stood looking down at the corpse for a minute without speaking. Enro had fallen atop the bridal-gown-clad corpse, his thick hand still reaching toward the charred bones of her arm as if to take possession of her.

Gosseyn stood breathing slowly and deeply, not letting the sensations of grief and rage overwhelm him. He forced himself to think, to think carefully. The true picture of these events was not yet clear.

The seventeen-year-old was saying, "I have all his memories, codes, and secrets. Not everyone has been mind-controlled. But each officer was set to watch the next one in the blackmail pyramid, with Enro at the top, able to watch all the secret dealings. Well, that whole system is now mine. I can order Commissioner Thule of the League Safety Authority to organize a bloodless surrender to the Greatest Empire.

"The Empire, once it envelops the League, will continue to exist in name only. It will be used as a basis to establish a true Null-A universal state.

"Since we can undo the Shadow Effect now, when we can use the graduates of the secret system of Games Machines operating through the Cult to select candidates to follow Ashargin—he will be surprised when the Games Machine of Corthid pulls him alive out of the shadow—to follow him when his expedition leaves to restore and repopulate the Shadow Galaxy. It will be to this galaxy what Venus was to Earth."

Gosseyn was squinting at a glitter of gold. He walked over. It was one of the marriage rings. It had fallen from the velvet cushion during the fight but had somehow escaped being melted.

He frowned at it, bent over, picked it up. It was slightly warm in his fingers. It was clearly that same ring he had just seen on Eldred Crang's hand a few minutes ago. Strange.

Aloud, he said, "One thing I don't understand."

The seventeen-year-old raised an eyebrow. "Only one? The universe is a confused place. Count yourself lucky."

Gosseyn said, "You are not the original Lavoisseur, are you?"

The youth shook his head. "No. I was made as a copy, with certain memories blacked out. As soon as the curative process concludes, you and I will be one, no matter where our two bodies might be. My mind was carefully made to fall back into sanity once my task was done. Made! Logically, I cannot be the real Lavoisseur."

"Then he is dead?"

"No. The Lavoisseur I killed in the Semantics Institute on Earth was obviously a copy also."

"Then where is the real one?"

The seventeen-year-old smiled quite a charming smile. It was the first innocent and cheery smile Gosseyn remembered seeing on his face.

"Come now!" said the boy. "Put the clues together. She has the skills to impersonate the body language and speech patterns of an emotional, highly-strung woman, but all her actions betray the cool calculation of a trained Null-A. This was all done according to plan. Think! *She* is the one who gave the order to fire when she was still in the line of fire. Why do you think she picked the name Patricia? Ptath-Reesha. The name of the mother of the Gorgzid race, the Eve of her world. No matter how far-fetched a 'long-lost sister' story sounded, the first ancestor could pass the biological scans needed to prove herself a member of the Royal Bloodline. She founded it! She was the fourth passenger of the Gorgzid migration vehicle. Where do you think she is?"

Before the youth was finished speaking, Gosseyn stimulated that buried cue attuning him to the spot he had memorized on the floor of Patricia's apartments on Gorgzid.

The apparatus was still there, behind the panel Gosseyn had cut free from the wall. The panel had not been repaired, so the medical coffin and its associated neural machines, broadcasters, and cell stimulators were still visible.

What had not been visible before was the panel to the rear of the medical coffin, hiding from view the second and smaller coffin hidden beneath. It was from this that Patricia, blinking and wiping nutrient fluids from her flesh, climbed on unsteady legs.

Her hair was plastered to her skull. Her new body was still pink and tender as a baby's, although she looked to be in her early twenties.

She glared at him. "What a stupid plan! Next time, come up with a better one!"

Gosseyn blinked at the naked, wet, dripping, angry Empress. "Whose plan?"

She raised an eyebrow. "Still slower at this than we all assumed!"

Then her gaze fell upon the ring in his fingers. Suddenly her expression turned soft. Patricia plucked the ring from his grasp and stood toying with it, turning it over and over in her swift, finely molded fingers.

She turned away from him, still toying with the ring, and she pulled a sheer silk robe from her closet to throw nonchalantly over her shoulders.

"The Chessplayer, Inxelendra, Gorgzor-Reesha, the Bride of Gorgzor, agreed to help you with the whole duplication process. She is the biology expert. She is the one we will have to go to next to get you outfitted to look like Crang. We cannot go to her until we visit the old site of the temple complex, and get her husband's sleeping body."

Patricia opened her bureau, drew out a holster that she strapped to her inner thigh, and slipped her miniature electric pistol into it.

That done, she sat at her vanity and brusquely toweled dry her hair, attacked it with a brush.

"She doesn't like you much, but she knew that once you became a time-traveler, and returned through these last two years as a copy of her hired man, Eldred Crang, you'd be in a position to get the cell samples you need from the Crypt of the Sleeping God, make a duplicate of the medical patient you are going to kill, and set up a serial connection using your method so his brain-patterns and personality (what remains of it) will flow into the next body. Since this one will be undamaged, and will have a working secondary brain with Yalertan training imprints, it should be able to automatically reach back through the centuries to its past, and establish a connection to its current brain, recovering all the lost memories.

"Gorgzor will be alive again, and his knowledge of

specialized political-economic callidetics is what the galaxy needs to be guided smoothly to a unification."

Patricia applied a small amount of lipstick, pursing her lips in the mirror, smoothing out irregularities with her pinkie.

She was still speaking. "Long, long ago, we all agreed. Everyone else, the whole galaxy of migrants, allowed themselves to be reduced to amnesia and barbarism, so that no future history would ever lead the Ydd to them. We three were spared. We were left with our memories intact, to watch and wait over the millennia for signs of the enemy.

"There was only one way to find him.

"You see, the strain of galactic civilization, the complexity of the modern understanding of the universe, was forcing man back into the psychological and neural patterns of the Primordials, bringing out potentials they had encoded there. The ancient neurochemical structures were beginning to reappear. Traces of the secondary brain, in primitive form, were cropping up in many places every few generations in the galaxy, but three planets in particular had a higher statistical potential. They were selected for our purposes.

"On Earth, on Yalerta, and on Gorgzid, over many centuries, the three of us introduced three different variations of the Primordial technology. We watched to see who or what would come to destroy us.

"On Gorgzid, it was easy for the Observer Machine, during his interment in the Crypt, to introduce false memories into Enro to convince him I was a long-lost sister, kept in hiding since birth. On Yalerta, Inxelendra could pick up the thoughts from the younger-universe version of herself, Leej, who went to the island where the Follower had established his retreat. And on Earth . . .

"It was the year that Hardie hoaxed the Games and won the world presidency that we finally knew who was behind the tampering you had detected in the Games

Machine you had built, and so you and I moved to Cress Village. Living on a small farm only a few miles from the Hardie country mansion, with the Observer-designed amplifiers in our basement, we watched the conspirators.

"But even with Eldred Crang, and me, and X infiltrating the inner circle, it was still not enough to tell us who was the real leader behind the Follower, that mysterious shadow-being serving the Ydd, determined to wipe out Null-A before a Null-A political philosophy became galaxy-wide.

"And so one last desperate move was made, a sacrifice move, meant to show the unknown man behind the Follower that the rebirth of the Null-A galaxy could not be stopped, not even by a galactic war. You had to show the enemy 'Chessplayer,' whoever it was (we now know Ydd was working through Enro), that the secret of immortality was about to reappear in this galaxy.

"So you decided to step onto the cosmic chessboard yourself.

"The false memories of being married to me were only made to seem false in order to convince Enro not to kill you, but enough of the memories had to stay intact to bring you to the notice of the Hardie gang. Even as it was, it was a near thing. For obvious reasons, we kept our marriage secret. Even Nordegg, the man who ran the store on the corner, did not recognize you, once you took off the flesh mask you had been wearing for two years.

"You made an older copy of yourself and put him in the Semantics Institute, and also a maddened copy of yourself to infiltrate the Hardie gang, and then you subjected yourself to the amnesia process. And so one afternoon, you simply walked from our little house in Cress Village to the air terminal to go to the City of the Machine. You had forty dollars in your pocket. I packed your lunch."

She opened a small drawer, drew out a fine gold band, and slipped it onto the ring finger of her left hand.

Then she rose gracefully, and her silk robe slithered as she turned toward him, one eyebrow arched, her eyelids half closed, her expression one of impatience held in check by amusement. She was trying not to smile at him.

Gosseyn had almost not been able to listen after the words "recovering all the lost memories." Because the method had been clear. The Observer had told him, although, in the press of events, he had no time to act on the knowledge.

Now she picked up the other ring, his ring, from where she had laid it on the vanity table. She took his left hand softly, and ceremoniously placed the ring on his finger, grasping his hand with her hand.

The contact was like a shock. The energy, the space-warping force of an emotion that had persisted though the death of one galaxy and the birth of another, was a reality he could feel with his extra brain. It reached from her to him . . . and elsewhere.

Time and space were not barriers to this, the fundamental force. Even the primal particle of all universes was nothing more than this. Love reflecting itself. Attention.

It was a simple matter to reach out back across less than two years following the path. The seventeen-year-old version of himself, now Enro's heir and running his empire, was connected to Patricia through that emotion, and so was the version who lay dying on the floor of the Semantics Institute, two years ago . . . and so was . . .

. . . the version of himself that paused, a month before that, before going to sleep in the hotel room, a sleep of less than a minute, but enough to trigger the final amnesia. Even as his eyes closed in sleep, that version could hear the floor loudspeaker already beginning to sound: *"The occupants of each floor of the hotel must as usual during the games form their own protective groups. . . . "*

No matter where they were in time-space, it was still his brain, identical with him. Lavoisseur and X and Gosseyn had sufficient similarity that the memories could be reintegrated: And, in an illusion universe, no signal, no memory, could ever really be lost.

It took only an effort of will to force the similarity.

And then . . . oneness.

He opened his eyes and saw her staring at him.

Her eyes shined with impish good humor. "Do you remember who I am, now?"

"Patricia Hardie."

"Patricia Lavoisseur. *Mrs*. Patricia Lavoisseur. Your wife."

He kissed her. It seemed the sane thing to do.

TOR

Voted

**#1 Science Fiction Publisher
20 Years in a Row**

by the *Locus* Readers' Poll

Please join us at the website below
for more information about this
author and other science fiction,
fantasy, and horror selections, and to
sign up for our monthly newsletter!

www.tor-forge.com